POSSESSION OF A WITCH

THE SAVANNAH COVEN SERIES

SUZA KATES

ICASM PRESS
SAVANNAH

Published by Icasm Publishing LLC
5710 Ogechee Rd. Suite 200 #278, Savannah, GA 31405
www.icasmpress.com

Library of Congress Cataloging-in-Publication Data

Kates, Suza
Possession of a Witch / Suza Kates
    p. cm.

ISBN-13:978-0-9849030-7-8
ISBN-13:978-0-9849030-8-5 (ebook)
I. Title

Printed and bound in the United States of America

10 9 8 7 6 5 4 3 2 1

Acknowledgments

I am overdue for a few words of thanks to the people who supported me when the idea of writing a book was just a crazy dream, and I also owe the ones who I've met along the way.

For this book, I want to give special thanks to Steve and Tex for the crash course (ha ha) in aviation basics. I hope I got the details right!

A big thank you to my brother and sisters for their encouragement, even when they had no idea what paranormal romance really even meant. Also to my stepfather, Woody, and stepmother, MaryAnne, a second parent can be a precarious thing, but I struck gold with both of you.

And my mother and father, though Dad has passed on, they provided the perfect mix of discipline and why-the-heck-not? Thank you for letting me have ideas and for giving me the will to see them through.

I really need to acknowledge the one person who made my dreams possible. In addition to helping me with all things technical, my husband, David, is a fiend when it comes to researching trends, business practices, and how the industry is changing or will be in the future. He also knows how to build an awesome website, and I am grateful he knows how to speak code! My best friend and greatest support (and butt-kicker extraordinaire) he has given me the courage to put my words out there. So thank you, and I love you.

Lastly, I could never have imagined the community of people I would come to know through— of all things—a social networking site. To my friends on Facebook, some of you have been around since the very first book and others just joined in last week. You guys make my days fun and hopeful. You share jokes, pictures, and your thoughts on the books, and I still don't know how I got to be so lucky.

Thank you for all the kind words and for creating a small family both with me and each other. It's like we all share a secret, and the rest of the world doesn't know what they're missing! From the bottom of my heart, I am grateful. Thank you just isn't enough.

Special Acknowledgement

I also want to give a huge thank you to Mina Dudenhöfer for helping with the Spanish included in this book. She is an awesome translator and a pleasure to work with!

To my brother, Wade
Thanks for being such a good black sheep
and making me only seem gray

THE COVEN

Anna St. Germaine
Hair: Long, straight, sable brown
Eyes: Sapphire blue
Color: Sapphire blue
Cat: "Ivy" gray female with lime green eyes

Anna sees visions of past, present, and future. She is the coven's head witch and is a descendant of the three women who originally banished the demon Bastraal three centuries ago. Her ancestral home is on an island off the coast of Savannah, Georgia and now serves as coven central.

Claudia Grant
Hair: Straight, long, flaming red
Eyes: River green
Color: Coral
Cat: "Rowan Von Ashbi" coloring of an American Wirehair with yellow eyes

Claudia is a history professor who only needs to touch an object to sense its past and previous surroundings.

Hayden Wells
Hair: Brownish red "caramel"
Eyes: Golden brown
Color: Pale pink
Cat: "Daisy" black tortoiseshell with yellow eyes

Hayden is a medium from San Francisco who sees and talks to spirits/ghosts.

Kylie Worthington
Hair: Long, wavy golden-blonde
Eyes: Hazel
Color: Yellow
Cat: Sassafras "Sassy" also a long-haired blonde but with bright yellow eyes

Kylie is a college student who's "on a break" to do her part for the coven and is able to control electricity in any form.

Lucia Ruiz
Hair: Long, wavy deep brown
Eyes: Brown
Color: Red
Cat: "Iris" black Persian with blue eyes

Lucia was born to privileged wealth in Spain and has the ability to find anything that is lost. She is an adventurer, world-traveler, and renowned relic-hunter.

Paige Reilley
Hair: Shoulder-length, white-blonde with ragged bangs
Eyes: Turquoise blue
Color: Turquoise
Cat: Tiger Lily "Tiger" brown and gray with white chest and belly, bright green eyes

Recently discharged from the military, Paige is a soldier in every way with the added abilities of super-strength and speed.

Shauni Miller
Hair: Long, straight, black
Eyes: Emerald green
Color: Green
Cat: "Cuileann" black short-hair with green eyes

Shauni is a nature-loving biologist from Colorado and communicates with animals telepathically.

Viv Sakurai
Hair: Shoulder-length, black, angled bangs
Eyes: Gray
Color: Purple
Cat: Kikoku "Kiko" orange tabby with yellow-green eyes and a grumpy disposition.

Relocated from Chicago, Viv is a physicist searching for an explanation for her own special power of telekinesis.

Willyn Brousseau

Hair: Wavy, shoulder-length, light blonde
Eyes: Pale blue
Color: White/cream
Cat: "Snowball" pure white with golden eyes

Willyn is a nurse, a mother, and a Christian. Raised in Alabama, she uses her healing powers to help those in need. She came to Savannah with an additional package, her young son, Tadd.

THE GUYS

Dr. Michael Black   *Whisper of a Witch*

This tall handsome veterinarian fell in love with Shauni in the first book of the series. He has dark blonde hair and gray eyes and is able to read a person's aura. He's a pretty calm guy until someone messes with his witch.

Dare Forster   *Conviction of a Witch*

Dark and handsome with deep blue eyes, this male witch came to the coven's island with his own plan. He wanted to partner with one of the women, but he never expected to fall in love. Especially with a gentle, Christian soul like Willyn. Now married, the two have made a family with Willyn's small son, Tadd.

Nick Reagan   *Binding of a Witch*

The coven likes to hang out in their favorite pub, and the owner of the bar always liked looking at Viv. His eyes are the color of the whiskey he sells, and his past is one of struggle. One night Nick finally got the nerve to approach the Asian beauty, but he got a lot more than he bargained for. The demon Bastraal had been destroyed once before, and his remains had been buried. Beneath Nick's very own pub.

Trevor Roch   *Haunting of a Witch*

One of Savannah's finest, this homicide detective clashes hard with the coven's ghost whisperer, convinced she's a con artist. Hayden has no choice but to work with the annoying man and find a serial killer who's working with the Amara. Staying true to form and following the coven's pattern, the two fall in love. Against their better judgment.

Quinn St. Germaine

Quinn is the younger brother of the coven's head witch, Anna. With sable hair and cobalt eyes, he is the masculine and handsome version of the siblings. His knowledge runs to occult history and magical languages. He assists the coven in all things, and though he has his eye on a particular witch, he does his best to deny it.

1

The world of night had always called to her. She found solace in the dark, the silence, and the sheer immensity of open sky. Whatever crisis or fear beating at her door, Anna could always count on the stars.

Though sandy beaches were but a walk away and a balcony opened off her top floor bedroom, the St. Germaine witch's favorite place for gazing was still a simple garden path.

Rubbing her arms through her shirt, she sensed the first tendrils of spring as warmer, lighter air flirted with the remaining cold, sweet-talking the remnants of winter to run along and let the flowers bloom.

Soon the green would surge and thrive in Savannah, bearing lilac-hued wisteria and rampant azaleas in an array of pink, white, and coral.

Anna breathed deep and sighed. Soon the seasons would change. Soon. But for now the darkest days weren't willing to let go. Not quite yet.

There were things to be learned on this mysterious night, and as a hereditary witch and gifted clairvoyant, she listened when inner voices spoke. Particularly since she and the other eight women in her coven had been called together to fight an evil greater than most. Summoned to fulfill an ancient prophecy, and each to risk her life in an individual challenge.

Four of her sisters in magic had faced their trials and won, but with every victory, the danger increased. So now, especially now, in her vast gardens caught between winter and spring, Anna obeyed the sudden urge for a nighttime stroll.

Moonlight cast its pale beams over the stone walkways, providing both visibility and enchantment. Wintergreen hollies reflected the illumination, their full leaves a promise that life would return to her well-tended beds.

She came by her green thumb naturally, as both her parents had worshipped the earth, tilling the island soil to expand paths and shrubbery. High walls of foliage encased most of the area, giving the gardens a sheltered, fairy-tale quality. Her mother had loved her arbors and the climbing vines that winked with flowers.

But the addition of koi ponds, that had been Anna's idea. Another bend in a very old but unbroken family line. As she eased closer to the water, the only stars she saw now were glimmers reflecting on its surface.

Even the brightly-colored fish remained below, uninterested or unwilling to disturb the tranquility. Gone were the water-lilies that would grace the meandering waterway when the weather warmed, leaving only dark water to gleam beneath a clear sky and round, white moon. The shiny pond was pure and peaceful. Glossy. Entrancing.

Her eyelids fell to half-mast as muscles relaxed, and her skin hummed with anticipation. Soon Anna felt a familiar pull, an opening door of light and transcendence, and as the vision came upon her, she knew.

A witch was being chosen.

Brisk, icy air rushed through her pursed lips to fill her lungs. Magic clutched then released inside, telling her this premonition was strong. Demanding.

She blinked her eyes twice. Slowly. And opened them again

to swirling, silver mists. The fog enveloping her danced and teased, alive with wisdom, and protective as it circled her bare legs.

She walked through the sparkling vapors, and as they cleared, the temperature began to rise. Thick, humid air settled on her skin as the cool gray was exchanged for a happy green. The environment came alive with sounds of wildlife, birds crying and bugs skittering. She would swear she heard the slow, groaning growth of towering trees and long, twisted lianas. Light fought to find its way to the forest floor.

Glancing around to gain her balance, Anna caught a glimmer of gold through the leaves. Something waited for her back there. Deeper in.

She jerked when a voice rolled through the thick brush. Older than time, it spoke in a low, urgent tone. Sharing an important secret. *Sacramachaco. Iraca.*

Foreboding slithered in her chest. "I don't know that language. What does it mean?" Her question seemed too loud, and she feared her force would shred the thin walls of the vision. She spoke more softly. "What does it mean?" Her breath was harsh and hoarse in her throat.

The strange voice didn't repeat itself, and as she whirled to search for the source, shadows encroached on all sides, covering the idyllic scene. The flutter of butterfly wings was replaced with the sluggish sound of long, sinuous bodies forcing their way through the underbrush.

Snakes. They were everywhere, lying in wait for the foolish traveler. She couldn't see them, but they were there. Another slid through the thick mud. *Sssssss.*

Feeling the squish of the wet soil between her toes, Anna looked down to find the ground wet, mud thickening and rising around her feet. This world was no longer friendly. But she needed answers.

Trudging onward, she kept her blue eyes on the glimmer of

gold, the sparkle still beckoning from behind the leaves. With a burst of energy, she emerged and found herself in a clearing.

On the far side a single, golden birdcage hung from a tree. Wind rotated the cage so it caught the remaining light and flickered one blinding flash. When her eyes cleared, she saw a black bird staring from behind thin bars.

The sleek black animal fluttered in vain, too cramped to fully extend its wingspan. Trapped. Vulnerable.

Then the bird shrieked its outrage.

Anna stuttered forward, still reeling from the swiftly changing scenery. "I'll get you out."

The bird shrieked again, but this time its gaze was centered on something behind her, to the far side of the open area. She whirled, all senses on high alert.

A man slid from the forest with stealth, his copper-toned skin bared from the waist up. His chest and arms ran thick with muscle, his face hard with resolve. When he clamped his dark eyes on her, he smiled.

And raised his bow.

Anna's heart froze and shattered. *Tyr*. One of the Amara members who planned to raise a raging demon. He was a killer. An enemy.

Tyr aimed his bow toward the caged bird with clear intent, too far away for Anna to stop him. She raised a hand, but no magic flowed. She was bound from using her gifts here. So she spun and raced toward the trapped animal, each step a struggle against invisible shackles.

Sacramachaco. Iraca. The voice rang through the clearing with such force Anna drew up short, just as a streak of silver shot from the sky. The object impaled itself in the sodden ground.

A dagger, ornate and embellished with shining black stones.

Three things were required to defeat the demon Bastraal. Three things to save humanity. Her coven had already found the book. Then they'd discovered the burial ground. So only one more was needed.

Anna stared at the half-buried piece of metal and gasped. *The blade.*

The bird squawked again, jerking her attention back to the cage and the life trapped inside. Which should she choose? She could only get to one of them before Tyr crossed the clearing.

While she debated, the bird's cry began to change. From the screech of sheer terror it stretched and expanded, morphing into a glorious song, full of power and strength. As she watched, the black feathers ran with color, changing from onyx to a wonderful red. Like rubies in the sun.

With a thrust of its body, the bird freed itself from the cage, perching in the open door before soaring over Anna's head. Red wings spread wide now, bright, brave, and full of hope. Then with one final call, the bird disappeared into the rain forest canopy.

Anna whipped her head to face Tyr as that one bared his teeth in anger. Then she took two running steps toward the dagger and dove to the ground. She slid in the mud, smelled the stench of rotten soil, and kept her eyes on the target. The blade.

Her fingers curled around the silver hilt, wrapping tightly under a large, black stone. The head of a beast was etched there, a serpent. Maybe a dragon.

As she clutched the dagger, the mysterious words floated to her again. They brushed her face as the voice whispered. *Sacramachaco. Iraca.*

She tugged on the blade, but the wet soil held tight, unwilling to lose its prize. Then with one mighty pull Anna wrenched herself backward.

And stumbled against a stone bench.

The clean scent of the gardens blew around her, and the moon still hung high. She was back. Safe and secure on her own property, where the pond still shone in the starlight. Undisturbed.

Anna's heart ratcheted against her breast bone and her hand still clutched into a fist. Though the dagger was trapped in her vision, what she'd brought with her still had value.

She'd returned to her world with knowledge. With a mission.

And a name.

2

Striking a match and reaching down into the large, glass jar, Lucia lit the last of three apple spice candles. She'd put some in the large kitchen, the foyer, and now here in the grand hall where most of the females in the household had gathered to have a movie night. The sweet, homey scent was soothing, and the last of the winter stock.

She and the other women of her coven were taking a break from the study of martial arts, demon basics, and inter-dimensional portals. Since Hayden, the coven's own ghost whisperer, had completed her trial and saved some souls, the next item on their agenda was how to close the doors to the underworld and stop the flood of demons that invaded Savannah on a nightly basis.

The grand hall was roomy and boasted a huge, flat-screen television mounted on the wall. Lucia so admired the clever way an oil painting slid to the side to reveal the screen that she had plans to install a similar setup in her own house. Whenever she returned, that is.

She'd become accustomed to the cheerful— and sometimes not-so-cheerful—voices of her friends, so a television filled with sound and animation would help keep her company in her enormous *palacete*.

The Spanish mansion would always be her home, but centuries-old stone walls, wide, cold hallways, and vacuous rooms often made her feel like the only person in the world.

Yes. She'd get the biggest television the market had to offer, and if she was still lonely? She'd fly her friends over for a huge post-prophecy party.

"They've made a breakthrough in the remote control of quantum systems," Viv said suddenly, making Lucia's head spin from the change in topic. With her nose still buried in a scientific magazine, the Asian physicist spoke from the crimson chair she nestled in. The opulent velvet contrasted starkly with the serious and straight-laced witch.

"You don't say," Lucia answered, smiling at Shauni who was stretched out on the floor playing with her dog. Skid was almost fully grown but still full of puppy energy. He pulled at the thick rope and shook his head, growling for all he was worth. But he looked like he was smiling.

"Yes. I knew they'd make a break soon," Viv said. Still absorbed in the article, she missed Shauni's quick shake of the head and Lucia's wink as they silently agreed not to encourage a discussion of quantum physics.

A feather-light stroke on her leg told Lucia her cat was still playing shadow. Iris, her black Persian, had been behaving strangely all day, unwilling to let Lucia out of her sight for more than a few minutes at a time. "What's the matter, sweetie?" She bent to pet the cat, smiling when bright blue eyes blinked lovingly.

Iris had been named for the goddess of the rainbow, who rode on a ribbon of colors from earth to heaven and back again. Lucia considered the name a celebration of beauty as well as travel. Two of her favorite things.

When she'd named the little black ball of fur Iris, she'd had no idea she was simply falling in line for destiny, calling her cat by a botanical name, just like eight other women who hadn't even met yet.

Now she and those women were family, living in Anna St. Germaine's ancestral home on a barrier island off the coast of Georgia. Summoned by magic, they'd all come together to learn of a prophecy laid out three centuries before and left strictly for them.

Lucia and the others were the chosen. They were the nine.

They were the Savannah coven.

A head-butt against her calf brought Lucia's attention back to the persistent cat. Iris usually got twitchy whenever Lucia was preparing for an expedition, but she wasn't going anywhere now. Why was her pet clinging like a feline burr? "No worries, pretty girl. Everything is fine." She patted the silky, black head. And hoped she was right.

Was something in the air tonight? A hint of the mystical that Iris was sensing long before her human? Another demon invading their sanctuary?

"Hey witches," Claudia called from the kitchen, pulling Lucia from her daydreams. "What do you want to drink? We're taking orders." Claudia was wearing her fiery hair free tonight, letting it fall straight as rain to her lower back. She wore dark-denim pants and a white silk blouse, her definition of casual.

Lucia grinned as she touched her own top. She'd been in the mood to glam up as well, pulling out black pants and an embellished blouse. Beads were stitched into the fabric and shimmered in candlelight like polished onyx.

She examined her fingernails, glossy with "Poppy Field" red. The same hue glossing her lips.

Lucia thoroughly and unapologetically loved being a girl.

Especially since she spent half her life digging into dirty, forgotten spaces. Hidden caves or buried tombs. There was nothing wrong with enjoying the good things in life. They were often fleeting. "I want root beer," she told Claudia. "The calorie-loaded kind."

The others put in their drink requests just as Kylie bounded down the wide, mahogany staircase. She was on the phone, bopping her head up and down. "Yes, Sir. I will." She sighed as if the sky was falling and rolled her eyes. "I promise. Tell Mom I love her."

Ending the call and shoving the phone in her pocket, the college coed on a prophecy-filling break from classes trudged to an empty chair and flopped down. "My father. Ugh. He is so not happy with my current life choice."

Now Viv did look up from her magazine, sending a tender look to the youngest of them. "He wants to know when you're going back to school?"

"Yeah. I don't think he's going to buy my independent research story much longer. But at least I managed to stop him from coming to Savannah. He wanted to bring my mother for a visit. Can you imagine?" She twisted her riot of long, golden curls into a messy knot on her head. "I don't know what I'd tell them."

Viv's jaw dropped. "You mean they don't already know or at least suspect?" She sat up straighter. "They don't know you're a witch?"

"Whatevs." Kylie waved a hand and grimaced. "My father the general would freak if he knew his daughter was a sup."

Lucia was walking to her favorite spot on the couch but stopped in midstride. "I'm sorry, but is this a translation thing? Why are you soup?"

After staring blankly, the light dawned on Kylie. She broke into laughter. "No, no. Sup, as in short for supernatural." She curled her legs under her. "Come on, Lucia. I would expect such stodginess from Viv but not you."

From the floor Shauni stifled a giggle, clearing her throat and pointing at poor Skid when Viv raised a brow. "The dog did it," Shauni said, her green eyes twinkling.

Claudia came out with a tray of glasses, followed by Hayden, who'd also volunteered for kitchen duty. When drinks had been passed around, the women all gathered to talk and kill time until the food arrived from the mainland.

Island life was private, quiet beaches, peaceful woods, and Anna's castle-style mansion to prowl around in, but sometimes the distance to civilization was an issue. Especially, Lucia determined as her stomach growled, when she was waiting on Thai food. *Yum.*

Her stomach rumbled again at the thought. She lived for all things spicy.

A door slammed at the far end of a long corridor before quick female footsteps slapped across the floor. The sounds had all heads turning to watch as Anna breezed in the room. She appeared anxious, her usual serenity gone. Urgency flowed straight from her cobalt blue eyes.

"What is it?' Paige demanded, rising and ready for battle. She was a soldier from the tips of her fair, blonde bangs all the way to her solid, black boots. Ass-kickers, Lucia had heard them called.

Anna waved her hands and smiled, though her deep breath belied the attempt to hide her fluster. "Nothing. No threat, at least." She put a hand to her chest and closed her eyes. "I'm sorry. I'm not usually so demonstrative."

"Ya' think?' Kylie said. "I've never even seen you break a sweat. I swear, Anna," the young blonde widened her eyes, "you were almost...running."

Willyn, the healer of the coven, was immediately at Anna's side. "Come sit down. Tell us what's wrong." She took Anna by the shoulders and guided, practically forced, the head witch to take a seat.

"I'm fine, really." Anna used both hands to brush her long, sable hair, making sure she was no longer flyaway. Then with the folding of those hands in her lap, she resumed the dignified and composed aura they were all used to. "I was taken by surprise."

"In the garden?" Paige said. Her hands were on her hips, and she hadn't sat back down.

"Yes." Sipping the glass of tea Hayden brought her, Anna explained. "I had the urge to go for a walk."

"Oh, no," Shauni said from where she still sat petting Skid. "Urges in this coven usually trigger big events."

"But it's not time for another trial," Hayden said. She was also still standing, next to Paige. "I just finished mine a little over a month ago. We should still have weeks before another witch is picked."

Anna shook her head and plunged right in. "But we don't. The pattern has changed on us again." Setting her drink aside, Anna rose and began to circle the large room, her elegance fitting easily into the scenery of rich, dark wood, antique furniture mixed with modern, and slate flooring laid over a hundred years before.

"I took a short walk and found myself staring into the ponds. The reflective surface, as well you know, is a perfect medium for divination."

"You had a vision," Viv said.

"I did. A vision unlike any I've ever experienced." Anna told them of her unexpected trip to a faraway jungle, the way the light changed and how she struggled to find the golden cage.

Then she told them about Tyr.

"He is also a seer with the talent for prediction." Anna stopped moving and clasped her hands together. "He and I shared the same vision."

Claudia looked up from where she sat next to Lucia on the couch. "You mean he was actually there? As much as you were?"

Anna nodded. "He knows what I know. He probably heard the voice and what it told me." Her knuckles went white as her fingers clenched. "The Amara will be searching for the blade as well. I'm sure of it. That's why we can't waste any time."

The middle of Lucia's stomach started to tingle. She glanced at her cat, who was still hovering underfoot, then to the red candles burning all around. When she allowed her gaze to travel back to Anna, she found her friend's soulful blue eyes on hers.

Anna smiled. "I wasn't sure until the bird turned red." She pointed to the amulet hanging from a silver chain around Lucia's neck then walked over to touch the ruby-hued stone at its center. "The color of the bird, once it found hope and freedom, was bright and bold. Radiant with strength." She held Lucia's stare. "Like some others I know."

The grand room blurred at the edges before righting itself again with a rush of air and tinkling of distant bells. Feeling her feet solidly on the floor, Lucia drew a deep breath. She touched Anna's hand where it rested against the necklace. "It's me, then," she said in a firm tone.

Anna nodded.

After allowing herself a moment for the truth to sink in, Lucia dropped her hands to her sides and said, "Okay. I need to start researching. We need to locate any mention of the dagger you described. A name is good, but a photo is better."

She whirled to seek out Claudia and Viv. "You two. Put those brains together and find the words Anna heard in the vision. Your guess is as good as mine on the spelling."

"Right." Claudia saluted before elbowing Paige in the side. "I think she's after your job."

The lean and mean warrior only smiled. "I'll believe that when she cuts those damn nails."

A male voice joined in the chaos when Quinn called from the top of the stairs. "Joe just called to say Joseph was headed out and had Ethan with him. Guess he made good travel time."

"Ethan?" Kylie said. "Your friend from Harvard?" She rubbed her hands together. "Another man on the island. Finally."

Quinn glared.

Lucia laughed, and with the release she felt another emotion fighting its way into her heart. "Easy, girl," she told Kylie. "It's my turn, and if the pattern the others have set holds true, this guy could be a contender."

Anna had been right about at least one of the qualities she'd listed. Lucia did have hope. And for something that might surprise the fireballs out of her sister witches.

Kylie winked and leaned to Lucia, speaking under her breath. "I wish my turn would hurry up and get here. I can't stand the suspense any longer." Her big, hazel eyes shifted to Quinn as he strode across the slate floor towards the kitchen.

Drawing back in surprise, Lucia asked, "Not in denial anymore?" Kylie and Quinn had been caught in a dispute of attraction versus loathing for almost a year. That kettle had to be close to screaming.

Kylie sighed. "Why bother when all of you keep pointing it out?" She raked a hand down her arm to clasp her own wrist. "I don't see why I should have to wait for my trial, but considering how bull-headed he is, I'll probably need fate to give him a kick in the right direction."

Lucia grinned. "Well put." And exactly what she had been thinking. While the others who'd been challenged had different responses to the whole trial-equals-love scenario, she wasn't worried about the romantic aspect at all. In fact, she welcomed it. She rejoiced in the possibility.

If fate had chosen a man for her, she would trust the decision. Not many people in life were reliable, and she, for one, would gladly accept the gift of love. Signed and sealed by providence, with a mystical good-for-life warranty.

Lucia hugged herself, and then with a spring in her step headed for the powder room to check her makeup. She let Iris trail in behind her, happy to share the moment with her favorite confidante. With the lovely smell of apple crisp in the air, she looked into the mirror and re-applied lipstick. Then she puckered up for the hell of it.

Tonight she could be meeting her soul mate.

3

Lucia returned to the grand hall to see Claudia tug Viv from her chair and toss the magazine aside. "Come on. Let's get started on that research," she said with a flip of her red hair. "Two witches are better than one."

Viv straightened her black glasses. "I'm on it."

"Me, too," Lucia told them. "The sooner I know details about this dagger, the sooner I can get a lock on it." Plus, she could use a distraction, anything to keep her mind busy. Eagerness to meet their incoming guest battled with nervousness. What would he be like?

Handsome, please. And definitely smart, since he'd attended Harvard with Quinn. Outgoing? Surely. He studied and tracked demons for a living. Lucia grinned. So maybe he liked to see new places.

She fell in behind Claudia and Viv, walking to the library with purpose, but they all froze in various stages of movement when someone pounded on the front doors.

"Oh, it must be locked," Willyn said, jogging to open the massive slabs of oak. "Can the research wait a little bit?" she called out. "Joseph's here with dinner."

Lucia wiped her palm down her hip. *Oh. He's brought a lot more than that.* She wiggled her fingers to release jitters, plastering her best friendly-but-not-too-obvious smile on her face. The new guy was about to walk through those doors. *This better be good.*

But the curve forming on her lips faltered when a tall, dark-haired man stepped inside after Joseph. Her skin tingled with heightened awareness. Her nerves all but sang *Haaal-le-lujah!*

Wow. She'd hoped he would be handsome, but nothing could have prepared her for what swaggered into the foyer.

He was called Ethan, she remembered, and now she had a picture to go along with the name.

His hair wasn't simply dark, but black as a raven, and long enough to fall into his eyes when he bent over. As Lucia watched, Ethan greeted Willyn with a hard nod of his head and a smile that could only be described as reluctant. He set a large black suitcase on the floor, but a carry-out bag of food remained in his arms.

And what an amazing set of arms they were. His gray, thermal shirt showcased a well-developed upper body and a lean waist that narrowed to blue-jean covered hips. Lucia rubbed her fluttering stomach. *Turn around. Turn around.* Yes! She almost shouted with joy.

He looked just as good from behind.

Joseph took the bag then, directing their guest to make his way to the grand hall to meet the others.

If Lucia had once pictured Quinn's friend as a scholarly bookworm, someone who spent more time studying than experiencing, that assumption was destroyed. This man's fierce and guarded expression told her he'd seen plenty of action as well. Battling against the evil that men do. And demons.

Ethan's posture was rigid as he swept dark, scrutinizing eyes around the mansion. He was an observer, taking everything in and storing the data for when and if it became necessary.

When his gaze settled on Lucia, she held her breath, as nervous as she was excited. She felt her lips quiver as he raked his eyes over her from top to bottom. Then Quinn called his name, and he looked away.

Breath expelled in relief when those scorching eyes turned away. *María santísima.*

"I know what you're thinking." The voice near Lucia's shoulder made her flinch, and she barely bit back a squeal. Viv was standing beside her, one side of her mouth hitched up in amusement. "You wonder if he's going to be part of what you have to figure out," she said, patting Lucia on the arm.

"A girl can dream," she said on a sigh before meeting Viv's rain-gray eyes. "We deserve some sort of bonus for saving the world, don't you think?"

Claudia had joined them now, and the history professor with dead-on fashion sense was ready to share her opinion as well. "That's definitely my kind of bonus," she said, indicating Ethan as he shook hands with Quinn and smiled. "Mee-ow."

Viv smirked and slipped her glasses off. "He has an interesting educational background, too. Theology before he got into studying the occult."

Panic welled in Lucia's throat. "But he isn't wearing a collar. He's not a priest." She shook her head. "Please say no."

Viv laughed and wrapped her arm around Lucia's shoulders. "I think Quinn would have mentioned it. Besides." She smacked Lucia's behind and gave her a gentle push forward. "If any female was blessed with the attributes to convert a man of the cloth, it's you."

Lucia sent her a grateful smile. "Nick loves you for more than your looks, and that's what I want, too."

"You'll have it," Claudia said, pulling her down the hall toward the appetizing smell of food. "You deserve it. We all do."

Walking with her friends to join the others, Lucia swallowed against uncertainty. Against doubt that nagged and old fears that clambered. Deserving love was fine and good, but having it was something else.

Children deserved the love of their parents, but hers had somehow forgotten that credo.

She closed her eyes and forced the pain from her chest. *Forget about them. They're damaged*, she told herself for the millionth time. *I'm not.*

And her insensitive parents had nothing to do with her life anymore. Nothing to say about her destiny.

As of this evening Lucia had been called to trial, and she intended to reap the benefits in addition to fighting the fight. After all, she was due some good luck.

Now she too could have a partner in life. Someone she could count on. She could love. *Finally.*

Fate had made sure of it.

~~~

Ethan splashed cold water on his face, wondering if he should bother with the five o'clock shadow darkening his jaw. He'd taken a flight from Poland to his home in Virginia to repack, then had continued on to Savannah without stopping.

Redness made his dark brown eyes seem somewhat sinister, predatory. Combined with hair that needed a trim and his unshaven face, the overall look was...well, exactly what Ethan was.

A man best suited for chasing monsters.

He replaced the navy hand towel in its hanging ring, noting the marble of the counter and quality of bathroom fixtures. He'd been friends with Quinn for years, and the guy was salt-o'-the-earth. His sister Anna seemed all right, too. An amazing thing, he mused, considering how loaded they were.

Ethan turned to survey the lavish bedroom he'd been provided, ambling to the majestic bed and wishing for a nap. He was well beyond simple sleep deprivation and into hallucination territory.

He shook off the urge to close his eyes and ignored the soft bed that called to him. There was work to be done. There was *always* work to be done.

Because unlike humans with their frail, needy bodies, evil never took a break.

From the other side of the bedroom door, Quinn called out Ethan's name then gave a perfunctory knock. He opened the door before Ethan could answer. "You ready? We've got food, and your timing is perfect, because my sister had a vision she wants to share with you. You know, pick your brain along with mine and the girls'."

"Girls?" Ethan hiked his brow. "You call witches charged with defeating a major demon 'girls'?"

"Hey. I'm an honorary coven member." He notched his chin up. "Plus, they can't do without me."

Chuckling low, Ethan shook his head at his friend. "I see your ego remains intact."

"As does your denial to admit my greatness. But never mind that. You need to come meet everybody. And before all the food's gone." He twisted his mouth to the side. "These witches don't play around when it comes to eating."

Deciding to leave his unpacked duffel for later, Ethan blew out a breath and ran a hand over his face. The shadow would have to stay.

Downstairs, the kitchen sounded like a late night pub minus the music. Ethan sent a sidelong look to Quinn as they crossed the grand hall to join the action.

The women had spread a Thai food feast out on the spacious granite counters, and chairs had been positioned around an island of the same gray stone. The centerpiece of the room curved to form a huge crescent, affording plenty of space for seating.

Sniffing the air, Ethan allowed himself a long drag of the scrumptious smelling food. Curry, ginger, and a bevy of exotic spices teased him, but he reminded himself he'd already eaten.

Anna was passing around white tableware with a woman whose hair color was somewhere between brown and red. A younger female, long blonde curls and energy that practically buzzed off of her was distributing forks and spoons.

Quinn was shoulder to shoulder with him and leaned his head closer to say, "You know Anna, my sister, and the blonde is Kylie. She hasn't been called yet." He lifted a finger to point. "Hayden just finished her trial. She's the one you want to talk to about the demons, since she's seen the most."

"She talks to ghosts?" Ethan was memorizing as he went, a particular talent that aided him in his chosen field. Writing down notes was hard to do when you were running from a succubus.

"The redhead is Claudia," Quinn continued. "She not only teaches history but senses it in objects. The shorter woman next to her is Viv. She's already passed her challenge, too and can send a bus flying with the flick of her pinky."

"How about her?" Ethan asked, indicating a woman with blonde hair to her shoulders and gentle blue eyes.

"That's Willyn, our healer. And she's the one who married a witch. Dare is probably around somewhere running roughshod on his new stepson. Six years old now and filled with power." Quinn laughed. "Thankfully, Tadd can't make fire. Yet."

When his friend paused in the introductions, Ethan tore his eyes away from the tall, curvy brunette with her back to them. The one he'd noticed in the hall before.

Quinn gave him a knowing smile and laughed.

"What?" Ethan demanded.

"Um...the Spanish lady you were just scoping is Lucia." Quinn's shit-eating grin spread.

"I was just learning faces." Ethan scowled. "Besides, you know better."

The smile fell from Quinn's face. "Yeah. Anyway, the one

with the long, black braid is Shauni. She converses with animals, who, by the way, can be real opinionated. And last, but hell and far from the least, is Paige. The woman with light blonde hair and serious biceps, she..." Quinn gave a light punch to Ethan's arm. "Well, why don't you try pissing her off and see for yourself?"

When the coven started taking seats and motioned for the two men to join them, Ethan dredged up a friendly face and pulled out a chair. He'd been acquainted with the supernatural world from a young age and was well versed in the ways of paranormal oddities.

But this was his first coven of witches.

He'd spent years educating himself, since childhood really, though that hadn't been by choice. Gathering data and figuring out what worked. What didn't. And what to avoid at all costs. Despite the injuries and near misses he kept going, for a singular, driving reason.

He'd like to salvage what was left of his life.

So while he was glad to help the women with their demon infestation, he would never stop looking for that one critical piece of information. The detail that would send him in the right direction. The answer that would set him free.

Ethan knew Quinn and was sure the mansion library held plenty of documents. Added to that, the women gathered here had amazing talents. He would assist the Savannah coven all right.

And he hoped they could help him in return.

He waved away the offer of *po tak* soup from the sweet-looking blonde, preferring to stick with his glass of water. He was ready to start the meaningful conversation but would allow a few minutes of polite get-to-know-everybody time.

Quinn spoke up as he loaded his plate with garlic beef. "So this is the guy I've been telling you all about. Expert on demons and other night-crawlers." Quinn switched to rice and began piling it on as well. "Coven, meet Ethan Drake."

Kylie stopped dousing her plate with soy sauce to beam at Ethan. "Ethan Drake? Like the video game...well, almost. That's so cool." She looked to the Spanish witch. "Remember, Lucia?"

Lucia gave a short, embarrassed laugh. "Sure." She shook her head slightly. "I only played it that once. Because you were sick and wanted company."

Ethan found her reaction curious. Why would she care if others knew she'd played a game? Or did his presence make her nervous?

Maybe he should work on his smile. He'd been told it could come across as a sneer when he was irritated. Right now he was simply exhausted, but aggravation would show.

He wasn't given a chance to say anything, because the woman with white-blonde hair Quinn had jokingly warned about shot him a question. "Has Quinn told you about our prophecy?"

"A little." He cleared his throat and said, "I know the original three St. Germaine witches banished the demon Bastraal once before. About three hundred years ago, and that they left a prophecy behind to handle him when he tried to return."

"He's determined to make a comeback," the red-headed Claudia said, her voice tight. She stirred the vegetables on her plate. "And every time one of us has to do our part, his attacks get worse. Every time we defeat the Amara, they come back stronger and with newer, better tricks than before."

"The Amara." He leaned onto his elbows, engrossed by the supernatural super storm building in Savannah. "Their leader is some sort of witch as well?"

"Yes. A Nordic seior." It was Anna who answered him. "She's been granted immortality by Bastraal in exchange for setting things into motion up here. In our world. Her followers range from other witches, to shape-shifters, and the woman Quinn told you about before you came down here. Searenn. She's a Droehk."

Rubbing his neck and leaning back against the wrought iron of his tall stool, Ethan said, "A demon master." He flattened his mouth into a grim line. "I'd heard they'd all been wiped out. Bad news that one's still alive."

He wished he could get his hands on the Droehk. He'd make her talk, whatever it took. She'd have plenty of info to share.

Lucia sat across the island from him and stuck a dish out, waving it in front of him. "Care for a spring roll?"

Still caught up in his own musings, he brushed her off with a wave of his hand. "No."

She shrugged. "They're so good. How can you resist?"

He leveled her with a blank stare and said, "Self-control."

She set the food back down and looked away but not before Ethan saw the flash of hurt in her eyes. Yeah, he'd been right. Fatigue was swiftly becoming annoyance.

Why was she so dressed up anyway? Hair, clothes, makeup. Maybe she had plans to go out later, but the shiny shirt was a little much.

Not to mention the way the shimmers kept drawing his eye to her chest. He fumed and forced his attention away. Guess every coven had to have a Buffy.

And hell, he hadn't slept in over twenty-four hours.

More than lack of sleep was getting to Ethan. He knew better than to abuse his body. To let his defenses down. So he would find out about this vision of Anna's and get to bed.

Maybe he'd rest peacefully. With no nightmares.

"Quinn tells me you had an experience tonight," he said to the woman who had eyes the color of cobalt, a trait she shared with her brother.

Those eyes shifted to her sibling before Anna wiped the corner of her mouth with a napkin and set the cloth beside her plate. "Very well. I had a revealing premonition, but we haven't had time to research all of the specifics."

"Such as?"

Anna took the time to take a drink of her iced tea, but Ethan didn't miss the cool look that passed over her regal features. He was doing great. Alienating these women one by one.

Ethan was used to all kinds of monsters and curses, but he might want to reconsider making enemies of this coven. In all his travels he'd heard similar tales of prophecy and saviors. He'd even come across a diary that had mentioned "The Nine." And as he considered Savannah's description, location, and current problems, he had a deep suspicion he was facing those nine women now.

He gave a tired sigh followed by a groan. "Look, I apologize. I'm jet-lagged beyond lucidity, but that's still no excuse for rudeness."

He received a few grins and nods, telling him he was forgiven, but the woman called Lucia, still leaning back in her seat, let out a laugh that sounded like relief. "Good. I mean..." She held her mouth open before adding, "we understand."

"I heard two words while I was there," Anna finally told him. "*Sacramachaco* and *iraca*. None of us recognized the language."

He took a moment to consider, though he recognized the words and knew what they meant. He knew them well. "Incan," he said with confidence. "A dialect found in Peru."

The dark-haired Lucia pursed her lips, and all of a sudden she didn't look so timid. "You think it's Quechuan?"

Ethan tilted his head before acknowledging her with a slow nod. He was impressed. There just might be more to the sexy witch than he'd originally thought. Not that it would matter to him.

She shot a look to Anna and spoke with a rolling accent that now sounded sharp instead of exotic. "If he's right, we need to focus on South America. At least in regard to the dagger's origins. Who knows where it might be now?"

"Dagger?" Ethan had to stop himself from appearing overly-enthusiastic. "Can you describe it?"

Anna's eyes narrowed slightly before she described a silver dagger with black stones.

Ethan held his breath.

Then she told him of the design. A dragon swallowing an arrow.

"Hell," he said, "it's beginning to look like I'll never get a chance to sleep." But energy washed through him. "I know the dagger you saw. In fact I'm very familiar with both its history and purpose. If," he added with a wry grin, "you believe in that kind of thing."

Lucia put her hands on the granite. "Have you seen it?"

"No," he said. "I've never seen it in person and don't know where it is."

"That doesn't matter. I just need a picture." She reached to touch his forearm before realizing what she'd done. She jerked back as if scalded. "Or even a sketch," she added.

He noticed now that her eyes were a rich, velvety brown. But as she waited for his response, they were piercing. Determined.

"Right. We've got our own tracking system," the woman with long caramel hair said. Hayden, Ethan remembered. She grinned softly. "And one of the world's best relic hunters."

Ethan glanced around at the gathering. He did fine on his own, but wouldn't mind another able body and experienced explorer to give him a hand. If an expedition was required to locate the dagger, then he was damn well going to be on it.

The coven just didn't know it yet. Neither did Quinn. Watching as his friend ate his beef and rice, Ethan felt a trickle of guilt.

Then Ethan shoved the self-reproach aside. He planned to tell them tonight anyway, just as soon as he knew who his traveling companion would be.

He remembered Quinn's earlier comment and turned to the

one called Paige. Fearless. Tough. She had to be the one. He met her eyes of aqua-marine and nodded. "Tell me about some of your finds."

She frowned at him. "What?"

"Your discoveries. Any artifacts worth mentioning?"

After a moment her light-blonde brows shot up before she laughed short. And she wasn't the only one of the women who seemed amused. Why did he suddenly feel like the butt of a joke?

"Not me, bud." Paige snorted and jerked a thumb to her right.

Slowly Ethan trailed down the table to find the dark-haired vixen in the black shirt. The one with the distracting spangly-spangles. His shock must have been evident, because she lifted one impudent brow and crossed her arms.

Her smile was brittle when she said, "*Hola.*"

4

Lucia lounged on the sofa in a leisurely pose, almost defiantly so. How dare Ethan judge her so harshly when he knew nothing about her? And if his brusque attitude hadn't been proof enough, the surprise on his face to discover she could do more than paint her nails had closed the case. With an insulting bang.

Things were so not going the way she'd hoped. Not to blow her own horn, but men were usually nicer to her. Sure, romantic fun and games were fine, perfectly natural to her way of thinking, but she'd always been well aware of the depth of most men's feelings.

Often measured somewhere between thigh and cleavage.

And that was how she'd liked it. Not too much involvement, therefore no broken promises or broken hearts. She was particular in choosing lovers, of course, but flirting? She could wink and flutter every day. It was enjoyable, and best of all... nobody got hurt.

She knew she'd recognize the one for her when she saw him, and then she could get serious.

If only Ethan would cooperate.

His frank dismissal of her hadn't been painful. Exactly. But it sure hadn't felt good either. She'd expected a little more from destiny's blind date.

Claudia gave her an encouraging wink as she took a chair to wait with the others. After Ethan had stunned them all with his information about the dagger, they'd decided to reconvene in the grand hall while he went upstairs to get some materials.

Lucia found it odd that the very dagger Anna had seen, the very one Lucia was meant to find, was mentioned in a book that Ethan just happened to have with him. Of all the materials he'd accumulated in his life's work, how was it the key to her challenge was stuffed in his black duffel bag?

From beneath lowered lids she watched him stride across the floor. Proud, sure of himself, and with features set in hard lines, Ethan Drake emanated strength. An invisible aura seemed to pulse around him, defensive, with an energy born of strife and survival.

Or maybe that's what Lucia chose to see, instead of having to admit he simply didn't like her.

Iris meowed near her feet, so Lucia patted the couch in invitation. The cat put her front paws on the green velvet but stopped mid-leap when Ethan spoke. Glancing between him and Lucia with shrewd blue eyes, the Persian finally settled on the stranger to follow his every move.

Ethan took a position in the center of the seating area to address the coven and Quinn.

Then as Lucia watched, her traitorous cat pranced across the room to sit adoringly at Ethan's feet. *Hmph.* Guess pets really were reflections of their humans.

Maybe she should follow her cat's lead and fawn over Mr. Hostile. Let him know she could be friendly, too.

Determined to start anew, she flashed an encouraging smile as Ethan held up a worn, brown book. "I've got that picture you wanted," he said, espresso-hued eyes directed at her. "But first, I want to give you the dagger's history."

"Glad I made popcorn," Kylie said, only to receive a

chastising tap on her shoulder from Quinn before he told her, "Pay attention."

"I'll take some of that," Anna said, reaching into the steaming bag of microwavable goodness. She rubbed Kylie's arm and almost glared her brother into the ground.

Ethan took advantage of the tense silence to start his history lesson. He spoke to Anna. "The stones you saw on the dagger are rumored to be obsidian. A dark, shiny material formed after lava cools. It's called volcanic glass, and many cultures revered it for its beauty and ability to be worked to a razor-sharp edge. For arrows."

"Arrows again," Claudia said. "Hmm. Symbolic of something specific, I presume?"

"Sure." Ethan nodded. "The arrow is often used to represent power, and sometimes the act of hunting. I believe the hunter allusion fits best in this case, but I'll get to that in a moment."

He clutched the brown book as if protecting a secret. "The serpent you described is in fact a dragon, and while it's been found in many different societies, the use of it on this dagger refers to a specific entity. A mythological beast." He paused for effect. "*Sacramachaco*. Bad snake."

The lamplight in the room blipped off then on again, sending shivers over Lucia's shoulders. It was never a good thing to have menacing words echoing in the air just as darkness fell.

"There's a storm coming up from south of here," Quinn said in explanation. "Go ahead, Ethan."

Pulling a set of keys from his pocket, Ethan dangled a credit-card shaped flashlight. "Just in case." For a moment Lucia thought he was joking, but his firm lips didn't smile.

"The story of this dagger began hundreds of years ago, during a time when people were much more accepting of things they couldn't see, hear, or explain," he said. "Legend has it the dagger was forged for the specific purpose of killing this entity. This demon. A destructive force that wreaked havoc on natives in the land we now know as South America. He was called The Earthshaker."

"I'm going to go out on a limb and say that was because of earthquakes." Viv stood behind Kylie, her big brain probably working double-time. "Ancient civilizations often attributed natural disasters to displeased gods or monsters."

"True," Ethan said, taking a few slow steps in the Asian woman's direction. "But this time they were right. And the term earthshaking didn't apply to tectonic shifts but to a journey. A transference."

He gestured like a college professor would while giving a lecture, and Lucia allowed a small smile. Ethan seemed to enjoy the role of teacher.

His soot-black hair was pushed to the side, giving her a clear view of the straight brows that gave his eyes a hawkish quality. Of wide firm lips that could be severe yet tempting at once. Lucia shivered as pure attraction racked her body.

She sat up straighter, ignoring the sudden ache to kiss him so she could focus instead on his words.

"Earthshaking," he continued, "is the act of passing from the underworld to the upper world."

"When a demon takes corporeal form," Anna said, her hand still in her lap, cupping the popcorn she'd been about to eat. "So my ancestors weren't the first to have this problem. I suspected as much."

"You mean there are more Bastraals in the world?" Shauni asked, causing Skid to whine from his favorite spot on the upper walkway. The dog had detected fear in his person's voice.

And Lucia shivered from that same feeling of dread. "Just how often does this happen, or has a demon been successful?" The idea of anything as strong and vicious as Bastraal walking among humans was terrifying.

Ethan shuttered his expression. "More often than you want to know, so let's focus on one issue at a time."

Lucia snapped her mouth closed. She definitely wasn't imagining things. He was being ruder to her than anyone else. Was it her fault he was so prejudiced about glitz and glam? "So what does *iraca* mean?" she asked. Better to get him talking again.

He lifted a careless shoulder. "It means blade. Which I believe is explanation enough."

After that comment, Hayden looked at Lucia and widened her eyes in question. At least Lucia wasn't imagining things, but that didn't help the problem. Why was Ethan being so antagonistic?

"At any rate," he said, sliding his eyes back to Quinn, "the makers of the dagger were successful in defeating The Earthshaker, and supposedly hid the blade after their victory. Like your prophecy, there are others. The dagger was secreted away for many years. Concealed until the day it was to be used again. In fact there's an expression."

Now he opened his book and read from the pages. "And shall the blade rest beneath the veil, interred until it meets the hand of she who may wield its power. The priestess of the hunt."

"Priestess could definitely refer to a witch," Claudia said, tucking her feet under her and smiling.

"Lucia." Willyn eased to stand beside the couch. "Your profession is to search for things. To hunt them."

Lucia searched the faces of her friends, from Hayden's soulful warmth to Paige's steadfast intensity. Kylie's youthful wisdom around again to Willyn's serenity. "You can understand why I'm not thrilled to be this priestess," she said. "It follows that I'll have to wield the blade. Against a demon."

Quinn indicated the brown book in Ethan's hand. "Not necessarily. You might wield a blade in several different ways, and even if it is to defend yourself or kill, the phrase said nothing about a demon."

"Either way, I know my task is to find this dagger," Lucia

told him. She stood to walk to Ethan, meeting him almost eye to eye in the middle of the floor, since technically she had to look up.

She ignored the flutter in her belly. It took an awfully tall man to make her feel smaller. More feminine. "I need to see what's in that book," she told him firmly.

Ethan drew back with no small amount of surprise. Now he knew claws could be painted Poppy Field red.

After beetling his brow at her with irritation, he opened the book to a marked page. A sketch older than the slate beneath her feet was there, on paper gone yellow and ragged at the edges.

When she reached for the book, he kept it just out of her reach. "I'll hold it," he said. "It's important to me."

"Fine, but I need to get a good look." Making a show of clasping her hands safely behind her back, she leaned forward as he spread the pages again. The weapon was just as Anna described, a dragon with an awful look in his tiny eye was bent around himself to swallow an arrow.

As she stared at the picture, the world began a slow heavy throb around her. A deep sound pulsed in her ears, whooshing back and forth like a gigantic metronome in a sea of tar. Images flashed at her, as they always did when the place she sought was far away.

The dagger was nowhere close to Savannah, of that she was sure.

Air, clouds. A blue sea beneath. Travel by plane would be required. She flew in her mind's movie screen, over jungle and river, mountain and valley, until the electromagnetic chips in her body all swung in one direction. She felt a long pull then snapped to a stop, where she wavered and fought to get her bearings.

Cracked stones came into view, decorated and placed with precision many, many years ago. Blinking to clear the apparition, she stared at the ruins around her, and knew where she was.

When Ethan's hand grabbed her shoulder, she shook off the lingering images and said, "Kuelap." Then she was looking into his dark-chocolate eyes. Too bad they were bittersweet.

She laid her fingers over his and grinned. "Well. That was new. I've never had quite so much information and as many clear pictures."

"Are you steady on your feet now?" he asked in an impatient tone before pulling his hand out from under hers.

Rebuked once again, Lucia sniffed and did her best to look down—actually up—her nose at him. "I'm always steady on my feet."

With his handsome face still flat and unreadable, Ethan repeated the word she'd spoken. "Kuelap." He nodded and rubbed his jaw, pacing away from her as he thought aloud. "The cold place."

"You know it?" Lucia prodded as she took up her position on the couch again, pretending her shoulder didn't still tingle from where he'd touched her. "The name means cold place," she explained to the others, "but only because it's one of the few places in the Amazon jungle that isn't warm."

She went back to the couch and sat back against the green velvet. She faced Anna. "Now I know where I'm going and can start prepping."

She held up her hand and started ticking off her fingers. "My plane is at the hangar, so I need to call and let them know I'll be coming. My pack is..."

"Hold on," Quinn jumped in before anyone else could, and a few of the witches looked as if they wanted to do just that. When Lucia swung her eyes to him he said, "You can't go by yourself."

"Of course I can. This is what I do. I know how to get around, and if I need any assistance I can hire extra hands on the ground."

"Quinn's right," Willyn put in, her normally soft voice hardened by immovable concern. A tone she'd perfected as a mother. "We know you're capable, but things have changed. This trip won't be like the ones before."

Lucia scoffed. "Why?"

"Because you never had the talented Ms. Ronja and her psychotic friends to deal with, that's why." Paige had her don't-even-argue face on, and Lucia could see she was going to be outvoted.

Huffing loudly, Lucia shrugged and said, "What about the portals here in Savannah? The beasts slipping in every night? Our coven is already going to be down one witch. We shouldn't lose another."

"I disagree." Shauni was standing with her hands on her hips. "We've learned that our individual challenges are paramount to success. Take one of us with you to increase your odds." In a rare show of obstinacy, the raven-haired woman drilled Lucia with pure, green eyes and insisted, "I'm the best choice. Tell me what I need to pack."

"What? Why you?" Kylie asked. "Shouldn't we take a vote?"

"Okay." Shauni was trying to sound reasonable. "Then let's vote. Anyone with objections to my being the one to go with Lucia, raise your hand."

Sneaky witch, Lucia thought and grinned. "No one is going to object. And that's what you were counting on."

"Then it's settled," Shauni said, rushing the decision before anyone thought to change their mind. "Now I just need to tell Michael."

"That I need to take some vacation time," the man in question said as he strolled into the room. Wearing his uniform of jeans and a button-down with sleeves rolled up to his elbows, Michael took off his glasses and hung them in his shirt pocket. "I took the second boat out and heard the tail end of the conversation."

He smiled with as much willfulness as Shauni had used to make her argument. "Where are we going?"

Laughing at the turn of events, Lucia told the tall, blonde veterinarian, "Peru. And you'll need to take clothes for warm and cool weather. Bug spray, of course, but don't worry about food or water. The Caravan will be stocked with what we need and any emergency supplies. I'll plan our route tonight."

She was surprisingly relieved to have arrangements to make. Her ego was still bruised from Ethan's curt words and obvious disregard. She'd let herself be optimistic. Maybe too quickly?

Now it looked like her trial would be carried out in Peru. With Ethan nowhere in sight.

She pretended she didn't feel like she'd been kicked in the throat.

Foolish really, all this worry over a man when there were much larger problems to solve. But Lucia had taken heart when the others before her had ended up happy and cherished by someone. The real and aching need to be loved was nothing new, but having her hopes dashed so quickly made her feel like a spindly-legged eight-year-old all over again.

Ugly and alone. Unworthy.

"I should go as well," Ethan said, causing Lucia's head to jerk up to see if she'd heard correctly. She held her breath then expelled it in a controlled rush, trying to stay quiet and listen.

Anna studied Lucia for a moment then Ethan before she asked him, "Why?" Simple and straightforward.

"There's more to the legend of the dagger, and if you do find it," he said for Lucia's benefit, "you might need my help. When The Earthshaker was destroyed, he cast out one final curse before he vanished. He killed his human harem and left their souls behind to guard the dagger."

"Then maybe I should go in your place." This from Hayden. "Besides, you should be here in Savannah to help with the demons." She brushed caramel-colored hair from her cheek. "Right, Anna?"

Their leader considered the question. "I wish I knew more, but for once we may have to let instinct be our guide. Mr. Drake seems determined, and he is the expert, apparently, on this dagger and the evil associated with it." She nodded and glanced to Lucia. "You have the final say, though. This is your challenge."

"These aren't your average spirits we're talking about. If there is any such thing," Ethan said, pressing his argument. He turned to Lucia and squared his jaw, ready to convince her. "The souls were changed by their demon master. They were... twisted."

Mrs. Attinger chose that moment to breeze into the grand hall from the kitchen. She held a crystal vase full of crimson roses. The silver-haired woman and all-around caretaker of the extended family stopped when she realized everyone was staring at her. "Oh, I apologize. Seems I've interrupted."

Lucia was relieved to have the interruption, but then she took in the huge bouquet and their meaning. "Mrs. Attinger. You've already started on the flowers." Her eyes burned suspiciously. "No dust ever settles on you."

The older woman smiled. "I do what I can, and since the color is a personal favorite of mine, I'll be happy to fill the mansion with vibrant reds." She winked and moved to set the vase on an end table.

Lucia stood and walked to her side. Leaned over and smelled the flowers. When Mrs. Attinger pulled her into a hug, Lucia sank right in. She was never one to pass up a maternal embrace. "But I won't even be here," she said against the woman's shoulder.

Pulling back, Mrs. Attinger touched her cheek. "But your flowers will be, and every time we stop to touch a petal, you'll know."

Blinking to clear her vision, Lucia said, "And you'll take care of Iris while I'm gone? You know how she likes her treats."

"Of course I will." She squeezed Lucia's hands. "We all will." Then she turned and left as quietly as she'd come.

But she'd given Lucia the boost she'd needed. To make a decision and take whatever fate decided to throw at her. "You can go," she told Ethan, and could tell by his frown he didn't like the fact she was *allowing* him to accompany her and the others.

Then for one tiny bit of payback, she told him, "But this isn't going to be a pie walk."

Her moment of superiority disintegrated when Claudia laughed. "Um. I think you mean a cake walk." She gave a conspiratorial wink. "Those damn colloquialisms."

Lucia swallowed against embarrassment then laughed despite herself. "So, we have some work to do. Ethan," she said suddenly, "I think you should get some sleep. I'll handle the travel plans, so you don't have to worry." She took in his tired eyes, hoping some rest would improve his jet lag.

And his attitude.

Lowering his head in acceptance, he said, "I appreciate that." He said his good nights to the women and slipped off toward the stairs.

Holding herself in place, Lucia didn't turn and watch him leave. Tomorrow would be a fresh start, and if she just breathed deep and did what she did best, everything would work out fine. Two of her primary skill sets would be required for this task, so really, she was as prepared as a witch could get.

Ethan's aloof and devastatingly handsome face flashed in her mind.

Locate an ancient artifact and make a man fall at her feet? *Hmph.* She snapped her red-tipped fingers in the air and smiled. *Easy as cake.*

5

The airfield was humming with activity by the time Ethan arrived with Shauni and her boyfriend Michael. Though barely seven in the morning, the air was already warm enough for him to slip off his brown, leather jacket. Savannah weather was like a temperamental woman and swung with mercurial tendencies.

A golf cart buzzed across the tarmac and rolled to a stop in front of them. The young man inside told them he'd be their escort and would take them to the hangar. Ms. Ruiz had left word of her guests' arrival.

Ethan ordered himself not to be too impressed with Lucia's efficiency, though he grudgingly admitted a kernel was growing inside where the Spanish witch was concerned. Respect. He recognized how hard she must have worked to line everything up for this impromptu expedition, and he understood the value of having a competent person as leader of such a trip.

He knew, because he'd gone on plenty of excursions himself, and had seen how quickly a misstep could turn to crisis if the guide was inept. So far Lucia Ruiz seemed up to the job. But he would reserve judgment for the time being. He'd just wait and see.

Squinting against the sun as they neared the open hangar,

he searched the area for a brunette with outlandish fashion sense. He almost skipped right over her white T-shirt and khaki pants, but the long ponytail of loose brown curls gave her away.

That and the way she filled out the khakis.

Too bad, he told himself. He couldn't go there.

He was still having a hard time putting together the siren from last night with an explorer willing to get her hands dirty. He exited the golf cart, and when Lucia turned at the sound of Shauni's voice, he almost laughed at his own analogy.

Her hands were filthy. Apparently she was a hands-on pilot, adding another line on her resume for Ethan to chew over. Gorgeous and accomplished. *Aw, hell.*

"Muy buenos días," she called out in her flowing accent. She wore no make-up and the long red fingernails from the night before were shorter and unpolished. She actually had a smudge of grease on her face.

And Ethan was uncomfortable with how cute that was.

"I'm so excited," Shauni said, jogging over to peer into the open hatch with Lucia. "What are you doing?"

Michael hauled a small, beige duffel onto his shoulder as he moved to stand with Ethan. "Do you even know what you're looking at?" he called to his girlfriend, the raven-haired witch who reportedly talked to animals. Ethan would like to see how that worked.

Shauni tossed her boyfriend a challenging look. "Do you?"

Michael let his eyes travel down to her backside and said, "Always." When he winked, she only laughed and whispered something to Lucia. If Ethan were guessing, he'd say it was probably something about men and one-track minds.

He wished he could disagree. And that thought drew his attention right back to his pilot for the day. The exotic version from the night before had drawn his eye a time or two, but the natural Lucia was a far more dangerous entity. Worse than attractive. She was intriguing.

No one would ever describe her as ethereal or dainty. Those words weren't quite right for the Spanish witch. She was more...earthy.

And in a way that was far too sexy to be ignored.

Murky ground, Ethan warned the hot-blooded male just beneath his own skin. There was a reason the women he pursued were only borderline interesting. He had rules for a reason. Safeguards. His failsafe isolation method.

He didn't spend time with females who were any combination of smart, attractive, funny, ambitious, or kind. The extended time spent in such a female's company could never be worth the risk.

Only one, maybe two good qualities could be allowed, and Lucia was hitting on more than one level. He almost wished she'd shown up today in a completely inappropriate outfit. Then it wouldn't be possible to take her seriously.

Unfortunately, she seemed to know her stuff, and there was nothing he could do now but bite down on the strap and withstand her presence. Her proximity. Hopefully, she wouldn't smell as intoxicating as she looked.

"Nice Caravan," he told her, for want of anything better.

"You like her?" Lucia stroked the underside of the narrow, silver nose. The plane was detailed with two stripes, a thick one of bronze and thinner black beneath. "I found her a few years ago. Great storage capacity below, and the flexible design is perfect for landings. Grass, rocky terrain, or uneven airstrip. The nose gear absorbs lateral and vertical forces and shifts it to the fuselage."

A wrinkle of confusion formed between Shauni's black eyebrows. "I take it that makes things less bumpy?"

"You should enjoy the ride," Lucia replied, looping her hand around Shauni's elbow to steer her towards the back. She pointed to the underbelly of the Caravan. "We have plenty of emergency materials stocked, including water and dried food packs."

"I brought my own food packs," Ethan said. "I like to eat healthy."

She forced a smile and added, "We also have satellite phones, for communicating with Anna and the others if the need arises."

"I thought we were only going to be gone a week," Shauni said. "Or even less."

Lucia nodded and patted the side of the plane, causing a low, metal reverberation. "I just like to prepare for any eventuality." She slid those warm, brown eyes to Ethan then. Was her smile a bit mischievous? "But I expect everything to go smoothly."

Frowning, Ethan turned his attention to the rest of the plane. He hoped she was right. If she could do as she claimed and find the dagger quickly, the four of them might be able to get in and out of Peru within three or four days. Plenty of tourists visited Kuelap Fortress, and the surrounding countryside was fairly safe. Hopefully there would be no run-ins with drug cartels or tribes angry over land disputes.

Fly in, search the ruins by night, and fly back out. Simple.

And if all went as planned, Ethan would come away with his own prize. Ten years of searching was long enough, and he'd finally gotten a taste of hope. The first real chance he'd been given since his tumultuous childhood.

Since the curse.

So he was grabbing that chance. With both hands. And no one would stand in his way.

"The weather report says we're all clear, and I've done my check list." Lucia pointed to the bags being loaded underneath the plane. "So if you have all your things, we can get started."

Shauni grabbed Michael's hand and pulled him around to the opposite side to board. She laughed and clapped her hands twice once she'd taken her seat. "I've never flown in a small plane before."

Michael lifted her hand and kissed it, his gray eyes full of love for the woman beside him.

Ethan grinned despite himself. He could appreciate the happiness of others and had learned long ago to compartmentalize the desire for something as deep and real as what Michael and Shauni seemed to have. Another survival measure, because he wasn't destined for the same and would waste no time on envy.

Left with the choices of taking the front seat next to Lucia or going for the back and snubbing her outright, Ethan reminded himself he'd dealt with tight situations before. He climbed in the front and waited.

"First things first," Lucia said after buckling her lap strap. Then she pulled out a small pink tube and twisted the cap.

Ethan's jaw dropped when she swiped a little brush over her lips, smiled and said, "Watermelon. Hmm."

He waited for her to put away the tube, waited for her to notice his stare. When she finally glanced at him, he said, "Our lives are in your hands, and the first priority of your takeoff check list is lip gloss?"

She tossed the end of her long ponytail over her shoulder. "I know what I'm doing. This is my routine. I don't travel without lip gloss." She tilted her head down slightly, daring him to argue.

With an exasperated sigh, all he could come up with was, "Why not lipstick?"

She shrugged and slipped on her headset. "Not the right consistency, and glosses have pleasing scents to choose from. They make me happy."

Michael tapped Ethan on the shoulder. "And we want a happy pilot."

"Fine. Whatever." Ethan tucked his bag away and sat quietly. When the teasing scent of watermelon struck straight to the core of his gut, he did his best to dislike it. And to not think of Lucia's lips. They were fuller than average, lusciously so. He thought the term was *bee-stung*.

"Savannah ground, this is November-four-three-four-Sierra-Charlie, ready to taxi." Lucia's voice was firm and confident, and he couldn't stop himself from shifting his eyes to study her profile. Here was a woman of the world. Ready to take life by the yoke, literally, as was the case, and steer herself to whatever destination suited her.

The plane rolled out of the hangar with Lucia speaking as needed into her receiver. When they came to a stop at the end of a strip, she said, "Tower, November-four-three-four-Sierra-Charlie, holding short of runway one. Ready for takeoff."

"I'm so impressed," Shauni said from the back. "This is a whole other side of you, Lucia."

Ethan gritted his teeth and looked out the window. He was impressed, too.

Lucia smiled back at her friend then Ethan. Her grin was feral as she smacked her lips and said, "Ready?"

"Sure," he replied in a smooth voice. When she released the brake and they started to move, he tore his eyes away from her competent hands and lean, curvy physique.

Was he ready? Ethan breathed deeply. *I'm not sure I am.*

6

Lucia and the others must have taken the sunny weather with them, Anna mused as she hurried in from outside. Overcast now, the day had turned cool, so she was delighted to find Paige building a fire in the grand hall.

As the lean blonde stoked the growing flames in the hearth, she tossed a comment to Anna. "We won't have reason for these much longer. I thought we should take advantage and huddle inside today." She tossed the stick she'd been using onto the logs and added, "Or we could plan the first stage of our attack."

"You mean defense," Hayden said, strolling in from the kitchen with a tray of snacks. "Since technically we're the ones being invaded."

Spying the medium's assortment of offerings—cheese squares, mini-sausages, veggie tray with sauce—Anna gave her friends a suspicious onceover. "Why do I feel like I've walked into a trap?"

"Because you have." Hayden smiled unapologetically. "But if we're all feeling restless, we knew you'd be catching up to us soon enough."

Anna barked a short laugh. "More than. In fact, I think I'm lapping you and about to win the gold. I've been trying to let Lucia clear the continent before plunging into the home field disadvantage, but apparently you're all as eager as I am."

"We do have a job to do," Paige pointed out, ready as ever to war plan.

When the rest of the coven trickled in with their own additions to the snack extravaganza, Viv took a seat beside Anna on the couch. "Mrs. Attinger is making tea." The telekinetic witch tilted her head to the side. "She said you'd need some Dragon Jasmine for calm. Does she have the gift of sight like you?"

Taking a piece of broccoli and dipping it, Anna shrugged. "She won't admit anything, but she does pick up vibes. Having lived with her in the house during my teenage years, I'm sure of it."

"Ouch." Viv grimaced. "Having a mother for a witch and see-all-know-all Mrs. Attinger around at the same time? Did you ever get away with anything?"

"Sure," Anna said, grinning smugly. "I just blamed Quinn a lot."

Kylie was the last to come in holding a large frosted mug with a foamy top. "I blame Quinn a lot, too," she mumbled before catching the surprised looks and smiling broadly. "Never mind that. Moving on."

"Is that actually a root beer float?" Paige asked.

"Uh..." Kylie stalled and sized up the soldier. "If I say yes are you going to hurt me?"

Paige shook her head. "Now I want one, too." She zipped to the kitchen in a blur of movement.

"No using your skills inside," Claudia called out from her position in front of the fire. She was warming her backside. "You might break a vase or something."

Paige was back in less than a minute, with foam gracing her lips. "Yum."

"Now that our bottomless stomachs are being filled," Willyn, their gentle healer, said with her chin resting in her palm as she curled up in a chair, "what are we going to do about the demons?"

"Straight to the point." Anna smoothed her shirt. "I like that." Pausing to gather her thoughts, Anna looked at her hands. They were so like her mother's. *Now where did that come from?*

"Anna," Kylie said. "Are you all right? You look like you've seen a..." Holding her mug out toward Hayden, she finished with, "Well, you know."

With a chill from both nostalgia and premonition coursing down her arms, Anna answered, "Yes. I'm fine." She straightened up and said, "Ethan did have a few suggestions before he left this morning. Unfortunately, what he thinks we need, we still don't have."

"What's that?" Viv asked, gray eyes frowning behind her black glasses.

"If we're going to clear the demons out, specifically the ones affecting humans, we have to know more about them. We need to identify their...breed, for lack of a better word."

"You mean he couldn't tell you?" Paige set aside her empty mug. "All due respect, isn't he the specialist?"

Anna saw she'd started off with the wrong lead. "He is, and he was able to show Quinn and me a list of what kind we're dealing with. The ones that can either look like or possess and use human forms."

She stood now, feeling more confident. "The good news is he says these..." here she stumbled on the word, because the significance of it was huge, "that these *clans* don't usually get along with each other, having once been closely related in the other world. So whichever ones are in Savannah, are probably all the same."

"It is just so freaky to hear you say things like that and know they're true." Kylie stared into the fire and popped a cheese square in her mouth.

"I know." Anna put a hand to her stomach. "Believe me, this

is all far more than even I expected. At any rate, all we have to do is identify the type of demon, and we'll know how to combat them. They each have their own essence, Ethan said, and we need to know what it is."

"The list is up in my room," she explained, working herself up to a more energized state. "Ethan pointed me in the right direction, but that doesn't solve our first problem."

"Which is?" Hayden asked.

"We have to catch one of them, don't we?" Viv wrapped her arms around her mid-section. "Or at least get close enough to scrape off some of their skin, or hair. I don't even know how we determine their essence in the first place. Excuse me, deadly demon, would you mind rubbing this swab on the inside of your cheek?"

Paige nodded. "Yeah, and that's if we can even spot one. We could go around staring at people until we see a face flip over to the ugly side. Then what? Grab them off the street?"

"Even Trevor won't be able to save us if we do that and we're wrong," Hayden said. Her detective boyfriend was back on the beat and protecting his city. But now he knew to keep an eye on the shadows for real monsters.

Kylie threw up her hands. "Man, it's too bad we don't have Frodo's sword or something."

"Huh?" Viv swiveled to give the younger witch a baffled look.

Anna, however, shared the love of cinema with Kylie. "How do you mean?"

"You know. The way his weapon lit up when Orcs were near. We need a something-wicked-this-way warning system." She huffed, tearing her attention from Anna and back to Viv before she hissed, "You don't know Frodo? Seriously, Viv? Seriously?"

Anna held her hands out now for a full inspection. The chill raced down her body again, but this time she recognized the omen. *My mother's hands.* She dropped them and took a turn around the room, tapping her finger to her chin. "I'm working up an idea," she told the others. They were all watching her intently now.

"I think we can use what Ethan gave us, but it will require some work." And some courage, she thought when her gaze traveled down the long, dark corridor. When she visualized the old, wooden door that stood at the end. Locked tight.

"I promise to fill you all in once I work out the details." Anna wished for that Dragon Jasmine tea, since her insides had gone cold. "But first I need to talk to my brother."

7

Dabbing just the right amount of perfume on her pulse points, Lucia took one last look at herself in the bathroom mirror. She practiced her best come-hither smile and reveled in the joy of being female.

Then she ran her palm over the ruby-red halter dress, satin with a high waist and Marilyn pleats that fell to mid-thigh. In the mirror her reflection gave a decisive nod before she twirled to test the effect.

Now her grin was one of satisfaction. Kylie and Claudia weren't the only ones who could rock a Valentino.

She wore her brown hair loose and her heels high, and the sounds her steps made on the marble floor only amped up her confidence. If this outfit didn't catch Ethan's attention…well, then she'd check to make sure he had a pulse.

Snagging the matching clutch from a night stand, she left her posh villa and walked to meet the others at the main building. Sure they could have stayed at a less expensive hotel, but it wasn't every day a girl got to host an intercontinental expedition to help slay a demon and save the world. So she wanted to make her guests as comfortable as possible.

And if the outdoor lounge just happened to come equipped with a dance floor and hot, Latino band, all the more reason to wear a little, red dress. Especially one that gave such good twirl.

As soon as she entered the breezeway of the main lobby, she crossed paths with Shauni and Michael. Shauni, bless her, was wearing a white dress that fell to her knees and was trimmed with vibrant green embroidery. She looked like a jungle princess.

Michael wore a black linen shirt, which was ridiculously sexy on his tall, muscular frame. Lucia gave him an appreciative growl and winked at Shauni. "I need to get you two out of the country more often."

"Look who's talking," Shauni said as she trailed a finger down the red satin pleats. "I know hunting gear when I see it."

Michael nodded then said, "Huh?"

"Never mind," Shauni took her blonde hunk by the arm. "The less you know the better."

"I agree," he uttered, moving with her and Lucia toward the lounge. "That seems to be a theme with you and your friends, and one I'm beginning to fully embrace."

"Which theme is that?" Lucia asked, kicking up one half of her lips in a smirk.

Michael shot her a look that said *You know what I mean* before backing it up with a grunt. "Plausible deniability."

"Good plan," Lucia said on a laugh. The band chose that moment to kick off a quick-tempo song and the wind blew warm and salty from the ocean. She gave a whoop then asked Shauni and Michael. "Do you know how to do a *paso doble*?"

When she received two blank expressions in return, she waved her hand. "Never mind. You will before the night's over. Which reminds me." Lucia scanned the crowd. "Where is my partner?" She was nothing if not persistent.

Then she saw him, and her stomach rolled like a midnight tide. Dark as the devil and twice as handsome, Ethan sat alone at the crowded bar, focusing on whatever he was drinking. He had the dangerous loner routine down to a science.

The only problem, Lucia worried, was that it wasn't an act.

Tiki torches were scattered around the perimeter, adding another layer of mystique. Here she was in an exotic locale, with a tortured soul pulling on her heartstrings, and all she could do was stare. Where had the daring Lucia gone?

She stood like a freshman at prom, trembling all the way down to her strappy heels. She couldn't stop looking at him, memorizing every curve of his wide, thick shoulders under the black of his shirt. The way his raven hair hung to his collar, and how he brushed the length of it out of his face when the wind blew.

Lucia had almost collected the shreds of her composure when Ethan slowly turned his head. He glanced past her before doing a double-take. Lucia smiled. Even from this distance she saw his eyes darken, and not with the dislike he tried so hard to convey.

His stare narrowed slightly, as if he were sending her a message. *Back off.*

But Lucia wasn't receiving. Instead she tossed her hair over her shoulder and lifted her chin in challenge.

She thought she saw his jaw clench before he turned away.

Ethan whirled back to the bar and flattened his palm on the glass bar. "Whisky. Now."

"Do you have a preference?" the man behind the bar asked.

He shook his head. "Anything." He curled his upper lip. "As long as it's not Spanish."

The woman was trying to torture him. *Jesus.* What else could explain her wearing that dress? She was the one being put through some sort of supernatural test. She was the one with everything at stake.

So why did he feel like he was dangling over hot coals? *Red* hot coals.

Five hours in a small compartment had been bad enough,

trapped and unable to get away from the very female scent of her clean skin. He'd never imagined the smell of basic soap could be so tempting, but mixed with her essence and the barest hint of watermelon?

He took the short glass of yellow liquor and didn't bother asking what it was. He downed it and motioned for another. The bartender gave him a wary look, as if he recognized trouble when he saw it.

When he poured, Ethan worked up a smile. He had to keep the guy on his good side if he wanted an unending supply of liquid resistance.

If he had to look at those long, toned legs in red high heels for the rest of the night, he was going to need some backup.

He heard Shauni's voice as she and Michael came closer. Then he smelled what could only be described as expensive sex, and he had a feeling Lucia was right behind him. And she'd added perfume to an already potent female package.

"You won't need too many of those," she said close to his ear, tapping her fingernail on the side of his glass. "I promise not to make the night too painful."

He jerked his head to the side, away from her warm breath. "Too late," he muttered into the glass before tossing back the rest. The whiskey burned his throat and all the way down until it hit his gut. But at least it took his mind off of other anatomical parts.

"Come on, Ethan," she put a hand on his shoulder and every muscle in his body clenched. "Won't you come dance with me?"

Her voice was full of teasing laughter, another thing he'd discovered about her on the flights. She had a sense of humor, wicked at times, yet charmingly sweet when she misused an expression. She spoke perfect English, probably better than his own, but Claudia had been right about the damned colloquialisms.

"I don't dance," he said, drumming his fingers on the

polished wood as he waited for the bartender to finish with a group at the far end. "But you go ahead." He didn't like the bite he heard in his refusal, but it had been there just the same.

No matter. He had to keep his distance, and the Spanish witch with smiling, brown eyes just wasn't taking the hint.

Hell, he'd be surprised if she would take a verbal shove. She bounced back like putty, and damned if he knew why.

Ethan had been in a plane with her all day, spending much of that time dodging her attempts to draw him out of his shell. He had a hard exterior for a reason, and that's how he intended to keep it.

Lucia had a rhythm. She'd prod him lightly, good-naturedly until he would start chatting with her due to his own curiosity. She was a likable enough person. Then she'd subtly shift and get too personal. Too close to the very issues he had to hide.

So he'd snap himself closed again and fall silent, reminding himself he really couldn't afford to like the witch. Especially with her sneaky advance and retreat method. Why was she so determined to make a connection with him?

"Okay," Lucia said, trying to make her tone light when Ethan continued to ignore her. He could tell her pride had taken a blow, but from what he'd seen so far, she was resilient. And persistent.

Damn, could the bartender be any slower?

"How's it going, Ethan?" Shauni asked, clearly trying to ease the tension after Lucia sailed away.

Finding Michael seated next to him and Shauni leaning on her boyfriend's back, Ethan pressed his mouth into a grim line. "I'm making it. If I can avoid hurting anyone's feelings." He met her pure, green stare. "Why do I get the feeling this trip is going to be much more complicated than I expected?"

Sliding her eyes to meet Michael's look of *Oh, boy*, Shauni sighed and said, "Lucia's facing her challenge, and I can tell you from experience, the trials never go as we expect them to."

"That's fine, but I'm only here to share my expertise. Basically just a consultant." Ethan sat back and crossed his arms. "I really have no part in this whole challenge thing."

At this Michael gave a short, deep laugh. "Yeah. That's what I thought." Shauni elbowed him in the ribs, but he just rubbed the sore spot and added, "That's what we all thought."

"Please." She rolled her eyes. "A group of happier men I've never seen. Poor smitten saps, the bunch of you." She faced Ethan again. "And another thing I've learned?" She rubbed his shoulder. "That old adage about the bigger they are has never been truer."

Ethan gave her a smart-ass grin. "Good thing I'm not the falling type, then." He caught the bartender's attention just as he heard Michael say beneath his breath, "That's what Trevor thought."

Deciding to remove himself from the disturbing conversation, Ethan took his third drink and swiveled his bar stool, glad to feel shots one and two kicking in. The air was slightly thicker, tangy with that ocean smell, and the music had slowed to a less arousing rhythm.

He had a hard enough time forgetting Lucia and her outfit without imagining what she and those hips could do with the right song.

Michael had turned around as well, and Shauni stood between his legs, leaning back against his chest. They made a pretty couple, the intelligent blonde veterinarian all wrapped up in his green-eyed witch.

But that kind of connection wasn't meant for Ethan. Even if something waited for him in Peru, he wasn't sure he could ever risk falling for someone. He thought of Lucia's dress. Of the amulet that hung from her pretty neck.

Red might be the color of love. But it was also the color of danger.

When he saw a couple swaying together on the dance floor,

Ethan forgot all about symbolism. His eyes hardened as they focused on the brawny man holding Lucia like she might be his conquest for the night. *Ridiculous. I barely know her.*

He shook his head and forced himself to take a calming breath. He wanted absolutely nothing to do with Lucia. He had no business letting his body or his male pride respond to her.

So what if she was dancing with someone else? Moving her hips in a seductive way. Smiling up at her partner.

Ethan had wanted her to go away. To stop giving him so much of her attention. She was like a forbidden treat that kept getting shoved too close to his hungry mouth.

The flirtation had to stop.

And when the man dancing with Lucia slid his hand suggestively low on her back, Ethan decided to take care of two problems at once.

He knocked back the whiskey in his hand with one slug and slammed the glass on the bar behind him. Without looking to see anyone's reaction, he stood and made his way across the dance floor.

His instincts allowed him to weave through the other moving couples with agility, and his well-practiced restraint kept him from tapping the man's shoulder too hard. "I'm cutting in," he said, but the stranger didn't step away. Instead he gave Ethan an angry frown.

Lucia said something in Spanish before smiling sweetly to her dance partner. He gave her a gallant bow and kissed her hand. Then he smirked at Ethan before edging away.

Even with every piece of good sense inside of him screaming not to take her in his arms, Ethan was helpless to stop his hands from slipping around Lucia's small waist. Her shoulders were a soft, golden-brown, satiny in the torch light, and he ground his teeth at the thought of another man touching that skin later on tonight. "What did you say to him?"

Her eyes crinkled, and her red lips lifted as if on the verge of a smile. Her damn mouth was always on the verge of a smile, and Ethan found himself wanting to taste the full, curving temptation.

"I told him you must have had too much to drink," she said, her accent even more pronounced after speaking her native tongue.

Then her eyes sparkled devilishly. "And that I preferred lovers over fighters."

"So I'm not the only one getting your blatant invitations," Ethan said, tightening his embrace and dropping his gaze to her cleavage.

He arched a brow when her smile faltered and her body stiffened. "What? Did I misread the signals? Because you've been doing your best to turn this business trip to pleasure since we left Savannah."

Lowering his head, he stopped just shy of kissing her. "What's your game, Lucia?" He rolled her name off his tongue with a Spanish flavor.

She drew back as if he'd slapped her. "I'm not playing a game. I've done nothing to be ashamed of." She tried to extricate herself, but Ethan held firm.

"Not yet, anyway," he said. "And I came over to make sure you kept it that way." He told himself he wasn't lying. To her or his own conscience. "I don't care what you do on your own time, but you're the leader of this mission, and we need your head in this. All the time, all the way. We can't take chances with your fooling around or picking up strange men."

Lucia's eyes changed from warm invitation to brittle stone. "This might surprise you, but I'm selective in who I choose to take to my bed." She licked her lips, rimming the inside with the tip of her tongue. Then she pressed against him and purred, "I like to flirt." Her fingers found his hair and stroked. "So sue me."

Ethan muttered a curse and straightened his elbows

enough to hold her back, leaving a mere inch of sultry air between their bodies. For his protection now more than hers. "You're saying you don't take many men as lovers?" He filled his voice with derision and doubt, trying to rebuild the wall that had to remain between them.

He'd gotten sloppy. Time to rebuild, even if it was with animosity. "Your behavior says something different," he all but snarled.

"And your behavior suggests you've spent your life in a monastery. A very angry one." She tilted her head and offered a mocking look of sympathy. "How many lovers have you taken?"

He laughed low, but probably not in the way she thought. "You might be surprised."

Lucia continued to twine her fingers in his hair while she pushed her chest closer again, delivering a one-two punch of seduction and insult. "That's not very specific," she whispered, looking at his mouth.

Ethan twirled her out then back again with dizzying speed. "No," he said. "It isn't." And when she looked up at him, the mutinous vixen was gone. Losing her balance unexpectedly had banished the mask and allowed her true feelings to flash across her face.

Ethan was instantly contrite.

Another slow song began playing, so he took the opportunity to redirect. "You asked me to dance before." His arms relaxed and his grip on her eased. "Does that offer still stand?"

Lucia took a moment before she answered, studying his face for any hint of anger. Looking for answers. Or for a trap. "I guess it won't hurt," she said finally. "Maybe we can get through one dance without biting at each other."

His depthless eyes were focused, as if he didn't understand what he was seeing. Maybe she was as big a mystery to Ethan as he was to her. "You speak English well," he said. "Did you study in America?"

With the last bits of tension leaving her body, she moved in time with Ethan, the easy sound of a bolero soothing to her mind and their shared mood. "No, I went to a boarding school in England during my primary years." She added in a perfect, British accent, "Only the best are admitted to Leweston Abbey. Or that's the story my parents sold me, anyway."

Refusing to slip down that slope, Lucia reminded herself to look to the future instead. Ethan had shocked her with his heated response and how quickly he'd disposed of her former dance partner. She'd only taken the man on the floor to get Ethan's attention, but his fast ignition had been a surprise.

Goddess bless the whiskey for prying open a door she'd begun to think was welded shut. At least Ethan was talking to her. *Really* talking to her.

Not to mention all the touching.

Lucia shivered when his hand readjusted on her lower back. The man not only looked hot and dangerous, he felt that way, too.

Taking a leap and hoping Ethan decided to jump along with her, Lucia said, "I do like to flirt, that is the truth." She licked her lips, but this time due to apprehension. "But I wouldn't do that with you if it weren't important. No, that's not what I want to say."

She looked up into his dark, brown eyes. They were almost black. "I wouldn't do anything to jeopardize this trip or my trial, but I think you may be part of it."

"Of course. I'm here to assist with the dagger and any paranormal entities we encounter." He firmed his full lips into an obstinate line. "That is my part. My *only* part."

Dragging her hands down his shoulders to rest on his forearms, Lucia squeezed, hoping he would understand. "Ethan, I believe fate has brought us together. This is all new for you, I know, but after what I've seen happen to my friends, why would I ignore what is so clearly in front of me?"

He looked uncomfortable now, like the older boy gently trying to let the younger girl down. To end her crush before she got hurt. "No, Lucia. I'm sorry, but I don't see what you do."

Stubborn man. Wasn't he the one who'd barreled out here to pull her away from the competition? Was he that blind, or did he just think she was? "What are you so afraid of?"

"I'm not afraid," he said quickly. "Just experienced. Besides, I'm not a big fan of fate. She's screwed me over before." He stepped away when the song ended, and she could tell he was looking for an out. "Fortune is no friend of mine."

"Why not?"

Instead of answering Ethan heaved a breath. "Lucia, you're a gorgeous woman, and I know you don't need me to clarify that. But this idea you've got in your head." He waved his hand between them. "You and me? It's never going to happen."

Shaking his head slowly, he reached out to graze his knuckles along her cheek. For a moment, just a moment, he seemed sad. "And you're going to have to trust me on that."

When the man from before moved up beside Lucia and asked for another dance, Ethan stared at him with an unreadable expression. He lowered his head in deference and backed up. "Thank you for the dance," he told Lucia with the hard expression she was beginning to know so well back on his face.

Instead of going to the bar, Ethan went in the opposite direction. He walked toward the beach with its pounding surf and wide, white sand. There he could avoid the noise and light, the frivolity and human interaction.

Out there with the sweeping ocean he could find what he apparently wanted most. Solitude.

Trying not to take his rejection personally, again, Lucia stiffened her shoulders and tracked Ethan as he walked away. She watched as he entered the shadows. And disappeared.

8

The next morning saw others rise early in Savannah. In the Amara plantation house, a bedroom was still banked in darkness while cool, pale light made its way through a crack in the heavy drapery. Lifting a French-manicured hand to shield her face, Ronja said in a calm voice, "Close the curtains."

Tyr obeyed his lover's simple request then turned to await the next directive. Few could command the Kiowa warrior, still living after hundreds of years. Few had the strength, power, or hard-wrought respect.

But this woman did. The gifted seior who made his age seem a small snap of time. The witch from an ancient land, filled with black magic, and consumed by vengeance.

Beautiful, he mused, was never the right word. Ronja was so much more. And while he appreciated the long, lovely curves of her form and her cream with honey skin, these filled him with only basic human urges.

But her eyes. They were the color of the Norwegian Sea in winter. And almost as cold.

Ronja's unrepentant thirst for destruction fueled his raw, male lust, not only for her body, but for the depraved and thrilling cruelty that lay beneath.

This is why he followed her. Why he loved her. The only one

who craved blood and death even more than he did.

When her hand rubbed the navy, crushed velvet cover, Tyr sat beside her on the bed. Rarely did he see her so at ease. Her golden hair was in a smooth chignon, and her lips were their own natural pink.

She took his hand in hers, bronze against milky white. "You know what you must do."

Tyr gave a swift, curt nod. "Yes."

"We have two opportunities," she said. "First, you've been given your gift of prophecy for a reason." She smiled now, waving her hand so flames sprung to life in the boudoir fireplace. "I'm chilled," she explained before continuing. "The coven fails to realize that our side has help from beyond, too."

"I know where to go," Tyr said, wanting to assure his love that he would win this round for her. For Bastraal and the awful power the demon would grant them. "I saw the fortress." He paused before adding, "But the only witch I saw was Anna."

The soft pads of her fingertips circled on the back of his hand. Ronja always told him how she loved the feel of his toughened skin.

She also enjoyed the feel of his flesh between her teeth, but Tyr didn't mind. The pain she gave him was exquisite.

"Don't worry about that. You'll know who is at trial soon enough," she told him with a lick of her lovely lips. "As I said, we have two opportunities. You've been given information and will use it to retrieve the dagger."

A shadow formed in her eyes then, tiny storms covering up the blue. "And when I have the blade I'll bury it so deep inside the ground that the core of this planet will melt it into oblivion. That cursed weapon will never be used to put one of our kind down again."

"Second," she snapped before he could respond. "I owe the coven an excessive amount of pain. A gift, you might call it. Passed on to them through me." Now she snarled. "From

Bastraal."

Tyr almost flinched to see the agony flicker across her face. He didn't know what Ronja's master demon had done to her after their last defeat, but the punishment hadn't been pleasant. "You want me to kill her," Tyr said, trying to steer her back to the current battle.

"If you have the opportunity, yes. But we have another plan." Ronja waved a hand and opened her bedroom door. Scarlett glided in, in her usual stylish getup, but the red-haired witch didn't look pleased.

Another person came in after Scarlett, a smaller female, shrouded in a gray, hooded sweatshirt. Searenn's face was cast in shadow, but the stench of unleashed rage poured from her tense, lean body.

"You aren't the only talented one among us," Ronja told Tyr in a matter-of-fact tone. "And we will use everything in our arsenal." She looked to Searenn and asked, "You've found the materials you need?"

A raspy voice like the sound of glass beneath a boot answered, "I have."

"Good." Ronja's face shifted from stern to happy again in a flash. She threw aside the heavy velvet blanket, leaving herself exposed but for a sheer, white gown.

There was only one reason Ronja ever wore white, and Tyr immediately grew hard.

"It's warm enough now," his lover said, smiling just for him. Her fingers tightened on his. "You have long days and nights ahead of you." Then she leaned across his lap and pulled a straight-razor from a bedside table drawer.

Holding her gaze on his face, Ronja eased the white gown up her legs and over her hips. Then she spread her thighs.

Tyr heard Scarlett adjust her position as she watched from the corner like a voyeuristic wraith. For once the woman was silent. She was jealous.

He waited as Ronja gripped the handle of the razor and impaled him with her stone-blue stare. "Drink your fill," she said. "Then drink more." In a quick move she sliced her femoral artery with surgical precision.

Tyr's voice was coarse with need when he said, "But you will be weak." His mouth watered as he recalled the taste of her blood. Of demon essence. He was well acquainted with the searing power and could barely wait for his veins to convulse as it rushed through him.

"Only for a time." Ronja let her head fall back against the pile of pillows, and as Tyr lowered his mouth to her pulsing flood, she looked over his head to Scarlett. "I'll be safe here. Protected." She pressed her hand to Tyr's black, braided hair, holding him closer. Harder. She moaned in ecstasy.

"All that matters," she whispered as he drank, "is that you will be strong." She gasped when he got rougher. When his pulls became greedy. Violent.

As Tyr sucked the vital magic from his woman's thigh, he heard Scarlett ask Searenn, "You have what you need to communicate with the guardians?"

Only silence. But that was Searenn's way.

Then as Tyr felt himself throb and climb toward orgasm, Scarlett's voice whipped angrily from the doorway. "Then go," she ordered Searenn. "It's time to wake them up."

9

After more than six hours in the plane, Lucia's passengers had been lulled into a semi-catatonic stupor. The constant drone of the engines tended to do that to a person, and on the second day of travel, even Shauni's excitement had dimmed. In the back, she leaned her head on Michael's shoulder and dozed.

Ethan had been broody all day, an extra layer of grouchy added on top of the quiet reserve Lucia had already become accustomed to. Considering last night's crash-and-burn at the lounge followed by a restless night's sleep, she was willing to give him some space.

Now as he stirred from an hour's nap, he actually looked a little more peaceful. Maybe a bit more receptive?

Ready to start anew, Lucia would take a new tack. She'd stop the full-speed approach that had failed her so miserably and institute Plan B instead. The strategy that never seemed to fail when the male species was involved.

She'd make it all about *him*.

"Have a good rest?" she asked in a pleasant tone, careful to appear hospitable yet not overly interested. Yes, she was still fully determined to land her soul mate, but he didn't have to know that.

A sleepy murmur was his response before he shifted to look

out the window and the landscape far below. "Where are we?" he asked.

His hair was like black silk, gilded by the sunlight, and his roughened voice caused a whirl of desire in Lucia's belly. She tamped down on the lovely sensation and said, "About thirty minutes north of the Chachapoyas airport." She saw his brows hike as he realized they were close to their final destination.

When Ethan fell back into silence, Lucia casually adjusted her headset and spoke again. "It's a good thing you're so familiar with the dagger. I'd say that's a coincidence, but I don't believe in chance anymore."

She waited. No response. "So, how do you know so much about it?"

"The blade was forged for the specific purpose of killing demons. Very powerful masters of the underworld." He nailed her with a look. "That is my specialty, as you may remember."

Gripping the yoke almost as hard as her lips were clamped, Lucia forced herself to breathe. Patience, she told herself. Patience.

"Yes. You are the demonologist." She cut her eyes to the right, taking in his hard profile. "What is the established course of study for that title, and does it come with a Ph.D.?" Smiling broadly to soften the impact of her sarcasm she added, "Seriously. How did you do it?"

"The established study has been around since a pile of mud grew legs and started to crawl." He turned to face her full-on. "Life. That's what I study. And all the things of this world and others that try to crush that life in a bloody fist."

Lucia nodded sagely, her forced cheer sagging in the face of his dismal honesty. "Were you always interested?" she prodded. "I mean, did you like scary movies growing up? Or were you just an inherently morbid kid?"

The humor in his voice measured at around negative fifty when he said, "You have no idea."

Lucia waved a hand at him. "Okay, I give up. Then what made you decide to study monsters?"

When he reached down to his brown satchel, Lucia feared she'd pushed too hard again and had lost him. He'd probably bury his nose in a damn book for the rest of the flight.

Then to her surprise, Ethan dropped the bag and sat back in his seat. "I have my reasons," he said.

It was the rapid pulse of his temple that kept Lucia from pursuing more info. He didn't want to talk about it, and she reminded herself she was supposed to be backing off.

She sighed. So much for Plan B. What else was there when the man didn't even care to brag about himself or his exploits?

As they flew through a cloud, Lucia took a moment to check her instruments. A glance at the artificial horizon. Compass. Altitude. Soon she was free of the white mist and full visibility was restored.

Too bad she couldn't say the same for Ethan. Very little was clear about this man. Other than the fact he wanted nothing to do with her.

"Steering clear of professional life, then," she told him before letting the ends of her lips curl up. "Where are you from, Ethan?"

No answer. And was that an annoyed grunt she'd heard?

"Fine." Now Lucia was growing impatient. "I'll assume you're from the States. Northeast, if I'm a gambling woman."

"Betting," he said. "If you're a betting woman."

"*Gracias*. No work talk. No home town disclosures. So I'll keep it simple. How about siblings?" She saw his jaw jerk. Then again. He was grinding his teeth. A sore point.

Instead of retreating—as she'd promised herself she would do— Lucia bore down and followed the scent of blood. "You have a brother," she said, quietly observing his reaction. His mouth stayed relaxed and his eyes didn't flinch.

"Okay. How about any sisters?" she nudged.

Ethan threw up a hand, fingers barely bent at the knuckles and stiff with tension.

Pay dirt. Lucia held her breath, sensing the sudden rise of emotion in her dark-eyed companion.

"Leave it," Ethan snapped, dropping his hand again. "Just leave it alone." When his eyes whipped to hers they were bright with turmoil, though whether it was angst dancing there or fury, Lucia couldn't tell. "We're not playing meet-the-family here, witch. Just do your damn job and fly the plane. We get to the fortress, you do your hocus-pocus trick and find the dagger, then we're done."

She would swear his glare grew hotter as he looked at her. He was extremely pissed over the mention of a sister. And his jaw was at it again, jumping as he clenched his teeth so hard Lucia was afraid they'd grind to chalk.

"*Sí,*" she said in an easy tone. She faced forward, giving him room to unspool. She couldn't blame him, either. She was the one who'd stalked the wounded animal. And had unwittingly backed him into a corner.

"*Lo siento,*" she added, as out of nowhere remorse swamped her. How would she like it if someone came along and picked the scabs of her life? "I'm sorry. I shouldn't have pushed. But you see, that's what I do. I hunt. I pick. I dig."

Ethan blew out a breath and shrugged as a dark cloud suddenly rolled across the sun and cast them in shadow.

"You intrigue me, Ethan Drake. In so many ways." She swallowed and licked her strawberry lips. "I don't understand why that is such a sin." The truth just popped out, and she never even saw it coming.

With another unidentifiable expression on his face, Ethan glanced at her. "It's not a sin. I just don't want to you to get any ideas." He tried to smile, but it was an epic fail. "I'm a dead end. That's all you need to know."

"But..." Lucia started to ask him what he meant, but when

a sultry, female voice whispered in her ear, she flinched and stared forward. She held her breath.

Shaking her head, she blinked twice and glanced aside to Ethan. He appeared unbothered. Had she imagined it?

Again the voice slithered into her ears as if coming from her head set. She rattled the piece in her ear, and just as she determined the headset was malfunctioning, Shauni bolted upright in the rear seat. Her emerald eyes were wide and aware. "What was that?" she asked, leaning forward. "Did you say something in another language?"

"You heard it, too?" Lucia asked, praying she conveyed calm.

"I don't suppose there's some sort of air travel phenomenon that causes auditory hallucinations?" Shauni chewed her bottom lip as if she already knew the answer.

"What are you guys talking about?" Now Michael was concerned as well. He hadn't heard the sound, which in most cases would bode well. Considering the fact Lucia and Shauni could see and hear creatures others couldn't...well...that boded crappy.

Ethan was hunched against his window as if searching the outside of the Caravan. Then he swung back to look out across Lucia on her side. "I don't see anything." His eyes fastened to hers, black brows gathered. "This can't be what I think it is."

"Whoa, what?" Lucia's bottom lip dropped before she coughed a breath and said, "Did you hear the voice, Ethan?"

Though they weren't in a crisis, she scanned her instrument panel. She and her coven had been dealt some deadly blows by the Amara and had recently battled a posse of demons. They'd proven they could handle themselves, take a hit, and get back up again.

Lucia glanced at the altimeter. But they'd never had to do any of those things at ten thousand feet.

Ethan was scrambling for something in his satchel. "I heard it. Damn it." He pulled out his book, the one with the information on the dagger. He flipped through it then stopped to drag his fingers down a page. Then the next.

"What's happening?" Shauni asked Ethan.

"They shouldn't be able to come out this far," he muttered, flipping more pages. "They are bound to guard the dagger."

Deciding she'd worry later about how Ethan was able to hear the voices when Michael couldn't, and why he'd jumped straight to his demon guidebook in response, Lucia zeroed in on her first concern. "The guardians of the blade? Is that what we heard?"

"I can't be sure, but the voice was female, and I believe it was speaking a pre-Quechuan dialect." He looked to her for confirmation. "It only makes sense, but I don't understand why they're here. Why they're contacting us."

He shoved the book back in his bag. "It's like they knew we were coming."

"I hope contacting is all they do. Are they demons?" Lucia said, cursing herself for not insisting Ethan fill them in sooner. The plan had been to have a quick Incan-monster-tutorial before they hiked to Kuelap. Now they were in the thick of it and were—she hated to even think the pun—flying blind.

He shook his head and frowned. "They're…demon-ish."

Lucia tapped the back of her head against the seat since she couldn't exactly hit the steering wheel. "That's good enough for me, and we can guess why and how the guardians are here." Then in perfect time with Shauni she said, "Searenn."

"Oh, no," Michael said, patting Shauni to make sure her lap belt was tight before checking his own.

Ethan nodded. "I couldn't agree more."

"Maybe they just want to communicate. To warn us off or something." Shauni was sitting back now, holding onto Michael's arm.

"Maybe," Lucia said, but she couldn't take any chances. She needed to get them down. Fast. "I'm going to divert to…"

She started to lay out a plan but stopped when ear-piercing laughter rang out all around them.

Soon the lone voice was joined by others. Then a few more before so many screeched at them the number was impossible to count. The coarse yet sharp sound vibrated into her bones.

"This can't be good," Ethan said.

"I'm landing us as soon as possible," Lucia told him. She looked to verify that his shoulder harness was on correctly.

No one spoke after that. The potential for danger was evident, and the air was heavy with fear.

Even witches could die if they crashed to the earth from this height.

Lucia steadied her mind and continued to draw full, even breaths. Three lives were in her hands, and thank the goddess, her training and many, many previous flights made her actions second nature. She could do this.

After the storm that had swooped in to surprise her off the coast of Canada one fall evening? A little fly-by in the warm jungle was nothing.

Then she caught movement in the corner of her eye. *What the?* The artificial horizon was turning upside down. She glanced out in front, but the plane was still flying upright. A faster whirling motion drew her attention to the compass. The dial spun wildly.

María santísima. "Those bitches are in my avionics."

"Okay, no problem," she added quickly, trying not to alarm the others. "But I'm not going to take any chances."

"Please don't," Shauni said, her lips tight and eyes grim.

As she readied herself to radio their position, Lucia heard the very worst sound a pilot could ever hear. *Brrrr-Brrrr.* No, no, no, she chanted in her head. Please no.

Brrrr-Brrrr. This was happening. *Brr-Brr-Brr.* It was really happening.

The abrasive noise died out suddenly, leaving only the

wicked sound of wind as the plane cut through the air.

The quiet rush meant one thing, and terror exploded in the back of Lucia's mind before crawling down her back with a cold ripple.

"What was that?" Shauni squeaked.

Ignoring Shauni for the time being, Lucia spoke instead to Ethan. His eyes were huge. Fully comprehending. "I need you to keep an eye out for a clearing."

When he jerked his eyes to hers, she asked, "Do you know what I need?"

"Yes. Yes," he said, biting off his words to hide his alarm.

"Just hold tight back there," she told Michael and Shauni, Then, using her radio, Lucia made the call she'd hoped never to have to make. "Mayday. Mayday. Mayday. This is November-four-three-four-Sierra-Charlie. We are experiencing engine failure. Our current—" *Whush!*

The instrument panel sparked one time, then sizzled and cracked. Lucia tried to raise another channel, but she knew. The radio was gone, too.

She made a growling noise in her chest, somewhere between anger and utter disbelief.

"These guardians aren't fighting fair," she said, hoping she sounded more assured than she felt. "But we're going to make it."

She looked to Ethan and saw her own steel will reflected there. Good. She'd need the support.

"We have to find an open area. Look around for breaks in the tree line." Based on what their altitude had been before her instruments had gone haywire, Lucia figured they had about five miles of glide time.

She adjusted the flaps, saying a silent thanks that the guardians hadn't destroyed them as well.

Determined to get her passengers to safety, Lucia thinned her lips and scanned the horizon. Soon Ethan smacked her arm with the back of his hand and pointed toward the west. Lucia nodded. Then she banked.

"I got it," she said to no one in particular. She saw her chance and had no choice but to take it. No matter how rough the terrain might be. She was out of options.

"I'm taking us down."

10

"We're at about seventeen-hundred feet," Lucia said. "We're committed now." So far luck was with them as the clearing in the forest seemed to be mostly grass. The stretch wasn't nearly as long as she would like, but she'd have to make do.

She couldn't make out any trees, but only touchdown would tell her how rocky the ground there really was. The wheels of the Caravan were suited for natural air strips, though a gap in the Amazonian rain forest barely qualified.

"Shauni," she said as they descended, "You're going to have to help me slow us down when I say."

With her brow furrowed, Shauni swallowed hard then asked, "What do you want me to do?"

"I'm going to stand on the brakes when we land, but the runway is still too short. I need you to help slow us down and keep the plane steady." She worked up a half-smile for her friend and turned to her. "Help control the speed. Witch style."

Shauni nodded. "Guess we should have brought Viv with us." The telekinetic wonder of the coven could control objects much better than the rest of them.

Shauni and Lucia together might be able to smooth out some bumps, but an airplane was a little more substantial than the wooden spheres they practiced with.

Now they were coming in over the canopy of the forest, and Lucia's knuckles whitened as she gripped the yoke. The drop into the clearing would take some maneuvering. As soon as she cleared the trees, she'd have to go for it.

Flaps down. Landing gear down. The closer they got to the tree tops, the more she could feel the speed. Green streaked by, the panorama blurred by how fast they were still going.

A low moan came from the back, but Shauni shut it off as soon as it began and whispered, "I'm okay. I'm okay. Just tell me when."

The wind sounded like a gale now, or was that only Lucia's imagination? There weren't enough simulations in the world to prepare for the reality of a crash landing.

To see the hard, unrelenting ground coming up at you. Knowing you had the bare minimum to work with.

Lucia lowered the plane as the forest started to give way. Beside her, Ethan gave a small, surprised grunt when the wheels struck the top of a tree and the aircraft shuddered.

Lucia couldn't spare a word of encouragement. She was in the window now, and every ounce of concentration had to be on the terrain rising up to meet them, which was much closer than she'd estimated from above.

The landscape screamed by them now, and Lucia guessed they were still at about thirty feet. Seconds until they touched down. "Get ready, Shauni," she said, her voice tight from the eruption of adrenaline she couldn't quite tamp down.

Instead of holding her breath, she blew out long and slow when the wheels found purchase. The impact jarred her spine but she kept her bearings, holding the wheels steady as the Caravan rumbled over uneven land.

And just as she'd promised, Lucia stood on the brakes, trying to slow them, hoping the impact with the approaching forest would only result in a minor collision. They were belted in and the frame could handle it.

"Now, Shauni," Lucia said evenly, though her throat felt constricted. "Just focus on slowing us down. I'll handle the rest."

"Got it," Shauni said, sitting up straighter in her seat and focusing a flat stare out the front window.

Lucia could sense her sister's magic working, but the pilot in her could only see the growing threat right in front of them. They were still going too fast, so she threw her power in with Shauni's, straining the muscles of her gift as she fought to decrease their speed with her mind while still stomping the brakes and managing the yoke.

"Lucia!" Ethan cried out, his fist pounding once into his seat as he stared straight ahead.

Then she saw it, too, but knew there was nothing to be done.

A crevice in the ground stretched across their path. She couldn't tell how deep it was, but it sure wasn't shallow. Too wide for the wheels to roll across undisturbed.

"Keep her steady, Shauni!" Lucia yelled, channeling all her strength to the mystical net she and the other witch had cast around the hulking plane. Would it be enough?

She heard Michael curse just before they hit the ditch, then all of them slammed forward and to the right as that wheel hooked into the fissure. As they circled to the right, careening out of control, Lucia held tight to the yoke.

Knowing it would do no good.

The right wheel had come off or had been wrenched out of alignment. Ethan was below her now as the aircraft continued to cartwheel toward the trees. A powerful, grinding shudder told her the wing was scraping the ground.

She heard Shauni scream before they crashed into a tree and bounced back off to veer in the other direction.

They were out of control, and the forest that had once threatened them was now their only chance. The multiple blows would eventually slow their momentum. How many hits could the fuselage take before they grated to a stop?

The sounds were unimaginable and too many to identify. Finally Lucia let go of the yoke.

And took hold of her magic instead. She put everything she had into slowing their speed. Controlling the roll was beyond her.

As they started to tip to the left, Lucia saw a great trunk coming toward her. The plane skidded and gave its last great groan as the left wing got caught up in something sturdier than itself. Then the nose curved around and toward the massive tree trunk.

Por favour no nos dejes morir. Please let us live.

The craggy pattern of the bark was the last thing Lucia saw.

~~~

Ethan opened his eyes to a low creak and the feel of weighty metal rubbing against itself. Once his sight adjusted and he could tell the cabin was semi-upright, he moved to unfasten his safety belt. A starburst of bright pain set off in his shoulder, making his breath hitch uncomfortably in his chest.

The injury was likely from the tree they'd rampaged into. Or one of the many they'd met up with.

Testing his arm and the aching joint, he determined there was no break and probably no tissue damage. A deep contusion was likely.

When a masculine groan came from behind him, Ethan realized the women were both quiet. "Michael, you okay?" he asked even as he leaned across to check on Lucia. Her head rested against the far side since the plane tipped in that direction.

"Ugh. Mostly okay," Michael answered before talking to Shauni. "Are you hurt?" he asked, his voice filled with angst until his woman answered and confirmed she was unharmed.

"I think so," Shauni whispered. Movement from them told Ethan the two were adjusting and doing the same self-check he'd just performed.

Rubbing her cheek lightly, Ethan spoke to Lucia. "Hey. Wake up. You need to wake up, Lucia."

Her dark lashes fluttered against skin that was too pale for his liking. And when she eased her head up to face him, his heart bumped painfully to see her velvety brown eyes were clear. *Thank God.*

And as swiftly as relief flooded his system, sharp, putrid fear rode on the wave behind it. Enough of that, he ordered himself, cutting off the concern. The depth of fear he'd felt to see her crunched against the glass had shocked him.

Nothing more than the acceptable and expected level of compassion, he told himself. Given their situation, he'd be a bastard if he didn't care about another's health and well-being. They'd been in a plane crash, for Pete's sake.

Still, that didn't explain the extra jump his pulse rate had taken when he'd seen her lying in the crooked, unnatural position.

Calling forth the emotional barriers he relied on, Ethan spoke harshly when he nudged her arm. "How do you feel? Anything broken?"

Stretching her arms and grimacing, she rubbed her left hip before shaking her head. "Nothing a hot bath won't fix."

Ethan frowned. Lucia in a whirling, steaming tub of water was not an image he needed.

He jerked his head to the side. Did he feel something approaching? Had the darkness sensed that brief and meaningless tug in Ethan's heart?

No. No. He was just all stirred up from what had happened. He studied the couple in the back seat, relieved to find himself flinching at Shauni's white face as much as he had Lucia's. See? Normal level of concern.

He could call off the watch tower. Nothing was coming.

"Is anyone hurt?" Lucia asked, her accent heavy as she pressed a hand to her cheek. She'd probably banged herself up pretty good.

"I'm okay," Shauni said. Then her face broke into a happy smile. "You did it, Lucia. You got us down safely."

Making a face, Lucia replied, "In one piece at least. And you did it, too." She reached to grab her friend's hand. "If we had smashed into that final tree any harder..." She let the gruesome prediction trail off but put tentative fingers back to her jaw as if testing one more time for fractures.

"Then we should get out of here," Ethan said, scouting for the least mangled portion of the fuselage and the shortest drop to the ground. "Will your door open?" he asked Michael who was situated on Lucia's side.

"I don't think so," the vet said, allowing the first wrinkle of pain to cross his countenance. "Part of it is stuck in my leg."

"Michael," Shauni gasped, immediately bending around to survey the damage without jostling him. "How bad? I can't see."

"I think I can pull it out. My anatomy may be different from the animals I treat, but my guess is the metal missed any important blood vessels. I'm going to try to pull my leg...off. Because moving the door isn't an option."

"Are you sure?" Shauni asked, taking his hand to let him squeeze hers if necessary.

His gray eyes held those of the woman he so obviously loved. "Babe, we're somewhere in the Amazon. I don't have a choice. Besides, Lucia said she had medical supplies, and I need to get a better look at my leg."

"Wait one second," Shauni said. "I'm no Willyn, but I've been working on a spell to help some of the animals who come into the clinic. I might be able to dull the pain." Her eyes fell to his impaled leg and she added, "Some."

The black-haired witch closed her eyes and murmured an

incantation, and the air shimmered around Michael like a cocoon of golden dust. "Now," she told her boyfriend as a tear glistened in her eye.

With his face strained and neck corded, Michael used his hands to grasp his calf and pull toward Shauni. With a grunt and explosive yell, he wrenched it off the twisted metal. His leg released with a wet sound, conjuring images of ripped flesh and muscle.

Ethan flinched in sympathy but waited for the man to calm his breathing and open his clenched eyes. When Michael finally looked at them, his hand was still pressed to his wound. "Okay. Now we need to get out."

"Your door," Lucia said, motioning for Ethan to try his side. "We can't get out over here. It's all bent up."

Remarkably, Ethan's door swung freely, and he slithered out to find the drop not nearly as bad as he'd imagined. The wheels and landing gear were toast, but their absence reduced the height by several feet. The body of the plane was partially buried in the soft, moist soil.

The rain forest trilled and whispered in its lush, vibrant way, bringing the reality of their predicament to the forefront. Ethan glanced around as if a jungle cat might slip from the green depths at any moment.

Later. He'd cross that off his worry list later. First they had to tend to Michael.

With no small amount of struggle, they managed to help the tall, blonde man to the front seats and out the exit. There was no help for the fall he'd have to take, and Ethan did his best to catch him around the waist and soften the impact.

Michael landed on his feet, and while he didn't cry out, Ethan suspected he'd held it in for the women's benefit. The burning, gray eyes he raised to Ethan confirmed the suspicion, so he simply nodded to the other man and shared a mutual moment of male bonding. "Let's get you to a clean, dry place and check out that leg."

By now Lucia was out and after assisting Shauni down, she started the search for usable goods and equipment. The bottom portion of the plane had taken a beating. A trail of food, tents, and water bottles, among other things, showed them the haphazard path they'd beaten through the forest.

After a silent minute of taking in the destruction of earth and shrubbery, Lucia turned to find Ethan. They both knew their survival was nothing short of a miracle. Or of magic.

Working together, the two of them quickly located a tarp and enough material to make a comfortable pallet for Michael. After Ethan found a First Aid kit and was assured by the vet that he could care for himself. He left Michael and Shauni and resumed scavenging.

The sun was high above, so they'd fallen from the sky somewhere near eleven o'clock. Though the clearing they'd tried for was bright and yellow, the floor of the rainforest was shrouded in shadows. A sacred sanctuary. A temple of its own making.

By the time he and Lucia had gathered all they could find and made a pile near the base of a massive tree, Michael had cleaned and bandaged his leg. "How is it?" Ethan asked, noting only a small amount of bleed-through.

"Not bad," Michael said then blew out a breath. "Not great, either." He looked up as Lucia moved closer. "Our Spanish goddess had antibiotics in her kit, so I should be fine for a while. No major bleeding."

"He wouldn't take a pain pill," Shauni complained, putting the bedroll Lucia handed her behind his back.

Michael's smile faltered. "This isn't the place to be whacked out on drugs. Which brings us to the next issue." He looked up to their leader. To Lucia. "What now?"

Hands on her hips, she looked stern as she relayed their status. "The good news is the sat phones still work. I called in our last known coordinates, and the Caravan's black box will help them find the crash site. The Peruvian Air Force should send a team from Piura, on the coast. They should locate you in a day's time. Two on the outside."

"What do you mean, they'll find *us*?" Shauni asked, standing to look Lucia in the eye. "Where will you be?"

"There's no reason for me to stop. Ethan knows what he's doing and will stay with the two of you."

"While you head on to Kuelap," Ethan stated, joining the women as they hovered around Michael's pallet. "Lucia, we should all wait here for transport. We'll lose a few days, but as soon as we're able, you and I can get back to it."

"No. I'm the one who has to finish this and find the blade." She held up a hand in a traffic-cop motion when Ethan opened his mouth to argue. "This isn't about pride," she added, voice firm and eyes clear. "I'm the one headed for the dagger, so I'll be the target."

"The guardians," Shauni said. "You want to draw them away from us."

Lucia shrugged. "Who knows what they're capable of? You will be safe here. Plenty of supplies, and we can finish rigging up shelter before I go."

Unease crackled along Ethan's nerves, and he couldn't say why. He wasn't crazy about this plan. "What about animals?" he threw out. "You want to leave the two of them to fend for themselves?"

Shauni hiked a black brow. "I have that covered."

It took a moment for him to recall her animal-whispering abilities. "Right."

"And what do you mean 'the two of them'?" Lucia said, rounding on him. "You're staying, too. I won't have the three of you put in danger again because of me."

Ethan had more than one reason to head out with Lucia. He still had his own goal. But seeing to her safety was also a concern.

Even if he didn't want to admit it.

Taking a step closer, he held Lucia's hot stare. "If you're determined to go on foot, then I'm coming with you. I made a mistake by underestimating the evil powers at work here, and I won't let you go alone."

It was his turn to hold up a halting hand when her mouth opened to argue. "You need me," he said. "I'm part of your challenge." And admitting that out loud sent a tremor through his veins.

"He's right," Shauni said, drawing three questioning looks her way. "Michael and I will be safe here. The wildlife won't be a threat, in fact, they'll protect us if I ask them to. And as much as I hate to admit it, the real danger lies with the guardians."

"Either we all stay or the two of you go." She sent a warm look to her boyfriend on the ground. "We have to protect our injured."

Michael frowned back at her. "Why don't you just call me Nancy while you're at it?"

Ethan slapped his thigh. "Then it's settled. If Lucia intends to draw away the guardians, then it only makes sense for me to go along." He dared her to contradict him when he told her, "I'm the only one who understands what you're heading into."

After a slow-burn of assessment and what he could tell was internal struggle, she nodded once before pulling something out of her pocket and wrapping her hair up in a tail. "We'll set you two up before we go, and you'll have the sat phone if you have any trouble."

Ethan watched as Lucia shifted into work mode. He respected her more with every critical decision she had to make. She didn't shirk away from tough choices but stared down the crisis and barreled right through.

She was a woman who set her sights on a task and got it done. Ethan cursed himself for adding more support to the attraction he was beginning to feel.

Despite her strange need for lip gloss, Lucia had gained his admiration.

To Ethan's way of thinking, esteem was a much greater attractant than shiny lips or sparkly clothes. Or even long, long, curvy legs.

When the women set back to work, Ethan moved away from them to start building the shelter. He was trapped in an even worse situation than before.

He didn't want to be stuck with Lucia, but he couldn't let her reach Kuelap without him.

Ethan had stared down monsters of every make, yet the thought of sleeping near the witch made him shudder.

The more he got to know her, the more afraid he was to be alone with her.

11

A loud rustle above their heads made Lucia and Ethan stop to locate the source. When the body of a black spider monkey flashed from one limb to the next, Ethan sighed and Lucia laughed.

"Guess we're both on edge about anything coming from the sky," she said, choosing that moment for a much-needed rest. She moved to a nearby tree, the top of which disappeared high above in a dense mesh of canopy.

Around them the vibrant green seemed alive. Thick and lush, trilling with the movement of hidden life forms. Humidity clung to Ethan's skin as he surveyed their location.

Which was smack in the middle of nowhere.

He smelled the striking scent of cherries and found Lucia slicking a tube over her lips. She gave them a testing smack before slipping the balm in a pocket and zipping it up tight.

Couldn't lose the all-sacred lip goo, he mused, pissed more than he should be to find himself appreciating the bow of her upper lip and how her mouth always seemed to be ready to smile. His predicament had gone from uncomfortable to precarious.

He and Ms. Curvaceous would be together. All alone. For days.

At least they would be physically grueling days. That should keep her mind occupied. And her body.

When she felt his critical stare, Lucia held out her hands. "What? It has SPF." She muttered something in Spanish then, and he was sure he'd rather not have the translation.

They'd been hacking their way through the dense foliage for less than an hour, and his back was drenched with sweat. His hiking partner was a little frazzled around the edges but still looked decidedly too glamorous.

With naturally golden skin and long, shiny curls of rich brown, it didn't take much primping for Lucia to look good. Dammit. Ethan found himself thankful for the perspiration. Maybe he stunk, too. That would work. He could keep her at a safe distance with olfactory assault. Like a skunk.

Not that she'd made any real moves on him since he'd dropped the truth bomb on her on the dance floor.

Now they were struggling their way through the Amazonian forests in Peru, and despite her tempting mouth, they were both too tired and nasty-feeling to muster up an ounce of flirt.

Buttress roots covered the forest floor, providing plenty of opportunities for a trip or fall. Combined with the thick brush, navigating a mere twenty feet took strength and stamina. He raised appraising eyes to Lucia. She apparently had both.

With one foot resting on a gargantuan root, she downed half a bottle of water before offering him the rest. "You should drink," she said.

Ethan, too thirsty and irritated to argue, snagged the bottle and finished it before shoving it in his own pack with a crunch.

"Since we're in the southern hemisphere, the fall is just beginning. We're lucky to have dryer, cooler weather, but the humidity is still thicker than at home." She checked her compass again to verify their heading before putting it away and swinging her backpack around to her shoulders.

"Yeah," he allowed, well aware of the climate. "Fewer

mosquitos, at least. The value of that can never be understated."

"Was that sarcastic humor I just heard?" Her eyes were bright, lips wanting to curl.

Ethan brushed aside the warmth her charming personality had almost kindled. He bit out, "Simple observation."

"Oh." Her mouth formed a disappointed moue. "What was I thinking?"

She marched ahead and spoke over her shoulder, assuming he would follow. "I'd say we've almost made two and a half miles in just under an hour. We're fresh yet, but bruised up, so I suppose it balances out. We need to maintain this pace or even bump it up to three miles an hour."

She stopped to pivot. "I know I can do that. How about you?"

Was that challenge sparking her big, brown eyes? Despite the hazards, Ethan let himself enjoy how pretty she looked with her ponytail and dolled-up lips. Her lithe figure curving against the wild and verdant backdrop of a tropical rain forest.

She seemed right at home, and Michael had been right. Here, in her prime, doing what she did best, Lucia was indeed a goddess.

Then his mind took a dark turn. But was she the Priestess of the Hunt? Was the dagger meant for her skilled hand?

She could have the dagger, he thought. As long as she was willing to give up its matching piece.

He'd kept the pages in his book pressed together when he'd shown her the picture of the blade. As far as he could tell, the coven didn't need to know it was one piece of a two-part set. The witches didn't require the silver band rumored to rest alongside the dagger.

But Ethan did.

"I can keep pace with you," he said, showing no hint of the things ransacking his peace of mind.

Lucia turned away and set off again, saying nothing but, "Good." A clear dismissal from the female who less than twenty-four hours ago had looked at him with want in her eyes. Seemed like he'd gotten his wish. Her complete disinterest.

Forcing himself to focus on the trail ahead, Ethan let his body take in the bombardment of sensations the jungle had to offer. The scrambling monkey seemed to have found some friends, and they set up a chorus of excited cries.

The air here was moist, hence the name rain forest, and the rich soil permeated the dense atmosphere with its loamy smell. The nutritious dirt was like angel dust to the plants here, and the overgrown flora proudly displayed robust green leaves and trailing vines.

Cocking one eye toward the barely visible sky, Ethan returned to less pleasant observations. He and Lucia had left Shauni and Michael behind, in what had amounted to a fairly luxurious tent, all things considered. The two women had laid a ward to veil the crash site and tent from the vicious hags who'd downed the plane.

And despite what he knew about the ferocious creatures, he hoped they targeted him and Lucia instead of the two they'd left behind. Michael might be strong and fearless, but he was still incapacitated.

He realized he'd left out some crucial information and looked to Lucia. "If the guardians come back, we need to be ready," he said to her back.

After a few vicious swipes with her machete, she huffed out, "I'm listening. And while you're at it, why don't you explain how you're able to hear demons. Or…demon-ish beings."

Though she couldn't see the motion, Ethan shrugged. "I've spent my life around the things. After one too many demons, I guess they rubbed off on me." He lifted his eyes to gauge her response. There was none.

He figured his reasoning was close enough to the truth.

As he followed her along what could loosely be described as a trail, Ethan started from the beginning. Before the dagger's creation. "When the Earthshaker roamed this land, he created plenty of havoc. As much as demons seem to crave blood, pain, and death, they often have a pretty big ego to go along with their sadism."

Lucia gave a mirthless laugh. "I can see that. Bastraal has each of the Amara recruits ready to lick his boots. If monsters wear boots." She paused and breathed hard. "Even Ronja bows to her evil master, and her ego is massive."

Ethan nodded to himself as she spoke of the coven's enemies. The Amara, he knew from Quinn, were a collection of paranormal beings and humans who enjoyed brutal control over others. And hoped to rule the destroyed world alongside Bastraal. Their demon.

Their leader was a witch named Ronja. Immortal, cruel, and hell bent on seizing some dark power for herself.

Ethan had never crossed paths with a true immortal before. That he was aware of anyway.

"The Earthshaker," he said to continue the story, "took full advantage of the human population. He claimed women and created his own evil harem."

Lucia made a disgusted sound and trudged on.

"Yeah. I can't imagine either. Don't want to." Ethan swallowed at the first thought of nausea. He had come across stories of what underworld creatures did with their toys. And women were rarely more than playthings to a creature with disturbing appetites and an endless supply of victims.

"However," he told her, "it's been said that The Earthshaker picked female companions based on their willingness to perform depraved acts. He enjoyed encouraging their cruelty. Eventually the women discovered they could increase their strength. That they could gain power."

Lucia stopped to take a break from the arduous task of clearing underbrush. A V of perspiration had formed on the front of her T-shirt. "How did they get power? The demon?"

"No." Ethan held her stare and spoke in an even cadence, trying to sound like he was telling an everyday story. Instead of the stuff of nightmares. "The harem became known as the Qara Mikuna."

Her brows furrowed and she shook her head to show she didn't know the term.

"The words are Incan. They mean flesh eater."

Lucia curled her lips back. "Eew."

"Yes. They're similar to the Native American legend. Wendigos." Ethan didn't blame Lucia when she returned to the job of hacking greenery. Better to focus on anything other than cannibalism and the horrid way the Qara Mikuna gained strength.

"So when the dagger was created and The Earthshaker knew his time was limited, he fed his harem to improve their strength. He provided them with temple priests, virgins, the young, anyone he deemed special. After the harem had grown strong enough to withstand death, he ripped their souls from their bodies and cursed them to guard the dagger. They were forced to protect the weapon from any who would use it for its sole purpose."

Lucia stared at a particularly thick liana, like poison oak on steroids, and carefully pushed it aside. "So how did The Earthshaker die? Why didn't the Qara Mikuna protect him?" she asked, holding the vine back so he could pass as well.

"Who knows?" he said. "Vengeance? They were angry with the demon for killing them?" He lifted a shoulder. "Remember, this all originated from oral storytelling about six hundred years ago."

"Then how do you know it's all true?" Lucia waited, facing him in the dense enclosure of the jungle, staring up at him with curiosity mixed with a healthy dose of skepticism.

"How do you explain the attack on your plane?" he asked.

Laying the flat of her palm against his chest, she pulled her mouth to one side. "Good point."

Ethan forced himself to stand still. To hide his reaction to her touch. The hand she'd pressed against him seemed to burn, even through the fabric of his shirt.

He maneuvered away and smoothly reached for the machete instead, "Why don't I take point for a while?"

She nodded as heavy deep breaths racked her torso. "We should break out of this soon." She lifted her brows. "I hope."

When he started to lift the huge knife, she grabbed his arm. There was that delicious burning sensation again, but he waited patiently until her hand fell away.

"How does that prepare me in case the harem comes back?" she asked.

"It doesn't. I mean..." He looked over her shoulder and saw a big, prickly caterpillar. He didn't know the species, but the urticating hairs were creepy and often found on venomous types. The blinding, neon-yellow was also a bad sign.

Ethan tugged Lucia with him as he stepped away. Just in case. Thinking of danger and defensive mechanisms, he told her, "The Qara Mikuna do have a weakness. Fire destroys them. Completely."

"Excellent," she said, her eyes blazing with genuine delight. "Good thing I came equipped." She snapped her fingers then rolled them open to display a dancing flame in the center of her palm. "And that's just the warm up."

Ethan wasn't sure how to respond. His head buzzed suddenly from the strangeness of it all.

He was stranded in the Amazon, fleeing from dead, cannibalistic concubines while heading for ancient ruins that might hold the answer to his prayers.

Now he was watching the most amazing woman he'd ever met snap fire from her fingers.

And all he could think about was that worm. "I think it smells you," he said, pointing to the creepy-crawly as it turned and made its way along a thin plant limb. Straight for Lucia.

"Aw. He's a cute one." She leaned forward for a better look, but Ethan hauled her back, afraid she might stroke the thing. "Not that one," he said. "Not too close."

"I was only looking," she told him, mouth flattening. "Besides, he looks harmless."

"Did you forget where we are?"

She sucked in a breath. "You're right. Things here are not always as they seem."

And that includes you, he thought, once again realizing how he'd misjudged her that first night. Lucia Ruiz was more than top-of-the-line eye candy.

She laughed at his stricken face. "I won't touch," she said again, leaning closer to drive home the assurance. Then those lips curled at the edges.

And Ethan was charmed all over again. Top-of-the-line female is what she was. But still eye candy.

"I should have told you sooner. My mistake." He felt the wrinkle form on his forehead. "You should call Shauni and tell her about the fire."

"Right." Lucia pulled out the sat phone and dialed. She spoke briefly, because they had to keep moving, then she put the phone away and reported, "They're doing all right, and thanks for that. Shauni was glad to hear she had a readily-available weapon in case the guardians somehow find them."

"Good call," she said, thumping him on the shoulder.

When her face softened and her eyes became curious, Ethan should have taken warning. But he couldn't turn away fast enough.

"Are you this protective of your sister?" she asked, but as soon as the words were out her expression froze. Realizing she was treading on forbidden ground, Lucia bit her bottom lip and waited silently.

He ducked his head and moved away from her. "Even more

protective," he said, a double-meaning in the words, though he knew she wouldn't understand. He cut through the shrubs with renewed determination.

Her question had struck him like a ten-ton boulder, reminding him he had a job to do.

And that he needed to get away from this witch.

A long, hot breath shook his lungs. His temper flared as he thought of his sister, but he couldn't place all of the blame on Lucia.

Ethan always overreacted when it came to Grace.

But she was okay now, he thought. She was safe, going to college and living it up. She was a smart girl. Happy. Carefree.

She was alive.

Because Ethan had made sure of it.

A long, strange cry from above had his skin clambering to crawl off his bones. Were those monkeys?

Get your shit together, Drake. He and Lucia had a good three days in the wild together, at minimum. He couldn't start jumping at shadows for no reason.

Not when there was a perfectly good one out there. Somewhere.

Ethan made himself think of his sister again and her sunny smile. He wouldn't change a thing. It had all been worth it.

Then he cast a dark look to the woman trailing him through the thick vegetation.

It *had* to be worth it. No matter the sacrifice.

Ethan hadn't made a deal with the devil. Not exactly.

But he'd done the next worst thing.

12

Mrs. Attinger was wiping down the mahogany wainscoting in the grand hall when Anna found her. The scent of the older woman's special, lemony rubbing oil took Anna back to childhood days. She'd always loved the clean, fruity smell and the way the wood gleamed dark and rich after a swipe of Mrs. Attinger's cloth.

Anna smiled. The fascinating shine and the nostalgia were both a kind of magic. "Mrs. Attinger," she said, drawing the woman's gaze. "Can we talk?"

Silver hair cut like a pixie's and eyes just as sharp and bright, the sixty-something woman tucked her rag in a white apron pocket. "Of course." She narrowed those clever eyes now, studying the woman who'd come from the child she'd raised for the last sixteen years. "Why so formal, Anna?"

Anna put a hand to her chest and sighed. "I don't really know where that came from." Then she grew somber. "Maybe because you might not like what I have to say."

"Now you've got me worried." She came over and took Anna's hand. "Spit it out, child."

Child. Anna grinned. Here she was pushing thirty and the leader of a powerful coven, but when her beloved housekeeper called her child, that's exactly what she felt like.

"I know this will stir up memories," she began, "ones we'd like to forget, but..." she squeezed the delicate hand now and said, "I plan to open the tower again. We need it."

She didn't have to explain who *we* meant. Mrs. Attinger had been aware of prophecies and witchy secrets long before Anna or Quinn had been born. She'd served...no, she'd worked alongside Anna's mother in her younger days, then she'd cared for Anna's father after he'd married into the family.

He'd kept his name, Patterson, but it was a family tradition that the name St. Germaine be passed down to each generation of island witches, whether paternally or maternally. The name mattered. The family destiny mattered.

And now Anna knew she was the one. The St. Germaine witch fated to complete a mystical circle. To defeat the demon Bastraal, as her ancestors had done before her. Three centuries ago.

Instead of the sorrow she'd expected, Mrs. Attinger nearly burst with elation. She pumped Anna's hand up and down before patting her shoulder. "You wait right here." She hurried to a long side table that was covered in bric-a-brac, pictures, a crystal swan about to fly, a wide candle set in stones, to name a few.

She picked up a framed painting, a small oil that Anna had never found very appealing but kept and loved for one reason only. Her mother had made her promise never to let it go. To keep it here in the mansion and take good care of it.

Her mouth dropped open when Mrs. Attinger used the heel of her hand to punch the painting straight out the back of the frame. "What are you doing?" she nearly screeched.

Mrs. Attinger kneeled to retrieve the pieces from the floor, then looked up to Anna with glowing eyes. "Exactly as your mother told me."

When Anna only worked her mouth soundlessly, the older woman stood and made a *calm-down* gesture with both hands.

"I know this seems strange. I should have explained first, but I'm just so damn excited this day has finally come."

Well now Anna was just going to fall out in the floor. "Mrs. Attinger. You said damn."

"I'll put a quarter in the jar. It's getting dusty by now." She held out something, and at first Anna thought it was the painting. "This is for you," the housekeeper said gently. Lovingly. "Your mother said I was to give it to you at a very specific time."

The object in her hand was a small, dove-blue book.

"What time?" Anna whispered.

Now Mrs. Attinger's gray eyes shone with unspent tears. Her voice hitched when she said, "The day you asked about using the tower."

Trying not to cry herself, Anna reached for the tome. It looked like a diary, classy and feminine, yet a bit mysterious. Much like her mother. The pages were gold at the edges, and Anna imagined her mother writing, in her long, elegant strokes.

Anna closed her eyes and remembered her small hand being guided by a larger one, gentle and of the same shape as her own. *Penmanship is a dying art,* she remembered her mother saying. *Always use your hands, Anna, to write what matters most.*

And just what, she wondered, had her mother written here? Whatever she found between these pages would surely be important. It was no coincidence that the book had been guarded. Hidden in plain sight and protected on various levels.

A laugh found its way from her gut, though the sound was weak. "At least we can finally get rid of that mean looking goat-herder," she said, indicating the painting.

Mrs. Attinger shook the small portrait and agreed with a nod. "Amen." Then she sobered and answered the question she knew her young charge wanted to ask. "I don't know what's in it, but your mother said you would know." She sniffled. "That you'd know what to do with it."

Pressing the small book to her heart Anna sighed and said. "Thank you."

"Yep. Yep." Shooing Anna away so she could hide her tears, Mrs. Attinger pulled the rag back out of her pocket and headed to the wall where she would resume her painstaking routine. She wouldn't miss a crevice. Not a corner.

Mrs. Attinger always tended to what she loved.

More anxious than ever about broaching the subject of the tower with Quinn, Anna was certain she was on the right track. She had to bring the tower back to life, and her brother would understand.

She would wait until they could take some time and be alone. Together they would read the book. They would heed their mother's wishes. And if the time was truly right, the two of them might find some closure.

The tower, after all, had been locked for a reason.

13

By the time Lucia and Ethan broke free of the tightly-woven underbrush, the sun was sinking in the sky. As soon as they came to a reasonably clear spot, Lucia decided to make camp. "This place is as good as any. What do you think?" she asked Ethan, though she was already swinging off her pack.

Her shoulders were well beyond sore, and her back all but demanded she stop for the night. She was in good shape and no stranger to trekking, but she wasn't often required to put forth such effort after a roll and tumble in an airplane crash.

"Fine with me." Ethan winced as he let his own pack slide to the ground and land with a *thud*. He'd taken a beating as well but had impressed her with his fortitude. They had both agreed to hike until nightfall or until good sense made them stop.

And good sense had just arrived.

Both of them wanted to push themselves to their limits, but they were also experienced and knew they'd need a good night's rest as well as time to rehydrate. Hiking for ten hours a day was hard in any climate. In the humidity and heat of the Amazon, it was brutal.

"I won't argue if you want to skip eating and get right to sleep." He massaged the area between his neck and right shoulder. "We should set up the tent."

"*Sí*. But first." Lucia rubbed her lips together. They were rough and dry, no doubt from her loss of fluid, so she reached for her balm.

Ethan shook his head before putting his hands on his hips and assessing her from head to toe. "I've noticed all your lip stuff is red. Like your dress was." He indicated her amulet with a lift of his chin. "And the stone in your necklace."

Lucia felt warmth infuse her as she lifted the intricate silver setting with its bright gems. Wherever she traveled in the world, her sisters were always with her. "Each of the witches has one, with her signature color as the centerpiece." She took three steps, bringing herself closer to him as she held the amulet out for his perusal.

"See?" she said, using her fingertip to trail over the swirling pattern. "The eight smaller stones represent the others. Each of us individuals, yet united as one."

He didn't move away from her, but his look was disdainful when he said, "And your color is red. Dare I point out how appropriate that is?"

Instead of allowing insult, Lucia let a throaty laugh roll forth, low and—as she'd often been told—seductive. "Of course."

She let the necklace fall to her chest and trailed her finger along Ethan's chiseled jaw. The whiskers there were inky black, like his hair, and while she'd never cared for bearded men, the rugged look made him even more devilish.

And definitely sexy.

"Red," she whispered, still testing the scratchy yet soft feel of his stubble, "is strong and bold."

He still didn't step away but stood his ground instead, wrapping fingers around her wrist, bands of steel, and forcing her hand down between them. He didn't hurt her, but she was good and caught. "You might see it that way," he told her in a threatening tone. "But your kind of red is like a caution sign."

Controlling her breath so he wouldn't see how his gravelly voice and firm, full lips affected her, Lucia gave him a cocky smile. "I can work with that."

Ethan shook his head slowly side to side, his wickedly dark eyes never letting go of hers. Then he released her wrist and moved toward a tree.

Lucia could tell his feelings toward her were shifting. Evolving. Yes, he still treated her like a carrier of the black plague, but something had changed.

She'd felt his heated stare on her more than once, and every time he seemed to catch himself and tense up. He appeared angry, as if being attracted to her was the worst kind of torture.

She could understand such a reaction if she weren't just as interested in him. But she was. And she'd done everything possible to make sure he knew it.

Her pride had taken a worse beating than the plane, but still she kept moving forward. Hoping Ethan would slip up and give her something she could understand.

She kept telling herself he must have an excellent reason for snubbing her.

Because it hurt too much to believe he found her lacking.

Ethan was supposed to be hers, and every one of her sisters who'd faced their challenge had found love. So what was his problem?

¿Cómo podría una hija mía ser tan fea? The words still came back to haunt her. If a man told her she was beautiful, sexy, funny, none of the compliments ever really mattered. Not compared to her mother's harshest criticism.

¿Cómo podría una hija mía ser tan fea? How could a child of mine be so ugly?

Lucia had never forgotten.

Her parents had regretted bringing a child into the world, afraid little Lucia would cramp their lifestyle. So they had taken steps to make sure she didn't.

POSSESSION OF A WITCH

Boarding school and Beatriz, her beloved housekeeper and the only real mother she'd ever known. These were the two things that constituted Lucia's young life.

And when she'd seen the pattern emerge from the challenges her friends faced, when she'd witnessed the awful ordeals that ended with love, Lucia had discovered hope.

She would have a turn at the wheel. So she would find romance.

Too bad her greatest challenge was convincing the man he was *supposed* to fall for her.

Ethan had his back to her, still staring into the darkening forest. Suddenly he gave a short laugh and said, "Don't worry, witch. You aren't the only deceptive creature in the jungle."

Deceptive? She opened her mouth to protest his description, but when he motioned for her to join him and pointed out toward the trees, curiosity made her forget his rudeness.

When she sidled up next to him, he put a finger over his lips in a *shhh* gesture, then he parted the leaves. "See that bit of red?" he whispered.

"Yes."

"Looks harmless, right? Cute little frog," he said in a way that told her the small leaf-rider was anything but. "I can't be sure, but I think that's a strawberry dart frog."

"Poisonous," Lucia clarified. And now the insult was back. "I get the analogy, but you're wrong, Drake."

He turned those dark eyes her way and hiked one black brow.

"I'm not deceptive," she said, walking away from him to lay aside her pack. "I've been up front with you. I never hid my intentions." Anger began to bubble inside her, pushing her to a precarious place.

She'd tried being honest. Then direct. And finally subtle. She hadn't had any luck with those tactics, so what did that leave her but one option?

Down. And. Dirty.

Taking a sip of water from her bottle as if nothing were amiss, Lucia smiled to herself. She put the drink down and stood with a long, sinuous stretch. She lifted her arms above her head as she slowly pivoted. *Damn. He's not looking. Probably still spying on that tiny amphibian and comparing it to me.*

Before she could make a move, Ethan muttered something to himself about being filthy and started lifting his shirt. The hem started its climb from his tight backside, then cruised over a muscular back and up, up, up to shoulders that spread wide and looked as if they could easily ram one of these hulking trees to the ground.

He must be tired if he's letting me have this peep show. Guess I'm not such a concern after all. Lucia imagined sending out her own poisonous darts, a love spell that would make him want her above all things.

Yet she held still as he massaged his upper arm. She observed. Appreciated.

The man was definitely packing, and she didn't mean ordinary guns. If the ripples across his shoulders weren't enough, the sensual curve of his lower back was. She couldn't stop herself then, walking silently over to stand a foot behind him.

He stilled when he felt her approach but didn't move. She reached out and let her finger glide over the taut muscles just above the top of his pants.

She thought he might have expelled a breath, but he whirled too quickly for her to be sure. He captured her hand in his.

"Lucia," he said, tone flat in attempt to hide whatever emotion she'd stirred. Was it fury? Desire? The two were so closely related, how could she tell?

She licked her lips and leaned forward, her intent clear as she closed the distance between her own mouth and the heavenly fullness of his. She so wanted to know what he tasted...

"Be good," he said more firmly, setting her away from him like an errant child.

Lucia made a noise of frustration when he hastened away and held up a finger, again, like she was a naughty youngster.

"Why?" she asked, her hands up in supplication. She had finally met the one man she truly wanted, for more than a flirt and laugh, or even a short relationship, but he spurned her every time.

She knew her hurt and confusion shone through when he gave her a look akin to pity. She was here with an extremely virile man, and all he wanted was for her to be good?

Then Lucia's stomach lurched and her head seemed to drop to the ground. Oh no. "But you can't be gay," she sputtered. "No way would she do that to me."

"She?" Ethan asked, and damn him, he was about to smile.

"Fate. Fate. Even she wouldn't mess with someone so bad as to send them a destined mate who just couldn't...wouldn't..."

His smile vanished. "No."

"No, you're not gay?" She could feel certainty slipping away. She'd been so sure.

"Yes...I mean no. I like women, but, no." His face hardened. "I'm not your soul mate."

He threw his soiled shirt down and stalked to her, his strides long and purposeful, eating up the ground until he was close enough to touch her. But he didn't. And this time, she didn't reach for him either.

"I'm going to say this once, and as clichéd and stereotypical as it may sound, it's not you." He angled his head down to stare at her. "It's me. It truly is me. There's nothing wrong with you, and I'm not trying to hurt you."

She ran his monologue through her head a few times before latching onto one important factor. "So you do find me attractive?"

His groan was half growl when he moved around her and

headed toward the shrubs. "I'm going to try to find some collected water in a trunk or something. I need to wash up."

Realizing his patience was stretched to the breaking point, Lucia thought fast, trying to figure out how to turn his mind to other things. He didn't understand her flippancy, or that humor was just part of how she dealt with things that hurt.

Particularly being dismissed, cast aside as if she didn't matter. Like she wasn't even there.

Ethan Drake, it seemed, was turning into the King of Rejection. As she watched him stride away from her, she squelched the eruption of tears that suddenly wanted to break loose. She'd seen others walk away too many times to let the familiar ache take control again.

She'd handled the world's worst type of dismissal, the most cutting humiliation, so there was no way this willful man could top that.

"Wait, Ethan." When she called out he stopped and turned his head to the side. He waited, just as she'd requested.

"I can help you." She held up her hands when he faced her fully. "Bear with me. Let me get back on your good side."

He blew out a breath and turned. "I didn't say you were on my bad side. It's complicated, and I'm just trying to keep you..." He trailed off and shook his head. "Never mind."

Lucia grinned and held up a finger. "*Espera*. You're going to love this. And you won't even have to get naked...no, actually. You will." She ignored him when his eyes widened, then she moved to retrieve the tarp from her pack.

Silently she chastised herself for the curse of having no filter. Whatever she thought just rolled from her head to her tongue.

Ethan was likely as tired and dirty as she was, and cranky to boot. She could fix at least one problem and hopefully distract him from their previous conversation. She had to try and undo the damage she'd caused.

Had she really told him she thought he was her soul mate? *Mierda*. Any man would balk at that. Even a fated lover.

"What are you doing?" he asked when she started scoping the trees. She finally chose three that had enough clearance between them and formed an almost perfect triangle.

Humming softly, she proceeded to tie the tarp to the first trunk, and after the knot was secure, she pulled the tarp around the middle tree before tying it to the third. With the olive-colored plastic hanging to the ground, she'd effectively created two walls.

"Now go behind there and strip." She dusted off her hands for a job well done.

He shot her a doubtful look. "I thought we'd moved past that."

Throwing up her hands and rolling her eyes, Lucia said, "Trust me. You will be very happy in a minute." She crossed her arms when his face grew even more stubborn. "And I promise I won't touch you or even get too close."

They had a staring match before she snapped out, "And I won't peek."

Studying the tarp as if searching for clues, Ethan finally relented and made his way to the other side of the makeshift dressing screen. His head was visible over the top. "You stay there," he warned before the sounds of sliding fabric and a few bumps of the tarp told her he was undressing.

Lucia simply shook her head. No man had ever considered her such a threat before. She frowned. Why was that?

Did he have an aversion to witches? Spaniards? Brunettes?

She could make herself crazy trying to guess, but luckily Ethan finished taking his clothes off and fixed his eyes on her. "Now what?"

"Either toss your clothes to the side or give them to me."

With a mulish expression he threw them in the opposite direction to land on a limb. She grunted to herself. *Honestly.*

Where was the trust?

She started to lift her hands but stopped. "Ooh. I almost forgot." She raced to his pack and kneeled. "Where is your soap?"

His handsome face was blank for a moment before a comprehending gleam bloomed in his eyes. "Front pocket in the plastic bag. What are you up to, witch?"

Lucia found the small bar and returned to stand a few feet away, holding the soap for ransom. "One of my talents happens to be control of the elements." She held up her hands and spoke to the air, the trees, the earth and clouds. "*Que venga la lluvia y que caiga sobre él.*"

Then she smiled at Ethan. "Water, come rain on my friend." The space a foot or so above Ethan's head began to whirl, mixing the greens and golds of the forest like paints under a brush. Glistening streams of water started falling on his head, turning his hair to shining onyx before sluicing over his amazing shoulders and down his chest.

"Heads up," Lucia said to get his attention. He'd dropped his head backward, so the water would hit his face, but he snapped upright at her command. She tossed the bar of soap to him before giving him her back and leaving to start working on the tent.

She'd allow him some privacy.

Ethan didn't abuse her gift, but cleaned up quickly then asked her to bring him clean clothes. "I forgot to grab something to wear."

With a smirk on her face, Lucia sauntered closer, handing the pack over to make sure he didn't think she was trying to sneak a peek. But as usual, she couldn't control her tongue. "Are you absolutely *sure* you want to get dressed?"

Surprisingly, his face didn't tense up with annoyance, but he didn't quite smile either. "I'm positive," he told her, but his hand snaked out to grab hers as he took the pack. "But thanks for giving me this. I feel much better."

She shrugged. "I'm not going to intentionally deny you comfort. That would be cruel and petty."

"And you're neither of things," he said, still gazing at her as if he didn't know who or what she was. "Are you?"

Not sure what to make of his calm scrutiny, Lucia laughed and said, "Not today. But wait until tomorrow morning. We didn't bring any coffee."

"Damn. That's right." Ethan returned to his normal attitude of straight forward and get-the-job-done. But at least he was less stern than he had been all day. Since the crash.

The memory of tumbling through the forest reminded her of her own bruises. "Was the water warm enough?" she asked, swiftly taking his place behind the screen when he stepped out to pull a shirt on. "I tacked temperature control on at the last minute."

"It was wonderful, Lucia. You're very skilled."

"Ha. That's what I keep trying to tell you," she quipped and was delighted to see one side of his mouth lift. Not a full grin but not a curt dismissal either. "Do you ever really smile? I mean, all the way?"

He tossed a question back at her. "Does your mother know how bold you are?"

And as if sensing the change in her mood, the water she'd just conjured turned from warm and soothing to a punishing cold.

She quickly refocused her energy and heated the showering streams. "No, she doesn't," Lucia said. "She doesn't know much about me at all."

14

Ethan stopped what he was doing when he heard the stiffness of her voice. With everything they'd gone through in the last couple of days, he'd never heard her sound so brittle. So empty.

He dropped the tent pole he'd been about to slide into place and went back to the shower. "I'm sorry. I can tell I scraped a raw spot."

She said nothing, moving closer until her face was visible over the tarp. "You and your mother aren't close?" He saw her bite her bottom lip and felt even worse. Why was he pressing her? He didn't need to know more about her. He didn't give a damn about her personal life or past. He shouldn't care.

"Oh, she could probably pick me out in a crowd," Lucia said, her inflection tense. The terseness showing her anger. "And that's only because I look like her sister."

Ethan made a scoffing noise. "Surely a mother would know her own child." He couldn't imagine. His mother was the epitome of maternal. She'd almost sacrificed herself to save Grace, his sister.

Ethan had just beat her to it.

The silence from behind the curtain was deafening. Rarely did Lucia have *nothing* to say. No comeback or passionate rebuttal. No witty remark.

He took a chance and moved even closer, putting one finger on top to pull the tarp down, creating a slight indentation.

Don't look down. Don't you dare look down. Ethan forced himself to do as he'd commanded her earlier. He made himself be good.

But when he saw her faraway stare and the complete vulnerability in her doe eyes, his heart hurt for her. Just a little stab in the very center.

And that's when a foul wind blew into the camp, shaking the leaves and silencing the jungle around them.

Lucia gasped and made Ethan jump inside his own skin. "What is it?" he asked, ready to rip aside the plastic and sweep her up.

Just what type of naked female would he have in his arms then? Spitting mad or softly compliant?

He spared no time to consider it, glancing around instead for any encroaching danger. He could smell the evil in the air. Probing. Testing.

"I...guess it was nothing," Lucia said as air blew out of her lungs. She was relaxing visibly, and that told him just how startled she'd been. "I thought I saw something."

"What?" he demanded. "Tell me exactly."

"It looked like a pair of yellow eyes, but now that I rationalize it, they were too big and sort of floating right here in front of me." She gave a nervous laugh. "If I'm hallucinating, my blood sugar must be low. I'm not going to skip dinner after all."

"No," Ethan said in agreement. "Neither am I." He knew better than to even suggest it as he had before. He'd not only run himself into the ground by the exertion of traveling so far on foot, but on top of that he'd allowed himself a moment of weakness. Just a split-second of true emotion, and it had almost brought hell down upon them both.

Got to be more careful, Drake. "I'm going to pull out some health bars while you finish up."

"I don't really like those, and I have some freeze-dried packs," she said. The water flow had ceased, and she sounded like she was drying off with her field towel.

"You'll eat something good for you," he said, hoping she heard the order in his voice.

"Yes, Captain," she replied, the good humor already back in the way she spoke and moved. That hint of a smile was on her lips and in her eyes when she came around the plastic barrier. "I'll take down the tarp and use it to help seal the outside of the tent."

"Ah, so that's why you said we wouldn't need a hammock." Ethan busied himself with the meal, knowing her shirt was slightly damp. That it clung to her. Gorgeously. "If we can keep the tent sealed, we can sleep on the floor," he added.

Some beasts would be kept out by plastic. But not all.

Ethan warned himself to stop being so fatalistic. To not get so worked up. He'd probably imagined all of it, just as Lucia had thought she'd seen eyes. Yellow eyes.

Lucia tugged on the last knot and freed the tarp before tossing it over a low-lying branch. "The cover can dry while we eat." She spied what he held in his hands. "Health bars. Yum."

Fighting the relief that coursed through him when he realized she was really all right, Ethan shocked himself when he said, "I'm glad we'll be sleeping together."

Lucia froze where she stood. She gaped at him. "Excuse me?"

Waving a hand and focusing on the package that promised *Fruit and Nuts for Good Nutrition*, he told her, "Not like that. I meant for safety."

Her laugh was light and full when she asked, "Why, because a little strawberry frog might get you?"

He sighed. "Yes. Exactly that."

"How did you recognize what kind it was anyway? There are so many species here, many still undiscovered, they say."

"I got lucky, really, but I do have an interest in the smaller creatures. Their methods of defense and camouflage are fascinating." *And you'd be surprised how some demons use similar methods.* "There's always something new in the worlds of entomology and herpetology."

She came to sit beside him. "Okay, the first one I got. The study of insects. But what's herpetology?

He handed her a bar and saw her make a *yuck* face. "Like the word herpes from Latin. It literally means to creep."

Now she dropped the bar in her lap. "Ugh. I'm going to file that under disgusting trivia that I just didn't need to know."

Ethan turned his head when she said the last, because for once, he'd let her charm sneak its way through. Past his barriers and into his gut where the remnants of his childhood sense of humor lay dormant.

And no matter how much he told himself it was reckless to enjoy any small thing about Lucia, something inside him needed to feel that joy. It yearned for the freedom of laughter and the ability to connect with a woman. In a way he hadn't for so long.

Lucia was relentless, and if she wasn't killing him with those voluptuous curves, she was delighting him with her wit. She was dangerous, no doubt, and red was a most appropriate color.

But for now he would take just a little of the warmth she wanted so badly to share.

As he rummaged in his backpack, he made sure to keep his head down. He made sure Lucia couldn't see his face.

Because he was actually smiling. All the way.

~~~

The night was crisp with early autumn chill, that clean, invigorating feeling reminiscent of high school football games.

A glowing orb rode steady in the distance, a full white moon, sharing her power with the insignificant humans below.

The moon was rumored to have effects. To cause erratic behavior, coerce magical beings to come out from hiding, or to give that little extra push and make someone fall in love.

And it was the last that worried Ethan as he surveyed the low-rolling hills and their moonlit glow.

He remembered this place and had come here often in his youth. He moved his gaze to a lone maple tree, its colorful leaves hidden by the dark, yet somehow he knew they were a bright mix of about-to-fall yellow, red, and burnt orange. Then like magic, a blanket appeared on the grass beneath its bowers.

And he knew this night.

His footsteps didn't quite touch the earth as he moved, closing the distance much faster than he should have. Part of him knew he was visiting a dream, but the other part of him didn't care.

He had to make it to the blanket and the still form lying there. Did he know her?

At the edge of the light-blue blanket, its paleness frosted even more by moonlight, Ethan studied the woman. Her hair was long and dark, waving over her shoulder and halfway down her back. Clarity hit like a lightning strike.

His first love had been a brunette. His only love. "Oh, God," he said, his voice broken with pain. "Jessica? Is that you?"

She didn't stir, but the wind rustled leaves across the grass around him, above him the tree trembled. Did it know something he didn't?

As he looked around for what felt like an enemy approaching, he saw nothing but the idyllic country night and noticed two twinkling stars had joined the great moon.

The woman made a sound, a soft sigh of contentment. Her hand slid down her hip to rest on her thigh.

She rolled over, but Ethan still couldn't see her face for the dark strands of hair. "Jess?" He reached for her with a shaking hand, slipping one finger beneath the brown. He pushed her hair to the side.

Not Jessica he realized as the glow across the land turned a sickly yellow, like a god's hand had put a color screen over the pure, sweet moon. Lucia was sleeping on the blanket. The same one he'd shared so long ago with a different female.

The night he'd lost his virginity and given his heart.

"No," he said, finally finding his rage. "No. This isn't possible." As the putrid light changed even more, the pretty scene became drenched in red, everything tainted by the color of death. Of blood.

Lucia's eyes fluttered open, confused and unfocused, then she called Ethan's name. He could hear the question, the fear in her voice.

"I won't let this happen," he said, fists clenched at his side. He didn't know if he was telling her or the entity he knew was close by. Watching. Always watching.

He raised those fists to the sky, shaking his wrath at the now-oily moon. "I am still in control!"

A sound permeated the air around him as if in answer to his yell. A sliding sound of silk against grass, and with no further warning the thing was there. Huge yellow eyes materialized in the reddened darkness, staring at Ethan with their serpentine slits.

The beast gave a horrible hiss before flicking its tongue to test for scent. "Ethan," it said smugly. "You called?"

A hand clamped over his mouth and a female voice spoke close to his ear. "Shhh. Ethan. Wake up and be quiet." Looking around wildly, he saw the inside of the dark green tent. He smelled the richness of rain forest.

And he felt the warmth of the woman at his side. Lucia. She was here. She was safe.

And she still had her hand pressed to his mouth. He gently

pulled her fingers down and asked in a hush, "What's wrong?"

She was leaning over him, body taut and unmoving. Her head was cocked as she listened.

"They're out there and getting closer by the minute." She withdrew her hand and sat up. "But if we break camp and hit the trail we can lose them."

The last streamers of sleep cleared his brain and he sat up with a bolt. "Who? The guardians?"

"The Amara. I can't tell how many, but I'd feel their stench anywhere." She looked to him as she raked her fingers through her hair to untangle it before tying it up with an elastic band. "The women of my coven can sense the Amara, and now that I've got a bead on them, I can track their location."

She gave him a grin, and it wasn't sweet. "As long as they don't lay eyes on us and actually see us, we should be able to dance around them."

She chewed her bottom lip. "I bet Tyr is with them. Their seer," she added before he could ask. "He probably saw our location in one of his handy visions, but you and I can make good time. Keep far enough away and avoid them altogether."

"They're headed our way now?" he asked, rolling up his sleeping bag like a pro. Thankfully, he was.

As he tied the strings to keep the bag tight, Ethan closed down the chill from the nightmare, because that's all it amounted to. A bad dream.

Lucia stretched her arms in front of her. "I'd say they're less than a mile out, and Tyr is exceptionally strong. He'll be able to cover the distance faster than most." A thin wrinkle formed between her eyes. "I wouldn't be surprised if he's a tracker, too, considering he's an Indian."

"Come again?" Ethan stopped in the middle of slipping into his leech socks.

"I forget in the States you say Native Americans now." Then her face lit up with realization. "Oh, yes, I forgot to tell you he's somewhat immortal."

"Somewhat?" he said before climbing out after her to help dismantle the small tent and gather up their other belongings. They were both neat campers, so it wouldn't take long. "Isn't that like being a little bit pregnant?"

She laughed, a low throaty chuckle. "Fine. He's not a true immortal like Ronja. She's the real deal, but if Tyr drinks her blood," she paused and gave him a mischievous look, "let's just say he's on borrowed time."

Shaking his head and marveling, Ethan helped her finish up with the tent and looked around to make sure they hadn't forgotten anything. "We're being hunted by more paranormal entities than I can count on one hand, and you're still making jokes."

Dawn was breaking in the distance, and the jungle glowed with an otherworldly light. Calm. Peaceful.

Magical.

Ethan took in the scene then looked at Lucia as she put something fruity smelling on her lips. "You're an enigma, Lucia. You really are."

She smiled. "What a sweet thing to say."

Ethan hiked his pack onto his back and held out a hand. "Lead or follow?"

She pursed her lips and gave him a flirty wink. "Since we don't have coffee, I'll need something to brighten up my morning." Her eyes travelled to his booted feet and back up his tan pants. She circled around to stand behind him. "I'll follow."

He looked to the brightening sky. "Save me from audacious witches."

Then he readjusted the straps of his pack and took off, tossing over his shoulder, "Let's move."

15

Anna knew where to look for her brother when he needed some alone time. The coven had sparred hard yesterday, so today had been declared free time. She stopped outside his door and knocked.

"Come in, Anna," Quinn called from the other side.

She pushed inside to find him at his desk, a slab of reclaimed wood that had been sanded and polished before being set atop two thick, marble columns. She hadn't been able to picture the idea when he'd first explained it, but she'd been proven wrong.

The finished product was a work of art. Brown and gray whirls in both wood and marble were masculine, the columns sturdy, and the design showed an appreciation for the past. She grinned and crossed the large room, realizing the description of the desk would also fit her brother.

Though a few years younger than her, Quinn was in his own way...wise. "How did you know it was me?" she asked, turning her head to see what he was reading.

"You always knock the same way." He kept his face down until he finished the paragraph he was on. Then he looked up. "I've been reading some of the things Ethan suggested. These demon clans are disturbingly well-classified. Wonder if there's an evil version of Darwin down there."

Anna grimaced. "Now that is disturbing." She rubbed her hands together and moved to the ceiling-high shelving unit behind his desk. She picked up a framed picture of their parents from when they were young, full of hope, and newly-married.

She and Quinn both had their mother's blue eyes and their father's sable hair. Their facial features had been passed down haphazardly with Quinn getting the full lashes—damn him—and Anna the arched brows.

She'd teased him mercilessly when they were younger, and she still remembered the trouble she'd gotten into when Quinn had decided enough was enough. He'd cut all those long lashes off with Mrs. Attinger's sewing scissors.

But they'd grown back. Eyes that had been pretty on the boy were arresting on the man. And it still caused a pang in her chest to think of him that way. All grown up.

He sat and watched her with those perceptive eyes, knowing her well enough to wait until she was ready to say what she'd come to say. She'd always admired that about him. His gift of patience. The art of being still.

"I want to open up the tower again." She heard his sharp intake of breath. Heard him clear his throat as he processed her unexpected announcement.

"Does this have anything to do with our little bug problem?" he asked, picking up one of his expensive pens and rolling it between his fingers.

"The demons hulking around Savannah, yes. The timing is just too perfect for there to be any other answer." Anna had been clasping the book in one hand and now held it out to Quinn. "I had my suspicions about what Mom and Dad were working on up there. Before they..."

"Yeah. Got it," he said in a clipped tone. Quinn didn't talk about the tower room. Or the accident. "How long have you had this book?"

"Only recently. I mentioned using the tower to Mrs. Attinger, and she gave it to me. Mom left instructions for this specific occasion."

Quinn's eyes were an odd combination of anger and injury. Anna's heart felt the same way. Furious her parents had been taken so early in life, yet aching deep inside from the loss. "What occasion?" her brother asked.

Anna drew a breath. "When you and I take up where they left off."

He sat forward quickly, causing his chair to squeal in protest. "Are you crazy? After what happened, why would you even suggest it? You have to lead the coven." He stabbed a finger at her. "You have to make it to your trial and defeat Bastraal."

Quinn stilled abruptly. "Because you know you'll be the one called to end it."

"Yes," Anna said in a small voice no one ever heard her use. "I've always known." She indicated the book, so small and fragile looking in her brother's hands.

Internally she pulled herself back together. Forced her spine to grow rigid again. As it should be. It had to be. "Look over it if you like. Mom kept notes on their progress."

She took a turn around the room while he studied the journal. Quinn was a man of varied tastes, and she smiled to see he had a copy of a gruesome comic book on his nightstand. He'd always loved that kind of thing. Maybe he should have been the one destined to fight the king of demons.

"They were trying to store magic in metal. They tried several kinds and made progress but only titanium was light enough and strong enough for their ultimate purpose." He closed the book with a snap. "Our sweet, loving parents were making weapons up there."

"Yes, and the more they tried to force the metal to accept their magic, the stronger the combustion. They couldn't find a way to get around the natural resistance."

Anna strode to stand in front of his desk. She put both hands on the wood and leaned toward him. "We can finish it, Quinn. We have our own arsenal now. An army of smart, versatile minds."

He gave her a tired smile. "From Greek myths to Gucci. We've got you covered."

She held his stare, unwilling to look away. She had to have Quinn's participation, but more important than that, she wanted his blessing. Finally he handed the book back to her. "Then we know what comes next."

She took it and released a quivering breath of relief. "We take it to the coven."

~~~

A gaggle of women awaited them as Anna and Quinn descended to the great room. Anna's hand was still on the mahogany railing when Kylie called out, "They're here," before turning her vibrant face up to them. "Mrs. Attinger told us to fill you in when you got down here."

"Is everything okay?" Quinn asked.

"Yeah. Yeah. She told us to send for Nick and Trevor, since they would need to hear what you had to say." Kylie lifted her blonde brows with curiosity. "I certainly hope you know what it is you're supposed to say."

"I do, yes." Anna said aside to her brother, "I told you that woman gets vibes."

Quinn grinned and stuck his hands in his pockets. "Yes, she does. And whenever she caught me doing something I shouldn't, I always blamed you."

Anna laughed loud and full, startling both herself and her brother. "I bet she never believed either one of us."

"Oh," Kylie said, holding up a finger. "And she declared it pizza night. We ordered your favorites."

There was a hum in the elegant room, almost palpable, and

it spoke of anticipation. Of a battle about to be waged. Though the others couldn't know what Anna and Quinn were going to share, there was no doubt they could feel the importance of tonight's meeting.

Even if it was going to be carried out over slices of pepperoni pizza.

As soon as Nick and Trevor walked in, Paige jumped up from her seat and started handing out paper plates. "I want to get straight to the plan, so everybody grab some food and find a spot."

Nick walked over to give Viv a sound kiss and touch her cheek before taking a comfortable chair. He'd come straight from his pub and looked worn out.

Trevor, on the other hand, was wired, his blue eyes eager to share something. He stood next to Hayden and waited with his arms crossed over his chest. When everyone started to settle down, he looked to Anna. "I have something to share, too, and I hope it will play into whatever you've got going."

"All right," Anna said, musing over magic's choice of men for her sisters. Each was steadfast and intelligent in his own way. And each seemed to bring something to the table to help fight the fight.

Forgoing any pizza due to a clutch of nerves in her stomach, Anna spoke from a standing position. "Quinn and I have outlined a basic concept, but there are still pieces to be worked out. We all talked before about these demons coming through the portals and how Ethan left behind some leads for us to follow."

"And the first thing we have to do is identify the type of demons in the city," Paige said. She didn't roll her finger in the air in a "hurry-up" motion, but the way she jiggled her leg practically said the same thing.

"Yes, and the information Ethan left us includes common elements, metals mostly, that will react to certain breeds."

"And will help us identify them," Quinn finished for his sister. "So we have the basics that could lead to both detection tools and..."

"Weapons," Paige said. She clapped her hands together. "Now we're talking."

Viv wiped her hands on a napkin and took a sip of cola before asking, "When you say elements, what exactly are we talking about? I imagine some of them are hard to come by." She lifted a hand. "It's not like you have a stockpile of metal lying around here."

Anna and Quinn exchanged a look. "Actually, that brings us to the second part of tonight's proposal." She smoothed her moist palms down the front of her jeans. "Our parents were experimenting with this type of work. They weren't testing demon essence, or however we want to refer to it, but they were working on imbuing magic into metal."

"We think we can do both, now that we have Ethan's list." Quinn slid his eyes to Anna, so she nodded. She'd let him tell this part. "Our parents set up their metallurgy workshop in the tower."

Anna saw Willyn grasp her husband's hand. She and the others knew there had been a fire in the tower once, they just didn't know specifics. Dare rubbed his wife's hand and his shoulders lifted as he drew a deep breath. He'd been friends with Quinn and Anna since their youth, so he knew everything.

Quinn stood firm with his legs apart. "They had an accident in the tower. There was a fire and they were killed."

The room was silent, no one sure what to say. What to ask.

Finally Anna said, "We've talked this over, and not only do Quinn and I want to move forward on this, it was something our parents wanted for us as well."

"Despite the risks?" Claudia asked, her hands clasped in her lap. The history professor could be all-business when necessary. Even when it stung.

"I think they understood things would be different for us." Anna indicated Quinn and herself. "The magic passed to us is stronger than what our parents had."

"And you believe you can control it," Paige said. "With our help." The statement brooked no refusal.

Anna smiled at her loyal friend. Paige would take on a lava flow to help her new family. They all would. "Yes. With your help. All of you. Which is another reason we think we can do it."

She gestured to Trevor. "And that brings us to you, Detective."

"Right," Trevor said with a decisive nod. "My partner Cole and I have been keeping an ear out for strange goings-on, stranger than the usual Savannah fare, I mean. There are stories on the streets about a warehouse. We don't have a location yet, but they're saying some people who go there... well, they come back different." He paused. "Or not at all."

"Just perfect," Kylie said. "They've set up a demon factory."

"That remains to be seen," Anna said, her previous anxiety gone now as the idea of innocents being used by evil washed away any personal conflicts. "I assume you'll keep looking," she told Trevor.

"Of course." He was a good man and determined not to let his city fall.

"I'll plant a few careful seeds, too," Nick said. "I can ask a few questions around the bar. Listen to the daily chatter for anything out of the ordinary."

"Excellent," Anna told him. "Quinn and I will get the tower back in shape, because we want to start on the first experiments. I have an idea for how we might identify the demons." A fire was burning in her gut now, and she was ready to be proactive for a change.

She sent a conspiratorial smile to Kylie. "Then we can get to work on swords even Frodo would be proud of."

16

"No, let's go this way," Lucia said, staring down her nose at the meandering stream of water that probably fed into a larger tributary of the Amazon River. "Too much water that way, and we only have leech-proof socks. Not full body armor."

She saw the side of Ethan's mouth kick up momentarily. "You're the professional explorer," he said in a way that told her he was trying to push her pride button.

"Yeah, well." She brushed her shoulder against his as she passed him and stopped to speak near his ear. "We all have something." She marched on, already scouting another area that would be traversable and keep them heading toward Chachapoyas then Kuelap Fortress beyond. And this way was drier.

She shivered and said, "Blech," before she could stop herself. Leeches, she believed, were straight from the bottom of the evolutionary barrel.

"You know one of my phobias, so what does a fearless demon-seeker put at the top of his list of Things To Be Afraid Of?" She shifted her eyes to Ethan, glad the landscape had opened up enough for them to walk side by side.

She stopped to admire the beauty of an orchid, bright fuchsia and so graceful. The blossoms begged for her to pay a little attention to them, and the flowers would become fewer as they moved farther from the area of Moyobamba. The town appropriately referred to as "Orchid City."

The land was becoming more mountainous, and the great peaks that would provide their greatest challenge loomed in the distance. Their purplish-gray rode majestically against the blue sky.

After a long silence that told Lucia he was choosing his words carefully, Ethan looked up into the afternoon sun and said, "Seeing others suffer. That's what I fear."

The admission surprised Lucia, and she felt her brows shoot up. The man of mystery had plucked a juicy plum from the tree and shared it without sidestepping. Of course, one reveal wasn't going to be enough.

She wanted more. She needed to know what made him function. Why did he live the way he did, chasing down monsters and picking them apart? What made a man study evil?

Ethan's soul had been wounded, and Lucia was sure, if she figured that out, everything else would fall into place. So she was even more curious after his last statement. She was greedy for more fruit.

"Did you see Jessica suffer?" she asked.

Ethan's right foot skidded in the dirt when he jerked his head toward her. He found his balance quickly, though, turning a withering stare on her as if she'd betrayed him. "How do you know …never mind. I guess I talked during my dream. Not the first time."

Then he seemed to recall how mad he was. "Why do you have to do that? I very carefully weighed whether or not I should answer your question with the truth." He started forward again with every intention of leaving her far behind.

"Why wouldn't you be able to tell me the truth?" she called, speeding up to match his pace.

He pressed on stubbornly. "You think honesty is so great,

why don't we talk about you for a while? The topics that make you go deeper inside yourself to hide. All's fair, right?"

"I don't see what my past has to do with anything, but okay. I was born to parents who are beyond wealthy and spend their lives wringing pleasure out of every cent they have. I grew up attending the finest schools. So expensive they must surely have been good enough to raise a child." Lucia's lips clenched with anger, but she shut it down straight away.

"You lived with your parents sometime, though," he said as if trying to call a bluff.

She narrowed her eyes in thought. "Approximately two days every year during *la Navidad,* at least until I was ten and considered too old for such sentimentalities. So that adds up to...oh, I'll pad it a little and call it a month."

Ethan halted suddenly and stared in front of him. "Are you saying you've spent a grand total of one month living with your parents?" His forehead wrinkled as he tried to ram that square peg into his sensible version of a round hole.

His expression turned kind, as if the wind had changed directions. "Lucia," he said, "you didn't have any family growing up?"

A loving face materialized in her memory. "Not of blood. But I did have Beatriz, our housekeeper. She lived at the main estate full-time and eventually became my nanny, then guidance counselor, and before I knew it..." Lucia trailed off on a thoughtful pause. "She was the only mother I ever knew, and I am so grateful she came into my life."

Lucia worked up a smile, though it felt overly-bright. "Have I donated enough blood for today? Time for a fair exchange?" She prayed he didn't pursue the subject, because she never talked about her parents, or their neglect, and speaking the horrid truth was like rubbing alcohol on a cut she thought had healed.

She decided not to give Ethan a choice and went for a

diversionary tactic. "So who is Jessica? Is she your sister?"

"You're right," he said brusquely. "Enough spilled blood for now."

Lucia felt her jaw drop as he shut her down and walked away. "Why...you rotten *cabrón*. I should never have trusted you."

She wanted to throw something at his handsome face. But everything was in her backpack.

"I don't need or want your trust." He held a hand up. "Correction. We need to trust each other for the basics. Survival. But only for a few more days."

This time her accent rolled as she said the word with heart. With heat. "*Cabrón*."

"Look, Lucia," his tone was weary as if he didn't feel he needed to justify himself. "I don't spend a lot of extended time with people. It makes it easier to stay on track, do my job, and avoid difficult entanglements."

He drew himself up straight and an imaginary veil of ice seemed to cover him. "Especially romantic entanglements."

Huffing through her nose, Lucia felt her Spanish temper rising from the polite and proper ashes. So much for private school decorum. "You have made it abundantly clear that you aren't interested in a romantic involvement. And while it may be taking a long time to penetrate my thick *cabeza*, there's no reason to be cruel."

In a blast of anger, she grabbed his arm when he attempted to move away from her again. "But we're in this together, whether you like it or not."

"I don't like it. In fact, I resent it. Why do you have to know about my personal life?" He jerked his arm free. "Why can't you just let it go?"

"Because you're holding something back." As soon as she spit the accusation out, Lucia realized the idea had been nagging at her for a while. She'd been too blinded by the cartoon hearts blocking her good sense to see the truth.

Ever since Ethan had been unwilling to let go of his book with the dagger's picture, she'd had a small, niggling concern. "Let me see the drawing of the dagger again."

His expression turned dangerous. The denial fell too quickly from his lips. "No."

"Why not?"

"Why do you want to?"

Gripping her hands into fists, Lucia channeled calm. "Why won't you let me see the rest of the book? That night at the mansion, your fingers were almost white from clamping the pages together. My life is on the line here, Ethan. So is yours. How dare you keep anything from me that has to do with my trial?"

Now she stalked away. "Then you have the gall to get pissy about a few personal questions."

His long, powerful legs closed the distance between them and then he was in front of her. His hands grabbed her upper arms to slow her down.

Instead of resisting and letting things get further out of hand, she stopped in her tracks and stared at him. Waiting.

Ethan's arms tensed and flexed, though he held her gently. Then he dropped them and hooked one thumb under the strap of his pack. He turned to take in the view of the mountains, now that they were on a small rise.

She could see he was struggling, weighing his words. Deciding how truthful he could afford to be? She crowded him and spoke near his shoulder. "Don't mess with me, Drake. This isn't about you and me, but my challenge. Lives are at stake in Savannah, and if we lose the battle there, the rest of the world will fall."

Ethan kept staring into the distance. Then he finally heaved a breath and said, "There is something else, and if it has anything to do with your challenge or the coven's prophecy, I swear I'll hand it over."

"What is it? What does it have to do with the dagger?" Lucia's skin felt chilled, even under the weight of the hot, humid air. Wind caressed the spattering of trees that stood around them, but she couldn't fully appreciate the wonder of nature or the scene that stretched before them.

How much had he kept from her? Could they have avoided the guardian attack? The plane crash?

"My friends are back there in the jungle. Michael is hurt, so if you could have done something to prevent that..."

"What? No." He thumped a fist against his chest. "I wouldn't let harm come to you or any of your friends. Anyone at all. Is that what you think of me?"

"I don't know what to think! And why should I? You're like a damn vault, Ethan." She kicked a stray rock and sent it tumbling through the grass and dirt. "A very prickly vault."

Ethan sighed. "I'll tell you this much. For once I'm close to getting something that I need, something that could change... everything. But if it's meant to be part of the prophecy, then I'll relinquish it." He looked away from her. "No matter what it costs me."

"What do you mean? What will it cost you?" A jumble of feelings collided inside Lucia— doubt, compassion, resentment— yet she could see he was grappling with his own conscience.

Whatever he was after, whatever he needed, had to cut to the core of who he was. It had to be the missing piece.

"What it may cost me is irrelevant." His stare was empty when he looked at her. The depths of his dark brown eyes seemed bottomless, void of any telltale signs. "And you'll get all the answers you want when we find the dagger."

With that he turned and left her.

For once she didn't follow. She let him crest the small hill and start down the other side.

"What is that supposed to mean?" But she was speaking to the wind.

Frustrated and with more questions than she'd had before, Lucia mumbled to herself and went after him. In the vast and wild terrain of the rain forest, she didn't want to lose him.

Though she would be able to find him with a lift of her palm if it came down to it.

Remembering her gift, she decided to scope the vicinity for the Amara. Her argument with Ethan had distracted her, and she'd shut down her internal radar.

As soon as she set out her mystical net, she knew that had been a mistake. *Damn.*

She hurried to catch up with Ethan but soon realized he'd gone further than she'd thought. She ran faster, pushing branches aside as they whipped at her, ignoring the small scratches.

"Ethan," she said in a hushed voice when she saw a flash of his pack through the leaves.

A few more paces and she was close enough to snag his shirt. "We have to be quiet. The Amara are close." She glanced around. "We need to keep going. Same direction but faster."

He sucked in through his teeth. "See what happens when you let emotions get in the way? Shit." He continued on but carefully, trying to move swiftly but quietly.

They'd been making headway for about ten minutes when a mechanical ring screeched into the fragile quiet. "Holy...it's the sat phone," Lucia said. "*Mierda. Mierda.*"

Panic pulsed inside her like a strobe light, and until she could get to the phone to stop the noise, she and Ethan might as well be flashing, too. A bright sign for the Amara to follow.

She answered in a whisper and motioned with her hand for Ethan to hurry up and go forward. They might still be able to lose their enemy, but if Tyr and whoever was with him hadn't known Lucia and Ethan were nearby, they definitely did now.

Shauni was on the phone letting them know the Peruvian rescuers had found them and were loading Michael for transport as they spoke. Lucia could hear the relief and happy tears in her friend's voice. "I'm so glad," she said. "I'm so glad."

They ended the call quickly when Shauni had to get on board as well, but Lucia felt like a bus had been lifted from her chest. Even if long-dead demon harlots *had* ransacked her plane, she still felt responsible for the safety of her passengers.

She told Ethan, "Michael and Shauni are being taken to a clinic for immediate care then on to a hospital in Lima, since they're foreign nationals. It's protocol."

"Then they're safe." Ethan shocked Lucia's system then when he looked right at her and smiled. His rugged face became so blindingly attractive, and yet still so *male*, she couldn't think straight for at least three heartbeats.

"I was worried, too," he said, telling her he'd read her clearly. "That's great news."

But their moment of relief was short.

A woman's wild cry rang out, causing the small skittering animals around them to freeze and grow silent. The phone had given them away, all right, and now Lucia knew who had accompanied Tyr.

Carson was his sidekick on this adventure, and her presence made a twisted sort of sense. She was, after all, an Amazon.

"Do you think that means they've spotted us?" Ethan asked, pulling out the machete that had been strapped to his back.

"I'm not sure." Lucia stood close to him and looked back the way they'd come. "Sound can be tricky in this thick vegetation. But that's Carson. I'd know her crazy, hostile voice anywhere."

Ethan put his hand on her shoulder and tried to shove her behind him. The action caused a spurt of warmth in her stupid, romantic heart. *Oh, boy.* Guess she really couldn't take a hint.

"We don't have to fight, but we can if you want," she said, getting her mind back on what was crucial. "Tyr's strong and tricky. He may also be hyped up on Ronja's blood."

Lucia was tired but not so exhausted she couldn't spare some blue light for her enemies. "I can take Carson, but...I don't know. Maybe we should just keep trying to evade."

Ethan was the kind of guy who looked like he could handle himself in just about any situation, but if something went wrong out here, they were far away from any kind of help.

She envisioned Tyr's hateful eyes.

A hospital could be right around the corner, and it wouldn't make a difference.

If she or Ethan went down, Tyr and Carson wouldn't allow them to be nursed back to health. They'd kill them then and there.

"I want to go," Lucia said, urgency making her speak faster than normal.

"Don't you want to get them off our tail once and for all?" Ethan glared into the jungle. "We still have the Qara Mikuna to deal with. There's no predicting when they'll set their sights on us again."

"No. We should go." Another sensation was troubling Lucia, and she couldn't pinpoint the cause.

Then a roar shattered the stillness of the forest, some sort of great cat. It sounded ferocious.

And it was on the hunt.

"I know that voice, too," Lucia said, hooking her hand around Ethan's elbow and tugging insistently when he just stood there. "Ross is with them."

"They have a predatory feline named Ross?" he asked. But at least he was moving with her.

"No, Ross is a shifter."

"Uh. That could be bad." Ethan gripped his machete more meaningfully. "What do you want to do?"

When the roar sounded again and threatened to shake the trees above their heads, Lucia let go of Ethan's arm and took a deep breath. *"Tenemos que correr,"* she said, terror causing her to fall back on her native tongue.

But Ethan had gotten the message and was moving with her.

Heart thrashing and blood flowing, Lucia told him again in English. She told him to run.

17

Ethan moved as quickly as possible, but even the less dense jungle was thick with hanging vines and slapping fronds. The natural world was unruly compared to the neat and trimmed gardens of civilization.

He tried to keep his voice down when he spoke to Lucia. Staying close on her heels helped. "Why would they be here? Why would the Amara attack us out here instead of lying in wait at the fortress? It doesn't make sense."

Lucia also spoke in a hushed voice. The predator stalking them had both keen hearing and smell. "I have a feeling this is about more than simply finding the dagger. Ronja's lost four times now, and she can't be happy. She's a ball of fury covered by injured pride."

She stopped to face him, lines in her forehead telling of her seriousness. "This is about payback."

Ethan subconsciously reached for the machete handle to make sure it was still there. "Out here they can do whatever they want, rip us to pieces even, and no one would know."

The image of what a panther with human intelligence could do made his insides stutter and run cold. He jerked his head to indicate the semi-path they were on. "Keep moving."

They hadn't heard anything from the shifter and were only

assuming he was still in cat form. He might just as easily have changed to a bird, flying above to spot his quarry. If he found them, Ross could drop down and turn to any creature he chose.

As if to support Ethan's morbid thoughts, dark clouds overtook the sun and cast the already shadowed forest into a darkness that pulsed with warning. The hulking trees looked more sinister, and the sounds of life became screams of alarm. "Where is he, Lucia? Can you get a bead on Ross?"

Lucia stepped aside as Ethan swung around her to take the lead. Latching onto his pack, she let him guide her as she closed her eyes and brought the locations of their enemies into focus.

Her breath hitched before she said, "Ross is closing in, closer than he was before. And the others are spread out to the sides, not as near but..." She opened her brown eyes and now they were dark with apprehension. "Tyr and Carson are coming around the edges. They're flanking us."

Ethan kept pushing forward, internally weighing their options. The shifter was gaining on them, and racing through the jungle this way was only wearing him and Lucia down. The end result was predetermined, and a wise man would make the best of the predicament.

If he intended to survive.

Thunder broke through the sky with an earth-splitting crack, and as Ethan swept aside a leafy branch, he saw they'd come to a small opening in the underbrush. When Lucia pushed free from the bushes behind him, he faced her. "We have to fight."

He could tell by the sour look on her face that she'd already come to the same conclusion and was none too happy about it. She slipped off her pack and walked to the far perimeter of the clearing to drop the heavy load. She would do better without the weight on her back.

Slipping the machete free from its sheath, Ethan eyed the black metal and accepted the gruesome truth of what he might have to do with the long, fearsome blade. "Who's the greatest threat?" he asked her. "Of the Amara, if they come at once, who do we need to take out?"

Lucia spun around slowly, her palm out in front of her like a rotating satellite dish searching for signals. "Ross is still closer than the others, so I'll use my magic against him. Even with your strength and weapon, he can shift into any creature he chooses. I've seen him take the form of a grizzly."

Ethan nodded. "Supernatural against supernatural. Your witch to his shifts. Fine. The next one will be this Tyr person you mentioned. He's a warrior. Any other talents besides his visions?"

Lucia shook her head. "None that I know of."

A roar carried to them from the forest, startling birds from their hiding places in the canopy. Howler monkeys gave a sudden, whooshing cry as if their voices had dried up from fright. Then they too made a hasty getaway, the rattling limbs above giving away their path of retreat.

The predatory cat was tight on the trail of its prey, his thrashing steps growing closer. His growls lowered and became fiercer as he advanced. Ross could smell how close he was to catching Lucia and Ethan, and his demeanor had changed. He was no longer simply tracking his prey.

He had found them.

Rain chose that moment to fall from the gray skies, hampering what little visibility they had. Now every leaf was shaking from the pummeling water, making it harder to tell where the cat was coming from.

Without a word, Lucia and Ethan put their backs together, each facing the opposite direction.

Ethan wiped rain from his eyes and stared into the jungle. Waiting for the great cat to spring from the shadows. Why wasn't the shifter on them yet? He'd been close, enough to have them between his jaws if that's what he wanted.

"He's stalling," Lucia said. Her hands were loose at her

sides, her breathing harsh but evenly drawn. Ethan could sense her apprehension, but there was no physical sign. She was prepared for just such an occurrence. She'd trained for hand-to-hand combat and seemed more at ease than he felt.

"You think he's waiting for the others so they can attack at the same time?" Ethan continued to scrutinize the dark spaces but could only see a few feet into the tangled green.

"Yes." Lucia said nothing else, but the message was clear. They might not have the luxury of choosing who to take out first. They would be forced to defend themselves against whoever came for them.

And that might be all three at once.

Lucia stilled suddenly and threw a hand back to slap Ethan's side. He turned and followed her glare to a man standing just within the shelter of the trees. This had to be Tyr. His skin was the color of an aging penny, his hair and eyes were black as sin.

He smiled with malice at Lucia, then, just as Anna had described in her dream, the Native American warrior raised his bow.

And aimed for Lucia's chest.

As she lifted her hand to call forth magic, Ethan slashed his own arm across hers and knocked it back down. "Save it!" he yelled over the rain before taking one step forward with his left leg, essentially blocking her from Tyr. Then he followed through with his other leg while arcing over with his right arm.

The machete bulleted through the air and landed with a dull thud in the middle of Tyr's gut.

There was no sound in the clearing other than rain as Ethan looked at the dark-skinned man, and he stared back, stunned. Slowly Tyr spread his arms so he could see his stomach, the expression on his face morphing from astonishment to fury.

Ethan didn't have time to think but ran toward Tyr just as an angry growl sounded from behind him. He knew Lucia would be ready to take on the powerful cat, and Ethan had to make sure Tyr was out of the fray for good.

The woman Lucia had spoken of could be anywhere right now. Carson, the wild Amazon with brutal fighting skills. Her teeth would rip flesh the same as the cat's, so Ethan would have to be ready.

He leapt through the air when Tyr tried to bring the arrow back to his bow, catching him around the waist in a perfect football tackle. Once on the ground, Tyr tried to roll out from under him, but the blade in his abdomen only drove deeper with the struggle.

Soon the two men were slippery with dark mud, making it difficult to keep hold on one another's skin.

Ethan grunted as he fought to keep his grip. If he could get his hand on the blade again, he'd drive it into the bastard's heart.

At least that's what he was thinking before an elbow caught him in the jaw, clipping him so hard he saw black and red starbursts. When he finally blinked his eyes clear, he found himself flat on his back, the rain pelting his face.

And Tyr had somehow found his feet.

The Native American man was bracing one hand against the trunk of a tree, clenching the other around the hilt of the machete still buried inside him.

The rain was thrumming with a vengeance now, but on the far side of the light gap, Ethan could make out bright blue flashes. Lucia's magic. Judging from the erratic bursts, she was nailing the shifter over and over again.

Then a terrifying thought struck. She might be pitting herself against two different people.

Ethan got up and started to rush to her aid but logic rammed into him. He stopped and weighed the odds. Tyr was already hurt, so it only made sense to finish him off. To level the fighting field.

As the man pulled on the blade and screamed in pain, Ethan

channeled every ounce of mercilessness he possessed. He made his way to the tree and wrapped both hands around the hilt. Just as he'd imagined, he retracted the machete far enough to shift the angle to an upward slant.

Then he plunged the thick steel into Tyr's heart, ignoring the man's wet, gasping breaths and widened eyes.

He could allow no pity. This was the man who'd almost planted a bow inside Lucia's chest. He'd tried to kill her.

With a wrench Ethan pulled out the machete and let Tyr topple to the ground. He spun to locate Lucia. She was still firing off blue streaks, but they seemed to come less often and were more controlled.

They were also weaker, as if she were tiring. He stumbled out into the clearing and immediately saw why. She was battling two challengers, and only one of them was human. A blonde woman was diving behind trees and down to the ground, avoiding Lucia's power surges.

The roaring cat must have shifted to the hawk-like bird that was dive bombing Lucia's head every time she whirled to face the oncoming woman. From his vantage point, Ethan could see that the two were only feigning attacks, forcing Lucia to use up her strength.

With the bloody machete still in his hand, Ethan ran across the slick ground to her side. "They're baiting you," he said, voice raised over the rain.

The pissed-off glare she slanted him gave him renewed hope. "I know. That's why I backed off." She fired a shot as Carson looked out from behind a thick trunk. "What about Tyr?" she asked as Ross dipped from the sky to distract her.

This time when the vicious bird came close, Ethan whipped the machete into an arc to nip the tail feathers. The shifter screeched then landed in the cover of the rain forest.

"Tyr's dead or well on his way," Ethan told her. He was impressed to discover yet another facet to Lucia. One he'd never seen before.

She stood fierce and hard as she engaged her opponents, with sharp eyes trained on the trees and legs in a battle stance. He'd thought her sexy at first glance, pretty and natural without her makeup, enchanting as she teased him.

Now all of those personalities were wrapped up into one package. Inside the brave fighter who stood by his side.

In a word, Lucia was marvelous.

"Good kill," she said, referring to Tyr. "But we need to figure a way out of this. Now that we're two against two, we can take them on together." She studied the crimson stain of his blade. "Maybe you can score another for team coven."

Ethan nodded, but a sense of unease crawled down his spine. He'd never hurt a woman before, evil or not. He wasn't sure how he'd feel about killing one, so he said, "I'll take the shifter."

As if he'd been heard, a wet, tearing sound came from behind the leaves. He had a bad feeling he knew what that meant.

When the sleek, black panther strolled out of the forest, Ethan quirked a brow. What do you know? The shifter had shifted. Again.

The muscles that flexed in the cat's shoulders were nothing short of awesome. Huge, velvet paws thumped in the mud while Ross bared his thick, sharp fangs. He was huge, larger in real life than Ethan could have pictured. And more menacing.

The eerie color of the cat's eyes reminded him he fought something far more sinister than an animal. A supernatural monster was literally licking his chops and moving in for the kill.

The panther's pupils were vertical slits, but they were encased by an eerie and unnatural blue. Like the clearest of swimming pool water, they zeroed in on Ethan, never leaving his face.

Ross rumbled deep in his chest. If Ethan didn't know any better, he would say the hulking predator was mocking him, laughing at the machete in his hand. The one that now seemed so small.

With a leer that spoke of confidence and eager blood thirst, Carson crept from her hiding place as well. "You didn't think we'd make the same mistakes, did you, bitch?"

Her eyes were filled with hate as she stalked Lucia. "I rushed your kind once before. I underestimated the punch behind those pretty little faces." She snapped her teeth like a gator. "I won't make that mistake again."

"The witch is mine, Carson."

Ethan whirled to find the male voice and faltered a step. He didn't believe what he saw.

"Lucia. Time to revise the strategy," Ethan said, bracing himself as his brain struggled to make sense of the impossible.

The man he'd killed with own hands had risen. Tyr was back in the fight.

18

Tyr's torso was still smeared with blood from his own grasping hands, but the deep wound from the machete looked like it was healing. In fact, it was almost closed up completely.

As the rain washed away more grime and blood, Ethan could see the skin stitching back together. "What the hell?"

Lucia rammed her back against his again. "He's been drinking from Ronja. Damn it. He's stronger. Immortal. And I have no idea how long the effects last."

"I hope you've got some ideas, because I'm all out." Ethan held the machete out in front of him, both hands aching from the tight grip. "I messed up. I shouldn't have wasted time on Tyr. I'm sorry."

Ethan could tell Lucia was shaking her head as she said, "No. I wasn't sure, either."

She paused, and as Ethan slowed his breathing and readied himself for the fight, all he felt was the heavy rain hitting his clothes. Stinging his skin.

All he could smell was blood mixed with the wet, rich soil. And he envisioned the many ways he and the woman behind him might die.

None of them were pleasant.

"Ethan, I'm sorry we got you into this." Lucia's voice hitched.

Now it was his turn to shake his head. "My choice, all of it. And Lucia," he said, "I want you to know, in spite of everything, I'm glad to have you at my back."

Ethan steadied himself then and glared, eyeing the dark-skinned Tyr as he approached.

Lucia's throaty chuckle was a welcome sound. "And you, demon hunter. You're a lot more than book smart. I'll give you that. Too bad I never got a chance to...."

She cleared her throat. "But enough with this talk. I'm not done yet. *Jamás.* Never." She spoke in a way that told him she was wearing her wicked smile. "How about you?"

The cocky smile he felt forming was his own version of a red flag, And he'd wave it in his enemy's face until he took the final fall. "Not a chance, witch. But I will be a gentleman and let you have first strike."

Lucia laughed into the rain. "I appreciate it. Just be sure to duck."

As if incensed by their banter, the panther roared his displeasure and crouched to the ground. Muscles bunched and thrummed as Ross prepared to leap.

But Tyr was swifter on the draw and had already nocked an arrow. He aimed for his target.

"Lucia, at your six!" Ethan yelled, throwing out the warning before he ducked and pivoted, clearing the way for her lethal blue light.

He let her have a shot at Tyr, who was too far away for Ethan to take. And there was no way he was letting go of his machete again. Not until they were safe, or the Amara were all dead.

Or at least down long enough for Lucia and him to make a break for it.

Holding onto the weapon turned out to be a good thing, since he lifted his head to find the huge, black cat flying through the air, jaws wide and claws outstretched. Ethan lunged forward and to the side, swiping at the cat's massive chest. His arm and hand reverberated when the strike landed, but he held onto the machete as he fell.

The panther bellowed, telling Ethan he'd struck true. The cat landed beyond Ethan and Lucia, where it stumbled and whirled to fend off another blow. But Ross didn't seem inclined to take another pass at either of them.

Carson had also come at them at a clip, but from the ground all Ethan could do was roll and trip her up with his feet. She crashed and skidded into the mud but kept going, clambering back to her feet.

Her murderous eyes were pinned on Lucia.

With one hand still streaming magic at Tyr, Lucia flung out her other arm and threw another ray toward Carson. Blue lit up the blonde woman dead center of her chest, but she wasn't as strong as Tyr and flew through the air with a scream.

Ethan was up again, ready to defend. But Carson stayed where she was, crumpled in a pile and being soaked by the storm. Ross's blue, panther eyes took in his fallen comrade as if he was debating his next move.

The panther stalked the edge of the clearing but kept his distance, content to roar his fury at Ethan. He must have been badly injured from Ethan's blow.

In a diving roll, Tyr changed positions to escape Lucia's light. Wrath filled his black stare when he stood and yelled at her. "I will have the dagger!" He strode toward her, unafraid, despite the beating he'd already sustained. "And in Ronja's name, I will have your life!"

This time he kept the arrow locked in his fist, raised high above his head as if he'd drive the weapon into Lucia with his bare hands.

Seeing the man's intent, Ethan felt the first trickles of terror. Not fear for himself but for Lucia. Clearly Tyr would sacrifice his own life if it meant taking her down with him. His glare burned with vengeance.

"Lucia," Ethan barked at her, "hit him again."

When she didn't respond with a strike, Ethan moved to her and put a hand on her shoulder. "Damn it, he wants to kill you. Hit him again, or I will."

He didn't understand the stillness that had come over her. Or the slight lift of her lips, a sure sign she was smiling inside. She turned her head to him and said gently, "I feel something coming."

When he would have spoken she put a finger to his lips. "Listen. Don't you hear?"

Fighting the panic as Tyr came closer and Ross circled to their back side, Ethan did his best to close out the two still after their blood. He opened up the tainted gift inside him and listened as she instructed.

He heard the sinister shrieks she was talking about, far away. Distant. But they were moving in fast.

And as they grew closer, the sounds began to change. The angry screeches grew louder, more determined. When the owners of the savage voices were close, and Ethan was sure they'd been found, the evil women began to laugh.

"The guardians are coming," he said, glancing from Tyr to Ross then casting a wary eye to the sky. He shot a questioning look at Lucia. "Why the hell would that make you happy?"

Now her smile was fully formed. And vengeful. "Because," she said, indicating Tyr as he too looked up, "we aren't the only ones after the dagger."

Giving him a roguish wink, Lucia held her palms to the sky. "Don't worry. I have a plan." With her face lifted to the rain, she started to chant, speaking what sounded like Latin and... apparently any other language she felt like using.

Then she switched to English, to reinforce the spell she was casting. "From flesh and spirit we seek to hide, I make a shield so none can see. Strike blind the ones who mean us harm, as I will, so shall it be."

When the air around them heated, a rush of static filled Ethan's ears. Then was gone.

The next thing he heard was a cry of rage as Tyr shook his fists. "Where are you, witch?" But as soon as the words spewed from his twisted lips, he threw a sharp look over their now invisible heads and shouted at whatever he saw above.

"We should go now," Lucia said, grabbing his hand and heading for their discarded backpacks. The spell must have included anything they had on their person, because none of the Amara noticed the action.

Then again, Tyr and the panther Ross were too busy fending off the vengeful Qara Mikuna as the spirits dipped and dived, raking claws through skin or clothing. The demon-cursed harem was toying with the Amara thugs.

Ethan couldn't suppress his grin. The flying cannibals were playing with their food.

Tyr had made a mistake declaring his intent to find the dagger. They were much too close to Kuelap and the hidden blade for such boasting. The warrior had brought the guardians down on them all.

Now Ethan and Lucia had to get away, get lost again. Before her charm wore off and the harem came for them, too.

"Don't worry about making noise," Lucia said, urging him on as he hacked at anything standing in their way. "The rain will cover us, so we should take advantage and get as far away as we can. Then we would do better to veer slightly off course and find a place to hide."

"Okay." Ethan saved his breath, needing every bit of energy he had left to slash his way through the wet and clingy rain forest. They'd taken a turn toward thick underbrush again, and his arm was burning from overuse.

When they broke free enough to run, he slid the steel blade back into its sheath and took Lucia's hand. They ran together, leaping fallen logs or protruding roots until their breath scraped out of their lungs and their sides ached.

They burst from the brush to discover huge, moss-covered stones with a small stream running through them. Ethan pointed to the other side and a particularly large rock. "Behind that. The bushes are thick."

"Fine," Lucia bent and rested with her hands on her knees. "I can't go any farther anyway."

Traipsing across the small creek, they curved around the back side of the boulder. The stone angled up and to one side where it touched another. A small crevice formed beneath, so Ethan shined his light into the darkness to check inside.

"Only dead leaves, but the place is a little wet," he said.

"I don't care." Lucia was panting. "I just want to catch my breath for a few minutes and see if I can detect the Amara. With any luck they're still tangling with the flesh-eaters."

A shout sounded nearby, and they both whipped their heads up to listen. Lucia whispered, "I couldn't tell if that was an angry scream or one of pain."

"Me, either, but it wasn't the guardians." Ethan put his hand on her lower back. "Get inside."

He followed her in to discover the space was tighter than he'd thought. They tried lying side by side, but Ethan's half of the space angled sharply. Not enough room for his shoulder. After some twisting and maneuvering, he found himself on top of Lucia. "I'll crush you."

"No. I'm okay." Her voice sounded odd. "Just...try not to move."

Propping himself up on his elbows to alleviate his weight, Ethan found a comfortable position. The rain continued to pound the earth, despite the forest's attempt to catch every drop. Steady and soothing, the storm's patter helped him relax, and soon his respirations slowed.

Lucia's breathing calmed as well. She took deep, slow draws

that Ethan could feel moving against his chest. Her presence lulled him into a sense of security. Of comfort.

As his eyes adjusted to the low light, he could see the spread of her rich, brown hair, long wavy strands made darker still by moisture. Her lashes held droplets as well and were especially lush against her cheeks.

Lucia's lips were parted a bit, and though he couldn't see their color he knew from memory that they were a deep blush, caught somewhere between pink and red. Like the two sides of Lucia. One a fragile bud, and the other a brave, flourishing bloom.

Maybe it was the tremble of her lips as the wet chill set in, or the way her dampened clothes molded to her curves. But Ethan was suddenly very aware of the woman lying beneath him. His body responded to every inch of her heated flesh as it pressed against his own.

He'd fought to ignore the way she made him feel, how she called to him. Pushing her from his thoughts time and again, he'd wanted so badly to despise her, or at least find her irritating.

But with her quick wit and athletic body, her deep stores of knowledge and experience, and chocolate eyes that could shift from defiant to wounded in the space of a heartbeat, Ethan saw something in Lucia he simply couldn't deny.

When had his defenses started to crumble? When had he begun to view her as something other than a problem? Because that's what she was, only now even more so.

Lucia was a huge problem.

But after watching her come alive with the rush of battle, never afraid, never wavering, Ethan couldn't lie to himself anymore. Despite the risks, she'd slipped past his guard, and somewhere along the way, he'd started to—damn it all—he'd started to *like* her.

Images had started creeping in, the kind of fantasies he

could never allow. Yet he'd played a starring role. With Lucia.

He could picture himself waking up to her impish grin every morning. What a way to start the day. Or taking her out to dinner, a movie. Then she could wear one of her flashy outfits, and only he would know the warrior that lay beneath the glitz and glamour.

Only he would know what she felt like ...

Get yourself under control. He berated himself as he looked at her and felt her voluptuous curves beneath him. His lust for her was a threat to them both.

But his body wasn't listening. The close, cramped quarters, the veil of shadow, the thrumming rain, and God...Lucia's clean, natural scent.

He had to separate emotions from physical need. He'd done it before.

As Ethan's hand found its way to her tiny waist, he gave in and let himself picture her naked. He wondered what secrets he would discover with no barriers between them. No defensiveness or fear holding them back as he touched her.

Would she whisper to him in Spanish when he took her? When she cried out in the dark?

Enjoying his illusion of what they could make together, he forced the familiar dread aside. Foreboding followed him everywhere, like a painful shadow, but just this once he would tell himself it was okay. He could have just a moment. Nothing more.

Focusing on Lucia's face instead of the dire warnings screaming subconsciously, Ethan let his eyes fall again to her luscious mouth. He watched her bottom lip quiver sweetly. He heard her sigh.

It was all he could take.

He lifted her chin with his hand and looked deep into those pools of brown. "Damn you," he said, before lowering his head, hovering so close that they breathed together. Hot, wet breaths.

Then he tested her lips with his, caressing in a way that begged for entry yet gave him one last chance to pull back.

But he didn't.

Taking her with a kiss meant to ravage, to punish as much as taste, Ethan took what she'd offered so many times. He was half mad with desire, half mad with resentment.

He'd expected her to meet him with the daring, spitfire attitude she embodied, to rise up and meet his challenge. Instead she whimpered softly.

The sound made him grow even harder, want her even more, but then her hands were between them, pressing against his chest.

Ethan cursed himself for being so forceful. He reined in the kiss, easing off but maintaining his hold on her. His tongue slid against hers teasingly, testing her response.

Suddenly Lucia's hands came up to grip his hair, holding him in place as she finally kissed him back. With vigor. With the boldness he knew she owned.

One of her long legs snaked around his, so she could lift her hips and push against him. The exquisite pressure made Ethan groan into her mouth, but still he couldn't stop. Her tongue was so slick and sweet, with a hint of the strawberry she'd painted on her lips earlier in the day.

Sweet. Natural. Daring.

The thrill of her punched right through him, and the ever-present voice inside his head withered away beneath the pure taste and feel of Lucia. He'd known from the start she was a burning candle to his lost and wayward soul. She offered him honesty and solace.

But all he could bring her was deceit.

And death.

The nightmare from before came upon him then, and all he could see was Lucia's scared eyes, their innocent brown coated with the crimson light of encroaching evil.

Ethan knew what would come next, and he wouldn't let it happen. Not again.

Not to her.

He ripped his mouth from hers and jerked his head, rapping his crown against the stone above them. A warm trickle told him he'd drawn blood, but as he studied Lucia's confused expression and swollen lips, all he could think was, *Better mine than hers.*

19

Lucia's lips felt too cool now that Ethan had taken his warm mouth away.

He'd shocked her all the way to the tips of her boots when he'd kissed her so forcefully. Here in their miniature cave, with demon-ish things flying around, the Amara on their heels, and a thunderstorm beating the rain forest into submission. Here he'd finally put that wonderfully full yet firm mouth against hers.

And oh, he'd been even better than she'd imagined.

The male, woodsy smell of him had invaded her senses when he'd first rolled on top of her. Then when she'd felt all those thick, rigid muscles against every inch of her body, she'd actually gotten light-headed. It had been too long since she'd felt the hot, corded tension of a male form.

Now, realizing what she'd been missing was harder than never tasting him at all.

Ethan still stared down at her. Transfixed.

"What's wrong?" she asked, realizing he'd shifted moods again and was far back in keep-your-distance territory.

He held himself above her, so quiet and still, as if afraid to move. "I shouldn't have done that," he said, his voice raspy with an emotion she couldn't name.

Lucia still tingled from where his weight had held her down. Where he'd pressed against her core.

When he started backing out of the hole, he scraped his leg down the inside of her thigh, and she hissed in a breath. Of pleasure.

"Sorry," Ethan muttered, probably thinking he'd hurt her. "We can find a better place to take cover."

You mean a place where you won't be forced to deal with me. Lucia was confused by what had just happened. Both the kiss and his quick withdrawal.

At first she'd been shocked when his lips assaulted hers. Then aroused. And just as she'd let herself start to enjoy his fevered touch, Ethan had jerked away as if burned.

Lucia huffed to herself and ground her teeth, wanting nothing more than to stay in the cramped, wet space and feel Ethan's hands on her one more time.

But at least she'd been given something. A very valuable and encouraging piece of information.

Ethan wanted her. And judging by his abrupt loss of control, he wanted her pretty badly. *Good. Serves him right.*

When he was finally all the way out of the enclosure, Lucia was able to sit up and maneuver more easily. She eased from beneath the stones to find him kneeling on the ground. His expression was as grim as the sky above, a combination of torment and wrath. He was suffering.

Lucia felt a jab between her ribs. A shot through the heart.

Here was the down side to caring about another person. When they hurt, you hurt.

Perhaps his previous refusal had actually kept her safe. Ignorant. Maybe she'd been better off not feeling this very real connection to him.

Her flirting had been all fun and games before. An adventure with a great-looking guy, and a warm and fuzzy idea about true love.

Right up until he'd kissed her.

Now her world had been rocked, shaken from the foundation and turned on its side. With his fierce then gentle kiss, he had all but reached inside to wrap his strong hand around her vulnerable heart.

The idea of Ethan, the fantasy of him had suddenly become reality. When his big, solid body had her pinned to the earth. When he'd studied her with his espresso-dark eyes. She'd felt something spark to life.

Lucia no longer wanted a pre-determined soul mate just because he would be a sure thing. Because he would be destined to love her. To never leave her. Guarantees were worthless now if they didn't come from the right place. From him.

Don't get a girl wrong, she still wanted Ethan Drake. Hard-assed occult specialist and man of many secrets, with a body that was swoon-worthy.

This was who she wanted to love.

But in return she wanted him to love *her*. Despite her flaws or insecurities. She wanted real, honest love, given freely from him to her.

Not shrink-wrapped and special-delivered from that mysterious force called fate.

She stared right back into those depthless eyes, so deep and rich she feared they saw straight into her. To who she really was, beneath the flirtatious smiles and deflecting laughter.

Lucia's heart jolted like a rabbit, because now she knew him, too. She'd grown to care about more than an imaginary hero. The ideal soul mate she'd crafted in her mind.

Ethan was real, and her fictional idea of the perfect man simply couldn't compare.

She'd been hacking away at his steel exterior, and bit by bit she was seeing what lay inside. Pure, shining, treasure. A prize to be sought above all things. He was a good man, strong, intelligent, and loyal.

"Ethan," her voice shook with awareness of what had passed between them.

Hardening his face, he stood and stepped away, putting distance between them and using it to regain composure. He threw his head back and spread his arms, allowing the rain to wash his sculpted face.

And, Lucia imagined, the taste of her from his lips.

When he came back to her, his black brows were drawn together and his jaw was tense. "I changed my mind. We won't stop but keep pushing on. The risk of being found again is too great."

With trust and disappointment sparring like tiny soldiers in her mind, Lucia took his hand and let him pull her to her feet.

He acted like one kiss was going to summon an apocalypse. This self-punishment he put himself through had to be about more than crossing professional boundaries or whatever code of honor he might be trying to sell himself.

Lucia slid her gaze to his backpack and the book she knew was shoved inside. Everything went back to the dagger. His past and possibly his reason for insisting on coming with her to Kuelap.

His *real* reason.

Yeah, Lucia told herself as she fell quietly into step beside him. She still considered him a good man, but they had some work to do on the honesty thing.

He was still holding back.

~~~

"Ethan it has to be early morning. We have to sleep sometime." Lucia's feet were almost dragging. She was exhausted, hungry, and soaked through. The rain had lessened but had continued to drizzle on them for hours.

She could feel the blisters forming on her heels, the bottoms of her big toes. "Besides, you're the one always talking about the importance of taking good care of your body. Eating right. Exercising. Getting enough sleep. Emphasis on the last," she said, driving the point home with a wide-mouthed yawn.

"I'll be good for another couple of hours." He said, shifting his eyes to study her before flattening his mouth into a thin line. "You should be safe, too."

"Safe?" she echoed the word. "Not if I twist an ankle in the moonless night out here. I'm a witch but not a healer, and if I were, I wouldn't waste any of my power on an injury that could have been avoided by simple common sense."

After her diatribe, Lucia stopped as if convinced by her own argument. "I'm pitching the tent."

Ethan heaved an annoyed sigh. "Here? Now?"

"It's not ideal," she said, wrenching off her pack and grunting when her shoulders chafed. "We should have changed out of our wet clothes, too, but you insisted we keep moving. We aren't going to make Kuelap Fortress by tomorrow anyway. We've lost too much time meandering all over the place."

She rubbed her sore skin through her still-damp shirt and hissed from the tenderness. "I'm no wimp, but it's reckless to purposely abrade your own flesh in this environment. Open wounds, even small ones, can get infected."

Ethan took off his pack and threw it against a nearby tree. "This is impossible!"

Holding out both hands and feeling her mouth opening and closing like a fish, Lucia wondered, *What is going on in that head of his?* His outburst was about more than a rainy night hike.

Something much worse, much more deeply rooted, was bothering him.

Then she finally found her voice. And her indignation. "What is wrong with you? I've told you the Amara aren't close. They aren't even a blip on my radar! They, unlike us, probably did the smart thing and headed straight for Chachapoyas."

She crossed her arms. "Carson is probably nursing her wounds in a hot bath right now." She whirled and started pacing in a circle. "When did I lose control? Of myself? Of this expedition?"

She shook a finger at Ethan who was ignoring her and staring off into the jungle with hands on hips. "And I'm taking control back. Starting right now!"

Raking her hands through her hair and feeling the disheveled mess only fueled her temper. "Ugh. I feel disgusting, and for no good reason."

Ethan still faced away from her but said, "Then strip and go take yourself another magic shower. We can rest for a few hours."

Lucia fumed. "That's what I said I would do. Stop making it sound like you're giving me permission." She knew she was being petulant, but the last twelve hours had finally started taking a toll. A battle, the guardians, running through the rain forest while constantly looking over her shoulder.

The brief taste of heaven before being shoved aside. Again.

And having to do all of that while wondering why Ethan was back to being so foul-tempered. He'd gone right back to the first leg of this trip from hell, pretending he couldn't stand her. And now that she knew he was lying, vexation almost strangled her from the inside out.

She'd been so close.

Putting a finger to her lips, she remembered how he'd put his hands on her in their temporary hideout. How he'd used his mouth. He'd dangled a fat, juicy apple in front of her then snatched it back before hurrying away to glare at her.

He acted like she had coerced him or something.

Curling her fingers so hard her short nails bit into her palms, she said, "Maybe I will get naked." She could feel herself growing more and more spiteful, but good goddess, she was tired. And in pain. And *frustrated*.

On many levels.

It was only fair that he feel the same dissatisfaction.

Channeling her inner temptress, Lucia spoke in a husky voice. "*Sí*, Ethan. I want to get completely naked. We're all by ourselves. Out here in the lush. Uninhibited. Jungle." Now she took slow, undulating steps toward him, though his back was still to her and he couldn't appreciate her seductive act.

"Mmm. I can just imagine how good it will feel to be all warm. And soapy." She ran a finger over his shoulder, testing the barely-leashed hostility in his muscles. He thrummed beneath her touch, and now she knew his strain was from desire as much as annoyance.

She leaned close to his ear to whisper, "And wet."

He flicked her hand away and turned on her. "Stop it. Your behavior is unbecoming." He moved in to hold his face just above hers. For a moment she thought she might get another of his fiery kisses.

"Oh, I disagree," a man's voice said, driving a verbal wedge between them. Ethan shoved Lucia behind him to face the group of men who'd crept up on them as they'd argued. "I'm enjoying her behavior," one of them said. Then he gestured to Lucia. "And those promises of getting naked."

The man was smiling, but his expression was hard. "What are you doing here?" he asked, the ominous look in his eyes belying the friendly question.

The other men, five of them in addition to the one who spoke, emerged more fully from the darkness. One of them had a lantern, the yellow light shadowing their features so they appeared even more sinister.

Lucia had thought Ethan's new, black machete looked threatening. But the ones these men held, with nicks and stains from use, were positively unnerving. She wondered if the long blades had sliced through more than vegetation.

"We don't mean any harm," Lucia said, edging out from behind Ethan. "We are traveling to Chachapoyas. Our plane went down northeast of here."

"There are cities closer than Chachapoyas." He took a step forward then spoke to his companions in a language Lucia didn't understand but recognized as Quechuan. When the men came over to pick up their backpacks and rummage through them, she realized the leader's order had been to search their belongings.

"We aren't here to take anything from you," Ethan said, grasping the danger they were in just as Lucia did. "We aren't prospecting, and we have no interest in oil or disturbing the forest."

One of the men spoke excitedly, and Lucia's lungs shrunk in on themselves when she saw him shaking Ethan's book. He took it to the leader and flipped through the pages, pointing and lifting cagey eyes to Ethan and Lucia.

"Why do you have this?" the leader asked. His voice boomed now, face darkened with rage and suspicion. "What do you want with the Earthshaker's knife?"

Ethan walked forward to meet the man on equal ground, halfway between his group and where Lucia stood. "Because the dagger is needed again."

The man's mouth formed an O shape as he looked furtively between Ethan and Lucia. She could imagine what he was thinking. A woman talking about getting naked in the jungle was here to help conquer evil?

She'd have a hard time buying that one herself.

The leader went back to speak in hushed tones to his friends. Not that she and Ethan would understand what they said anyway. She lifted a brow and scrutinized her fellow traveler. Maybe Ethan did speak Quechuan.

At this point, she had no idea how many secrets the demon hunter might be keeping.

"You will come with us," the man said as two of the others picked up the backpacks again. The one with Ethan's book put it back inside the pocket he'd taken it from. He did so carefully. Almost reverently.

Lucia was caught between hopefulness and dread. What was going on here?

"Where are you taking us?" Ethan asked, and Lucia could see he was wound tight, ready to spring himself on all six of the strangers if the answer was one he didn't like.

The man waved his hand impatiently. "You must come to our village." His eyes changed, as did his smile, filling with anticipation and...welcome? "We have food and fires. Shelter. You can eat and get out of those wet clothes."

He furrowed his brow and chastised Ethan. "You should take better care of your woman. You will need your strength to recover what the Earthshaker left so well protected."

"You know the legend?" Lucia asked, already dreaming of real food. Ethan could shove those protein bars.

"*Ari*. Yes." He nodded and offered his arm to Lucia. She smiled sweetly and took it, beaming at Ethan to point out how a gentleman was supposed to treat a lady.

Her new escort explained as they walked. "For many generations we have known another evil would rise, and it was predicted strangers would come one day, seeking the knife."

He twirled his fingers in the air. "There have been signs recently, and now we have found the two of you." He smiled broadly. "I have the great honor of escorting the promised ones to our village. We will prepare you for the rest of your journey."

"I'm sorry," Lucia said, putting two fingers to her temple. Everything was happening so quickly, and even after all she'd learned of her own destiny and prophecy, it was difficult to take in what he was telling her. "Are you saying Ethan and I are the promised ones?"

She shook her head, frantically trying to grasp his meaning.

"But how do you know we're the ones? What makes you so sure?"

The man laughed. "We have long been told that two people would be found in the forest. Saviors who had lost their way. Now," he gestured with a flowing hand, "it is our job to set you on the right path again."

He continued. "There is no mistake, my lady. Everyone knows what to look for." He tilted his head to Ethan then to her. "An angry man and a bold woman. So you see?"

Lucia swallowed a frantic laugh, imagining what she and Ethan must have looked like to the group of men when they'd stumbled upon their argument. With a wry half-smile on her lips, she remembered how she'd taunted Ethan about her planned nudity.

Her actions might be considered bold.

Then she glanced over to see that Ethan was still scowling. Angrily.

"No," she admitted on a sigh, her boots squishing with every step she took. "No mistake at all."

20

With a trembling hand, Anna slid the brass key into the door's heavy lock. The patina of both gave away their age, a mix of green and brown that was both nostalgic and accusatory. Mr. Attinger would clean them both properly, but Anna wished she'd never let them go so long without attention.

She and Quinn had been young when their parents had died, and an unspoken agreement had existed between the orphaned siblings and their housekeepers. The tower room would not be spoken of, so the tragedy of their parents' passing could be forgotten, along with the place that housed such pain and loss.

And so the room had been forgotten. Overlooked and deserted. Until today.

She gave a soft push on the arched door, surprised by how quietly the old wood swung open. The unmistakable scent of dust hit her first, but beneath she detected traces of other things. Verbena, for protection and peace, one of her mother's favorites. And the deep, rich smell of Irish moss. For luck.

Morning sunshine did its best to light the room, but struggled to push past filthy windows. The stone floor and walls had been cleaned years before, and all burned items removed, but the remainder of their parents' tools and books had simply been shoved into boxes or empty shelves.

The look of the place reflected its treatment. Abandoned, and somehow forlorn, buried by a layer of gray dust.

Anna breathed deep and rolled up her sleeves. She and Quinn would reclaim this room and make it shine again, in the literal sense through housekeeping. And in the mystical sense. With magic.

They would bring the dirty, neglected tower room back to life. For their own use as a workspace, to meet the very real needs of the coven and help defeat the demons, and last but hardly least, for her parents.

She went to the window, though she could barely make out the sprawling gardens through the murky glass. From below she'd often studied the stonework of the tower, standing tall and isolated, bare and lonely. Pink, teacup roses had once encircled the grand column, but the vines had fallen away over time.

Anna firmed her lips and nodded. That would be rectified as well.

The first thing to do was organize any usable items, so she looked over the books, some stacked and others leaning at a slant. Those she could recover with tender care, and the stone mortar and pestle would work just fine, as would the newer glass version sitting beside them.

Quinn had either purchased or ordered any equipment they would need for the metallurgy, but magic would help them save time and cut corners. Fire wouldn't be the only way they could melt the chosen minerals. If needed, she and her brother would call on their gifts.

No, working with metals wouldn't pose much of a problem. The danger would come after they identified the demon clan wreaking havoc in Savannah. Then she and her sisters would force their magic into the specialized weapons, creating a supernatural alloy that would be highly combustible.

And potentially deadly if not handled correctly.

Anna felt a pinch at the base of her skull. No amount of herbs or oils would protect them if they didn't get the combination right. Her parents had made a crucial mistake, and had paid with their lives.

Shaking off the creeping dread, Anna picked up a box to search through its belongings. Inside she discovered natural elements, dried herbs, crystals, and rocks, each in individual containers and labeled. Some of this would be salvageable.

At the bottom she found branches, just the right size for making wands. That had been her father's hobby, so she was sure the material was Rowan, or witchwood. Their father had gotten a kick out of using the very thing that was supposed to dispel witches.

Anna grinned, thinking of her father's keen sense of humor and his booming laugh. It was nice to remember.

She heard footsteps on the stone staircase, recognizing the heavy tread as her brother's. "We've avoided this too long, I'm afraid," she said when Quinn came in behind her with supplies. "We have quite the job ahead of us."

He set cleaning supplies on the table and nodded. "Looks like." He stood and scrutinized the mess of a room. "I don't think we should ask Mrs. Attinger to help, though."

Anna's lips curved in a sad smile. "No. You're right." She lifted the box with her father's branches and other items. "This is for us."

Falling into a mostly silent but well-orchestrated form of teamwork, Anna and Quinn sifted, sorted, and organized the room's contents, saving what they could and tossing the rest. When the worst of the trash had been cleared, they started with the really dirty business.

Over a decade of grime covered the floor, shelves, table, and even the walls. They paused long enough to eat the sandwiches Mrs. Attinger brought up, and once again assured her they could handle the clean-up on their own.

All in all, the task only took them a few hours, and after much needed showers, they returned to the newly-ordered tower room. Ready to craft their design.

Quinn had arrived a while before Anna, and had used the time to set up the metallurgy tools. With his bark brown hair still damp, he fixed his blue eyes on her and spoke excitedly. "I've got a sample of each of the metals Ethan listed. We had all of them in stock but one."

Anna smirked. "Let me guess. Meteorite iron?"

"Yeah. Who would have thought that'd be hard to come by?" His tone dripped sarcasm. "And don't ask who I had to call to get it."

She held up her hands. "I won't."

"So," Quinn said, hands braced on the aged oak table. The wood was thick and sturdy. "Should we do it the old-fashioned way?" He gave a lop-sided grin. "Or the St. Germaine way?"

"Well. Time *is* of the essence."

He clapped his hands once. "I was hoping you'd say that. Fire is so damn hot."

"It tends to be."

After preparing what they would need to melt the metals, Quinn lined up five molds. One for each of the demon-sensing minerals. Everyone had discussed possibilities, and a simple yet reliable piece of jewelry had been decided on. Small, easily portable, and inconspicuous.

"I think this is genius," Quinn said, eager to take the first step toward ridding Savannah of its bug problem.

Coming around the table to stand next to her brother, Anna put a hand on his shoulder. "It almost seems too easy."

"But this is only the first part." Pointing out the five bowls set to one side, he told her what each of them was. "Nickel. Bronze. Copper. Silver." He thumped the last. "And the elusive meteorite iron."

"All malleable and appropriate for jewelry," she raised

steadfast eyes to her brother, "or for blades."

Quinn nodded solemnly. "We'll get to that. Soon enough." He picked up one of the bowls. "First, let's make the rings."

21

The clouds have gone. Lucia's first thought was of clear skies, since she woke to a small room filled with pale, glowing moonlight. She turned her head to survey her surroundings and recognized the small wooden house where she and Ethan were to spend the rest of the night.

An angry grunt came from the far side of the room, so she sat upright to get a better look. Ethan was still sleeping, but restlessly. Caught in another of his nightmares.

"Damn you," he uttered, and for a second she thought he was talking to her. *Now what have I done?*

But when she slipped from under her blanket to tread softly over the bare, wooden floor, she saw his eyes were shut and his jaw was clenched. "Stay away," he hissed, and now she was sure he spoke inside the dream.

"Shhh." She gently touched his face before sitting beside him on the small bed. Pushing his black hair out of his face she continued to caress him, concerned over the strain she could feel in his neck and shoulders. He'd removed his shirt to sleep bare-chested, and she had to clamp her hand into a fist to keep from touching him there.

He was utterly gorgeous, with his long, muscular torso and chiseled abs. Though she wouldn't put her hands on him the way she longed to, she could take advantage of the moment to appreciate the amazing man she'd been partnered with.

His midnight hair only enhanced the sculpted cheek bones and full, firm lips. She remembered the way he'd smiled when Shauni and Michael had been rescued. How the cold steel had melted away, revealing a happy affectionate person beneath.

Yet Ethan governed his emotions with a strict hand. Never allowing much to seep through, especially when Lucia was around. *So many secrets.*

He jerked abruptly and cursed, prompting Lucia to begin her ministrations again. "It's okay, Ethan," she said close to his ear, stroking his hair. "You're safe. Shhh." She kissed his forehead but only in tenderness and concern.

"Go back to hell, you Seraphim bastard." His jaw bit down brutally.

Seraphim? Lucia searched her brain for what she knew of the word. Weren't they some sort of monstrous deities? No, not gods, but angels. Fallen angels.

She continued to sooth him until he relaxed. Why would Ethan have nightmares about fallen angels?

There were too many evasions or denials on Ethan's part. Chunks of his past he not only refused to talk about but staunchly ignored. As if he could will certain facts to simply go away or even cease to exist. But no one could erase the past, no matter how painful it might be.

Pieces started clicking together then, and she didn't like the image they formed.

Ethan's study of demons and black rituals. His reaction to any mention of his sister. And how adamantly he'd insisted on coming with her to Kuelap.

He told her he wanted something that would be found with the dagger but for what reason? And why did he need this mysterious item?

He was specifically keeping Lucia uninformed, but his

secrecy made no sense. She could help him if he would only let her.

But that had been their problem all along, hadn't it? Ethan and his inability to share. To trust.

Well, she had a huge part of the puzzle now, and he would damn well tell her the rest of his story. And if she had to find this item herself and hold it for ransom to gain answers, that's exactly what she would do.

His sister, was she the Jessica he'd dreamed about? Did she have something to do with what awaited them at the ruins, or were his nightmares unrelated? His grueling, torturous nightmares.

And if all of that wasn't enough, now he was raving about Seraphims.

She gazed again at his handsome face as he relaxed and eased into a calm sleep. *Ethan Drake. Why so many secrets?*

A yawn overtook Lucia and her eyes fogged from the need for sleep. She was so tired. Why was she this tired? And her head was beginning to throb as well.

Blasted wet clothes and too many hours trekking.

With Ethan rolled on his side and apparently quieted, she made her way back to her own bed and crawled under the covers. Almost immediately, a dark curtain covered her. The sleep sprites were casting their nets, and she was too exhausted to struggle.

Tomorrow, she told herself as she floated away. She would confront Ethan tomorrow.

~~~

The next thing Lucia knew, light was streaming in through the square, glass window of the house. From the warmth of the air and heavy gold of the sunbeams, she guessed the day was at least half gone.

Stretching and feeling kinks release in her body, she could tell she'd been in one position for too long. Taking a deep breath she felt a tickle of guilt. She wasn't a girl who was ashamed to take advantage of Saturday morning, but even she never slept *this* late.

Sounds of quick breaths being pushed out and sucked in drew her attention to the floor. If she thought last night's sleeping version of Ethan had been alluring, the sight that greeted her now almost made her fall out of bed.

He was doing sit-ups, and judging by the quiver of his rock hard stomach, he'd been at it for some time. After a great heave he let himself fall back on the floor, resting on the wooden slats to catch his breath. He didn't look her way once.

Finally he rolled onto his stomach, and Lucia's heart leapt with glee. The man was about to do push-ups. Shirtless but wearing khaki cargo pants, he held his body in textbook position for the upper body exercise.

Lucia propped her head on her bent elbow and enjoyed the demonstration of fierce male fortitude. Every tight inch of it. His back muscles flexed and lengthened as he moved up and down. Thick arms bulged from the effort.

His black hair had grown damp at his temples, and the sight was somehow intoxicating.

Soon a sheen of perspiration formed at the nape of his neck as well as the lovely dip at the base of his spine. When he finally settled to the floor again to rest, Lucia could only stare at him and grin.

A whirling tingle was spreading up from her belly and down to her toes, and she thanked her lucky stars she'd woken in time to see this.

But with one maddening thought, her pleasure evaporated.

Why put so much work into that remarkable body if he was never going to put it to use? Didn't he know there were more important things than health?

Lucia dug her nails into the mattress and found herself wishing for some catnip. She would make her own body rub out of the herb, perfume and powder, too. If the stuff really did help attract one's lover, she wouldn't be averse to rolling in a pile.

She sighed as she imagined what she could do with a man like Ethan. Friskiness, caterwauling, and hanging from the ceiling. Play time wasn't just for cats.

Ethan must have heard her, because he scanned up the bed to meet her gaze. He started to glare at her, of course, but then he sat up and scrutinized her with worry in his coffee-brown eyes. "You look awful," he said, and totally made her day.

She flopped onto her back. "Gee, thanks."

"No, I mean it. Maybe you should get some more sleep." He was standing over her now, putting his palm to her forehead like a mother did her sick child. "Or some food. I'll get your breakfast and plenty of water to go with it."

"Do they have coffee here?" she asked with a glimmer of hope.

"Water first. Then I'll ask about coffee." Boy, she must really look awful. Because he'd suddenly turned into a mother hen. Or father hen. No, that wasn't really right, either.

He slipped a white shirt over his head, still speaking to her from his side of the room. "I'm sorry I made you walk so long in the rain. Good thing Wayra and his men found us last night."

Lucia had a vague recollection of climbing steps to a worn, wooden structure. Looking around, she saw the house was plain and small, but it was clean, and decorated with very few items. She and Ethan had been given an empty home, it seemed, but the villagers had made the space as welcoming as possible.

A colorful blanket hung on one wall with a small round table beneath. Two chairs sat beside the table, and a spread of orange flowers graced the center. Some type of bromeliads, she assumed, as the rain forest was thick with them.

Ethan snapped her out of her musings when he came and

again put his hand to her face, her cheek this time, much as she had done to him as he'd dreamed.

He was being so sweet and considerate. Had the villagers put something in his water?

"I should never have pushed you so hard," he said.

Lucia lifted one shoulder. "I hardly ever get sick. I don't know what's wrong with me. A little walk in the rain shouldn't have cut me down so fast."

Ethan frowned. "I know better, but I was weighing one evil against the other." He shook his head and clamped his lips tight, as if realizing he'd said too much.

"An evil other than the Amara and the guardians?" she asked, holding her breath expectantly. Would he spill? Finally?

"I'll get your breakfast," he said and walked to the door.

Lucia sat up, ignoring the raw scrape of pain in her head when she did. "Then you must be talking about the Seraphim."

He stopped with his hand on the handle, his shoulders dropping in defeat. And Lucia knew she had him.

Still facing away, he said, "I talked in my sleep again."

Raking a hand through her hair, Lucia scoffed. "You don't just talk in your sleep, Ethan. You're a real conversationalist." She went for the jugular. "Makes it hard to keep your secrets, doesn't it?"

When he said nothing more and jerked open the door, she raised her voice. "If you try to take the dagger from me, I will fight you."

He spun and slammed the door behind him, crossing to her in three strides. "I don't want the dagger. I told you I wouldn't interfere with the coven's business. I may be a lot of things, but I would never betray you and your sisters that way. Or Quinn."

"Then what are you after? Because your lies..." she censored herself. "Your *omissions* are beginning to leave great, gaping holes in a story that's no longer believable." She thumped the bed with one hand. "Why are you here, Ethan? For the piece that is supposed to be hidden with the dagger?"

"Dammit, yes! I need the other artifact." He raked a hand over a jaw shadowed by stubble. Then clenched that hand into a fist. "I told you I needed something from the ruins, but if I have to, I'll give it up."

"No matter what it costs, you said." Lucia stood to face him, but given his height, she still had to look up. "What is it, exactly? What does it do?" And if she had those answers, she might be able to figure out why he needed it. What had happened to him to make him so desperate? So closed off?

With grim resolution, he told her, "A piece of solid silver with the same lava rock as the dagger. It fits around a wrist."

Lucia couldn't help herself. "You mean it's a bracelet." She quirked one side of her mouth. "Really, Ethan, that doesn't seem like your style."

Amazingly, he almost smiled back at her but didn't confirm or deny that he would be the one wearing the band. "Made by the same priests who forged the dagger, it's said the band will protect whomever wears it from a demon's curse. In this case," he added, "A Seraphim. A fallen angel who shows himself in the form of a serpent."

Something tugged at Lucia's memory, but she lost focus when he continued to explain. "Their name is derived from the word *seraph*, which literally means to burn." He threw up his hands and turned from her. "I can't verify how he kills his victims. I only know the Seraphim is dangerous."

"Has he attacked you?" Lucia asked, moving to him to place her hand on his back. Anger coursed through him like a raging river. She could feel it.

He shook his head again. "I'm done talking about this. You have enough."

Ding. Ding. Ding. Lucia knew those particular warning bells. The ones that went off every time she got too close to a particular topic.

"Your sister," she said. "This demon has hurt your sister." A storm of sympathy raged inside her then. "*Dios mío*, Ethan. Why didn't you just tell me?"

He turned his head, giving her his profile. "It's complicated."

"What—" Lucia was interrupted by a knock on the door, and Ethan's leap to answer it. He had revealed far more than he was comfortable with, so she would let him go. For now.

The man who'd found them last night, Wayra, stood outside, a huge grin on his face. "You are awake. Good. Come with me now, and we will prepare."

Throwing up a hand in departure, Ethan slipped out the door and left Lucia standing there alone.

The small house fell silent as her mind replayed everything he'd just revealed.

Ethan had told her he wanted this bracelet, and that the artifact would guard its wearer from a demon. Clearly he wanted to find the silver band and defend someone.

So only one questioned remained. Who was he trying to protect?

22

Ethan could see the rising grayish-green peaks of what some called the Amazonian Andes, and the ever-present mists that hovered there. The ancient tribes who'd built high in the mountains had been named accordingly. The Chachapoyas. People of the clouds.

Wayra had shown him around the small village of Gwancos, and he'd been happy to learn they were only a few miles north of Chachapoyas. Evidently he and Lucia had meandered in just the right direction, losing the Amara somewhere in the jungle and heading toward their intended destination at the same time.

So Ethan could relax a bit more, knowing they had less than a day's travel in front of them. He didn't think the villagers would give him much of a choice regardless. A celebration had been planned for tonight. To honor the arrival of the promised ones. Ethan and Lucia.

He grinned as another man passed by and slapped him on the back, chatting jovially in the Quechuan language so that Ethan understood none of it. He could see the people here were excited though. Cheerful and content.

Their enthusiasm had penetrated even Ethan's foul mood, and the drink they kept pushing into his hand didn't hurt either. A group of giggling women had swept Lucia away earlier, and he assumed they were dressing her as the men had him. He wore one of their loose, white shirts, but had opted for his own beige cargos.

A large bonfire was being lit as he sat on a nearby wooden bench. This was the part of his job that he enjoyed, observing people of other cultures as they went about their ways. Performing rituals so exotic and unique, yet with the same core beliefs as any American household. Work, family, food, love, life.

And laughter, he thought, when several men made strange hand motions, thoroughly enjoying their own joke. Plenty of laughter.

On one side a lean-to had been set up, and underneath older women took long strings of meat and chopped them before adding them to simmering concoctions in large, metal pots. Oddly bulging potatoes went in as well, with a few other things Ethan didn't recognize.

Long strands of purple flower buds were strung all around, accented with blooms in saffron and fuschia. Village life might be simple here, but it was authentic. And honest.

When the sun began to fall behind the mountain tops, the light cast over the buildings deepened to rich amber. It was then he heard the female voices, so he turned to find them gathered outside the door of another house.

A white-haired woman came first, holding the hand of someone behind her. Lucia emerged from inside, her hair clean and gleaming, tumbling its glossy brown down her back. She too wore a white top, a peasant blouse in the truest definition, and a flowing native skirt in bright pink. Over her shoulders was a rainbow scarf.

Ethan smiled, remembering her tale of the mystical traveler, Iris. Lucia had named her cat after the Greek goddess, the brave woman who traveled by riding rainbows.

Lucia's eyes found him then. Her smile blossomed.

And Ethan's heart tripped all over itself.

A colorful bird swooped down to arc a soaring path through the village, surprising them all. Lucia laughed as she followed its flight, her beauty as natural and uninhibited as the flying miracle.

When Ethan realized he was staring he took his mug and drank long and hard. He emptied it.

Wayra was quickly there to hand him another, chortling low in his chest. "Not too bold for you now, eh, American?" He clapped Ethan on the shoulder. "And I think maybe you are not so angry?" He walked away, speaking loudly to the other men. Then they all laughed as well.

Lucia stood on the steps, her visage just above the licking flames of the growing fire. With her skin warmed even more by the setting sun, and rich, brown eyes glimmering, Ethan had no choice but to rise. And go to her.

Without question, she offered him her hand, and a silent agreement passed between them. No doubts or accusations just now. No evasions or fears. Together they sat where instructed, and waited while their hosts made various speeches and toasts.

Soon their bowls were filled with a hearty stew, and fruits were placed before them. The meal was one of honor and thanks, so Lucia and Ethan behaved accordingly. By the time they had eaten their fill, drums and stringed instruments were being tested.

"I think the party's just getting started," Lucia said then laughed when Wayra stumbled by.

Ethan jerked his head at the man. "I think the finder of the promised ones has been partying all day." He stood and held his hand out to her again.

He was beginning to enjoy the illusion of taking care of Lucia. Of being her man.

But that was all it could be. One night of fantasy. And

tomorrow, on to Kuelap.

As the night wore on, the surrounding land fell to dark. With no city lights anywhere to be found, the true and natural black of night covered them like a soft blanket. Torches were lit around the village, and the bonfire burned strong.

Everyone sat on benches or in chairs around the glowing heat. Ethan and Lucia sat side by side, enjoying the company of these strangers, and listening as Wayra translated for others who wished the travelers well.

The villagers offered many words of recognition and wishes for triumph over the Qara Mikuna.

Yes, they did know the legends here, and Ethan was almost sorry he'd been right. They would have to face the shrieking harem before this was over. He took Lucia's hand and rubbed one finger over the center of her palm.

He felt her shiver. "What are you doing?" she asked on a breath. He'd caught her off guard and liked the look of her flushed cheeks and rounded eyes. Her reaction to him was blatant, and he found himself aroused.

Lock it down, Drake. For her safety.

She pulled her hand away, sensing the change in him.

"I was just thinking how glad I am that you can make fire." He glanced around. "Although I wouldn't suggest you do that little trick here. Even our new friends might react badly to your being a witch."

"*Claro.*" Naturally. She tossed her head. "But that's not all you were thinking." She put a finger inside his cup to pull it toward her. "You're almost at the bottom of another one. Surely you're loosened up enough to talk to me by now."

Ethan growled but the sound was drowned out by the cheering, dancing crowd. He wanted to do a whole hell of a lot more than talk to her, but a vicious Seraphim and the deal Ethan had made long ago prevented him from taking Lucia by the waist and hauling her luscious body up against his.

Letting his eyes wander from her full, glossy lips to the golden skin above her neckline then down to the skirt he'd like to toss aside, Ethan indulged himself by imaging her long, toned legs wrapped around him as he drove into her. As she screamed his name.

Lucia snapped a finger in front of his face. "Are you trying to embarrass me?" she hissed.

The jolt made him realize he'd been about to act on the lustful idea, and his expression must have made his plans clear.

He muttered an apology and sat back in his chair again. Man. He must be drunk.

And knowing the weakness alcohol could bring made his blood chill and clog in its vessels. He was walking very close to the fire, and so was Lucia. They might both get singed.

"You said you're feeling better?" he asked, noting the circles under her eyes. He hadn't seen the bruising color earlier and was stunned by how quickly she was wearing out again.

"I am, yes." Looking down as she ran her hands down her bright skirt, Lucia added, "Anyway, I'm not going to bed until you tell me the rest of it."

He'd known this was coming, but damn did his throat close up suddenly. How much should he tell her? Certainly not all of it.

He needed her focused on the dangers lying in wait for them at Kuelap. Not worried about the one that could strike at any time. In any location.

"Truth can hurt sometimes, Lucia." He could smell her again, and this time her scent mingled with the aroma of burning wood. Exotic. Alluring. He closed his eyes and willed away the images of the two of them naked by their own fire.

He couldn't let himself fall for the witch. He had to block out this reckless sentimentality that was seeping into every part of him. But the more he tried, the more he wanted her. The deeper she burrowed into that secret part of him.

The one that must stay locked.

"You like to believe that love can conquer all." His laugh was scornful and derisive, so he didn't look into her eyes. He didn't want to see the hurt he knew would be in the rich brown pools. The insult she would feel as he mocked her pure faith in the very emotion he despised.

Love. He swigged his drink. *A death trap.*

The two of them were off by themselves, farther out from the fire and revelry, so Ethan let his hate reveal itself as he spoke. He channeled his strength but let his body go numb.

No way out of this problem, so he'd have to barge straight through.

Still avoiding Lucia's gaze, Ethan glared instead at the leaping flames. He let the melding hues of red and gold spur him on.

Fire wasn't the only thing that burned.

He stopped himself just short of growling as the memories assaulted him. He sucked cold air in through his teeth.

Then he told her his story.

"I was only eight years old when I first met the Seraphim." His hands rolled into fists. "And my sister Grace was only four when the evil bastard took her."

23

Ethan felt Lucia flinch when two village men tossed a long log onto the bonfire. The already searing wood beneath shifted from the new addition with a great rumble. "Where did he take your sister?" she asked, alert now despite her fatigue.

Ethan looked past her to the dark sky, a glimmer of moon shone between returning clouds. The weather on this side of the Andes was ever-changing, he hoped they could make it one more day without another storm. "When I say he took her, I should say he possessed her."

Lucia's hand flew to her chest. "How awful for her. Poor little girl. She must have been terrified." She held her amulet as if to ward herself from the horror of Ethan's tale. "That's why you study demons."

"Yes."

"Start from the beginning. How did the possession begin? How did you drive him out?" She leaned forward. "Oh, Ethan. He doesn't still attack your sister, does he? Is that why you want the bracelet? For her protection?"

Ethan chose his words carefully, neither correcting her assumption nor lying outright. "My sister is safe for now, but I've never forgotten how her tiny body was forced to battle a demon who was thousands of years older and cruel enough to impress Satan himself."

An alpaca startled them both when it gave off a high pitched scream from its corral, and Ethan wondered if the animal could sense the revulsion welling up inside him.

Remembering his sister's torment caused a visceral reaction in his body. Blood flowed to muscles and senses heightened. Ready to attack.

"She was so small, and one of the Seraphim's favorite tricks was to cause her body to convulse before sending her into a catatonic state. Her skin would turn white, eyes rolling back in her head, and her heart rate would slow until it was undetectable."

On instinct, he reached for Lucia, surprising himself with the need to touch her. She clasped both hands around his. "So many times my parents believed Grace had died," he told her, shuddering. "The worst torture a parent can suffer."

She held tight but didn't speak, allowing the silence to coax more from him. Ethan hadn't known how badly he wanted to share this, to alleviate the raw, scraping pain.

And the fact that he was lessening his burden with Lucia spoke volumes. Too much. He depended on her in ways he never had another person. He trusted her completely, and with his deepest fear.

Yet he couldn't be completely forthcoming with her. Not yet. Not until he knew for certain.

The depth of his deceit almost choked him.

Adjusting so he was leaning forward and resting his arms on his knees, Ethan withdrew his hand. "The short version is that we called a specialist. Someone who knew of fiends and monsters." That part was true, but he couldn't tell her the rest or why the demon had finally released his sister.

"He helped you end Grace's possession?" Lucia asked.

"Yes. He helped." Technically, that was true. "But I never forgot the vulnerability of a mere human when a demon from hell decides to make their body his playground." He dropped his head to his hands. "The way her skin would mark itself then heal again so the bastard could start over. He liked to inscribe messages on her tiny legs."

Now he reached for his mug again, refilled by Wayra, and bless the man for that. "The demonologist assured us Grace couldn't feel the pain, that everything done to her physically was more like illusion." Ethan looked to Lucia. "Something about inherent protection for the young."

"Gracias a Dios por eso." Thank God for that. Lucia shook her head, her lips pressed together in fury. Nothing stirred the heart of a warrior like harm to the innocent. Especially children.

Ethan took advantage of her words to segue the conversation. "You're a witch by birth with powers beyond imagining, yet you still turn to your religion. How does that work?"

A smile flickered on her lips. "Why does one have to nullify the other? Who made that rule?" Her chest rose as she drew a deep breath. "I don't like being told what to think or how to love." Her chocolate eyes reflected the leaping flames as she turned to Ethan. "Do you?"

Her question sliced his already bruised heart down the middle. She had no idea how close she'd struck to the truth. "No," he bit out. "Not one damn bit."

He perceived she was about to ask him about his sister again, but three young girls suddenly surrounded them as a new song flowed into the Peruvian night.

They seemed to be pleading with Lucia then one of them took her hand and tugged while pointing to the fire.

"Dance, bold woman, dance," Wayra said, his own feet scraping the dirt as he drunkenly spun around.

"Oh. No. I..." Trying to bow out gracefully, Lucia shook her head, but Ethan gave her a sound push and cut off her denial.

"Go. Have some fun. You might feel better." He reached out

to trail his fingers down her wealth of brown hair. "I know I do."

He was thanking her for listening, for pushing until he talked, but at the same time he cursed himself. Every link he forged with the seductive Spanish witch was one more step toward tragedy.

Ethan stared into his half-empty cup, seeing his own haunted reflection in the brown beverage. He was weakened by drink, and Lucia was ill from exhaustion, or something worse.

He watched Lucia perform the first tentative steps of the dance the young girls were teaching her. Her easy laughter was a balm to his troubled spirit.

He could bar her from his heart. One more day at least.

Sitting back and sipping the brew, Ethan allowed the anesthetizing effects to ride his bloodstream. He was centered again, or so he believed, and had years of experience fending off this particular brand of ruin.

He'd spent more time with Lucia and had shared more with her than with any other woman before her. And so far, nothing had happened.

Ethan was well into his cups and Lucia was weary. Yet there she was, smiling and laughing as she missed a hip-pop to the side. No harm. No foul.

Ethan smiled smugly. He would stay focused until they reached Kuelap, then he would find the band. Because hell and damnation if he was going to call the thing a *bracelet*.

Then a new element would be thrown into play, and he'd have one up on the Seraphim.

"I may have found a way, demon," he growled to himself. "I've beaten you all these years, and now I may very well put you down for good." He looked again to Lucia, wondering how he would feel to be unshackled at last.

A new song started, even faster than the other, with one player giving a loud yell. Drums pounded and cheers of delight rose along with the ash floating from the fire. After she spun one quick time, Lucia slowed her twirl and sought Ethan's gaze.

The smile she sent him was one of acceptance, and of familiarity. She'd broken into his inner sanctum, or so she thought, and he didn't have the fortitude to shatter the falsehood of it all.

Heat stole into him as he watched her dance. She knew the routine well now, and added her own sultry twist to the moves, tossing him that knowing smile on occasion and firing his lust even more.

Damn, she was a beautiful creature. And he was the man she wanted, without regard to his rejection and avoidance. How could one who'd been so injured by the absence of love, pursue it against all odds? Throwing herself on the proverbial sword again and again.

Ethan studied her neck as she tossed her head back and lifted her arms. He imagined trailing his lips down the lovely curve to discover what lay waiting beneath her white shirt. Perhaps he could separate sex and emotion, even with her.

Or was he just raging high on his drunkenness? Dangerously cocky as he drew near his ultimate goal?

He hardened for Lucia as he followed the sway of her hips. He'd never been a stranger to lust, as it held no peril. So why not? Despite her attempts to win his affections, he'd managed to keep the lines straight and firm.

Why not give her the one thing they could agree on? A night of passion. They both wanted it, and now Ethan felt sure he could stop affection from getting in the way.

Then Lucia changed her mannerism when a young girl came to her side. She slowed her dance and scooped the child up in her arms, spinning with a twirl of her brilliant pink skirt.

The little girl beamed at the pretty woman visiting the village, enthralled by her natural vitality and beguiling warmth.

Just as Ethan had been.

Like a bottle uncorked, everything he'd lied to himself about spilled out. All the tender feelings he'd crushed or knocked aside came together all at once. *No.*

He dropped his cup and stood, flexing his fingers as if he could capture the invading sensations and grind them to nothingness.

But it was too late. A vile taste swam in his mouth, an evil hiss rung in his ears.

"You're wrong," he said, knowing the beast would hear. "Not yet. You can't have her yet."

It all relies on you, he heard in his head, followed by a dry, sloughing noise he knew well. Serpentine laughter.

"But not yet!" He started for Lucia and saw her head snap back like she'd been struck. Holding her balance long enough to set the child down and step away, she put a hand to her head.

She teetered as if intoxicated. Ethan knew she wasn't. When her skirt brushed the edge of the fire, a woman beside her reached out to grab Lucia's arm.

But he was already there.

As he swept her up, the heat practically scalded him. She was burning up. Her skin was too hot.

With a nod for the gathered women, Ethan spoke to Wayra. "She needs rest. Thank you all, and please carry on." With that he hurried to their borrowed quarters, kicking the door open and depositing her on the bed.

She was drenched in sweat.

An older woman came in behind him with rags and a bowl of water. She handed him some type of fruit and mimed putting the food to her mouth then pointed at Lucia.

"I understand. Thank you," he told her, relieved when she backed out and closed the door, giving them privacy. "I know what to do," he said, though no one was there to hear him.

This was no normal fever, and Ethan shook with guilt. *All*

his fault.

He had to shut it down. To make it stop.

Yes, he knew what to do. And more specifically, what he couldn't allow himself to do.

He mopped her brow with a cool wet cloth and ground his teeth. Reckless! How could he be so foolish and irresponsible?

He'd put her in danger by being weak, and worse, he'd been so caught up watching her, wanting her, that he hadn't felt the evil approaching. Now it had its greedy fingers all over them. Searching, pulling, wanting more.

"Well you won't get it, you fucking snake." Ethan hardened himself at will, having practiced the technique for years. Ever since he'd been a teenager.

Since Jessica's death.

He would shutter his heart like a castle under siege, blocking Lucia out cold. And all the life she could bring to his pathetic, empty shell of a world.

There was no other choice.

Ethan held her in esteem and would continue to respect her, but from now on he could only view her as a friend. Admired and cared for but nothing else. He would think of her as a sister. Or cousin.

He glanced at her sleeping face, so strong yet delicate. And her mouth.

Yeah. Like a cousin. That was going to happen.

When she shivered in his arms, he positioned himself behind her, his body becoming her cushion. And her fortress. He would not let the darkness take her.

She turned on her side and murmured against his chest. Then she went slack.

Ethan wet the cloth as needed, cooling her face. Her neck. Eventually her respirations eased to a resting rate, and he was certain she slept.

Stroking her rich brown hair, he closed his eyes tight, willing his chest to stop hurting. Piercing emptiness had struck him when he'd seen her stumble, and the void still wouldn't leave him.

More proof that he cared about her, and more evidence of the hopeless cycle he'd fallen into. He was worried she'd be hurt. Worry evinced emotion. And emotion could kill.

He let her rest against him, feeling her heart throb in time with his. And hating the connection.

His nose flared and he steeled his spine, using the anger that rode alongside the fear. "Don't worry, witch. I'll stay strong. I give you my word."

He smoothed a stray lock of hair from her cheek. "The Seraphim can't come for you, Lucia. He can't hurt you."

The words were ash in his mouth when he said, "Unless I fall in love."

24

"We're all suited up, coach," Kylie told Anna, raising her hand to flash the simple silver band on her finger. Though plain in design, the magical mixture within the metal would light up if exposed to the right brand of evil. Demons, to be precise.

Kylie was one of the five chosen to wear a ring and perform *detection* duty. After dissecting the intel gathered by both Nick at his pub and Trevor through his police connections, the coven and their honorary male members had chosen one of Savannah's hottest spots.

Now they stood outside a brick fence preparing to reconnoiter.

"If you're looking for a wide selection of the opposite sex to choose from, this is the place," Nick said as a variety of people swarmed past them and music pounded from within. When Viv slid him a long, cool look he added, "At least, that's what I hear." He gave her one of his half smiles and a wink.

He didn't reach for her, since they were both playing the part of single-and-available for the sting they'd be running. Nick wore the bronze ring while Viv sported meteoric iron in hers. The other key players in the game were Claudia wearing a nickel alloy and Dare with copper.

Since the demons controlling Savannah's underworld might disguise themselves as male or female, the coven had to offer bait for both.

And there were plenty of sharks circling this particular social club.

After passing through the gate and getting their hands stamped, the men stood to one side while the women broke off into a group of their own. Less competition meant more hits.

Claudia raised one ginger brow as she surveyed the other females at the club. "Nick was right about the number of young, healthy bodies here. A playground for any monster looking for its pound of flesh."

Anna eyed a blonde dressed in a glittery dress that fell to mid-thigh, exposing long legs that ended in sky-high heels. She noted the thick-based shoes were covered with spikes. Interesting.

"We only have to get close enough to touch, and remember, these creatures don't play," Viv said, viewing tonight's plan with a scientist's mind, yet wearing leather boy shorts and silk top that hung off one shoulder.

Anna grinned. Her sisters didn't play, either. "Just put your hand near enough for the rings to pick up any demon essence," she instructed. "If your ring lights up, make sure one of the recorders is made aware. Then move on to the next target."

The sting operation was simple really. The five designated ring-bearers—ha ha—would scope out as many different club goers as they could. When a ring lit up, they would know 1) That they were successfully flirting with a demon. Yay. And 2) What species of demon they were up against. Literally.

Then the recorders— Paige, Willyn, Hayden, Quinn, or Anna— would write down whose ring had reacted. Hopefully, they would get multiple reactions from the same ring. Then they would know the kind of demon they fought and how best to handle them in battle.

Anna hoped the demon clan invading the town was of the humanoid variety, impersonating humans but squirming with evil inside. Then the knives could come out without fear of killing an innocent person.

Being able to store magic inside weapons would be another safety feature. Kind of a back-up generator for battles. Then the coven could start cleaning the streets at night, taking out any demon they stumbled across.

She and her friends would eradicate them like the pests they were, covering the city with ash. Demon ash.

Anna felt the fire of vengeance within. *Demon detritus*. She liked the sound of that.

She and the girls were still outside in a wide courtyard, standing room only and with a tent-covered bar on one side. People milled in and out of the building through an opening that looked like a massive garage door.

The once-industrial building had been successfully converted into a club, but an enormous one. So those testing the rings had each been assigned someone to stay close and observe. The recorders.

Trevor was the only one left to float, so Kylie had laughingly titled him the bouncer. But if anyone was qualified for the job, it was Hayden's detective boyfriend.

As the music changed and a cheer rose from the crowd, Quinn came to Anna's side. "We're all ready. Nick and Dare have gone in." He looked to Hayden and Willyn who would be keeping an eye on the men and recording any hits.

"We've got it," Willyn said before heading across the open yard with Hayden in tow.

Anna perceived Kylie's excitement as the young witch pursed her lips and moved a little to the music. With her long, blonde curls unbound and a short skirt on her petite frame, Kylie had already drawn a few interested glances. "Let's get to it, then." She tossed her hair over one shoulder. "Too bad Lucia's not here. I miss my hunting partner."

Anna wasn't sure if Kylie had been trying to get a rise out of

Quinn, but the comment struck home. Her younger brother set his jaw and glared at the blonde as she smiled at a man who looked military. Target number one.

"Your job isn't to hunt for men tonight, brat, but demons," Quinn ground out, his temple ticking dangerously.

Kylie fluttered her lashes and ran a finger over his shoulder then down his arm. "Aw, Quinn, don't you realize I'm female?" She narrowed her hazel eyes. "I can multi-task."

"Good luck," Anna said, cutting her brother off before he could reply. The tension between Quinn and Kylie was approaching red alert status. She almost wished the younger witch's trial would hurry up and arrive, but that was only because she believed her brother was fated for the coed.

When the muscular, military man leaned close to Kylie and she laughed like a coquette, Quinn's neck veins throbbed. If he wasn't meant for Kylie, the St. Germaine home would be seeing a great deal of pain before the prophecy came due.

Anna pulled Quinn away, sending a prayer to the goddess that her brother would remain unscathed. And Kylie. So beautiful, so clever, yet oh so green.

After a good push, Quinn went in pursuit of Claudia to keep track of her results, and Anna wound through the crowd to stand in a corner with Paige. The two of them watched over Kylie and Viv, looking for any ring illumination.

When Kylie stroked her current objective's neck, her silver ring remained unchanged. Whispering in the young man's ear, she flitted away to stand behind a group of girls. Since all she had to do was get the metal close to another's skin, she could also test females.

A quick pat on the arm while she gushed about loving a girl's dress did the trick. Then she pulled a similar stunt on the others standing in a circle chatting.

When she was finished she faced Anna and gave a disappointed shrug. Still no glow.

With a roll of her hips, Kylie moved away, only to be stopped by a hulking male with arms like tree trunks and soot-black hair hanging in his face. His look was stuck somewhere between a Goth and a frat boy, and somehow that made him more disturbing.

His arm slid around so he could grab Kylie's backside, but her small fingers latched onto the encroaching hand and shoved it firmly away. He leered as she wormed her way out of his embrace, winking and wiggling her fingers in a *ta-ta for now* manner.

Once her back was to the guy, she slapped her hand to her chest where Anna barely caught the fading silver light. She nodded and jotted on a small note pad. Score one for Kylie.

And one for the element of silver. Anna couldn't remember which kind of demon that meant, because she'd preferred to find out how much of a hell storm they were in after the fact. The experiment was far from complete, but if Kylie got a few more positive reactions, they would be sure.

She covertly observed Kylie, growing more optimistic when the younger witch's ring lit up two more times. Silver was a definite, and thank goodness for Ethan's formulary on how to blend the primary metal with others to make the perfect composite. One that created a mystical phosphorescence.

In the presence of monsters.

After an hour, most of the people at the club had been tested by the coven, and though new arrivals were still flooding the gate, Anna felt solid in her assessment. Kylie and her ring had gotten over a dozen reactions.

Anna shivered to think the number of demons here reflected the rest of Savannah. Hopefully the fiends gathered here more than other places. Young, drunken crowds were a hot bed of victims.

As some of the others came over to rejoin Anna, Dare looked at her notes and gave a long, low whistle. "Either Kylie has a good eye for demons, or she just gets around." The dark-haired witch tilted his forehead down to point Kylie out in the crowd.

Kylie raised her hand then and waved.

"See," Dare said, rocking back on his heels. "She just got another one."

Then Dare caught a glimpse of Quinn's seething expression. He grabbed Anna's brother by the shoulders and shook him, laughing. "Calm down, bro, she's only playing a role."

Quinn quickly smoothed his face into a mask, emotionless and hard. "I don't know what you're talking about."

Dare was saved from responding when Paige and Viv returned. The warrior with stunning, turquoise eyes was exuberant. Her partner Viv looked concerned. "We got a lot of hits," Paige said, her mind already geared toward weaponry and war.

"Uh-oh," Willyn said, standing beside her husband, Dare. "So did Kylie. In fact, she's still getting them."

Quinn growled. "We've got enough info. Someone grab her so we can get the hell out of here.

"I'll get her," Claudia told them, swinging away in her short black dress. She also drew stares, with her flaming red hair and mile-long legs.

Anna was grateful none of the other detectors had gotten responses, because the data they had was bad enough.

Just as Claudia came back with Kylie and they were all headed for the exit, a collection of seriously in-shape men filled up the gates, leaving no room for Anna and her friends to pass.

Paige blew white-blonde bangs off her face. "Looks like the one-seven-five is back in town."

"The who?" Claudia asked, eyeing the group of men in their tight shirts and jeans. Many of them had tattoos on their arms, and even the ones laughing and smiling had an certain aura about them. The kind that whispered, *Keep a safe distance.*

"Their battalion is stationed here in Savannah, at Hunter

Army Airfield." Paige looked to Hayden. "*You* know Hunter."

They all did, Anna thought. The military post where Hayden had completed her challenge and helped bring a member of the Amara over to the light side. Sylvie the hoodoo priestess was still in hiding, reclaiming her life and finding her way out of the dark with her spunky, little grandmother's help.

"You mean they're soldiers?" Kylie asked, craning her neck to see over Quinn's shoulder when he blocked her.

Paige crossed her arms and studied the men with a gleam of admiration in her eye, and if the coven's own female terminator paid a fellow warrior respect, he deserved it. "Not only soldiers," she told Kylie before a sly grin covered her lips. "Rangers."

"Oh," the young blonde said. Her father was a general in the Air Force, so she understood.

When at last the gates cleared of bodies, they started out. A lone male was coming up the sidewalk, but he had the look of the others they'd just passed. Paige was the last one to exit, so she bumped into the guy as he hurried in.

"Excuse me, Ma'am," he said, catching her forearms to steady her. Though Paige needed no one's help to stay balanced.

"Not a problem," she said, clearly intending to brush past and move on to catch her friends.

But the Ranger simply held on, his eyes scouring Paige's face. Entranced.

"Oh, hells no," Kylie muttered under her breath. Then she called out to the man, "Danger, Will Rangerson. Danger."

He didn't heed the warning.

"You can let go of me now," Paige told him, though she was facing the street with her back to the foolish man who still had one hand on her upper arm. Anna could read the tension in her body, and all of the witches held a collective breath.

"Wait. What's your name?" the man asked.

Paige whirled on him. "You're going to remember me as *Lights Out* if you don't peel your hand off this second."

He laughed at her and Anna groaned. *Here come the fireworks.*

Then the guy released Paige and stepped back, hands help up in surrender. "Roger. Now I've let go, so will your tell me your name?"

Before anyone could intervene, Quinn had moved to stand with Paige.

Anna frowned. Her idiot brother was just gunning for trouble, so he could blow off some Kylie-inspired steam. "Do we have a problem here?" he asked, looking...what was the phrase? Oh, yeah. *All bowed up.*

When several of the Ranger's buddies returned to see what was happening, Dare muttered, "Shit," and moved in to flank Quinn.

Then there went Trevor.

Anna sighed. This was not what any of them needed right now. The coven versus half the Ranger Battalion? That would be...*messy.*

Paige held a hand back to call off Quinn, but she stepped closer to fill the space the Ranger had just vacated. "You want to know who I am?" She was leaning forward. Not a good sign. Then she crossed her arms and took up a fighting stance. "Hooah."

The guy smiled even wider and his eyes, Anna noticed, grew shrewd. "I wasn't sure before, but now I am."

After nodding to the men standing behind Paige, the stranger tipped his head at her. "Have a good night, and sorry for the misunderstanding. Ma'am." He walked backward toward his friends but tossed Paige one last grin before turning away.

"What the hell did that mean?" Paige asked, putting her hands on her hips and looking like she might go after him.

"We don't have time to find out," Anna said, adding extra bite to her tone. "Kylie and Viv both got plenty of reactions to their rings tonight. We all know what that means."

"Yeah," Paige muttered, forgetting about the Ranger and coming back to her coven. And the battle at hand. "It means we got hits on two different essences."

"That is *not* cool," Kylie said with a hesitant glance toward the club. "We've got two kinds of demon."

25

"How are you feeling?" Ethan asked Lucia, for what seemed the hundredth time since they'd left the village. They'd gotten quite a late start, mid-afternoon if she were being honest. And all because she'd been tanked out, sleeping off whatever had made her ill.

Lucia gave him an obligatory nod of the head but couldn't lift her lips to smile. The truth was she ached from head to toe, as if rust was running through her capillaries and slowing down the works.

Ugh. She hardly ever got this sick.

But the misery was almost worth it to have Ethan's complete attention and nurturing. A chill racked her body, and her lower back muscles cramped in response. Almost worth it.

Ethan said she'd had a fever last night, and she believed him. All she remembered after his story about his sister was the way he'd watched her dance. His eyes had been so focused and his shoulders and neck so tense. He'd looked like a man waging a great war within himself.

And Lucia had to believe she was at the center of it.

But why?

She understood now why he'd been so driven to study demons, going to the most clandestine and secretive corners of the earth. The dark spots of this world where people still believed in dread and the crawling sensations on the back of their necks.

Where monsters were spoken of in hushed voices but were never forgotten. Always feared.

But there was more going on, because nothing he'd told her explained his reticence to let her get close. What did this bracelet or the demon have to do with the way he avoided relationships?

Ethan wasn't a coward, so his self-imposed isolation must be for good reason.

Lucia drank until her water bottle sucked in on itself with a crunching sound. Whenever she took a step toward the truth, he would throw a few bread crumbs on the ground. Then sweep them all away if she got too close.

She studied his long powerful legs and strong arms. What would a man like Ethan fear?

She rolled her shoulders so her pack would drop to the ground. They were only a short distance from Kuelap, after hitching a ride up the mountain road at Ethan's insistence.

They'd opted to stay away from towns and hotels, just in case the Amara went hunting. Lucia was in no shape to fight, so Ethan would be on the front line with his machete.

Not that he didn't cut one fine picture with rain pouring down and his weapon raised like an ancient *rey guerrero*. A warrior king.

The sun would set in less than an hour, and given how awful she felt, Lucia would take one more night of sleep before tackling the ruins, locating the artifact, and battling that heinous harem of hags for the right to the dagger.

"Enough cover here to suit you?" she asked Ethan. Already phrasing the words for her one-woman mutiny if he disagreed. She couldn't take another booted step. Not one.

She was even too ill to acknowledge the flare of lust in her belly when Ethan turned his sexy dark eyes her way. He'd shaved last night for the celebration, but now his jaw was shadowed again.

He carried off the rugged look far too well.

Lucia shivered. She could barely summon the strength to keep her eyes open, even with such a handsome specimen to look at.

Holy witch flu. She was *really* sick.

The hard day and night spent in the rain must have done it to her. For now, she was content to let Ethan set up camp and make their meal. He'd even brought along food offered by the village women. They'd been so concerned about Lucia leaving camp in her condition.

But Ethan was taking wonderful care of her. And each time he turned worried eyes on her or stretched his mouth into a line of concern, Lucia experienced a warm tremor.

She liked his gentle side, the one that held her arm to offer support as they climbed or made sure she didn't forget to take in the appropriate amount of fluids. In fact, if she ever needed a nurse maid again, he would be the first person she called.

She just hoped he would be close enough to answer.

When Ethan rolled out her sleeping bag and helped her take off her shoes, she let him. Then she climbed in to rest.

Soon he had a fire blazing and was heating stew in a camp pot. Lucia ate a citrus-type fruit while he pitched the tent, and by the time their meal was served, she felt good enough to converse.

"How much do you know about Kuelap Fortress?" she asked Ethan, hugging her sleeping bag to ward off the cold breeze at this higher elevation.

He tossed a twig into the fire then sat back against the base of a tree, one of many in the tropical, mountain woods. "I know the citadel is not strictly an Incan ruin but was built by the Chachapoyas, the cloud people. They built the fortress on the mountain somewhere around 500 to 800 AD and protected it successfully until the Incans overtook them in the fifteenth or sixteenth century."

Lucia sniffed and worked up a lazy smile. "I see you found time to read a pamphlet."

His responding smirk was as insincere as her own. "Once you told the coven and me where the dagger was, I did what I could to learn my way around."

"You said then that your main reason for coming was to help me with the guardians." Lucia huddled inside her warm bag, still feeling the sting of Ethan's initial deception. Though her resentment had faded somewhat, she would feel a lot better if he would just come clean. Completely. "Got anything else to offer besides their aversion to fire?"

"Not just an aversion. Fire will destroy them. That weighs pretty heavy in the how to save our asses column." He followed the snarky comment with a long, assessing study of her hunched up form. "If you still feel bad tomorrow, we'll hold off."

"No." The denial sprang from her lips. "I'm going in. I'm getting the blade. I'm taking it back to the coven."

He nodded. "And I'm going to help you."

"What else did you want to tell me before we climbed the rest of the way to the ruins? She gestured toward his pack. "You said you'd gone back over the notes you'd made about the dagger. Clues you'd picked up in various myths and legends."

As if relieved to be back on familiar ground, Ethan stood, refilled Lucia's stew bowl, ignoring her when she opened her mouth to protest, then he retrieved his journal and found the marked page. "Now that I look back through with Kuelap in mind, I notice details that fit. Several remarks about hiding in the sky could be interpreted to mean the height of the mountain."

"And the ruins are always covered with clouds," Lucia said. She could see connections he'd made and appreciated the additional knowledge.

"Exactly. Another repetition I've found is the mention of a bird's eye view of the twins. Sometimes when referencing the entrance to the harem's lair and others directing us to the dagger's hiding place." Ethan puzzled over the pages with a frown. "That makes me think the dagger is inside the lair where the Qara Mikuna can protect it."

Lucia grimaced. "So I'll be entering a den filled with sharp-toothed, concubine cannibals." Then she shrugged. "Not so different from sorority rush week."

Now he gave her a real smile, and her spirit practically took flight. "You were in a sorority?"

"I tried but discovered I was just too GDI."

Ethan's sarcastic laugh was a sharp shot in the dark. "You? Too independent? Shocker."

"Coming from the quintessential lone wolf," she said, watching as his face collapsed into its usual stoicism. "We've got plenty of time now. Why don't you explain why you keep me at arm's length?"

With a sigh that told of Ethan's immense and well-tested patience, he got up again to circle around their campfire. He kneeled beside her. "After we find the artifacts. I'll tell you everything, but until then, I am going to block your interrogation. Every time."

To Lucia's surprise, he placed a chaste kiss on her forehead and said, "Why don't you turn in for the night? We have to start early, and you still need to recuperate."

Hmph. If he was trying to distract her with such atypical kindness...well then, his underhanded ploy was working.

She closed her eyes and luxuriated beneath the press of his lips, realizing that tender Ethan was almost as compelling as ferocious Ethan. Dual sides of the same tempting coin.

Besides, he was right. Her legs ached and her stomach revolted as she uncurled herself to move inside the tent. As soon as she collapsed and zipped up her bag, she realized how cold the wind had been outside.

Cocooned in her little world, she chose to overlook the lingering doubts about Ethan and the things he still wouldn't tell her. Instead she dreamed about his heavy lidded eyes and how that rare smile of his made her heart flutter.

Regardless of his continued secrecy, she felt safe with him standing guard. As long as he watched over her, she would be safe. Able to sleep without dark visions or nightmares.

She snuggled in tighter and smiled. Yes, with Ethan by her side she could get some much-needed rest.

Here. With him. Nothing could touch her.

~~~

Ethan cast his gaze to the drab, olive tent. The plastic tarp draped over it glowed golden from the flames of their fire. And inside, Lucia slept.

He gritted his teeth and cursed himself again for being the least bit susceptible to her charms. And therefore exposing her to the hell that tracked his every step. His curse. His demon.

Every link Ethan forged with Lucia was like one more shovel of dirt on her grave. She could be as pissed off at him as she liked, but he'd show her his will was stronger.

His protective instincts went back far too many years and were honed to a cutting edge. Sharpened by his last hellish experience with love.

With Jessica. The young girl he'd given his heart to, only to watch in horror as she suffered immense pain. And died. Burned from the inside out.

Damn you, Seraphim. And that was all Ethan knew to call him, because the serpentine demon had never revealed his real name. There were rituals to help control black entities, to bind some of their powers. But the practitioner had to address the monster directly, or they could never be cast out.

There was no doubt in his mind Lucia was feeling the Seraphim's preliminary stages of attack. Which meant Ethan had allowed himself to weaken. To feel. And every tiny bit of fondness he developed for her meant the demon could seep that much farther into her spirit, her soul.

How long until he breached her fully?

No! Ethan shook his head and stomped off into the woods to pace alone, where his heavy footsteps wouldn't wake Lucia. *I just have to make it to tomorrow. The band will be there, and I can stop the Seraphim at last. Lucia will recover. And she'll be free.*

Ethan knew the bracelet...damn...the *wrist band* would only be a temporary fix. A mild relief. The object was still of this world, and therefore could be damaged like anything else. What if Ethan impaired it somehow, or worse, what if he lost it?

His line of work got physical almost half of the time. The other half he spent interviewing people about their societal lore or researching in a library. Either way, the risk remained.

For now he just had to keep his mind right and off of the witty, curvy, adventurous woman in his tent. The sexy witch who just wouldn't heed Ethan's very clear warning. In any of her languages.

With one final stare at the rising moon, he felt calm enough to return to camp. He didn't like leaving her alone for long anyway.

Just make it to tomorrow, Drake. The girl will get her dagger and I'll get my...oh, hell. I get a damn bracelet. Wondering what his vixen of a hiking partner would make of his internal dialogue, Ethan was practically grinning when he entered their camp site.

But his neck and shoulders stiffened with alarm when he saw Lucia standing near the back of the tent. She was staring into the dark woods, wearing only her long-sleeved T-shirt and panties. Ethan started forward with concern. *She must be freezing.*

Then she began a slow rotation, taking diminutive steps in place as she circled around to face him. Her velvety brown eyes were blank, staring through him instead of connecting. "Ethan," she said, the sound thin and weak.

"What's wrong? Are you sick?" He made another move closer but stopped when she tilted her head at an odd angle. "Lucia?" His blood felt like it flash froze before zinging back to life with a painful, forceful rush.

His head pounded, recognizing the signs even as the last of his shriveling hope forced him to say, "Are you awake?"

Her words purred now when she said, "Oh, Ethan," the syllables stretching fluidly as she spread her fingers and rubbed both hands over her stomach then eased them up to latch onto the hem of her shirt. Undulating her hips in a way meant to hypnotize, she lifted the material.

Just as the shirt cleared her breasts, a silken sheet materialized around her, the color of blood. Of passion. The red surrounded her as if worshipping her skin, and as she glided toward him, her panties fell to the ground.

This isn't real. It's all just an illusion. Ethan swallowed against the rising terror. *He's making me see this.*

She was naked under that wrap, and moving toward him with a wicked smile. As he watched, her lips developed a sheen. They glistened like wet berries, rich and sweet. Then the tip of her pink tongue ran over them. Teasing. Taunting.

Ethan heard his own groan but stifled his body's reaction with a douse of cold, hard reality. Lucia wasn't making her way over to seduce him. Something else was.

The witch may have stalked him in the past, but her gaze was fixed on him in a different way now. Her eyes were hungry. Predatory. And as he watched, they flickered to bright yellow.

With vertical pupils.

The serpent had taken his woman. Lucia was possessed.

Biting down on the fierce territoriality that raged in his chest, Ethan shoved emotion back in its lockbox. Where it would lie in wait until she was safe.

A response was exactly what the Seraphim wanted. The bastard was trying to stoke Ethan's feelings for Lucia, so he would ride in and try to rescue her.

But he couldn't show how much he cared about her. If he did, the demon would be allowed to take her life.

Every muscle from his arms to his abdomen corded tight. That was not going to happen. Not tonight.

Ethan let the artic wind of hatred blow through him. His enemy stood before him now. His most despised adversary. So that is who he would make himself see.

Not Lucia, exposed and manipulated in the worst, most invasive way.

"You have no right to her, Seraphim." Ethan spread his legs to shoulder-width, ready to defend Lucia, no matter what that defense entailed. "I do not love her."

The evil inside Lucia made her slide both hands up to cup her own breasts. "Oh, but you're so close." Her head fell back in ecstasy as she caressed herself. "So, close."

Then the demon's eyes snapped back to Ethan. "I know she stirs something in you, Ethan. You want to own her. To posse*sssss* her." He hissed the word.

The thing laughed in a horrible mixture of Lucia's voice and one filled with demented glee. Deep and rough, the beast's amusement echoed off the mountainside. "And it feels so good to be inside this particular body. Your tastes have improved. No more little girls for the foolish boy."

"Now you're a man, Ethan." Lucia's finger slipped inside her mouth and withdrew slowly with a sucking noise. "And you desire a *woman*."

Disgust battered his gut, but Ethan hid his repulsion. He addressed the Seraphim in a clipped, even tone. With cold, hard logic. "The witch is only a necessity. Her talent will lead me to the very thing you don't want me to have. That's the real reason you're here. You slimy fuck."

Ethan crossed his arms and forced himself to laugh. "Go ahead. Take her. She means nothing to me, and I'm about to find the bracelet that will block you from my life forever."

Ethan eased forward, lowering his voice to a menacing level. "I know you're afraid, demon. You reek of fear, because you know what's coming. That bracelet will defeat any demon, even one as strong as you. A fallen angel."

Ethan turned his back on Lucia, effectively dismissing the rotten entity controlling her.

There was more hiss in Lucia's voice when she/it spoke. Her throaty, sexy sound had been replaced with a coarse malevolence. "You say she is only a necessity, hmm?" the demon said skeptically. "You see, human, a flower blooming wild is no requirement for man, yet its beauty compels him to stop and wonder. To admire."

"Don't waste your riddles on me, snake." But Ethan's hands clenched as the Seraphim's words struck home.

"From a distance her petals burn bold and bright, but as you draw near, you find they are fragile, despite their daring blush." Lucia's body walked closer to Ethan, so he could smell the strawberry of her lips. The Seraphim didn't miss a trick.

He whispered with Lucia's voice to Ethan. "Yet you can't help yourself. You covet the flower so. You must touch it." Lucia moaned, and Ethan whirled to face her, afraid she was being harmed.

But he found her slipping a hand down to cup her sex. She smiled and said, "You must pluck the beauty that teases you. And before you realize what you've done."

The demon forced Lucia to rake the nails of her other hand

down her bare neck, leaving angry, welling scratches behind. "You've crushed her soft petals with your own brutal hand."

"You have no right!" Ethan yelled as the serpent left his mark on Lucia's flesh. He threw himself toward his backpack and the satchel waiting inside, searching for his silver flask.

The Seraphim was dishonoring their contract. Breaking their blood-drenched deal. Ethan hadn't fallen in love with Lucia. Not yet. So the demon could be dispelled.

With a fling of his arm, he doused Lucia's body with holy water and was darkly satisfied to hear the monster's angry cry. "Stay away from her, Seraphim. You are dangerously close to forfeiting our agreement, and if you do, then I'm free!"

"Never!" The thing inside Lucia raged. "I'll take everything from you, boy. I always have, and I always will." Shaking from the burn of the blessed liquid, the demon still managed to toss Lucia's long, brown hair over a shoulder. "You can't keep yourself from her much longer, and as soon as you find yourself between these long, lovely thighs..." The Seraphim made Lucia run her hand up between her legs. "Then I'll be back."

Her eyes flashed yellow one last time before her lips whispered, "And your witch will die."

Ethan ran to catch Lucia when she slumped, her suddenly naked body dropping like a stone the instant the demon fled.

He studied her face, ready to soothe her if she woke frightened, but she was sleeping soundly. Or was passed out from the strain of being possessed.

When the marks faded gradually from her neck, Ethan sighed with relief. He thanked every deity he knew that she would feel nothing. Seeing her ache from any more pain would rip him apart. She'd been through too much already.

Dressing her again in the clothes she'd removed, Ethan deposited her inside the sleeping bag. Then he threw more wood on the fire, building the blaze until the surrounding forest glowed orange. Deciding to leave the tent flap open, he positioned himself just inside.

With Lucia sleeping behind him, he made himself comfortable and settled in for the night. And with his reserve bottle of holy water in hand, he sat like a sentry with a watchful eye.

He would stay that way until dawn.

26

Ethan wiped his brow and looked up to the woman who was currently smokin' his ass as they climbed to the top of the mountain and the ancient fortress awaiting them there. It was as if Lucia had been storing up energy for the last day and half and was now putting the reserves to good use.

She'd sat up from her sleeping bag as soon as dawn had broken over the horizon, and damned if the woman hadn't been downright chipper. She had no recollection of the previous night's events and showed no residual effects of the possession.

Ethan was grateful for that. Absolutely he was. But hell, it's not like this was the Iron Man Triathlon of archaeological exploration. She was leaving him in the dust.

"Are we there yet?" he called once she stopped to survey their position with her hands on her hips.

He'd been going for humor but wouldn't shirk the offered respite. Pulling out a bottle of water, he took a slug and stood beside Lucia. "Oh, yeah," he said spying the yellow stone wall once he came around the bend. "We're there."

Ethan had known the outer walls stood approximately thirty-six feet in height, and the second level of walls inside were estimated closer to fifty feet, but seeing the amazing structure first hand was a true life experience.

He imagined the back-wrecking work of hauling ten thousand tons of limestone to this mountain top. The sheer will and effort it must have taken in 500 AD was staggering.

"She's beautiful," Ethan said, at a loss for anything more descriptive.

At his simple statement, Lucia turned to him and clasped her arms around his neck before laying her lips to his. His breath caught in his chest as the fear flooded back in, but she kept it brief and stood back to drop her hands again.

"I'm glad you're here with me," she said, vitality practically humming from her dusky-golden skin.

"Yeah," he massaged the back of his neck and said, "Me, too," before performing a mental inventory of his holy water, grave dirt, and other demon-wasters. He hoped he wouldn't need them, but Lucia was going to have to keep her distance.

Ethan was walking a sharp edge and trying not to fall off the wrong side. But if she kept surprising him like that, looking all fresh and luscious then pressing her chest against his for a kiss?

Hell, he might just have to drink the holy water.

Together they started walking, in sync and of a leisurely pace. They did, however, keep to the tree line as much as possible, scoping the area for the Amara. Tyr and his crew might be lying in wait.

"How big is this place again?" he asked her, enjoying the play of misty clouds around the base of the citadel. Brown and white goats grazed on the gentle green slope that was the last push to the top, and Ethan was having a hard time seeing the place as spooky or intimidating.

Lucia tilted her head then pointed. "The entire fortress runs north and south at a length of almost two thousand feet. A little over three hundred and fifty at its widest point. We don't have a choice but to cross the open grass to get to the main entrance," she told him, indicating the green expanse broken up by bulging gray stones that seemed to have stuck their faces out for a breath of fresh air.

"Can't you just pull up that handy internal radar of yours to see if the bad guys are lurking?"

She laughed lightly. "I have, but being this close…"

"I know." Ethan touched her elbow. "We've almost got what we came for. No time to get sloppy."

"And even with so few stragglers here looking over the ruins," she said, "I don't want to risk anyone getting hurt."

She made a half turn and sighed. "The name means cold place, and considering the winds, the description is fitting. But the orchids and bromeliads growing wild give the building a certain softness." She shrugged. "Let's hope we leave feeling the same way."

They took another minute to enjoy the twittering of monkeys in the surrounding forest, as well as the sweep of a colorful bird who perched in a tree and called out. Ethan swore the jewel-toned creature was saying, *Go on in. You're safe here.*

As they drew closer to the main entrance, they could see the walkway was enclosed by high walls on each side. The ground rose up like a ramp. Two great stones flanked the entryway, and Lucia patted the one boasting a serpent. "Think this is coincidence?"

Ethan flashed back to Lucia's eyes last night. How they'd turned yellow with narrow slits.

Then he shook it off. "Maybe. The serpent represented different things to various cultures. The Incas made your dagger, but the Chachapoyas built this fortress."

She tapped her fingers to the carving and murmured, "Hmm." She walked on, and after what must have been another hundred feet, the hall narrowed to allow only one person through at a time. Then they were inside the fortress, facing two lines of small housing units, most of them round and remarkably intact.

Various markings decorated the stones in the walls. Carved eyes, zig-zags, and rhomboids seemed to be the major theme. The inner ground was also green with grass, like a carpet spread for visitors.

Ethan watched Lucia lift her hand and follow her extra-sensory perception like a mystical metal detector. Moving in a slow, deliberate path, she meandered between buildings and looming walls.

As they moved farther into the interior of the citadel, the white mists grew thicker, swirling all around them. He understood why Kuelap was the city of the clouds.

Abruptly, Lucia stopped and looked around. Then she swung a disappointed look toward Ethan. "Good news or bad news?" she asked him in all seriousness.

He shoved his hands in the pockets of his cargos. After the sleepless and guarded night he'd had? "Give me the good."

"Okay. I know where the dagger is," she said, waiting for the question she knew would follow.

And it did. "Where?" Ethan asked, almost hesitantly.

"Well, that would be the bad news." She looked to the grassy ground and thumped it twice with the heel of her boot. "I'd say at least fifty feet that way." She pointed down. "In the belly of the mountain."

~~~

Discovering an artifact lay hidden beneath the ground was nothing new for Lucia. Her gift could take her to an object, but the pull that guided her didn't account for the twists and turns she might have to take to actually put her hands on it.

Her body quivered with the certainty. The dagger was absolutely beneath their feet. She and Ethan weren't prepared to dig to get to the blade, but based on past experience, she doubted they would have to.

"Whoever originally hid the dagger was human," she said when Ethan lolled his head back in frustration. "They had to have a way to get down there, and that's how we'll go, too." She blew out a breath. "This means we're dealing with a secret entrance."

"You can't just locate the secret entrance?" he asked, his eyes narrowed on her but with a spark of hope.

She shook her head. "Sorry. My talent doesn't work that way." She cocked one side of her mouth in a half-grin. "I can't set it like a talking car GPS and expect it to tell me when to turn."

She stomped her foot again. "Down. That's all I know. Once we find a way to go below, I'll be able to tell left right etcetera, but for now, all we can do is find a way in."

Ethan threw his arms out to indicate the great expanse of Kuelap. "Into what?"

"Relax," she told him, moving close to wrap her arms around him. He stiffened and warned her off with those dark, deadly-serious eyes.

Lucia couldn't stop the impish smile as she lifted the book from his back. She held it up and wagged it in front of his face. "Let's take another look at those clues you found. I hate to say it, but riddles and cryptic language usually exist for a reason."

He snatched the book away when she offered it. "I told you the basics last night."

Lucia felt her brow wrinkle. "Yeah. About that. I must have been torn up by whatever bug I caught. I can't remember much. Everything after stopping to make camp is foggy." She glanced at Ethan and thought she caught a flash of...relief?

With the muscles around her mouth and eyes feeling tighter all of a sudden, Lucia notched her chin toward the book. "So why don't you tell me again?"

She waited while he flipped pages, musing over his odd behavior. Had something happened last night?

His voice broke her concentration and dragged her back to the problem at hand. "We know we're trying to get into the harem's lair. The hiding place of the dagger protected by the guardians. The Qara Mikuna." He put his fingertip to a page and held it out for her to see. "And the entrance to the harem's lair is marked by the twins," he said excitedly.

Lucia read the rest of his writing. "From a bird's eye view," she murmured, mulling it over. "We obviously have to get up high, but we're already at the top of the mountain."

She put a finger to her lip. "There are two watchtowers. One at the north end, the other at the south. Also the *Tintero*, or inkwell, though the bulb is upside-down and appears to defy gravity. The Tintero has crumbled away some and won't be easy access."

"You have climbing gear?" Ethan asked, shoving the book back in his pack.

"The essentials." The familiar thrill of solving a challenge started buzzing in Lucia. "We should start with the accessible towers, and if we still haven't found the twins, we can try the inkwell."

"Sounds like a plan," Ethan agreed, relieved to have a task set before them. "We can't give up now."

"Give up?" She punched him lightly on the shoulder. "That is one phrase that *does not* belong in my vocabulary."

With renewed anticipation, they set off toward the closest of the two towers. Climbing the incline on the north end, they could see the towers here weren't like those found in ancient castles. Instead of being tall and columnar, the rise of land took them to a much taller portion of the wall. Wider as well, so that many men could have taken up position there to survey their lands.

Using a compact set of binoculars, Lucia and Ethan took turns combing the ruins for anything that might be construed as twins. Eventually they decided they were in the wrong spot and started toward the other end of the citadel.

Repeating the same exercise, they searched from every possible angle before Ethan huffed and said, "Nothing." He handed Lucia the binoculars. "Let's hope the inkwell is hard to climb for a reason."

"Like helping keep the underground entrance a secret? Making it hard for the average passerby to locate the twins?"

"Something like that," he said with a nod, taking her elbow as they started down.

Lucia tried not to smile. She'd been in tougher, dirtier, more perilous places than the top of this tower, but Ethan was escorting her as if she were fragile. She chalked it up to chivalry then let it go.

She had a feeling she'd have plenty of opportunities to demonstrate her grit before the sun set again. The wind was kicking up now, and bringing cold with it. Lucia was glad she'd switched to pants and a long-sleeved shirt.

Once they reached the inkwell, she and Ethan studied the inside and outside construction. The exterior was limestone and was sturdy, while the inner walls held dirt and clay. "More insubstantial on the inside," Lucia observed.

"But better hidden." Ethan looked around. "Still not many tourists and the ones that are here are nowhere to be seen. But why take chances?" He reached for her pack. "I'll go up the inner wall."

Lucia held tight to the pack. "Some parts of the structure have already crumbled. I'm lighter. This is my gear." She lifted one brow. "I'm climbing."

Ethan's jaw worked so hard she could see the side muscles bulge. "Fine. If you fall, I might break your landing. I'll let you know."

"I expunge my earlier thoughts about chivalry," she said, smiling as she readied her nylon rope and other equipment.

"You never mentioned it." Ethan stood with hands on his

hips.

"Oh." She popped back up and tilted her head. "Good thing I didn't, then."

Lucia could feel him checking her out as she climbed the inner wall, but didn't have time to gloat. She had very real obstacles to worry about at the moment. Mainly this crumbly, dirty wall that spilled dried particles every few feet.

When she coughed from an explosion of dust, Ethan asked sharply from below, "Are you okay?"

"Yeah," she called back down. I'm almost to the break in the wall. "I'll be able to see most of the fortress." She grunted as she pulled herself up to the hole, tightening her brake hand and securing her position.

Once she was safe, she pulled out the binoculars to study the walls and grounds like she had from the towers.

"Anything?" Ethan asked, his deep timbre echoing inside the round, hollow structure.

"No." Lucia blew through her clenched teeth, unwilling to accept the fact that they might have come to a dead end. They might have to regroup and come at the clues in his book from a different angle.

On her fourth pass of the farthest walls, she jerked the thick lenses back and adjusted them for better focus. "Wait." She strained her eyes, trying to make out two shapes that were distinctly different from the other tilted rhomboids and strange eyes carved into the walls.

The figures were inscribed in the wall but couldn't be seen by someone standing below. The stone just beneath protruded slightly, effectively blocking the drawings from view.

From up here, from the *bird's eye*, Lucia could see them plainly. Taking note of identifying factors, she made sure she could locate the stone again once she was back on the ground. "I'm coming down," she said in a hushed voice.

When her boots hit the ground, Ethan was there to grab her

by the waist. And he didn't let go when she turned to look up at him. "I found the twins."

He looked like he wanted to smile, but instead he backed away and shuttered his eyes, hiding any emotion that might have risen there. "Never doubted you would, Lucia." Then he nodded and helped her reel in the rope. "Never doubted you would."

27

Overcast skies and biting winds were turning out to be a blessing for Lucia and Ethan. The few tourists who'd come earlier in the day cleared out when the sky began to threaten rain.

Kuelap Fortress could be reached more easily due to recent road construction, but the trip up the mountain was still grueling.

"I think we're alone for the most part," Ethan said before giving Lucia a boost. She had to find purchase with the toes of her shoes on any available ledge. The limestone and yellow clay mixture was tightly packed, offering few footholds.

"Wow," she murmured when she finally got steady enough to study the "twins." She cast a look back down to Ethan. "You've got to come up here. This is detailed and sophisticated."

Scouring the wall with the flats of his hands, Ethan finally found two good grooves and hefted himself up by gripping the stone with his fingers. When his feet settled, he was able to stand and release his hold. He was on the opposite side of the two drawings from Lucia, leaning his upper body against the wall for support.

"What are those?" he asked, noting the many upraised points on the drawings, two people, etched to be identical.

When he reached to touch one, Lucia hissed, "Careful. Don't press on any of the protruding rocks."

As he studied the small stones embedded within the larger ones, realization dawned. "These are like buttons. An ancient version of numbers on a safe. A code."

"I think so," Lucia said, readjusting so she could see the man carved on Ethan's side. "Take a better look at your guy," she said, pointing to the drawing. "I can't make it out from here, but if I'm right, I know how to open this entrance."

Pointing lower, she asked Ethan, "Is there a button on the lower side of that figure? Just below his ribs?"

Ethan looked. "There is. Why?"

Lucia grinned and was happy to see Ethan's mouth quirk to one side when he said, "Spill it, witch." He was as eager to find the solution as she was.

Despite roiling, pewter clouds that menaced mountain top hikers, Lucia closed her eyes and let the breeze whip her hair from her cheekbones. This was what she'd been created for, and in place of parents who might spare her some affection, she'd been given other gifts instead.

An inquisitive mind, financial comfort, and the drive to go after the legends of lost worlds.

And she loved it all. The adventure. The thrill of discovery. No, she didn't hunt relics for fame or fortune. She didn't need money and didn't seek recognition. But she yearned for freedom, the chase, delving into the earth's secrets to prove to herself that she was worthy.

Lucia had learned she could face impossible challenges and with wit and determination, she could emerge the victor.

As she'd told Ethan before, getting to the right place was all up to magic, and for that, she would take no credit. But after she arrived? The digging, clue-solving, sweaty-muscle-straining work of truly uncovering the find?

That was what she lived for. What made her blood rush fast

and hard. Caused her body to tingle all over while her mind furiously clicked pieces of puzzles together to find the way. The next step. The next test.

How could she ever explain the feeling to anyone?

She found Ethan's eyes on hers, an eager grin teasing his firm lips, and she knew. She would never have to explain herself to him. He already understood.

Ethan Drake. Demon hunter and explorer by default. Guess he was more like Kylie's adventure video game hero than he realized.

"The Incan culture followed three simple and basic laws," she told him. "*Munay. Llankay. Yachay.*"

"I've heard of this," Ethan said as he inspected the carvings again. "And each of them relates to a particular chakra, similar to Buddhism. Chakras that are associated with parts of the body."

Lucia could tell by the rapid spill of his words that he'd reached the same conclusion she had. "These twins have far too many stones that might be pressed, and the number of combinations is astronomical. However, if we use the three laws as our guide..."

"And push the buttons at the corresponding body part in the same order as the three laws..." Ethan trailed off to scan the bodies inscribed on the wall. "This will work. The buttons aren't duplicated on both figures."

"That's what gave it away," Lucia said. She drew a deep breath then exhaled shakily. "What have we got to lose? The first law of the Incas was *Munay,* unconditional love associated with the *heart.*" Putting emphasis on the last word, she pressed the stone located in the chest of the carving closest to her.

"The next is *Llankey,*" she said. "This one is yours."

"I'm ready."

"*Llankey* is linked to our ability to do work, as well as our animal selves." Lucia nodded and Ethan lifted his hand. "The button below the ribs but above the groin."

He pushed and watched as the small stone sank into the wall, just as Lucia's had.

"The last is yours as well," Lucia told him. "*Yachay* refers to our wisdom and the perceptive third eye. The middle of the forehead."

"There's a button," Ethan said. "Hold on, because who knows what's going to open or where." He pressed the jutting stone at the top and in the middle of his twin's face.

A deep, grinding rumble sounded beneath them, and Lucia had to lean away from the wall to look down. "Something's moving down there." Then she recognized the heavy *clunk* that reverberated before the grinding started again but with a different tone.

"Jump!" she cried to Ethan. "The door is already closing!" She let go and spun to leap at the same time as Ethan. Landing then pivoting, she slung herself through the opening that was now beneath the carving. The space was only a few feet high, so she had to bend down to make it.

The door was growing smaller, and Ethan was twice her size. "Ethan!" she called, but his shoulders surged through the doorway before he did a diving roll. He barely made it through, with one foot scraping between the shutting stone and the waiting wall.

His momentum had saved him. The massive stone would have crushed his ankle and foot.

When the last bit of light was blocked out, Lucia thrust her hand out to find Ethan. "Don't move." With an ease born of practice, she found the correct compartment in her pack and retrieved two flashlights.

Ethan held a hand up to block his eyes when she shone one at him. "Can't you just light your finger?" he joked, taking the thin, silver tube from her.

Lucia sat back on her backside and took a glance around

them. She shrugged. "Some habits die hard."

~~~

Ethan was crouched down, his head and spine suffering the occasional painful scrape on the low ceiling. "Tell me the tunnel won't be this cramped the whole time," he said.

Lucia moved to look at him and banged her own head. "Ouch." She rubbed the sore spot. "Doubtful. They probably didn't waste much time excavating a secret entrance. Once we get to the working parts, we should have more room."

"Surely there isn't that much usable interior."

"This mountain towers almost ten thousand feet above the Utacamba River and the valley below." Her pack scraped along the wall. "Plenty of room in this big boy for tunnels and underground dwellings."

"Great," Ethan said, but he was secretly excited about the discovery.

Their optimism was rewarded when they broke free of the squat tunnel to find themselves in a much larger channel. The walls here were wide enough to allow large objects to pass through. Most likely early forms of equipment.

Ethan ran his hand over a side panel where several stones had been etched, like the ones above ground, only the inscriptions he saw now appeared to be writing. With the blackness waiting for them beyond the flashlight beams and strange markings in the subterranean tunnel, Ethan made up his mind.

The ruins were now officially spooky.

"This way," Lucia said, leading him to the left. "The path heads down."

Ethan fell in behind her, marveling at her steady hand and rapid assessment skills. She'd nailed the puzzle of the twins and their code in under a minute. With solid steps she barreled into the yawning cavern of millennia-old tunnels without a moment's hesitation.

The coven's prophecy and the forces that mastered it apparently knew what they were doing. No finer choice could have been made to guide him into hell's fury than Lucia Ruiz, the Spanish *bruja*.

And no other woman would he so gladly shadow, trusting every instinct or impulse she had.

Ethan was optimistic for his own reasons, though. He believed Lucia would guide them to the dagger as well as the bracelet, and then he could test the artifact's power.

Could the band truly override his curse? Even if it did, would he be brave enough to test it?

After all, his life wasn't the one in jeopardy.

He studied Lucia as she moved ahead fearlessly. If he'd ever wanted a chance at a real life, to share love with a good woman, there was no better opportunity than the one walking beside him.

But first he had to be sure.

Soon. Soon he would tell her everything. When the band was on his wrist and her death was no longer a possibility. At least, not at the Seraphim's hands.

There was still the very real threat of the Qara Mikuna to deal with, and Lucia was leading them straight to their den.

After almost five minutes of trailing lower and lower, Lucia stopped at a four-way juncture. "I can't tell which one to take," she said. "I can sense the dagger, but the pulse of it is still directly below.

"So we test each of them. Eventually we'll see which ones head up." Ethan took point and chose to go left, but soon they felt the gradual incline and decided they were heading back up. In the wrong direction. The same thing happened when they returned to the intersection and took the tunnel straight across from where they'd originally come.

"That was quick. So the right tunnel should go down." Lucia

jerked her head in that direction. "I have a good feeling about this one. Not my natural GPS kind of feeling. More of a women's intuition." She laughed lightly.

Ethan smiled and shook his head. They were about to face undead demon creations who wanted to eat them. Yet Lucia could laugh.

The pathway began curving after a few yards, winding around and around like a spiral staircase with no steps. Clearly the tunnel was constructed to allow faster descent, so Lucia's pace picked up, as did Ethan's.

He was sure they were about to find something meaningful. That they were indeed on the correct course.

At the bottom of the winding tunnel, the space opened up into a huge room, so large the soaring walls were reinforced with wooden beams. Flashing his light around, he could see an enormous door at the far end and what looked like chandeliers hanging from above.

"There must be a counterweight for that door," Lucia said. "It's too heavy to work without one."

Moving to her side, Ethan tugged on her hair to get her attention then directed his light toward the ceiling. "What are those?"

Lucia walked forward, shining her beam to get a better look. "They're braziers. Old style lanterns. They're massive." She rubbed her lips together, and Ethan could tell she was deep in thought.

"I think we should light them," she finally told him. "We've had to solve two riddles thus far. I can't believe we simply have to open the big door at the end of the room."

"Does seem obvious." He swung his light around some more. "What are we going to burn?" Then he spied misshapen piles off to one side. "Here. This looks like kindling and some sort of moss."

"And I've found the chains to lower the braziers." She

unfastened the thick chain from a hook embedded in the wall. "The Incas were amazing engineers, but they were wise to take control of the Chachapoyan fortress. With it already built, they just made themselves at home and started living. Then they had time to dig out all of this inside the mountain."

"But they weren't so lucky. They were eventually terrorized by the Earthshaker and his harem." Ethan filled the first brazier with the makings for a fire.

"Yet still they used their skills of technology to forge the dagger." Her body language changed as she took a pause before adding, "And the bracelet."

"Yeah." He quickly moved to fill the second brazier as she lowered it, hoping to avoid the discussion. "Let's light these then lift them back to their original positions and see what we've got."

"Ethan."

His shoulders tensed, because he knew that strain in her voice. A question was coming that he probably wouldn't want to answer. He went to her and grabbed the chain, stunned when she held tight and wouldn't let go.

"After we get the artifacts and are clear of this place, I expect to be told everything." She tossed the chain to him and went to work on the first light. In a severe tone she tossed over her shoulder, "And I mean everything."

Ethan knew he couldn't put her off much longer, and if things went as planned, he wouldn't have to.

How angry would she be when he told her about last night? That the Seraphim had possessed her. The danger she'd been in.

The risk he'd brought to her from the moment he first started falling in love.

Ethan paused as the acceptance hit him between the eyes. He was so close, yet he couldn't say it out loud. Hell, he shouldn't even think it.

The Seraphim couldn't get wind of Ethan's true feelings.

Would he ever be able to vocalize what he felt for Lucia? The fear of losing her might force him to lie to her. Forever.

Shame washed over him at once. No. He couldn't deny her the love she so desperately wanted. If that was in fact what he was feeling. But how would he know? He'd spent years eradicating any hint of emotion that managed to slip past his barriers.

But when he'd watched Lucia dance around the fire. When she'd held the little girl and smiled. When she'd lain in his arms, burning with fever. He'd known.

He did care about her, and so much more than he'd ever believed possible.

Then the Seraphim had come.

That was it then. Ethan had to find that bracelet and be free of the curse. He had to. And Lucia deserved the truth. Ethan had taken advantage of her faith for too long.

He began raising his brazier and had its chain hooked to the wall again before Lucia got started on hers. Various symbols were cast all around the room, onto the ceiling, walls, and floor. He took a quick survey but saw nothing that made any sense.

Lucia grunted under the weight of lifting the brazier as opposed to the easier task of lowering it, so Ethan went to her and gripped the chain. With his hands next to hers, they pulled and lifted the second lantern.

"Thanks," she said, dusting the rust from her hands.

The second brazier was still swaying above them, and so were the symbols it cast out. The pair of them studied the yellow pictures the fire produced from inside the large hanging lamps. "I don't see anything," Lucia said, sounding disappointed.

"Me, either." Ethan was beginning to feel the claws of frustration raking their way from his gut to his throat. *I have to have the band.*

Then Lucia snapped her fingers. "Look. None of the symbols

make any sense by themselves." She gestured to the middle of the two walls. "But look at what happens when the ones from the different braziers cross over each other."

She took tentative steps to one side as if lining up her sight. "It's all about the angle," she said, enthusiasm putting a bounce back in her stride. "There's a sun, with the circle being cast from one light and the rays coming from the other. And look." She pointed fervently. "There's a goat. Or horse."

Ethan went to align himself with her so he could see the symbols as she did. "Remarkable. Those Incas were sly, weren't they?" Then he found what they'd been looking for. "Lucia. At the base of that wall. One line a curve and the other straight with a point. What do they create when put together?"

She literally clapped her hands. "A serpent swallowing an arrow. Genius!"

Grabbing her pack to take along, because they remembered how quickly the last hidden wall had closed on them, Lucia hurried to the designated point and started running her hands over the stones.

Ethan joined her, and they felt one of the hefty, square stones start to give. Looking at each other and sharing a moment of triumph, they pushed together and were rewarded by a chain reaction that caused three stones to pull back and move to one side.

Taking Lucia's hand, he guided her through the breach in the wall and held her to his chest for safety. The stones crashed back into place right behind them.

They were in a sort of cubicle now, with one lone doorway at the opposite end. The entrance was clear, showing the way to a room on the other side. No apparent tricks or clues. Dragging his eyes up, Ethan discovered scratches above the door.

Still holding hands, he and Lucia edged closer, slowly, cautiously. "I don't have any idea what that says," he told her, "but somehow I think it's a warning."

Lucia tightened her grip in his fingers. "Beware all ye who enter here and curses, rot, and death?" She sent him a dazzling smile before swinging her pack up to her shoulder. "Yeah. I get that a lot."

When she readied herself to take the lead, Ethan put his hand on her shoulder and stopped her with his stare. "Don't forget. Fire destroys them." He kissed her quickly on the lips and enjoyed her look of shock. "And be careful. I bet they'd love to sink their teeth into a tasty witch like you."

She put her hand lightly over his then nodded. "I won't forget." She squared her shoulders. "I think this is it, Ethan. We're about to enter the harem's lair."

Stepping in front of her and ignoring her gasp of outrage, Ethan forced her aside. No way was he letting her go first. As a powerful woman and one of the prophesied nine, Lucia could definitely take care of herself.

But Ethan was suddenly overcome by the need to protect her, and if anyone was getting chewed on by a Qara Mikuna, it might as well be him. Then there would be no curse for the Seraphim to fulfill.

And Lucia would be safe.

Deciding he'd rather defeat his demon on his own terms, Ethan shook off the idea of dying beneath a mountain in Peru. After two decades of bondage, he was on the verge of uncovering the very artifact that would set him free.

He strode into the darkened room with his machete in one hand and holy water in the other. He could sense Lucia fuming from behind him, but for now he had other things to worry about.

His gut clenched and his nape tingled as he wondered what they would find on the other side of the door. *Brace yourself, Drake, because the witch was right.*

He cast himself into the shadows. *This is it.*

28

"Watch where you're going," Lucia told Ethan, unable to hide the bite in her words. His hero act of putting himself in front of her rankled. "Don't interfere with my challenge, Ethan. I won't have my mission hijacked."

"Relax, witch. I fully expect and want you to be here with me." He shot her a smartass look. "You've got the fire. Remember?"

"Yeah. I do." With that, Lucia sent a flame from her hand to light a torch on the wall. She knew it was a petty display of power and temper, but if the big man needed a reminder of who and what she was, then she'd be more than happy to give it to him.

"Seriously," she said as she lit three more conveniently placed torches. "Watch your step until we see what we've got. The Incas didn't exactly leave a welcome mat out or directions on where to find the dagger."

She scanned the room, looking for any type of shrine or monument. The dagger wouldn't be in plain sight, not after all the puzzles they'd had to complete just to get this far.

Lucia's hair tingled all over her body. She had a *un presentimiento malo* about this room. A bad feeling. The layout felt wrong. Like something was off. "Don't. Touch. Anything." She held Ethan's dark gaze with her own to ensure he understood.

She'd learned to listen to her gut during expeditions. Especially when it stood up and yelled at her.

"I don't see much of anything," Ethan said, but at least he was standing stock-still. "Maybe we're too late."

The possibility of someone else having beaten Lucia to the dagger made her stomach flip before she calmed herself. "No. I've followed the dagger all this way. I wouldn't have felt the attraction if it weren't here."

"That's true." He held out one arm to wave a hand. "Then where do we go from here? This place is completely empty."

"Give me a minute," Lucia said, easing forward but watching where she stepped. The longer she studied the room, which was at least twenty feet wide and over twice as long, the more she was able to define what bothered her. "In the far wall, some of the mortar between the stones looks darker." She shook her head. "But that's an illusion."

Ethan stuck his head forward, peering at the wall. "No mortar at all," he finally concluded.

"That's what I think. So there's a portion that moves."

"Then we should inspect it more closely." Ethan looked to her before taking a step, deferring to her judgment.

Lucia licked her lips nervously. She could use some lip balm but was too afraid to take her focus off the problem they were facing. The room might seem empty and safe, but a thread of caution still tickled her sixth sense.

She usually did this part of the job by herself, and having Ethan here only gave her something else to worry about. And she knew she was missing something. A big something.

But her brain felt slippery, and the pieces wouldn't click together. They just kept floating by each other. Not connecting.

"You stay where you are, and I'll make my way to the wall." She glanced to him, his tall frame still tense and unmoving. "I don't suppose you remember anything from your journal that might apply to this situation."

Ethan shook his head, slowly moving back and forth as if he were racking his own memory for a clue. "No. But you're right. This room seems off kilter, but I can't figure out why."

Lucia looked down to examine the floor. After a painstaking search for any telltale signs, she said, "I'll go first. For safety's sake, just step where I step."

"Aye, aye, Captain." He tried for lightheartedness but fell short. They both sensed the peril surrounding them, and the inability to target its source only increased anxiety.

Lucia placed a hesitant foot on the stone ahead and to her right. For some reason she felt better keeping to the center of the room. Nothing happened, and the breath rushing out of her told her how edgy she actually was.

Control your emotions, she chided herself, fully aware that panic killed more swiftly and surely than any bullet, stone, or plummet to the ground.

"When I move to the next stone, I want you to step on the one I'm on now." She took a deep breath as Ethan nodded. Then she faced the far wall again and studied the floor. There was a pattern here. She was sure of it! But damn if she could decipher the design.

Choosing the square that was directly to the fore of her position, she stepped solidly and felt a rush of giddy relief when again, nothing happened.

"I think the two stones you've stepped on are a bit lighter in color," Ethan said after moving to the place she'd just vacated. "If there are any cracks in the mortar, I can't see them, but I feel like you do. The floor is the danger."

"I'm going to try something," Lucia said. His words had triggered a memory. "I don't have a metal pole or I would tap the ground for any changes in tone." She looked over her shoulder to Ethan. "I do have a touch of telekinesis, though. Not nearly as strong as Viv, but the rest of us have been working on the ability."

"What are you going to do?" Ethan sounded doubtful.

"I'm just going to test for movability in the stones. If I get a reaction, I won't step there."

He gave a concerned groan. "I guess. Sounds risky."

Lucia waved him off. "I'll be careful. Just don't—"

"Move," he finished for her. "Yeah, I got it. I'm a quick learner that way."

"Smartass," she said with a grin, feeling more in charge of the precarious situation. Channeling a light and easy flow of her power to the next stone of her choosing, Lucia tested its stability but avoided pushing too hard. She wanted to see if the square would move at all, not shake the entire foundation on which they stood.

With no tremble or scrape of any kind, she felt confident moving to stand there. Then she applied her new experiment to another limestone panel. When it moved the slightest amount with a low, scratchy sound, she immediately stopped and said, "That one's no good."

She knew her smile was bright, and maybe a bit too cocky, but her plan was working. Maybe she and Ethan wouldn't die today. "All right." She pulled her pack up tighter and pointed to the floor. "What about that one?"

"Give it a try." Ethan was experiencing a break from the tension as well. His tone more at ease.

When Lucia sent a ripple of force toward the next stone, she felt a change right away.

"Stop. Stop!" Ethan yelled, holding his hands out like a man trying to find balance.

Too late, Lucia could feel it. She'd triggered something with the last stone, and a mild shockwave was shuddering from somewhere below the floor. Heading straight for them.

"Where, Lucia, where?" He was turning in a circle, looking for the break they knew was about to happen.

"I can't—" she broke off when the stones beneath her feet began to tilt then lost her breath as terror swooped into her lungs. Not an individual stone but an entire panel of multiple pieces! The last stone she'd tested had activated a chain reaction.

"Lucia!" She heard Ethan's yell right before something heavy hit her on her back. Tumbling forward, she landed and scraped her palms and knees but rolled to regain her feet as a loud wrenching noise filled the chamber.

Ethan was on his knees where she'd just been. He'd pushed her out of the way and was falling in her place. Falling! She threw her power out like a net, trying to hold him up until he could make his way to safer ground.

He tried to scramble up the huge piece of floor as it dropped from beneath him, the angle growing steeper every second. "Go!" he yelled at her as his hand slapped against smooth limestone. "Go!"

Then he was gone.

"Ethan," she cried, going to the very edge of the stable floor to throw herself down. She stared into the darkness but couldn't see him. She couldn't hear his voice.

With a shaking hand she grabbed her flashlight and held it into the gaping hole. The panel was rising again, shifting back into place, but she had just enough time to make sense of what she saw.

Not a straight drop down, but a deep slope. Ethan had slid down to... *Dios.* She couldn't let her mind go there. How far had he slipped into the mountain's core? Were there caves beneath? Caverns he could fall into? Or water?

As hysteria shrouded around her and sought to take control, she clenched her hands together and breathed. *Find him. Just find him.*

Ethan's handsome face swam into focus as she pictured his dark, stern eyes and the mouth that smiled too rarely. She imagined the way he'd looked at her when she was sick. The surprising concern he'd shown her, and the care he'd taken to make her comfortable.

She not only felt the pull that helped her find things, people, objects, or whatever she sought, but she experienced something else as she searched for Ethan's life force. A softer, gentler force was tugging as well.

And it was wrenching on her heart.

"Please, Ethan. Be alive so I can find you." As the tentacles of her special gift stretched their way through her surroundings, she let her thoughts drift to the hard man she'd come to care about. The stubborn, closed-off man who had more claim on her emotion than he deserved.

Damn you, Ethan. Be there!

Then she felt him. A kernel of warmth somewhere below but not directly underneath. He was alive, but she couldn't tell whether or not he'd been injured. "Hold on," she said to the empty room, more determined than ever to find the dagger and move on to the task of locating Ethan.

She prayed he was unharmed.

With a new and unbridled wrath sparking inside her, Lucia stood again and faced the wall. She had no idea how to open the hidden panel she felt sure was there, but at this point, she didn't give an Incan damn about the rules.

Strong emotion always heightened the power she and her sisters possessed, and now was as good as any time to use that strength. She held out her hands as if to grasp the wall itself, forcing a surge of telekinetic power from her fingers. When the stones started to tremble, she knew she'd triggered something again.

This time the mechanics inside the wall were activated, and a large, arched portion began to shift, ever so slightly. Then, as if a small obstruction had given way, the insert turned smoothly, gracefully, to reveal what looked like a shrine or memorial on the other side. All around the edges of the stone, engravings depicted scenes of carnage and death.

A picture of a giant creature with horns and dark fangs was among other representations of chaos and brutality. Women with profoundly voluptuous bodies were devouring people everywhere. Men, women, children, animals.

Judging by the artwork, the Earthshaker and his murderous harem had brought anarchy to the Incan people. And here, in a place of sanctity and secrecy, was the dagger that had finally brought the demon to his end.

Lucia sucked in a cool breath as she reached for the dagger. There was no time to waste on reverence, because Ethan needed her help. Still, she couldn't deny the connection to the warm metal—*how could it feel heated?*—and the gleaming black obsidian on its hilt.

Beneath the stand that had held the blade, Lucia saw a bowl-like shape carved into the stone. A silver band rested inside, also adorned with the polished lava rock. She allowed herself a moment of relief then she lifted the piece of jewelry from the indentation, storing it and the dagger securely within her bag.

And as soon as she'd removed the sacred objects, a familiar shrieking began to fill the room. If voices could quake their way through walls of stone, then the Qara Mikuna were doing just that. They had been summoned by the disturbance of their treasure, the weapon they had been ordered to defend.

Lucia didn't spend too long pondering the fact that they hadn't attacked until the pieces had been removed. She was too busy battening down any loose article on her person.

The cannibalistic bitches had come for her flesh, and their previous acts of horror would look like a day at the fair compared to what they would do to the transgressor of their temple. The witch who had taken their sacred bounty.

Planting her feet and readying her magic, Lucia saw

movement from the corner of her eye. A side door had opened, offering a way out of the deadly room. But could it be another trap?

She was about to make her way over and risk whatever lay on the other side of the opening, because she simply had no other choice. But a flash of gold and pink streaked through the air, cutting off her escape.

Another streak of gold and pale blue went over her right shoulder, slicing through her shirt and skin as it went. Pressing her hand to the wound, Lucia whirled to face her adversaries, searching the corners and ceiling for any trace of color.

These hags had more than sharp teeth at their disposal. And the proof was right in front of her. A transparent woman wearing a light blue dress, vaguely reminiscent of a toga, shimmered as she slowed long enough to take true form.

The spirit's body glimmered, her skin seemingly embedded with gold dust. She held up her vicious, golden claws for Lucia to see her own blood. Then the hag licked her digits like a human would greasy fingers. She said something in a gravelly voice, in what Lucia assumed was an Incan dialect.

Then the spirit held out her arms to scream, and Lucia's heart beat painfully. So many colors started to fill the room. *Mi dios, how big was the demon's harem?* The entire palette of the rainbow flowed around her. And then some.

Her amulet warmed against her skin, and she was reminded of her own magical color. She was red, the color of fire. And she would make these hags burn.

Then she thought of the other gemstones in her necklace, and the strength she carried with her. She saw her sisters' faces, the coven joined in a circle, conjuring their mighty forces.

I am a witch of the Savannah coven.

Lucia dropped her pack to the floor.

I am of the nine.

The Qara Mikuna started laughing and shrieking all around

her, one of them chomping her jaws like a shark, then laughing uncontrollably.

And will have what I came for. All of it. The dagger, my challenge, my destiny.

Ethan.

The man she loved was somewhere inside this mountain. Possibly injured, but definitely in need. She didn't have time to be dinner for a bunch of moldering, demon-ish whores.

"You think you want a bite of me?" she said, feeling the burn race down her arms. "Didn't your demon master warn you about me? My time has come, and I was fated to find the blade." Now Lucia smiled, feeling the ferocity of her own will.

"And I've got something none of your other victims had." Taking aim at the bitch who'd carved her shoulder, she opened her hand and torched the cackling fiend.

Screams erupted from the golden spirit, her light blue dress burned first then spread to her shimmering hair and skin. The process was not a fast one, and the cries of agony hurt Lucia's ears, but she was emboldened by her success.

Then the others started circling her, a swarm of monsters in pretty dresses, around and around in a blur of color. Soon she was in the center of a tornado, one with raking claws and snapping teeth.

"Let's do this," Lucia yelled, pumping herself up to spray the chamber with fire, burning every last stone to cinder if that's what it took.

Then she saw something that shook her to the depth of her soul. Two of the Qara Mikuna slipped through the stones, down into the floor. And she knew with dreadful certainty they were not fleeing from her.

They were going after Ethan.

29

Lucia started shooting randomly, blasting fire from both hands like a dual-stream flame thrower. The whirl of Qara Mikuna began to break apart as many of them combusted and screeched their final agonies.

As the golden monsters spread out, Lucia could see they were planning a new assault. With their transparent forms pressed high against the ceiling and flanking all four sides of the chamber, they started peeling off one at a time to come at her.

The first one, in a blur of golden skin and yellow dress, dove for Lucia's face with claws hooked and jaws spread. Her intent was clear, latch onto the mortal's head and eat whatever flesh those sharp fangs sank into.

But Lucia's reflexes were quicker, and she doused the hag with fire, experiencing a burst of satisfaction when the vile creature missed her and fell to the floor. The female rolled toward the corner where she continued to burn, and her gold-flecked skin soon transformed to a pile of charred and seared refuse.

Another caught Lucia unaware, sinking her claws deep into her left shoulder blade. "Ahh!" The scream was ripped from her as excruciating pain swarmed into her body. The sting of the sharp claws wasn't any normal penetration. Black, putrid poison oozed from those talons, destroying tissue like the strongest of acids.

So she didn't think to reach around with her hand but instead channeled her magic straight to the left side of her back where the thing was latched on, burning claws buried deep into Lucia's muscles.

The rush of her power must have worked, because the fiendish woman flew off her back, writhing and screaming as if tormented by an unseen attacker. The guardian stopped suddenly, pausing long enough to take one long look at Lucia.

Then she erupted from the inside out, exploding into flames and burning faster than the others before her.

Interesting. That was a new trick, for sure, Lucia thought, and now the area around her shoulder blade felt better, too, as if the flow of magic had somehow purged the hag's venom.

Taking out a few more of the Qara Mikuna with blasts of fire, Lucia started edging her way to the door. The exit was still there, waiting for her to make good on an escape, and she had to locate Ethan as soon as possible.

Bound by their curse to ever defend the dagger, the remaining Qara Mikuna had no choice but to follow Lucia, trailing after her as she stumbled through the opening and into a corridor. The pathway led in two directions. One way went up, and the other went down.

Ethan had slid into the bowels of the mountain, so she automatically veered in that direction. Two more harem females met their end through flame, twisting and turning as their pretty dresses and golden bodies burned.

Another came after Lucia but halted the chase and hovered. If long-dead demon spawn could get a calculating look in their eyes, this one did just that. What was she waiting for?

Lucia didn't intend to find out. She thrust a ball of fire right at the fiend and watched incredulously as the Qara Mikuna split herself right down the middle. Now there were two creatures, but not of the human—or used to be human—variety.

On both sides of the tunnel sat large, olive-toned reptiles, vaguely resembling Komodo dragons. Their skin was dry and wrinkly, and they were still transparent to a degree, just as the hags were.

They flicked long, thin tongues at Lucia, and she could see they still possessed sharp, jagged fangs. She'd had enough of being nibbled on, *gracias*. So she flicked both palms upright and incinerated the ghastly lizards.

Shauni would understand.

Throwing flames over her shoulder, she continued to decrease the number of her assailants and was thankful when they thinned out enough for her to slow and catch her breath.

She kept a watchful eye on the corridor behind her as she sent out another wave of her magic to search for Ethan. She'd gone much farther into the earth and wanted to make sure she didn't pass him by.

The occasional tunnel shot off to the side, providing new and unexplored passageways, but she opted to get as close to the level he was on before she started branching out. How far had the Incas dug into the mountain? She couldn't fathom the man hours it had taken.

Another hag tried to be stealthy, creeping close before speeding out from around the corner, but Lucia caught her before she made it halfway. She blew off the tip of her finger like the barrel of a gun then continued searching for Ethan.

He was close, and he was alive. Now all she had to do was navigate the twisting channels. They were much rougher than the ones far above, more dirt than stone, and not braced nearly as well. What kind of pit might Ethan have fallen into? She shuddered and made herself forge ahead. He was not much farther down.

Soon the tunnel evened out, and she could tell the area had

been cleared out for greater use. For something like building a trap, perhaps? A collection tank for any poor souls who fell through floors?

She scanned the level and sensed Ethan's location then barged down the corridor without a care for her own safety. She had to let him know she was coming. How horrible to be trapped down here in the dark. Possibly injured and in pain. If he was even conscious.

When she grew closer, she called out to him. "Ethan? Where are you?"

The creature that answered was not the one she wanted. A Qara Mikuna popped out from the tunnel wall in front of her. She'd probably been lying in wait for Lucia.

Knowing she was tiring from the rush of adrenaline and magic, Lucia waited until she had the hag in her sights before she tossed a conservative fire ball.

The guardian didn't just divide herself into two smaller targets to avoid the shot. She shattered into a hundred small forms.

Lucia jumped back from the sheer revulsion of the metamorphosis. Spiders. Everywhere. They covered the floor, walls, and ceiling, and were all skittering toward her.

So much for rationing power. She could just imagine hundreds of arachnid fangs biting into her. With the added bonus of Qara Mikuna poison. A hundred tiny fangs to sear her flesh.

Feeling like some guy she'd seen in a military movie—she couldn't recall the title—Lucia put her arms together in front of her with her hands side by side. The tunnel erupted with flames as she razed the creepy-crawlies until their jointed bodies shriveled into crunchy coals.

They dropped to land on the dirt floor, and she took particular pleasure in crushing what was left of them under her boots.

"Ethan?" she cried out, louder this time, despite the attention she might draw.

Soon she heard a dim but repetitive sound. A voice, a human voice, was muffled by the walls, but she had enough of a bead on it to follow the corridor to the next doorway. She pushed with all her might to open the stone door, and once it was clear, she could hear Ethan's yell.

"Lucia. Over here!" He sounded almost frantic. "Hurry!" then under his breath. "Damn things. Ow!"

Oh no.

The walkway in front of Lucia was narrow, the path a mixture of rocks and dirt that ran between two rows of roughshod rooms dug out of the stone itself. Small openings served as doors, but many of them still had metal bars preventing passage in or out.

As she skidded to a halt outside of the compartment Ethan's voice was coming from, she realized they were in a crude and primal type of prison. Kneeling to look through the door, if it even deserved the name, she saw Ethan fighting off swarms of spiders with his backpack.

Whichever hag had attacked him must have taken the precaution of transforming into so many small creatures to avoid Lucia's fire. *Sorry, you evil harem bitch. I'm still going to fry you. Each and every hairy, eight-legged piece of you.*

"Come toward me and put your back against this front wall!" Lucia yelled to Ethan. "Quick."

Without asking why, Ethan did just as she'd told him, and as soon as he cleared the mass of spiders that had gathered around him, she shot a stream of fire over the floor, lighting up most of the biting bugs with one shot.

There were still plenty scrabbling around in there, though, and Ethan would feel their poison acutely if he were bitten. Bitten any more, that is.

"Kill some more," he called out then. "I think you're helping my hand by destroying the guardian."

Lucia remembered how the pain in her shoulder blade

had disappeared. She'd thought her magic had cured her, but eradicating the source of the venom had. With a sharpshooter's eye, she took out as many as she could, searching for any signs of movement.

Finding every hidden spot in the room was difficult from her low vantage point. And she was still outside.

"I think that's most of them." Ethan's hand flew through the bars to grab Lucia's knee. "I'm very glad to see you, witch. Never say I'm too macho to appreciate being rescued by a woman."

"Glad to be of service," she said. "Now help me get rid of these bars." Shining her light on the enclosure, she could see a couple of the metal rods had already been pulled and broken off.

"They're weak from age," Ethan supplied, answering the unspoken question. "I felt my way around in the dark and was working on them when the guardian came. I could hear her laughing and taunting, but she didn't get serious until you started calling my name."

"Did you lose your light?" she asked, working on one side of the bars while he bent and broke the other.

"I must have."

Lucia handed him her flashlight to search for his pack and any items thrown free when he'd fallen. He found his flashlight, smashed and useless, so he tossed it. In no time they had the opening cleared enough for Ethan to wedge himself through. In single file they hurried back down the confined passage and entered one of the offshoot tunnels.

"What's the best way to get out of here?" he asked, leaning against a wall with a hand to his side. He must have worn himself out fighting off the spiders.

"I have no idea. We can try to go back the way I came, but I was rushing to find you."

"So no trail of breadcrumbs to find our way back?" He worked up a tired smile before his face hardened and he seized her wrist. "The dagger. Lucia, did you get the dagger? And the..."

She knew what he wanted, but as soon as he asked, anger and hurt made her shut down. "I have the dagger, but..." How should she put it? Because she wasn't ready to reveal her last bargaining chip.

"I'm ready to get off this, rather *out of* this mountain," she said. "Then we can talk." She took off before he could ask anything else.

They trudged up the slant of the tunnel in the hopes of finding their way out, looking for any type of exit. Lucia deflected Ethan's probing questions. He wanted to return to the chamber and search for the bracelet.

But when she left him standing in the pitch black, he cursed her and jogged to catch up. "Do you have the band or not, Lucia?" He was demanding an answer, and just as she was figuring out a way to stall, Ethan grabbed her arm. "Over there," he said from behind her.

"I told you I'm getting out of here first," she snapped. Tired, hungry, hurt, and almost out of magic, she just couldn't confront him here.

Ethan had omitted so many things since the night he'd first entered Lucia's life, and now she had no idea where lies bumped up against truth. Was there any truth?

"Over there, you stubborn witch." Ethan's commanding tone stopped her in her tracks. "I see light."

"Light?" Oh, that made her happy. A person could never be sure how they would respond to being underground for any length of time, and though Lucia had done her fair share of caving, this magic mountain from hell was going to be her last foray into the earth for a long while.

A manmade door, of wood this time, hung loosely in its frame at the end of a short corridor. Ethan delivered one swift kick to the rotten material and it splintered. He shoved the pieces out of the way and looked out.

Since he stepped through the portal, and she didn't hear his plummeting scream, Lucia followed. They were on the side of the mountain, and judging by the sun in the sky, they were on the same side they'd originally climbed to find the ruins of Kuelap.

"We're out." Ethan spun to confront her. "Now talk."

"Hell no," she said, putting her hands on her hips so hard she jabbed herself. "You talk. You tell me everything about why you really came on this trip with me. And," she held up a finger when he would have retorted, "you explain what the bracelet is for. If you need it to give to your sister, then just say so. But you haven't done that, have you? No. You haven't spoken clearly or sensibly since this whole thing started."

She shoved him out of her way and trudged into the woods to start the hike toward lower ground. They could camp tonight just like any other night, but she wanted to make a start toward town and civilization.

And a hot shower.

"Lucia, you owe me the truth about what you found in that room." She heard his steps behind her and turned in time to run her finger into his chest.

"You. Owe. Me. First." Each word was punctuated by a jab to his thick, solid muscles. With angry strides, she set off again. "Walk and talk, Drake, because you're out of options."

"You know most of it already, Lucia. You do," he added when she cast a hateful look over her shoulder.

Lucia kept her eyes forward, forcing herself to be strong. To be cruel, if that's what it took to get some honesty for a change.

"What I told you about my sister is true. She suffered for weeks. So did my parents." His breaths were coming in harsh bursts, so she moderated her pace. If she wanted to hear it all, the man had to be able to speak.

"We did call in an expert, but even he couldn't help. Not the way we'd hoped. All he could do was make a suggestion." Ethan mumbled and fought with his backpack before ripping it off his shoulders to carry in one arm.

Lucia slowed to face him, one of the straps was twisted, and Ethan was too upset to deal with it. "Here." She held out her hands and began fixing the strap while Ethan paced and continued his story.

"The man who helped us said the demon would take an exchange. If he was going to leave my little sister's body, he wanted something else in return." He was staring into the forest, his back to Lucia.

From where she knelt working on the backpack she could see the heaving breaths he took. She watched his wide shoulders rise and fall as he fought with the pain of his past.

A past that still affected him.

Without elaborating, Ethan came over to her and took his gear. He slipped his pack in place and gestured for Lucia to walk ahead of him again. Unsure what had just occurred in his defensive mind, she gave him a frown and walked on.

They hiked in silence for a few minutes, but when they came to a ridge on the side of the mountain, overlooking the wide valley below, Ethan stopped. "This is as good a place as any," he said, pulling out a canteen to drink.

When he swallowed what he would and looked at her, misery was etched into every line on his face. "Please," he said, dark eyes imploring and more wounded than Lucia had thought possible. "I need to know if you found the bracelet."

She couldn't add any more weight to his already burdened shoulders. "At least you're calling it what it is," she said, releasing her own pack to set it on the ground and rummage in the storage compartments. She pulled out the bracelet but held it tight.

"I have what you want," she said. "It's safe."

The relief that sailed through him and eased his tense

shoulders made her feel awful. Maybe she'd been wrong about holding out, but at least they were finally having a real conversation. She had to believe his short time of torment and worry would be worth it.

"What did the demon take in exchange?" she asked.

Ethan eased closer. "He wanted to take something from me, something I couldn't understand at the time. I was only a child myself, and the monster was offering me a way to save my sister."

He looked out across the valley as the wind ruffled his black hair. "I thought I was making a great deal. The Seraphim could never touch my sister again, and all I had to do was..." Swallowing hard, Ethan still avoided looking at her. "I swore to carry his curse with me always. And if I ever grew too close to a woman, if I ever opened my heart and fell in love..."

Now he did meet her stare, and his eyes were as cold and empty as a waiting grave. "If I loved a woman, he would come for her. He would kill her. Slowly."

Lucia froze in place and her breathing clutched. It felt as though a block of ice was lodged in her chest. Everything he'd said or done made horrible sense now. "What are you saying, Ethan?" A myriad of fears came at her, punching holes into the faith she'd so dutifully carried.

Was he saying to love a woman was to summon death upon her? Was that why he'd pushed her away so fiercely? Had his harsh rejections been his way of protecting her?

And if so, that meant Ethan was afraid he would come to love her. That he might be able to.

Lucia didn't know whether to be joyful or terrified. There was a chance Ethan could care for her, just as she'd dreamed, but would his affections end up killing her?

She began to understand his turmoil. There was no happy ending. A life without emotion, or love that equated to death.

"You can't be with a woman?" she asked, forcing the raspy

whisper through a tight throat. "You never have?"

Then some sanity returned as she realized she was clutching the answer in her hand. "Oh, God. I'm so sorry I kept this from you. For even a moment, but I had to hear all of it, Ethan."

He jerked back. "Hold onto it until I'm done. We've come this far." He stared at the silver band with a desperate longing yet a fierce hatred. As soon as he slipped the bracelet on, he would be bound to the artifact.

Ethan would be bound to the silver bracelet just as he had been enslaved by the Seraphim for so long.

She stepped closer. "You've lived all these years without a real connection to anyone else? Running from the possibility of love?"

"No. Not all these years." He pressed the heels of his hands against his forehead. "If you want the truth, you'll get it. But remember." His stare was heavy and cruel. "The truth isn't always kind."

She nodded and waited, too afraid to move, scared she might spook him. And she needed to hear his story now. She had to know if there was a chance for them.

"Jessica," Ethan said, his face gone flat and eyes lifeless. "She was my high school girlfriend."

Lucia's heart crumbled into a thousand pieces when she comprehended. "Oh, Ethan." *The nightmare.* "What happened?"

"Exactly what I allowed to happen." He went utterly still. "I killed her."

30

Ethan's hands were clammy and cold. Sweat gathered at the base of his spine.

The memories he'd fought to forget were now swarming back like angry bees. And they stung furiously. His mind, his stomach, down every nerve ending, until finally, they attacked his heart.

"I was seventeen and had never spent much time with any one girl. Years had passed since my sister's possession, and my body had grown, my mentality had shifted priorities." He barked a mirthless laugh. "Hell. I'd practically forgotten about my deal with the demon."

His gaze slid to Lucia, meeting the soft brown eyes that would turn scathing when she heard everything. "I met Jessica, and she was all that was naïve and innocent." He smiled. "But for her gentle nature, she had a bawdy sense of humor. Before I knew it we were an item."

"I'd started falling headfirst and didn't even know it." He remembered his own wonder and awe at the new experience. Elation just to think of that one special person, wanting to spend every available moment with them. Hearing their laugh, their hopes, their dreams.

The bittersweet crush of first love. He'd been too young to

know better but old enough to feel he could control that rush of pure joy. The kind that made the whole world glow.

"Then one Saturday night in the fall of our senior year, she gave me her virginity." Ethan's entire body clutched with sickening regret. "I told her how I felt, and the words were barely out of my mouth before the evil bastard showed up."

He felt Lucia's hand on him but couldn't bear to face her. "Maybe the turmoil of emotions and the thrill of sex with someone I cared about made me reckless. I know that sounds callous, but in the back of my mind I always thought of girls as recreation only. They had to be."

He pulled away from Lucia, unable to take the offered comfort with the stone of treachery still sitting in his gut. "Ironic, isn't it? The first female I showed true concern for was punished because of it."

Ethan watched as clouds rolled over the sky. Did he imagine the wind growing stronger, becoming colder and more brutal?

"She was still lying on the blanket we'd thrown under the trees when the bastard entered her bloodstream." Ethan jammed a hand through his hair. "He rushed into her body and flicked those yellow, snake eyes at me. Then he said, 'She will burn.' I tried to take the words back, the feelings I'd shared so selfishly. But then Jessica looked at me, she was there for a moment, feeling the shock, the agony. Her eyes were so wide, so confused. Then her mouth fell open and she screamed. Head back, muscles tensed until I thought she'd snap her own neck."

"She was burning, just like the Seraphim said. From the inside out." Nausea rose in Ethan's throat as the memory crystallized. The horror, the guilt, the helplessness. "I was such a fool, hoping the demon had just forgotten about me. That he'd moved on to someone else."

"Damn it." He whirled on Lucia. "But he will always be with me, watching and waiting. Taunting me with what I can never have."

"Ethan," Lucia began softly, "it wasn't your fault."

"Of course it was! I killed her with my own needs. I was short-sighted. Even though the bastard didn't give me any warning signs like he has with you, I should have known better. I should have been stronger!"

When Lucia's mouth dropped, Ethan realized what he'd said, what he'd let slip out in his rage.

Lucia frowned. "What do you mean he's given you signs? About me?" Her eyes darted as she let the new information sink in. She'd been totally unaware of the demon slinking around, invading her mind and body when it chose.

Now she would know Ethan had lied to her. He'd never warned her, fearing the truth would do more harm than good. Even as he'd come to admire her. Then like her.

And finally, letting her cause real emotion in his long-cold heart.

"The more I tried to push you away and tell myself you were the last female on earth I would want," he shook his head, "the more you dug yourself into my thoughts." Reaching out to her, he said, "I should have tried harder. I should have been more explicit, but you're so damned brave and confident."

She latched onto his arm when he would have touched her. She shoved him away. "What signs were there? Tell me."

He let his hands drop. "Your being sick wasn't from a virus, or exhaustion, or exposure to the rain," he said. "I tried to tell myself it was one of those things, but deep down, I knew better."

"You think it was the demon." Her expression was unreadable.

Ethan nodded solemnly. "And the yellow eyes you thought you saw while you showered."

He could see the fury coursing through her now, building as she became more incensed. Still, he couldn't afford to tread lightly. She had to understand that even a witch of her power would be at the mercy of the curse.

If Ethan fell in love with her, completely heart-wrapped around her love...

Then she was dead.

"Last night in camp," he said, his voice harsh and unflinching, "the Seraphim came to you. He was inside you, controlling your body, your mind, your voice."

Lucia shook her head and took a step back. "No. That's not possible. I would have known." She put her hand to her throat. "My magic would have stopped him. He can't touch me or he'll turn to ash."

"You're wrong. The world beyond this one plays by its own set of rules. You are part of my bargain by default. Your strength and abilities mean nothing." Ethan felt a punch to his stomach when her eyes turned vulnerable.

But he had to be ruthless. Lucia couldn't brazen her way out of this one.

"He took full possession of you, but he wasn't able to kill you or hurt you." Ethan looked at her neck. "Much."

With eyes wide, Lucia echoed, "Much?" But before he could answer, she moved her fingers to the side of her throat, trailing the tips downward, just as the Seraphim had raked her nails through that same flesh last night. "I thought it was a dream."

"I cast him out," Ethan said, as comprehension bloomed in her eyes. "He was breaking a rule by taking you. He should never have touched you, because... I don't love you."

Agony seemed to slice Ethan in half. "I'm sorry, Lucia, but I don't. I just can't allow it."

Putting her hand to her temple as if to stave off a headache, she clenched her eyes shut.

Then they shot back open, the usually soft brown crackling with fury. "Well that's just great, isn't it? So all of your carefully placed lies were for nothing." She held the bracelet up and shook it, making Ethan's arms jerk with the need to grab the artifact. To keep it secure.

"All this time," she said, seething as she advanced on him. "You knew the Seraphim was affecting me, and you said nothing." She put her hands on his chest and shoved. "You have a right to keep your secrets, Ethan, but not when they put my life and my challenge in danger. That thing was in my body! And you conveniently forgot to mention it."

She held out her arms. "And why? You lay it out for me in plain English that you don't love me." Her mouth trembled, but she hardened again and said, "So what's the problem?"

Baffled, he shook his head. "What do you mean?"

"You say you don't love me." She held the silver band up between them. "Yet the demon's targeting me." She moved her hands to mimic a scale that was unbalanced. "Which is it? Either you or your demon is breaking the rules."

She leaned close to hiss, "Or one of you is lying."

Raking a hand through his hair, Ethan had to fight to keep from revealing the truth. He wanted to tell her how close he was to giving up and letting go. How close he was to admitting that he not only wanted her. But that he was falling for her.

He couldn't. He couldn't! Even in the face of her anger over his betrayal. He had to keep silent. No chance could be taken.

Until he had the band on his arm. He had to know how it felt to finally wear the talisman. Would he feel free? At long last?

And would Lucia truly be protected?

"I'm sick of this," she spat suddenly. "All of it." She thrust the bracelet toward him. "You want your prize? The real reason you're even here? Fine. Take it."

She tossed the band in the air, and Ethan almost choked. He snatched the bracelet and held it between his hands. Almost afraid to breathe, he opened his palms, still cupping the silver respectfully.

He stared, mesmerized. How could anything be so pristine after all this time underground? How could the silver band and black stone shine the way they did?

With Lucia turned away from him, Ethan moved to slide the band in place.

The wind howled around him, and he thought he heard the demon's raspy voice beneath the keening breeze. The bastard Seraphim didn't want him to put the bracelet on.

And that was all the encouragement he needed.

"Go fuck yourself, snake," he growled, slipping the artifact around his wrist. The fit was secure but not too tight, as if the silver had adjusted specifically for his arm.

What felt like a flow of warm light expanded from his forearm, crawling inch by inch up his shoulder and across his torso. Soon the protective spell covered his entire body, and unbidden energy heightened his senses.

Was it some sort of mystical trick that he suddenly scented Lucia's natural female essence? The fruity lip balm she'd managed to apply even as they'd fought to escape the black mountain tunnels?

Illusion or no, he felt like he could lift the very mountain beneath their feet. For years he'd suppressed his very male desires. Not for sex, because he'd fulfilled physical needs when necessary.

No, it was the primal and basic need to take a woman for his own that had been imprisoned by the curse. Now those demands had been liberated. He was free to take a woman's body, and for the first time, maybe a little bit more.

Or everything, he realized, staring at the only woman he'd ever needed so badly it hurt. The only one who'd forced her way past his shields, reaching him on so many levels.

The days spent with Lucia had been hard, struggling to resist her and hating the demon and the deal he'd struck. Cursing the commitment with every breath.

Now he had the bracelet. His safeguard. And, whether through magic or freedom, the passion he felt for the Spanish witch came roaring to the forefront.

No, he might not love her now, but if he could unlock that last door. Open the last compartment that waited just for her. If given half the chance...

Forcing aside the internal debate, Ethan focused instead on the one thing he *was* sure of.

He had to put his hands on Lucia. Finally and completely, without fear of retribution.

"Come here," he said, the grate of his voice sounding strange to his own ears.

"Screw you, Drake." Her hands were on her hips as she surveyed the green valley far below. She'd thrown him the bracelet and had yet to even ask how he felt.

So he'd show her.

He raked his eyes over her very female curves. Long and lean, yet voluptuous in all the right places. Despite the dirt on her clothes and her irritated stance, she was the most erotic thing he'd ever seen.

"I'm ready to take a risk now, witch." He didn't care where they were. He'd have her up against a tree, like the wild things they both were.

"Too bad," she snapped, her head jerking to the side as she spoke, giving him a lovely view of her profile. Those full lips and thick lashes.

"You've hounded me since we met. Now we can finally give this artifact a trial run," he picked the right words, "and you're too *afraid?*"

He saw her tighten up, but she remained silent.

Ethan edged around her, blocking her line of sight and forcing her to look only at him. He put a finger beneath her chin and tipped her face up. "What's it going to be, Lucia?" He skimmed that same finger down her neck, feeling the need to stroke her there and erase the memory of the Seraphim's touch.

"Are you feeling brave?"

~~~

Lucia shivered where she stood, still in awe of Ethan's transformation. He was the same man, of course, but something inside him had been released.

How had he kept a leash on the wild and driving hunger she saw in him now?

Always the one in control, always the one to lead the way and set the standards, Lucia had never experienced such raw, primal...*quivering* need. Here was a man to match her boldness. Her untamed way of attacking life and drinking it dry.

"I'm not afraid. I'm pissed off." She kept telling herself that, too, trying to ignore the width of his shoulders as he towered over her, caressing her skin like she was made of porcelain.

"I don't blame you," he said, trailing his hands down her arms before slipping beneath them to capture her waist. "But you still want me to kiss you. You still believe destiny brought me to you."

Damn him! How dare he throw that in her face?

Especially when it was true.

He dragged her slowly, inextricably into his arms, and Lucia experienced a light flutter in her chest. He was so strong, so solid, and for the first time, she felt fragile.

The idea made her want to smile, and Ethan must have noticed the tilt of her lips. "There's my audacious witch. So ready to laugh at danger. To tell fate what *she* wants it to do." He locked her against his chest and lowered his head, the black silk of his hair falling over his dark, molten eyes.

He looked more serious than ever, and all of that intensity was focused on her.

Lucia's skin heated. Her heart hammered.

With his mouth an inch from hers, their hot breath mingling

and teasing, Ethan spoke against the sensitive flesh of her lips. "You're about to get what you asked for."

Her fingers curled into his muscular shoulders, and she imagined little claws forming to sink into the solid mass of him, staking her claim. She wanted to mark this man as her own.

Mine. Forever.

Then his mouth was on hers, and there was nothing gentle about it. He ravaged her, tasting, exploring, scorching her as he held her against him and lifted her to her toes.

The liquid pull she'd felt whenever she'd looked at him was now a surge of molten liquid. She had to feel him inside of her. The heavy, throbbing ache was too strong. Too demanding.

When she pressed her hips against the hard length of him, Ethan growled and took her mouth again. Deeper, more savagely. Then he lifted her, wrapping her legs around his waist as he carried her to an outcropping of rock. He used the solid wall of stone to trap her body.

Lucia gasped when he ground against her. The expression caught between a rock and a hard place had never sounded so deliciously erotic.

He held her in place with his hips, pressing his erection against her and making her cry out. He explored the shape of her legs, her breasts, then his roughened hands slipped under her shirt to cup her. He teased her nipples without apology.

Lucia moaned, afraid she might die if he didn't get her clothes off and take her fully.

"I can't get close enough to you," he said against her neck before taking a taste of her there. "All this time. Watching you walk around with this body, those curving lips," he bit her lightly, "and those velvet brown eyes always stripping me naked, telling me exactly what you wanted."

She let her head fall against the hard, cold rock, but she didn't care. No discomfort could penetrate the rising storm between them. His tall, strong body was like the sun, rubbing and touching her all over. Liquid heat making love to every part of her.

And she was still alive. No evil Seraphim would steal her body. Not when she'd just discovered how good it felt under Ethan's greedy and skillful hands.

Her hips moved against him in a rhythm older and more insistent than either of them. She'd known sexual attraction in her life, but never this overpowering urge to possess a man completely.

And to be possessed in return. Dominated in a way that actually gave her strength instead of stealing it.

This was more than sex. For both of them.

Bending the arch of his long, powerful back, Ethan ripped his shirt over his head. She'd caught a glimpse of his tight musculature, but having the steely strength bared and pressed against her was too much. His abs rippled and she had to run her hand over the hard ridges.

He lifted her arms and removed her shirt as well. Then he curved one hand across her chest to sink under the silk of her bra. He growled.

The wind whistled through the thick green canopy, and birds called out their exotic songs. This was so perfect for them, she thought. So right.

The jolting connection had been between the two of them from the first, but only Lucia had allowed herself to recognize it for what it was.

She and Ethan were meant to be together.

Be it fate or lost souls who'd finally found each other, here, at last, was her mate. And this reckless abandon was one more step toward unity.

Toward love.

She threaded her fingers into the cool, black silk of his hair and pulled him to her. "Make love to me, Ethan," she whispered against his ear.

His hands stopped stroking her, stilling in place as he breathed heavily against her cheek. She could feel the strain in his body, but he didn't move. He didn't speak.

Finally he lifted his face from hers and stared at her. She couldn't read his expression, but a cold blast of rejection tore through her when he shook his head slowly. "No." His brow furrowed, hardening his gaze.

And damping the fire that had burned in the deep, endless brown of his eyes.

Extracting his hand as if she were poisonous, Ethan put her bra back in place before smoothly lowering her to the ground. Cold wind raked her bare skin as he pulled away, and the void between them shattered what was left of her pride.

Something had changed, and she didn't know why. The magic they'd been riding was somehow empty. Broken.

"Ethan?" she asked, the timidity of her voice sounding foreign and weak to her ears.

"I can't do this." He thrust his hand out, warding her off. "I'm sorry. I lost control."

"You said it was safe now." Humiliation warred with anger as she watched him pick up his shirt and jerk it back on. "I don't understand. Did I do something wrong?"

Lucia again heard the pleading quality in her tone and bit her bottom lip.

She had to let sharp logic dictate her behavior, because tender emotion would not sway the hard, determined man standing before her. But why had he changed so swiftly again? What had happened?

He was out of excuses, so his sudden lack of interest could only be about her. The stark misery of that was crushing. Embarrassing.

Lucia felt like an unwelcome nuisance. And that was a sentiment she hadn't felt in a long time. Now the shame and disgrace were back. She wasn't what Ethan wanted after all.

She wasn't good enough.

She was unworthy of his affection.

"You have the bracelet now, Ethan." She pushed away from the wall of granite and picked up her shirt, flicking it twice to clean it off before tugging it on. "And you were all over me just now," she added, jerking her thumb at the rock.

"Wanting someone is easy, Lucia." His dismissive tone was a stab to her chest. "But I just got the wrist band, and I'm not sure of its power." He turned heavy eyes on her, blank and emotionless. "I was reckless. Heady with excitement, but you asked me to do the one thing I can't. That I won't."

"What?" she demanded, throwing up her hands.

He stalked to her and looked down before putting a friendly hand on her shoulder. He was distant. Unaffected. "I can't make love to you."

"You don't make any sense! You have the bracelet, the sole purpose of your life's pursuits. Which I found for you!" Her eyes stung suspiciously, but she told herself it was the biting wind thrashing against the mountain. "Now *you're* too afraid to use it?" she chided, tossing his words back at him.

"Yes. That's right." He left her to retrieve his backpack. "I am too afraid."

She rushed to him and grabbed his arm, wishing she had claws for an entirely different reason now. "You're lying again, aren't you? Just telling me what you think I need to hear. Was I just a handy female form to help you test your new toy? Does it work? Did the demon come or not?"

"No," Ethan said. "He didn't come, and he never will."

"Dammit," she pushed against his shoulder when his eyes shuttered over. "Don't shut me out now. We have something between us, and it's strong and true. Are you really going to just walk away?"

"What I'm going to do, Lucia, is proceed with caution. I'm not going to throw you down and have my way with you out here with no protection. I need to go back and do more research." He turned away from her.

"No," she said, anger squeezing her lungs until she thought she would pass out. "What you need is to man up! I'm the closest you've come to loving someone since Jessica. And you know it!"

At the mention of his high school girlfriend, Ethan tensed his jaw and leaned forward just enough to display his controlled fury. "Lucia, I said no."

He left her to head toward the forest, leaving her behind with a space in her chest that felt battered and bruised. The pain pulsed inside her like an open wound. Why was he doing this?

She'd felt his desire for her, and there had been more than just sexual need bouncing between them.

Or had she been fooling herself all along?

Her pride and certainty collapsed on itself. Time and again he'd told her they were just two people in a tough situation. Forced together by circumstance and necessity.

He had what he'd come for and had decided to play with the available female. The one who'd thrown herself at him shamelessly. Never taking no for an answer.

Well, this time she would listen. No refusal had ever been so clear. So final.

Tears welled in her eyes again, but with Ethan gone she let them stream. He was too far away to see.

With her heart a bleeding wreck in her chest, Lucia pulled together every bit of shredded pride she could find.

This was the last time she would throw her herself at Ethan Drake, only to have him play with her head and leave her behind as if she meant nothing.

He and fate had both screwed her over, and she was done putting faith in those that didn't deserve it. She would never trust him again.

She wiped her cheeks on her dirty sleeve. Never again.

31

Almost a week later Lucia walked off the dock to stand where a beige, sandy beach edged up to meet the island forest. Over the tops of huge live oaks, she could make out the jutting roof and tower of the St. Germaine island home.

Castle was a more apt description, she thought, as clouds passed over a waxing moon hanging low in the sky behind the house.

Inside the wood and stone structure, the rooms were just as majestic. Generations of family had lived here, generations of witches, and while Lucia wasn't of the St. Germaine bloodline, warmth and welcome suffused her as she set off through the woods.

As she made her way towards her family.

Michael and Shauni had opted to ride the golf cart around to the house with Joe. Michael's injury was much better, but Shauni had vetoed the idea of using his leg any more than he already had. They'd flown in from Jamaica that afternoon and had walked Atlanta's huge airport.

Lucia thought Ethan was somewhere behind her in the woods, but she didn't look back. She barely registered his presence these days, ignoring him as much as possible since he'd cast her aside on the mountain ridge.

He wasn't being forced to spend time alone with her anymore, so he no longer needed to pretend. He'd gotten what he wanted then shoved her away. Wham-bam. No, thank you, Ma'am.

And he hadn't even said he was sorry.

Oh, he'd made polite conversation with her and the others in Lima, where Michael was hospitalized. Then again as they'd travelled to and stayed overnight at the tropical island hotel in Montego Bay. But Lucia was channeling a whole new personality these days. Her behavior was much like Ethan's had been in the beginning.

She kept to herself and spoke to him only as necessary. In fact, she was practically frigid. In every sense of the word.

Occasionally he'd get frustrated and try to pull her aside, but Lucia was done with the ploys and mind games. She wasn't wasting any more time on him. He was hot then cold. Tender then rebuking.

Well, if Ethan couldn't make up his mind, she'd do it for him.

At least Shauni and Michael had gotten something from this doomed expedition. The two of them had fawned all over each other in their Jamaican paradise, almost effervescent with their love and devotion for each other on display.

But instead of letting herself get weepy when she saw the two snuggling and cooing, Lucia had only prickled with anger. Her heart had grown sharp barbs of defense against the one emotion that always seemed to get the best of her. Love.

She threw her shoulders back and sneered. Lying, cheating, misrepresenting love.

Well, she wouldn't be fooled again. *Bruja sola hasta la muerte.* That was her new motto. Single witch forever.

Glad to be rid of her torn and dirty backpack, she carried only a petite tote with her through the woods. She'd stored any salvageable hiking equipment back at her hangar space. Her now empty space.

But the bag in her hand held a very important box. Strong

and sturdy, inlaid with black velvet, as befitted an ancient, demon-killing dagger.

Lucia arrived just as the golf cart pulled up to the mansion and the double front doors swung wide. Kylie led the pack down the stairs and greeted her with a hug. Then she went to Shauni, while Willyn instructed them to get Michael to the couch where she could see to his injury.

Whatever wound was left would be healed shortly. Willyn didn't ration her gift when it came to the coven or those associated with their tribe. From estate caretakers to the new men being slowly inducted to their secret club, everyone had an important purpose. They all played roles to help fulfill the prophecy, even Willyn's small son, Tadd.

Lucia heard the crunch of booted feet behind her on the shell and sand driveway. Ethan. She breathed through her nose and ignored him. What purpose had he served in her trial? To harden her in preparation for future battles? To assist her with the guardians, or the perilous trip?

She would have been better off without him and his tagalong demon. Without the two days of illness. Or the heartbreak.

Who cares? she demanded of herself. *I've got my sisters and friends. I have Beatriz. I've gone most of my life without a real family, so I can handle being without true love for the rest of it.*

There was plenty of joy to be found in the single life, and she intended to reap every bit. From this day forward. She would hit the city life with Kylie and Claudia, giving new meaning to the expression about painting the town red.

Yes. That's exactly what she'd do. *Bruja sola hasta la muerte.*

Working up a bright smile, she held up the tote bag in triumph as her coven clapped and cheered. "One mystical blade. Coming right up!"

"We're so glad you're home safe," Anna said, her face showing more relief than even Lucia would have anticipated.

Quinn came down the stairs to greet Ethan, taking his

friend's bag and clapping him on the shoulder. "Good to have you back, man. And not a moment too soon."

Lucia grew cold. "Why? Has something happened?"

"Not yet," Kylie said. The college girl didn't believe in secrets. At least, not for very long. "We were all set to shove the coven's magic into a bunch of bi-glow weapons. But now that you're back, you can help keep us stable."

Lucia frowned at her, uncomprehending.

"What the brat is trying to say," Quinn explained—and since when did he call Kylie a brat?— "is that we're attempting some dangerous magic."

He looked to Anna, the others, then Lucia before adding, "Aw, hell. We're running out of time, so here it is. We need to imbue metal with that special blue light you guys can call up. We want to store it for use in demon confrontations."

Lucia beetled her brow. Did she really live in a world where the phrase *demon confrontations* fazed no one? "Why would you start without Shauni and me?" She hurried up the steps now, ready to take part in the ceremony or ritual or whatever the girls had planned.

"Like Quinn said, we are literally out of time." Anna swept in behind Lucia and gave her the rundown of events. "We've been working on a way to tackle the demon problem here in Savannah. As you remember, they've been invading human bodies, and well, we can't simply stand by and let that happen."

Quinn stood next to Ethan as the group moved into the grand hall to continue the briefing. "We used the list you left us," he told Ethan. "We were able to find out the type of demons that are inhabiting the city. Their numbers, by the way, are growing daily."

"Unfortunately, we've got more than one type of clan," Paige said, passing by Lucia to give her a light punch to the arm, the warrior's way of welcoming her home.

Lucia held out her hands to stop the flow of information

before it completely backed up in her brain. "Hold it. What did you mean when you said bi-glow weapons, Kylie?"

"Okay. See, we went to this club downtown, and man you should see the fine options they have there." The young blonde wiggled her brows then glanced at Ethan. "Oops. Sorry."

"Not a problem," Lucia said, waving the concern off. "We can go back and check it out after my trial."

She didn't look at Ethan but saw his fist clench as if he were irritated. *Good. Suffer the loss.*

"Anyway," Kylie said, baffled eyes bouncing between Lucia and Ethan, "we tested these rings that had different metals, and we got a hit on two types of demons. Similar clans that are working together to help the Amara bring us and the whole city to its knees."

Walking closer to Ethan, Anna explained to him, "We used your list, and the suggestions you made allowed us to make weapons with two different alloys."

"And they each glow a different color," Kylie added. "How cool is that?"

Quinn rolled his eyes. "We still have two problems, and you guys got back at the perfect time. We have to magically enhance the weapons. And we need to figure out how to drive the demons out of any humans they've possessed."

"Which is where I come in," Ethan said. "You can't attack the demon if it's still housed inside an innocent victim." He looked to Anna for clarification. "You need a way to expel the demon before you can destroy it."

"Exactly."

Moving behind Lucia, and clearly doing his best to stay away from her, Ethan motioned for Quinn to follow him up the stairs. "I've got some ideas to run by you," she heard him say to Anna's brother.

She refused to let his mannerism upset her. She'd made it clear he was to stay away from her and focus only on whatever the coven needed him to do. He'd helped Lucia fight off the Qara Mikuna, he'd found his bracelet so he could fall in love—with whoever he found one day—and now he and Lucia really had very little to talk about.

She was brought out of her wretched musings when Anna touched her arm. "Are you all right? I take it you and Ethan had a problem."

"That about sums it up." Pulling out the box, Lucia told her, "The dagger is in there. You should know also," she gave Anna the container, "that there was a second piece. A bracelet. But Ethan has claimed it."

She lifted her chin and narrowed her eyes, feeling like a fool all over again. "The wrist band is the only reason he wanted to go along. He needs it to fend off his own personal demon, which is another long story for later, and I made the unilateral decision to give it to him."

Casting a glance to the other members of her coven, she added, "I hope that decision stands. He needs it." She wasn't happy Ethan had rejected her, but she wouldn't be purposely cruel. Not like he had.

She'd send Ethan on his way with wishes for happiness and his ever-elusive chance at love. Even if it wasn't going to be with her.

"We trust you," Viv said, sliding her black glasses from her face to move closer. Sympathy flooded her gray eyes.

Feeling the threat of tears now that she was among her sisters, Lucia stifled the sob that rose up and cleared her throat instead. "I'm going to take a moment to shower and change clothes. Then I want to be filled in on everything I've missed."

"We missed you, too," Claudia said, as if reading an underlying meaning to Lucia's words.

Lucia had been lonely for her friends, more than she'd realized. She'd been too busy chasing an uncooperative demon hunter to notice.

Maybe if she'd had them with her she would have seen what Ethan had been trying to tell her the whole time. Maybe she wouldn't have made a fool of herself over the man. And her heart would still be intact.

Whatever. She shook it off. *Bruja sola hasta la muerte.*

She worked up a smile for the others and trudged toward the stairs. Her body and mind were both worn out.

As she passed through the grand hall, she took note of all the fresh flowers. Mrs. Attinger had been true to her word, but the promising red blooms didn't cheer Lucia as they had before.

She appreciated the support, in fact, she needed it more than ever, but she couldn't help remembering her words to Ethan. She'd proudly told him red was her color. That it represented passion. And love.

She should have listened to him, heeded his warning. Funny how they'd switched positions. Ethan was now free to pursue romance, and all Lucia saw in the crimson stain was a warning.

Love hurts. It teases and stabs, pricks and bleeds. It kills hope.

She felt a tug on her elbow and realized she was standing still and staring at a vase of roses. "Come on. I'll walk with you," Kylie said. Even the youngest of them could see Lucia's pain.

"Sure," she said, grateful for the company. "You can tell me what I need to know for this weapon ceremony and why we're on such a tight deadline to get them made."

Being back at the mansion had a double effect. She had the solace of her friends here, but their comfort made it too easy to let her walls down again.

And the pain pouring in was more than she could bear.

"Lucia," Kylie said when they'd made it to her room. "What did you mean when you said we'd go clubbing *after* your trial? You found the dagger, so why wouldn't you be finished?" Her hazel eyes consoled her friend when she said, "Unless you still have to fix something with Ethan."

"No. I doubt it. I just need to kill some demons." Lucia started stripping, eager to get to her own shower and her stockpile of scented soaps and lotions. She'd take any manner of escapism right now. As long as the smell wasn't tropical.

"But let's talk about that later. Once I get cleaned up I could use a little sisterly-bonding over a dangerous ritual with glowing weapons." She laughed but it sounded harsh. "And after that," she shot the younger woman a fierce look, "I'll be ready for a good fight."

32

Above Ethan's head was a pattern of intersecting, wooden beams that made up a pentagram. He studied the perfect design and marveled over the fact it had been constructed over three hundred years earlier.

They had come together in the great room, the oldest part of the mansion, and the most sacred. Here was the heart of the home, and the safest place to attempt dangerous magic.

As the women of the coven milled and prepared to do their jobs, he let his gaze drop to the one witch he couldn't seem to get a handle on.

Ethan had thought an intrusive, murderous demon was the greatest vexation of his life, but a certain mule-headed witch who couldn't go to the bathroom without putting on lip gloss was running a close second. Very close.

As if his fuming thoughts had penetrated that hard head of hers, Lucia cast him a fulminating glare before ignoring him once again to confer with Anna.

She had accused him of flip-flopping, but wasn't that exactly what she'd done? She'd spent the first half of their travels trying to wear him down with her potent sensuality and charm. Then she'd spent the second half turning up her nose and treating him like a parasite she couldn't cure.

His deceptions hadn't been nearly as confusing as her mercurial honesty. First he was her meant-to-be, and now she couldn't stand to be in the same room with him. She wouldn't spare a minute of her time to talk things over.

Damn headstrong female. He'd shown her how he felt on that mountain ridge, even if he hadn't been able to say the words. Didn't she understand? He'd been dragging the curse around with him so long it was practically a part of him.

He couldn't just drop the disabling fear that had plagued him for most of his life. The idea of caring for someone, especially the way he cared for Lucia, was terrifying. Even with the bracelet on his arm, her whispered plea to make love to her had struck him straight through.

Why had she said the word out loud? She might as well have dropped him into a freezing lake.

The lust he'd reveled in had been replaced. Terror had ridden in like a monstrous tide, drowning any chance of being with her that way.

There should be no question in her mind that he wanted her, not after his loss of control. Twice he'd been overridden by his need for her. Twice he'd staked his claim by taking her mouth if not her body.

She had to know how trapped he felt. How much he desired her, felt for her...yet feared for her safety.

Ethan heaved a frustrated breath. He would just have to find a way to start fresh. To start over. He had come too far and crossed too many boundaries to give up on Lucia. On them.

Once her challenge was complete, he'd take things nice and easy, romance her a little. He'd show her how he would do things if he had the proper time.

And if he didn't have to worry about the Seraphim turning her insides into Chernobyl.

Was it too much to ask for a little patience?

Nodding to Quinn when his friend held up a hand to wave

him over, Ethan gritted his teeth and told himself he'd figure it out. Lucia would just have to get over her mad and listen to what he had to say.

Besides, he'd rather have an angry Lucia still walking around than one he'd taken to bed and killed with his uncontrollable lust. He wanted to be with her, he could admit that now.

But he expected to have her for more than a single, erotic night.

He'd done his best to avoid feeling anything for her, so the fact that he did was all the proof he needed. Lucia was special. She belonged with him.

She might not believe in fate anymore, but Ethan had become its biggest fan.

He wrapped his fingers over the band to make sure it still rested there, a habit he'd formed since wearing it for several days. More than once Lucia had spotted him checking to make sure it was still there, and she'd either turned away in anger or given him a disgusted look.

If she only knew why he was so worried about losing the bracelet, or dislodging it. Since the night the Seraphim had crawled into her and tormented Ethan, he'd known.

He couldn't lose Lucia. For any reason.

If the silver band came off and the demon took her now? Ethan made a furious sound in his throat. No. That wasn't going to happen.

Quinn was holding out the duct tape Ethan had requested. If Anna was right about what the coven planned to do, then this room was about to get hectic. And he wasn't taking a chance on having the charmed bracelet blown off his wrist.

"We really have to come up with something better than this," Quinn said, hiking a single brow as Ethan wrapped the duct tape around the band to hold it in place. "You'd think a mystical artifact like that would have some sort of stay-put power."

Ripping the end off and trying to ignore how foolish he felt with tape around his wrist, Ethan said, "You'd think."

When Quinn walked over to the large round table in the center of the great room, Ethan watched curiously to see what was underneath the cloth. When his friend eased off the material, Ethan's brows shot up. He was impressed.

Quinn and Anna had been quite the busy blacksmiths.

Weapons of varying sizes and shapes covered the table, and on closer inspection, he could just make out the different shades of metal. He gave a questioning look to Quinn and at his friend's quick nod, he picked up a sword to run his finger down the center. "Beautiful work, Quinn. And how did you get the two metals to bind so evenly?"

Quinn shrugged. "Magic. Considering all the requirements we had, there was no other way." He gestured to the sword still in Ethan's hands. "The basic element is titanium, for light weight and durability." He pointed. "One side is alloyed with meteoric iron. The other silver."

"Specially treated to glow when near their corresponding demon."

"Correct. However, we had to add a colorant so there would be no confusion in the heat of battle." Quinn took the sword and set it back on the table. "Don't want to risk beheading a human on accident. The demons that possess bodies will light up a pale blue. Since it's the hue of the coven's magic, it will be like a waving flag of truce."

Ethan curled a finger under his chin. "Then you'll use my mixture to drive the demon out and slay him while the infected human remains untouched." He sighed. "Complicated."

"But necessary," Anna said, coming to stand with the two men beside the table. "Loss of innocent life is to be avoided at all costs."

"All costs, Anna?" Ethan knew his voice had gone hard, but he was a man who'd seen more collateral damage than anyone, human or magical, should have to witness. "You're fighting a war here. One that spreads to more people with every one of your challenges."

Anna's eyes slid to her brother, but Quinn simply lifted his hands. "What? You said Ethan needed to be up to speed, so I told him everything. We can't have anyone on our team operating with half information."

The wary look in her blue eyes soon changed to one of regret. "No, we can't," Anna said. "You're both right. We need someone with Ethan's background and pragmatism to balance us out. Paige has been trying to make us understand the same thing from the beginning. No matter what we do, we can't save everyone."

Quinn stared hard at the table of implements. "We already lost Jen, and who knows what that Droehk is out there summoning from the underworld. For all we know, other souls have already been sacrificed and harvested for Bastraal. To help strengthen the demon and prepare him."

"Then let's get started," Anna said quietly, and by her mannerism, Ethan could see she took every loss personally. As the leader of the coven and those fighting to stop the evil from destroying Savannah, Anna felt responsible for every life lost.

She'd better thicken her skin, Ethan thought, because he had a suspicion things were just heating up.

"All right," Quinn said loudly enough to draw everyone together. The other men had come tonight as well, brushing aside their women's concerns about detonations and fire. Michael, Dare, Nick, and Trevor had insisted on being here for the procedure, and none of them paid heed to the possible danger.

The men had complete faith in the coven. And in the witches they loved.

"We all know something bad is going down tomorrow night at this warehouse the demons are using." Quinn rounded the table to stand beside a piece of natural stone resting on a dais at the far edge of the room. "Nick and Trevor have picked up just enough information to figure out when and where."

"It's the *what* we just don't have yet," Trevor said, crossing his massive arms across his chest. Ethan was a big guy, but he wondered if this detective didn't occasionally rip out of his shirts like some kind of super hero.

"So we'll be prepared." Quinn indicated the pinkish rock beside him. "This piece of red sandstone is filled with iron and will help absorb any magic we can't control, or contain. The rock is our backup plan." He flicked worried blue eyes to Anna. "But let's hope we don't have to use it."

"We won't," she replied. "Now. Everyone has their assignment. Willyn, Hayden, Kylie, and Claudia will call forth the energy. They'll be responsible for keeping the source flowing." She looked to the four women as they each took up positions at the marks on the floor indicating north, south, east, and west.

Willyn and Hayden had the purest of hearts, one the healer of body, the other of spirit. Kylie brought youth and vitality to the table, where Claudia offered wisdom.

Anna gestured to Paige, "You and I will be across from each other. Then Lucia and Shauni will fill in the remaining spots. The four of us will channel the magic into the weapons."

When Lucia's name was called, Ethan couldn't stop his eyes from finding her. She moved in between Willyn and Claudia so the eight women formed a balanced circle. How rigid she seemed, eyes dimmed and jaw tense.

And he had wrought the change in her. He had caused the hurt.

The Asian witch was the only one left standing outside the circle. "Viv," Anna told her. "You know what to do."

Viv squared her shoulders and took a deep breath. "In case of explosion, I capture the blast and shut it down." She firmed her lips. "I can do it, but like Quinn said, I'd rather not have to."

"You won't," Paige said, her stance as tough as ever. She was pure soldier, just as Lucia had described her.

Quinn motioned for Ethan to move farther back from the circle, and as soon as he cleared the immediate perimeter, Anna nodded once to Willyn, then Hayden, Kylie, and Claudia. The four of them each looked up to a single point in space, directly above the array of weapons. Soon a mass of blue light formed, crackling and snapping with energy.

Ethan crossed his arms to watch, fascinated. The details he'd shared with Anna and Quinn on the mystical qualities of elements had given them the key to their metal alloy. Quinn said they'd tweaked the formula, including the magical elements involved, and were confident the coven's power would be absorbed by the metals. And held there.

"Ready?" Anna called out to Paige and the other two women who would help force the magic into the instruments of death.

Lucia and Shauni both said, "Yes," then their group directed the flow of blue down toward the table.

As if hungry for the power, an aura of silver hovered from the weapons to clasp onto the magic and pull it down, into the metal. Every piece on the table began to glow, but the illumination seemed to run liquid as the silver and blue whirled together, blending in a fusion of color.

Ethan wrinkled his brow. Worried. The two weren't mixing. Instead the dueling colors pushed off of each other like oil and water.

"Keep going," Paige yelled, though she and the others controlling the magic were already straining and sweating.

Ethan looked again to Lucia, her brown eyes were set on the weapons, the muscles in her neck corded as she struggled.

"It's not working," Quinn said, suddenly at Ethan's side. He too was shaking, but from a different kind of stress.

"Quinn," Ethan snapped. "You're one of the brightest guys I know." He grabbed his friend's arm, fully aware Quinn wasn't just seeing his sister and friends out there on a precarious edge. He was remembering his parents.

"You said it would work." Ethan glanced at the women as they fought to imbue the weapons. "You said they could do it, that they were meant to create the tools to defeat the demons."

He shook Quinn now. "Are you saying you were wrong?"

Moving his head side to side, Quinn drew a harsh breath. "No. No. I checked everything myself. Three times." He wiped his brow. "Anna and the girls are the strongest I've ever seen."

Then Quinn got himself under control, locking down the anxiety that threatened to take hold of him. "Thanks. I needed a kick in the ass."

Scowling, he marched to stand behind the warrior with short, white-blonde hair. "You hold it, Paige. You make it go where you want it."

"Screw you, Quinn," she uttered, but Ethan would swear she'd gotten a second wind and was almost grinning.

Quinn moved on to Lucia. "You laugh at everything, Luce. You've already mastered one dagger. Now take control of those."

And Lucia did the most unexpected thing. She threw her head back and laughed out loud, still holding her hands out in front of her and dominating the light.

"You're next, Shauni," Quinn moved on to the raven-haired witch. "Don't forget about the animals. I read some of the demons like to roast dogs up for dinner. Are you going to let that happen?"

Shauni's green eyes burst with an inner light, glowing brighter than was natural, and Ethan wondered if that had ever happened before.

Based on Quinn's gaping mouth, he assumed the answer was a negative.

With the other three women stepping it up, that left only Anna. But Quinn didn't yell or threaten. He looked at her and spoke low near her ear. A secret between brother and sister.

The light being channeled to the knives and swords abruptly surged with power, creating a blinding white light. Ethan shielded his eyes, just as the other men did, including Quinn. The witches stared straight into the blaze, their hair flowing back as if a gust of wind had burst over them.

"Hold it!" Viv cried, and instead of reserving her strength to capture any wayward blast, she joined in with Anna and the second group of women to help push the power into the weapons.

The brilliant white continued to swell, spreading and pushing at the boundary of the circle, until it covered them all.

"Anna!" Quinn cried, holding an arm up against a rush of heat.

My God, Ethan thought, afraid everything was lost and they were all about to die. The women were standing inside an inferno, or what felt like one.

Around him the rocks in the walls groaned as if waking to join the fight, the pentagram above their heads was awash with brightness until it looked like a star crashing down on them all.

Then the entire bulk of hot, white light sucked into itself and zipped into the weapons, leaving a vacuum of silence in the room. Other than the heaving breaths of the women, no sound existed.

Until Anna gasped and gave a tired laugh. She clasped her arms around herself and looked above. "Thank you," she said, and Ethan could only guess to whom she spoke.

When she stepped to the table and picked up a sword, she told them, "I'm going to test one." The sword glowed blue as she called magic from the metal. "They work. We did it."

Then she put it back down. "I don't want to waste any energy. We're too tired to make more tonight."

"But now we know how to do it," Paige said, her face splitting into a wide grin. "Did you feel the change at the end? Like we tapped into something new?"

Holding her bright red hair up to cool her nape, Claudia said dryly, "We're always tapping into something new."

"That was awesome," Quinn said, hugging his sister. "Awesome and terrifying." When he felt her sweaty back, he jumped away. "Ugh. You need a shower."

The other men went to their girlfriends. Michael was no longer limping as he embraced Shauni.

Seeing Lucia standing apart from the others, Ethan went to her, hoping she'd let him offer congratulations. That her success might soften the reception and open the door just a crack.

"How do you feel?' he asked, giving her a half-smile.

Her eyes shuttered as if preparing for attack, and she leveled him with her gaze. "I'm fine, Ethan. Thanks for your help."

And with that she walked past him, careful not to touch. She kept going until she'd exited the room, and not once did she look back.

Ethan followed her with his eyes. All the way out the door. He and Lucia were due for a conversation, and he would hold her down, tie her down, if that's what it took to make her listen.

He had things to say to his Spanish witch.

But first things first. He gave a nod to Quinn and made his way to the exit. A raid was about to be under way.

And Ethan had to make preparations of his own.

33

The next evening was crisp and clear as the last dregs of winter gave way to burgeoning spring. Lucia was sporting a simple gray T-shirt over pants of the same color, not unlike her casual hiking wear. The temperature was a pleasant sixty-five degrees and humidity was low.

The perfect night for a sneak attack.

She and her coven were all taking part in the operation sardonically named Warehouse 15. The joke came from having nine witches added to the six men who'd joined them and were ready to fight.

Much to Lucia's chagrin, that included Ethan.

Lifting her head to peer over the top of the brick wall, she sought his position down below, the next street over. From the rooftop perch, where she and Michael had been assigned to perform as lookouts, Lucia eyed the tall, broad form on the corner.

She could spot the irritating demon hunter anywhere and wished she wasn't overcome with lust every time she looked at him. He wore black fatigues and a tight black shirt. Far too sexy, and way unfair.

The demon hunter was playing dirty.

In an earlier, private conversation with Anna, she'd argued

against his coming along, but Anna wouldn't hear it. She had simply taken Lucia by the shoulders and said, "You know our trials are not only tests of mind, body, or magic."

Then she'd pressed her hand to Lucia's heart, and added, "We all have to confront fear or pain so we can truly master our destinies. Deal with Ethan, Lucia. Don't let injured pride cost you the man you love."

Too shocked to respond, Lucia had let Anna slip out the door as she'd come face to face with an extremely annoying reality. Had she let herself fall for Ethan?

Dios! She should have listened to him and just left him alone. Her plan had not only gone off the rails, it was another track entirely and about to run right over her.

She'd chased after the secretive, snarling man and had finally succeeded, only to have her hand slapped for the effort. But as angry and hurt as she'd been, she couldn't deny she still yearned for him. She still wanted the fantasy, the romance.

And she wanted to help heal the man.

She'd come to ache for his childhood trauma and the sacrifice a young Ethan had made for his sister. The grief and guilt he'd suffered when his first love had been murdered by the Seraphim. So heinously and right in front of his eyes.

Lucia had moved away from viewing Ethan as a gift of fate and a no-fail lifetime lover. Instead she'd learned who he really was. His past, his burdens, and his driving instinct to protect.

She just wished she could believe that was why he'd denied her yet again. That day on the ridge, while her lips were still tender from his ravaging kisses, he'd looked her in the eye and told her, "No."

And her heart had fractured.

Lowering the binoculars, she tried to put her mind back on the task at hand. Ethan could take care of himself, and no one really knew what they'd find inside the abandoned warehouse across the street. Abandoned by humans anyway.

They would need all the able bodies available, and Ethan had wanted to verify his demon-expellant worked correctly. A small sack made out of burlap hung on her belt—on all of their belts—with material woven tightly enough to hold the powders, crystals, and herbs inside, but porous enough to dispense as needed.

Ethan had assured them. One sprinkle in a demon's face and not only would it be forced to leave its human host's body, but it couldn't get back in.

She had to give him his due credit. Ethan Drake was a superb mixologist when it came to fighting evil spirits and their ilk, but a lifetime of having his own demon on his back had forced him to hone those skills.

Michael nudged her and jerked his head toward the street. A line of black vans were coming down the road, and the overwhelming number didn't scare Lucia half as much as how brazen they were. So many vehicles traveling together was an unusual sight.

So why weren't they being more covert?

Michael relayed what they saw to Quinn, who was in yet another concealed spot, spread out from the others. The point of entry to the warehouse would be decided on after the Amara and demons arrived. As far as Anna could tell, no one was inside the building at present.

So they were all awaiting orders from Paige and Quinn, each of them posted at different vantage points. "I see them," Paige's voice said in Lucia's ear bud. The entire team had been alerted to the procession of vans.

Black vans. Lucia made a dismissive noise in her throat. Could they be any more cliché?

The first van stopped right in front of the loading doors, and a man got out to unlock them. Once he'd spread the sliding doors wide, several more burly men and a couple of equally rough-looking females exited the first van and went inside as the vehicle left in a hurry.

Maybe they were trying to be circumspect after all. Using her binoculars again, Lucia watched as the men inside strode to the back of the empty building. She had to crouch behind the brick wall and was barely able to see what they were doing.

They were standing and staring up at nothing. "What are they looking for?" she asked herself as much as Michael.

"Not a clue," he said.

Then Lucia saw the wave of distortion hit, and if she hadn't been fixated on that area, she would have missed it. "I think I know what's happening," she said, looking at the line of remaining vans with a new sense of dread. "There's a portal in there," she told Michael. "Tell the others."

She looked again and could make out more movement in what should have been empty air. "It's becoming more active. There's definitely a portal." She eased back from the wall, her body awash in a cold, clingy sensation that made her ill. "And I know what they're going to do with it."

As if on cue, the second van rolled up to release another two men, but this time there was additional cargo. The two didn't go straight inside but opened the back door to pull out their captives. First a man with his hands tied behind his back, then two women and a teenage boy.

Michael stood alongside Lucia. "Let's go. We're to join Ethan and Claudia, since we can take the side exit out this building and slide up the alley without being noticed."

A lover and healers of animals, Michael was a gentle soul, but a mask had covered his face, and the normally kind gray eyes grew bitter. "They're going to give those people to demons, aren't they?" he asked, his assumption the same as hers.

"Receptacles for the new arrivals," she said, jerking open the metal door to descend the stairs. "That portal was gearing up to let more monsters cross over. To enter our world."

She palmed the hilt of her chosen weapon. A creation of

Quinn's, similar to a short sword but with a lean curve at the end. Just right for decapitations. "Well tonight we've got a surprise for them."

When they reached the bottom floor, she and Michael crept out the door and moved stealthily to join Ethan and Claudia. They stood on a corner that couldn't be seen from the street thanks to a large truck that had been parked there all day.

By the time she eased up to stand beside Claudia, Lucia could see the men were unloading the fifth and final van. "I doubt the guards are completely human," she said, making sure she kept her entire body out of sight.

"I was thinking the same thing," Claudia said. Tonight she sported black exercise pants and shirt, both a name brand. Lucia smiled. Even a nasty, bloody fight to the death required the appropriate attire in the fashion maven's mind.

But Claudia's next statement wiped the grin from Lucia's face. "I saw one of them face-flicker." The term used by the coven to describe when a demon's true appearance morphed into visibility. If only for a second.

Ethan could see them, too, without any help from the women. But he was the only male here who could. Luckily, the demons gathered here tonight masked themselves with human bodies, through possession or imitation, so everyone would be able to see their opponent.

Until Ethan's handy sacs of powder cast the possessors out. Then, well...they'd better hope a witch was handy.

"I hope the guys stick to the real demons. The ones who just look like people but can be killed instantly." Lucia thumbed her sword again.

"You're worrying too much, Lucia. Don't let your emotion get in your way." But Claudia put a hand to her dagger, as if taking comfort from its presence.

Falling into her own musing, Lucia frowned to herself. Why was she so worried? Not only were she and her friends better prepared than ever before, they had a greater number of fighters than in previous battles. Plus they held the element of surprise.

Her eyes tracked to Ethan to study his powerful body. Surely she wasn't worried about him? He was usually a solo act, and now he had plenty of backup.

Paige's voice came over the radio and into Lucia's ear bud, so she pulled herself away from the hovering doubt. "Dare and I are already at the top of the stairs on the backside of the warehouse," Paige said. "When Quinn gives the command, we'll be coming in up top and around the upper level walkway."

Claudia looked to Ethan then Lucia. "Ready?"

For the first time Ethan made eye contact with Lucia, his deep, dark eyes steady and true. "I'm ready," he said, and she sensed an underlying meaning to his words.

Instead of saying anything, she simply looked to the open cargo doors and narrowed her eyes. "Michael. We break for the doors when we hear from Quinn."

"Right." Michael was fully healed and ready to put the hurt on some vicious monsters. His stare was one of gray stone. "Quinn will wait for the optimal time, but if they start closing the doors, we have to go."

The last van pulled away after its load of victims and thugs had been deposited. Just as Lucia saw the doors start to move, Quinn's voice rang out over the radio, "Move in. Go!"

Their team of four sprinted across the intersection, just as the rest of their group burst in side doors and the one up top. Ethan and Michael pumped their long legs and beat the women by a few seconds, but they stopped to grab hold of the closing doors.

Lucia squeezed through first and found herself face to face with a large, thickly muscled man. A black tattoo ran up his neck and round the back side of his shaven head. Her sword was already free from its holster and in her hand.

And when the right side of her blade lit up a bright red—this time to truly represent danger and the permission to draw blood—she knew the man in front of her was an imitator. The body he used was all his, a clever copy of the human form.

"*Adios, demonio.*" Before the shell-shocked fiend saw what was coming, she placed the slightly curved tip between his ribs and thrust. He gurgled with eyes wide, blood spilling from his lips as he fell to his knees.

But he didn't turn to ash.

Afraid the monster in front of her would just stand back up after he had a chance to regenerate tissue, Lucia called forth the coven magic stored inside the sword. A small amount, because she didn't want to be wasteful.

A bare trickle of power tingled under her palm, and the man burst into ash.

"Are you done playing with that guy?" Claudia asked, her expensive clothes already sprinkled with gray. Looked like she'd fried one, too.

"Just testing," Lucia said. She looked round to get her bearings. The warehouse was mostly empty, but a few stacks of crates stood near the front doors. Overhead, round hangings lights cast a dim, yellow glow. The corners and back wall were shadowed, so they'd be wise to keep their eyes open.

Her head whipped toward the back as sounds of fighting grew louder and mixed with screams. The people who'd been brought here against their will were stumbling into each other. And based on their dazed faces, they weren't simply unbalanced by having their hands tied behind their backs.

"They've been drugged," Lucia said. "We have to get those people out of the way before they get hurt." The occasional expulsion of ash told her demons were being taken out but not quickly enough. The fighters in back couldn't fully engage for fear of hurting the kidnap victims.

"Hayden's already clearing people out," Ethan said as he and

Michael started moving forward with Lucia and Claudia. He lifted his weapon of choice, a machete, naturally, and pointed to the caramel-haired medium as she dragged people to safety beneath the metal stairwell. More crates surrounded the stairs to provide protection.

A woman came running at them as if she'd entered from a side door. Did the demons have a second tier of soldiers watching from afar? How many more were out there?

The black-haired female was screaming with the clear intent of bashing them with the wooden bat she carried, but Lucia sensed Ethan falter. "Still don't want to kill a woman?" she asked with a smirk, but inside she secretly cheered his code of ethics.

"Don't worry," she added. "I don't suffer the same sensibilities." Sidestepping and sticking out a leg, she tripped the advancing attacker but gained very little time when the agile woman rolled and bounced back up.

Lucia still had to figure out what kind of demon she was up against, so she ducked the raised bat and jabbed the blunt end of her sword into the woman's gut. She took advantage of the delay and laid her blade across the woman's back. It turned blue.

"Damn. We've got a possession." She looked to Ethan. "Time to see if those bags work." She shoved the woman upright by her shoulder and whapped her in the face with Ethan's bag, a quick way to spray its contents. With a bellow of outrage, a very big and very ugly demon shot out of the woman. Her now empty body slumped to the ground.

"Get her to safety!" she shouted to Ethan. He hefted the woman up and carried her toward the improvised shelter under the stairs while Lucia tried to keep the free-floating demon in her sights.

The monster was fast, and the growl emitting from his sideways mouth told her he was furious about being exorcised.

The color of his form, because he wasn't solid enough to have true skin, was dark green, almost black. But the deep hue only highlighted his wide yellow mouth.

Lucia thought she saw a flicker of eyes, but they were so small and dark she couldn't be sure. Why was his mouth sideways, and were there two rows of teeth?

The demon circled around her so swiftly she lost him for a moment. And then he demonstrated just why his mouth was that way. Elongating his body, the demon circled her with his top half and stretched his maw wide open.

She started to raise her arms to strike but was caught in the whirlwind of his twisting form. He was wrapping her up like an anaconda and about to bite down on her face. Just as Lucia gathered her blue light in one palm, another weapon came out of nowhere to slice through the demon.

While the multiple pieces of it wiggled and tried to reconnect, Lucia sent a flash of magic into it and pulverized the beast.

She found herself being shaken by Ethan. "Are you okay?"

"Yeah." She shook off her surprise. "Yeah." Footsteps clanged over their heads, so she turned to find Quinn wrestling with a guy who looked like a body builder. Paige and he were now separated, and the coven's warrior was struggling against two other demons with one coming up on her back.

"I'm going up," Lucia said.

Ethan paused and clenched his jaw. "I'll head to the back. There are still innocent people stuck in the middle out there." He gave a sharp nod. "Be careful." Then he ran toward the portal where most of the battle was still going on.

As she climbed, Lucia noted the group huddled under the stairs was getting bigger. Once the victims were away from the open area, the battle could really begin.

She'd made it to the top of the stairs and could see Quinn's weapon glowing red when it passed near the huge man. Good. No messy expulsion to deal with. She came up behind Mr.

Universe and all his muscles and yelled, "Back away, Quinn!"

When he shoved the hulking demon toward Lucia, she swung her sword and took off the monster's head. With the heat of her magic pooling in her blade, she pierced the body where it lay sprawled across the catwalk. *Phoof.* Nothing but ash.

She and Quinn clinked swords and grinned before going in opposite directions to veer around and come up on both sides of Paige. She was holding her own and had reduced the number of attackers from two to three, but a little extra help never hurt.

Lucia's entire being hummed with excitement. They were destroying these creatures, cleaning them out faster than predicted. The whole color-coordinated weapon plan helped speed things along.

Just when she felt the sweeping thrill of victory, Kylie's voice echoed from below. "The portal," she cried, and Lucia could see the young blonde was backed against the swirling mass of air. Only now the invisible wavelength of the portal had changed, rolling with a multitude of hues from crimson to purplish-black, a sickly mesh of heinous colors.

Kylie pivoted away just as a demon lunged for her then engaged her in a fight, striking at her again and again with a steel rod. Kylie dodged him before spinning around to hit him in the face with her burlap bag. The human body slumped while the demon rose.

But Kylie's focus was torn between her adversary and the disgusting colors roiling together in what looked like a putrid collection of bodily fluids. The tall oval shape bulged and spread along the edges, and the tempo of the churning energy was increasing.

Lucia stopped where she was when she understood what was happening.

The portal was activating.

34

Ethan heard a commotion behind him and turned to find a female demon. He shoved the woman away from him when she stumbled under Anna's attack, but didn't have time to see if she was possessed or a demon in both spirit and form.

Anna's dagger thrust forward in one swift motion, and he was suddenly surrounded by a cloud of ash. He waved a hand to clear his eyes, deciding she must have been one-hundred-percent monster.

Anna held on tight to the hilt of her weapon, made to assist a left or right slicing motion. Then she veered to Ethan's left to counter an assault just as he did the same for her.

After he'd hit the next guy in the face with herb powder, he caught the falling body. Viv was closer now than the other witches, so he yelled for her to take out the demon he'd let loose.

She held out two swords, just like a Samurai of old, and stalked in a circle as the freed demon hovered around her. When the beast tried to trap her and opened its gaping jaws to bite, she lifted both arms then brought the blades down at once, slicing the monster into so many pieces she simply chose the nearest one to stab.

She obliterated the whole thing with her magic.

Ethan and Viv shared a moment of satisfaction before putting their backs together to survey the area. The fighting had slowed, but the danger wasn't gone. "Too bad all the guys can't see demons like you, Ethan."

He wagged his machete in the direction of Michael and Nick who were standing guard around the rescued kidnap victims. "They do good work to be fighting blind."

Viv's eyes raked over Nick and warmed. "Yeah. They sure do." Then she laughed and gestured to the white powder on the faces of the captives. "They're free from the demons but are probably wondering why they got hit in the face with herb-scented bags."

"Keeps them safe from possession," Ethan said. "That's all that matters."

Dare had joined Michael and Nick as the other two men cut the binds from the captive's hands. Then Dare touched each of them and spoke into their ear, using his mind manipulation to cloud their memories of horror.

When Dare had finished, he, Michael, and Nick took them out the door. The three men were transferring the people to a safer location. Now that the fray was dying down and only a quarter of the demons remained, the coven could stand to lose a few warriors.

Kylie had yelled something about the portal earlier, but now her voice was heightened in alarm. "The portal is opening!"

Ethan jerked his head and saw the churning colors, like a machine that had been turned on.

He didn't want to imagine who or what was controlling it from the other side, but he started taking out the demons double-time. They needed to be rid of the monsters already on this side of the barrier. More beasts were coming through that portal at any minute.

He and the coven needed to be ready.

He helped Viv drag a newly-vacated body to the stairwell for the other men to find when they returned. Since almost all of their opponents were either expelled or destroyed, he searched above to find Lucia.

She and Paige were standing with Quinn, all three looking down at the portal and discussing the change in situation.

"Be ready to hit the mothers with firepower!" Paige yelled to the witches on the floor. Then she followed Lucia and Quinn down the stairs, three sets of boots banging against the metal.

He saw some of the women put away their weapons, apparently preferring to fight with their hands. Paige was right about firing at will, because anything coming through the portal would be fair game.

They would all be demons.

A blur on his side had Ethan lifting his left arm in a reactionary protective move. The door to a small office had opened before a man leaped out. He caught Ethan on the wrist with a pipe, but the bracelet caught most of the blow.

Ethan's machete flashed red, so he gutted the man with an underhand swing to the abdomen. Then he kicked him to the floor. Anna was there to zap the guy with her magic and turn him to dust.

And Ethan was grateful, because all his focus was now centered on the bracelet buried under a mound of duct tape. The pipe had made direct contact.

With his other hand grasped defensively around his wrist, Ethan searched again for Lucia. Had the bracelet been damaged? Could the Seraphim come for her?

Fear wracked his stomach when he saw her leaning against the rail at the base of the stairs. She had her hand pressed to the side of her head as if she had a headache.

The she raised scared brown eyes and stared at him.

"What happened?' he called, already running to her. He grabbed her by the shoulders, shaking her to get an answer then putting his arms around her. "Are you hurt?"

He felt her head move back and forth and her voice vibrate against his chest. He let her loose but didn't let go. "What did you say?"

"I heard something. A scream, but not of pain." Her face was the color of freshly-bleached sheets. She was shaken. "Anger. Fury." Her fingers curled into Ethan's shirt as she clung to him.

Then as if she realized what she was doing, she pulled her head up and visibly shook the emotion off. "We'll talk after," she said curtly. "Michael and Nick are back. You should go over there with them."

Ethan grated out a sound of frustration. "Fine, Lucia. I'll be on the sidelines, but if you look like you're in any kind of pain." He held up a hand to halt her rebuttal and pinned her with his eyes so she would know he was serious. "If you are in trouble, I *will* pull you out."

"Great. Whatever." She walked away then jerked back to look him over. The fire of anger in her eyes dampened and eased off, turning to something that seemed a lot more like concern. For him.

Then she rolled her shoulders and the worry was gone. "Just get to the side, Drake." She gave him a wicked smile. "Because we're about to light this place up."

~~~

Braced for whatever monstrosity came through the rotation of dark colors, Lucia stood in a semi-circle with her coven. They spread out like a wall of feminine power. Their faces were splattered with blood or smudged with ash, but she felt her chest puff with pride.

Her sisters had never looked more beautiful.

A pool of crimson caught her attention then, so she gave it closer inspection. Someone had bled plenty, as there was a puddle on the floor. Casting her gaze around, she assessed each of her friends and saw only minor gashes.

She whirled to find Ethan then cursed herself. Why would she suddenly have a vise around her ribs at the thought of his being hurt? He meant nothing to her.

Yeah, right. She tightened her grip on the sword.

Well, she definitely meant nothing to him, and she couldn't afford to let herself forget that.

A flash of red drew her gaze to Quinn. His sleeve was soaked in blood. She'd noticed him holding his upper arm as they'd walked down from the top floor, so he must have been applying pressure.

Judging by the stain, he'd been cut deep. But he was with Michael, and the vet could take care of it. If not, Anna and Willyn could tackle Quinn later and put him to rights. Healing under duress.

Just when her swaggering pride was about to surface—because so far they had kicked some serious demon *trasero*—Lucia heard something that chilled her marrow.

Screams and yells flowed from the portal, too many voices to count. The fearful sound was full of rage and menace, and the combined power of so many demons spewed from the other side. Lights shook and flickered above their heads, and Lucia prayed they didn't go out.

The yells suddenly grew louder, and without warning, hordes of possession demons burst from the ugly mass. The same nasty fiends that twisted around their prey before attacking with their sideways mouths.

The coven was ready for them, though, and Lucia's earlier prediction came true with a vengeance. No need to worry about the man-made bulbs going out, because she and her sisters truly were lighting the place up.

An image of battleship guns came to mind as she watched Claudia fire her right hand then the left. Back and forth, like a continuous one-two punch. And Paige, well she wasn't worried about finesse but blasted a steady stream of blue at the emerging monsters.

One by one the gruesome demons perished, turning to ash as soon as they broke free from the portal and were met with the coven's firing squad.

Really, Lucia thought. Where was the challenge?

But like suicide bombers and kamikaze pilots, she soon realized the side-mouth demons were dispensable. They'd been nothing more than a flood of decoys to draw the coven's wrath and drain their power.

Now another wave was coming.

Lucia's magic wasn't gone, but she was running on less than half a tank. "Slow it down, Paige. Conserve your power."

The blonde warrior shot a quick zap to a newly emerged demon then nodded. "I was thinking the same thing. Those war cries were meant to rattle us."

"They worked," Hayden piped up. "But now we know to save the magic." She unsheathed her short sword. "For the rest of them."

Lucia and Anna locked gazes before looking again to the portal. The sudden quiet was worse than the terrifying screams. The women stood there watching as the air in the warehouse grew warm and heavy, full of anticipation. Rank with fear.

What was coming?

Paige dropped to the floor when a projectile bulleted toward her head. She was blessed with unnatural speed, so she easily dodged the weapon.

The next whistled past Lucia, and she stepped to one side to see a metallic disk fly past. Shauni was beside her and raised her hand to blast the next one, but her ball of blue had no effect on the metal. The flat circular object only shimmied off course, biting into her shoulder instead of hitting her straight on.

Shauni yelped and clutched her sliced shoulder, but just as quickly, she made a face like a wolf about to attack. She too pulled out her weapon. As did the rest of the coven.

Time to find out if their titanium was tougher than demon-steel.

As soon as they made the move, a melee of noise and color broke free from the portal. More demons charged, but they were the ones who looked like humans. Not the possessors.

The blue assault started up again, and this time the coven used their magic sparingly. These were trained warriors, and their razor-sharp disks would kill instantly.

Lucia heard a familiar whistle and pivoted to see a disk coming for her face. She wouldn't be quick enough to catch it. She tried to lift her weapon but could already imagine the sharp metal embedding itself in her face.

Whack! Ethan's machete whisked in front of her, saving her bone structure. And probably her life.

She stood frozen, shocked and surprised, but as soon as she was able to draw air into her lungs, she muttered, "Thanks."

Then she returned the favor by zapping the demon at Ethan's back. "Get lost, Drake. You did your part, now move." Terror clogged her throat as she shoved at his chest. He could be killed as easily as any of them.

But he just narrowed those deep brown eyes. "I can see them, too, witch. I'm staying." He cleaved a demon through the side of its head before Lucia wasted it with some magic.

Swords sliced through the air to deflect flying disks or skewer demons. Blue magic flashed and ash flew all around. Despite the additional dark forces streaming from the mystical doorway, the witches maintained an upper hand.

Finally the demon ranks were diminished, and a handful looked at each other before deciding theirs was a lost cause. They turned to run back the way they'd come.

But thanks to Anna and Kylie, only two of them escaped.

Lucia was gasping for breath after the battle but knew her work wasn't over. Now the coven had to make sure this passage from hell was destroyed. Other gateways from the underworld existed, but the one in front of them had to be dealt with first.

Time to find out if their magic had any effect at all.

Lucia slid her sword home and held out her arms. "All together," she said, and the other women followed suit. "Focus on the portal."

"We'll have to use everything we've got," Willyn said, pushing her hair back from her face. Her blonde waves were matted with...*something*...on one side.

"If that's what it takes." Lucia let all the hurt and anger she'd felt over the course of her challenge flow through her body and out her palms. She channeled her power straight to the portal.

As her sisters joined in, the whirling mass of color was covered by electric blue. An unending wave of purity and strength. Then the portal began to shake from the absorption of their magic. "Don't stop!" Lucia yelled.

Maybe this was her final task, to learn that the coven could destroy the portals and stop the flood of monsters into Savannah. This was a big deal. Surely it would make her amulet sing.

The colors of the gateway stopped spinning but crackled with electric bursts of pale lightning. A low hum began then quickly escalated into a high-pitched whine. Energy was building inside, and Lucia prepared for an explosion. She prayed they could all withstand the blast.

But instead of bursting outward, the blob suddenly stopped shaking and *im*ploded. A tiny ball of blue rotated in midair instead of a door to the other side. Then a sound like thunder tore through the building, causing the entire warehouse to shudder.

The tiny ball had disappeared. The portal was no more.

Moving toward the empty space with her hand stretched out, Hayden tested the air for any remnant quality or imprint.

She cast her golden eyes to Lucia then the others. "I think it's gone. Completely gone."

As sighs of relief and a few moans of pain filled the room, Lucia stood stock-still and listened. She waited.

But no sound of triumph came from her necklace.

Trying to disguise her disappointment, she walked to the back of the warehouse, pretending to look around. Once she got her game face back on, she joined Anna and the others to help clean the building's aura.

When they were done with that, they got busy clearing the physical mess. No traces of magic or demon ash would remain when they were finished. Nothing to hint of the evening's ugly battle.

For whatever reason the Amara had been absent tonight, and Anna didn't want the coven's enemies to have a single clue about what had gone on in the warehouse.

Paige was the last one out and even made sure to turn off the lights and lock the doors. "Wish I could leave a note for the Amara," she said.

"What would you write?' Lucia asked, trying to keep her mind off her amulet and the dark-eyed man walking up ahead with Quinn.

Paige rubbed her chin before laughing. "How about... Detour."

Lucia laughed, imaging Ronja's face when she discovered her portal was gone. "No through traffic?"

Paige nodded as they headed out to follow the others. "Yeah."

Trudging slowly because her hip ached, Lucia waved Paige to go ahead. "I'll be right behind you."

She watched the warrior run to catch up to Kylie, and the blonde heads came together before breaking apart as the two women laughed. Lucia wished she could share their revelry, but too many things were bothering her.

They'd gained another victory for the coven tonight. Yet still no reward for her.

She covered her amulet as she walked, and as each minute passed, she longed more and more for the sweet, crystalline song her sisters had heard as they completed their trials.

Hadn't she faced enough obstacles? What did she have to do to pass?

Plane crash. Jungle trek. Amara blitz. Qara Mikuna. Even with some freaky see-through spiders. That bit.

And finally her heart had been crushed beneath Ethan's hiking boot, yet somehow she'd survived.

Now here she was covered in ash, and the red stone in her necklace remained stubbornly mute. Keeping her head down, Lucia watched her boots pound the sidewalk, letting the rhythm soothe her worried mind.

All she wanted was to go home, get something to eat, and sleep. She wasn't up for a victory celebration, and she sure as hell wasn't prepared for any questions.

Risking a quick glance, she took in Ethan's broad back as he walked and talked with Quinn. Then she tore her gaze away and let the cool night surround her. She let it wash away the strain.

No. Lucia wasn't ready for anyone's questions.

Because she had officially run out of answers.

35

After a quick trip to shower and change clothes, Ethan swung down to the kitchen for a bottle of water. He looked at his watch when he'd chugged the whole thing down, noting he'd waited twenty minutes.

That was all the time Lucia was going to get.

He marched back up the wide mahogany staircase, turning at each landing and continuing up until he reached the very top floor. Her bedroom was at the end of the hall, and he was sure she'd be there.

Knocking firmly, because he would allow at least that much of a warning, he gave her a moment before deciding to try the knob. Then he went in.

The door swung open to reveal Lucia's corner of the mansion, and he only needed a glance to know this was her territory. He cocked an ear and identified a low static-like noise as the blow dryer. So she was done with her shower. Good.

Ethan decided to take a turn around the room, as this was his first visit. He'd learned all he really needed to about the woman he was here to see, here to waylay, but still the tiny details were lacking. For example, he wouldn't have pegged her decorating style to fall right in the middle of Spartan neat and harem luxurious.

The wooden floors were bare, yet the tone of their medium gold grain was reflected in the bed's square headboard and bamboo blinds on the windows. More texture caught his eyes, and he studied what looked like packed and matted straw, cut into a rectangle to hang above her bed.

Ethan pondered the piece and decided he would ask her where she'd found it. Interesting artwork. Worldly yet contained.

Two marble-based lamps sat on the nightstands, one beside a brass clock. On the far side of the boudoir sat a sturdy desk of rich teak wood, the top graced by a brown-tinted globe and several stacked books.

And that's where the luxury took over. The chair held thick cushions of bold scarlet, plush enough for Lucia to sink in comfortably while she plotted her next adventure. The bed was covered in a similar color, though the mountain of pillows held a wild variety of gold and olive, the rich hues contrasting nicely.

Ethan cherished the idea of home, because his own travels always prevented his having one. Lucia's ability to make a single room feel like a haven was impressive, and a part of him yearned to build something with her. To see what the two of them could create together. As a team.

His eye was drawn to the red tulips on a corner table, and he realized there were things he would forever associate with the bright color. Strawberry dart frogs, wild Peruvian blooms, Lucia's passion, for life, for her duty, and for love.

Or had she abolished that last one for good? Had Ethan done it for her?

He rubbed the black stone on his wrist band, still disquieted when he thought of the risks of making Lucia his, but the magic talisman did him no good if he didn't use it. And the chance he'd been anticipating for almost two decades had arrived.

The fight at the warehouse had been the last push for him.

Seeing her take hits, wondering if she was hurting, and having her brown eyes lift to him when she'd been alarmed. Every time something had twisted inside his chest.

He could no longer deny the feelings he had for her. The emotions had grown stronger and more steady over the course of her trial, but his absolute fear of losing her had driven it all home. The respect he'd developed for her in the jungle, the fear for her well-being when she'd been sick, and tonight, when the lethal flying disk had almost found its mark.

He'd experienced the shock of realizing he couldn't live without her. He didn't just need her to be safe. He needed her to be with him.

Ethan was in love with Lucia, and keeping it a secret wasn't fair to either of them.

"What are you doing here?" Her voice cut through the air, slicing the atmosphere with its cold, sharp edge.

"How's your hip?" he countered. He'd seen her favoring one side after the battle, especially when she'd limped up the stairs. Fury sparked in her lovely brown eyes and made him grin. She thought to kick him out.

Well, too bad. Ethan had finally found his home. He wasn't going anywhere.

"I'm great, and any ache can be taken care of with one white pill." She crossed her arms across a heaving chest. How quickly he got a rise out of her just by being present. "Get lost, Ethan."

He shook his head. "No. You and I have things to discuss."

"You saved my life. I accept any forthcoming apology. Save your breath on anything else." She stomped to the door and jerked it open.

"I want to pick up where we left off on that mountain ridge, and you're right. I am sorry." He waited for her to acknowledge his confession, but she stood like a doorman waiting for him to leave.

"I handled the whole thing badly, Lucia," he said, halting

her when she huffed and started to walk out. "But you asked me to make love to you."

She gave him a haughty look. "Well, I must have been hard up."

"Don't," he snapped as anger heated his neck. "Just because you're pissed at me, don't cheapen what happened between us. Don't degrade what you felt for me because I was careless with you." He crossed the room and eased the door shut, so she steered around him and went to stand by her bed.

"You're crowding me, Drake," she told him, but her shoulders drooped slightly, the fire gone from her voice.

She was listening, at least, so he had to seize the opportunity. "Yeah, and I plan to keep on crowding you. You had your chance to be the aggressor, and I did a good job of running."

She snorted. "You don't say."

He would have laughed if he hadn't detected the sadness she was trying to cover. Her hair was loose, the gleaming brown trailing down her back. He moved closer and ran his hand lightly over the curls. She stiffened.

"Even when it mattered most, I fled from you," he said. "From what you offered." Then he captured her chin in one hand. "Now I have to convince you that you were right. And I was wrong."

She shook him off and nailed him with her gaze. Her lips were clamped tight but still trembled. "Why now? Nothing's changed."

"Everything's changed, and I don't want to be such a coward that I can't admit the most important truth of all." He chose his words carefully, still walking the knife's edge. "I do care for you, Lucia. That's what scared me the most. For so long I've avoided seeing a woman in that way, and just when things were most crucial, there you were pushing and beating your way inside. Begging me to let you in."

"I thought it was fate," Lucia whispered. "That destiny had

finally brought me someone I could love and be loved by in return. A man I could trust." She hugged herself as if forcing out the pain. "Then I fell for you because…you were you."

"And I cast you aside again, when you needed me."

She nodded and clenched her eyes shut.

"I'm truly sorry, and I don't say that very often." Ethan flayed his pride and offered it as sacrifice. "You weren't just another beautiful woman to me. You were my greatest fear."

"It doesn't matter anymore," she said, wiping a rogue tear from her cheek and rolling back her shoulders. Proud Lucia. Damn, she was something.

But her next words carved a chunk from deep inside of him. "I don't believe in love anymore. It's a rare thing and mostly unreliable. Parents, men, they've never been steadfast. Only friends have. Beatriz. Now my coven."

She put a hand on his shoulder and pushed gently. "I don't trust you, Ethan. I don't trust fate." She raised her head. "And I sure as hell don't trust love. Not anymore."

"I don't believe that," he said, capturing her hand. "You're the one who said love could conquer all and now you won't even give it a chance?"

"No. It doesn't deserve a chance."

"Liar." He pulled her against him, wickedly happy to see the fight burning in her eyes again, the stubborn set of her jaw. "You didn't stop having faith all of a sudden because I hurt your feelings. You're tougher than that."

"Then let's just say you were the final straw. My parents turned away from me, but I survived. They berated me and made me feel unworthy, but Beatriz was there to pick me back up. I never got close to a man for several reasons, usually because I was always jetting off to find the next relic or long lost tomb. But I also never felt a connection with anyone."

She tried to wiggle from his grasp, but he locked down even tighter. She sighed. "Then finally I found someone, and not just because of the prophecy and destiny. I felt more for you than any mystical force could convince me to feel. I gave you my heart, Ethan. Every time you told me no, I fought back, and not only for me. I fought for *us*."

She opened her eyes and the pain there made him ache. "You ran out of excuses on that mountain but still you wouldn't let me in. You weren't protecting me from the Seraphim." She put a hand to her chest and her voice broke. "You just didn't want me."

A shockwave rolled through Ethan. "Are you that blind, stubborn, or just plain stupid?" Her eyes flared as the gasp broke from her lips. She tried to pull away, but he wrapped one hand around the back of her neck, imprisoning her. "Foolish witch."

He stared at her full lips, the need to possess her overtaking everything else. Regret. Fear. Caution. All of it ceased to exist beneath the pounding urge to take this woman for his own. "You think I don't want you? Let me show you how wrong you are."

When his mouth took hers this time it was without hesitation, all reins had been cut loose, allowing his lust to rise up and take control. Because he didn't have a mere physical need for Lucia, he hungered for her affection. For all of her.

Her beauty was a given, and that long, toned body that curved in all the right places. But what drove him over the edge of reason was her dry humor and never-failing ability to look for the positive. Only Lucia could be trapped inside a mountain with demon-made cannibals and consider it just another day at the office.

Did she even know how fearless she was? How clever and bright? Her life force practically glowed with her strong and unwavering vitality.

It took a lot to put hurt and dejection in Lucia's eyes, so if Ethan had been the one to do so, then he would damn well stroke every other part of her until his previous betrayal was forgotten.

Until all she saw was what he could give her. And would give her.

She stood stunned and immobile as he ravished her mouth, but when his hands slid up to lift her shirt, she caught his wrists and pushed back. They had a brief shoving match before Lucia groaned and leaned back far enough to put some space between their torsos.

Then she slapped him.

The crack of skin on skin shocked them both into utter stillness. Ethan stared at her, his hands scalding where they rested against her soft flesh. So hot. So silky. But he wouldn't go any further until she allowed it.

"That's for the mountain ledge and leaving me humiliated." She was still frozen. "Just so we're clear."

"Good. We'll put that day behind us."

"Okay." She said her final piece and attacked him, kissing him aggressively, demanding he answer in kind.

The heat that had been flickering quietly inside Ethan burst wide open, and he knew he wouldn't survive another night without her.

Her shirt was gone in a heartbeat, and Ethan took a moment to appreciate her full, perfect breasts. Her hands were under his shirt now, stripping it away then returning to his skin to rake her nails ever-so-teasingly over his pecs.

"I've been dying to do that," she said before dropping her hand to the button on his jeans.

Ethan sucked in a breath then almost choked on it when her hand found the length of him and wrapped around greedily. "Careful, witch."

"You be careful," she said, giving him a seductive smile as she took a step backward. He saw now that's she'd only been wearing panties under the shirt, and the silken patch of red was his undoing.

Her body was worthy of poetry, and Lucia was a goddess of all things sexual. Fertile. Vital. He moved to her and ran both hands up her silken arms, caressing her shoulders, until finally, he wrapped her in his arms.

Taking in a deep draw of her natural scent, Ethan lowered his head and savored her mouth like a rare delicacy. "I have to be inside you," he whispered. "Now." Then with a growl he dove deep, making love to her mouth.

Her answer was to wrap one leg around his hips, holding herself in place by clinging to his shoulders. But he would keep her steady. She was the breath that filled him. The only food that could sate him. His female. His mate.

And no demon would take her from him.

When she brushed his wrist band, he flinched and tore his mouth away from hers. He looked to ensure the bracelet was still in place, then Lucia's hand gripped the side of his face and turned him back to meet her warm brown gaze. "Eyes on me, Drake."

He scooped her up and fell with her to the bed. "Not a problem."

Like a man gone wild, he positioned himself between her legs, then he sat up and slipped his hands beneath the straps of her bright red panties.

As Lucia watched, Ethan calmed and took a deep breath. He ran a gentle hand over her stomach before bending toward her. Then he shook her to the core when he kissed her injured hip.

She moaned lightly as the rush of potent sexuality erased any aches left over from the battle. All she could feel was Ethan's hands on her. All she could see was the way he devoured with his dark, dark eyes.

As he traced the outline of her body, worshipping her female form, Lucia let go of her last doubt. He wanted her.

Sudden and complete rapture burst inside, from a heart

that had been pummeled and left throbbing with need. Only one man had made her feel vulnerable and broken. And only one man could rescue her.

Ethan belonged to her, and she knew this not because of prophecies or plans, fate or situation. She knew it because her very blood came alive when he kissed her. His touch was like warm, liquid gold.

Ethan freed himself from his jeans, making her already busy heart throb faster. He was perfect. From his long, powerful legs, up past the chiseled torso, to his predatory eyes and silky, black hair.

A lock fell over his eyes and Lucia sighed with wonder. And raw, aching need.

She reached for him, and Ethan took her hands, intertwining his fingers with hers as he slid himself up her body. His thick, hard chest rubbed up her abdomen then brushed erotically over her sensitive nipples.

His hot mouth found her neck and laved her there. She shook out a breath of pure arousal and relaxed as he pushed his hips between her legs. He eased them apart. Slowly. Torturously.

She let herself drown in his warmth. In the whisper of her name against her neck. Her cheek.

When Ethan settled against her, the heat of his erection pressing against her, testing, teasing, Lucia didn't feel exposed or vulnerable, she was empowered.

Ethan looked at her again, his lids heavy, his breaths deep. "No more doubts," he said, and Lucia agreed.

"That's what I've been waiting to hear," she told him, keeping her eyes steady on his face as he slid into her and finally, fully, possessed her.

Need raged through her as she rocked with him, thrilled with how he filled her. Touched her so deeply. Their tongues tangled and tasted and she felt a straight shot of lust when his chest moved against hers. Male joined with female, straining and taking. Nothing had ever been more erotic.

Lucia was riding so high, so hard and fast, and Ethan's long, deep thrusts made her shudder with pleasure. She gasped when the liquid heat began to tighten, building that sweet, aching tension that told her she was close to ecstasy.

She opened herself to Ethan, taking all of him as he worked her body and cherished her spirit. She grabbed his neck and looked deep into his eyes.

And he was the last thing she saw before blinding rapture took her away.

Pleasure pulsed so strongly, engulfing her, and Ethan's name burst from her lips.

She heard his answering cry and felt the strain of his corded muscles as he spent himself inside her. Then the welcome hardness as he lay down on top of her.

After a moment, Ethan rolled to his back and pulled her across him to lie on his chest, drawing deep, rasping breaths as the two of them recovered.

Lucia had wondered about the true strength of his body and how it would feel to worship every lean, firm bit of it.

Now she knew. And he'd been so worth the wait.

Needing nothing but Ethan for warmth, Lucia cuddled into him, luxuriating under the weight of his arm as it circled her waist. He held her as if she was precious. Like he'd never let her go.

Good. Lucia smiled as her stomach fluttered. Because that was her plan as well.

Overcome by emotion for this man, the one who'd done everything in his power to keep her at arm's length, Lucia admitted to herself she wouldn't have done it any other way. Part of her had known why he'd rejected her that day on the mountain, but before she could risk her heart again, she'd needed to hear the reason from him.

As far as she was concerned, there were still a few more

puzzles to solve. More chains to be removed before they could start a life together. And when her eyes latched onto the band around his wrist, Lucia knew where to start.

With her head still nestled under his chin, she kissed him lightly, reveling in the warmth of his embrace, listening to his heart thud fiercely. "Ethan," she spoke against his chest. "I love you."

At once she felt him squeeze her tighter. She felt his hand brush down her arm. His lips kissed the top of her head. Yet Ethan remained silent, and she knew he was afraid.

Despite the love they'd finally discovered, he still couldn't say the words.

~~~

Lucia slipped quietly out the door of her bedroom, easing the lock shut behind her to tiptoe down the hall. She'd waited an hour for Ethan to fall asleep, so she could sneak out.

Her heart galloped as she hurried down the stairs, and a small spark of optimism was doing its best to flare to life. She smiled to herself as she crossed the grand hall.

Ethan wasn't the only one who could keep a secret.

Through the foyer she slid, feeling like a wraith in her long white gown. But when she drew near the library, she noticed golden light pouring from beneath the doors. Someone must have left a lamp burning.

Pushing her way into the expansive and elegant room with shelves of books running all the way up the high, high ceiling, Lucia spotted a lone figure bent over a desk. Quinn looked up from a thick and aged tome.

Lucia gave him a grin. She should have known.

"What's up?" he asked, getting straight to the point and forgoing any needless small talk. Lucia was still the witch at challenge, and all her friends knew...the trial wasn't over until the big gemstone sang.

Pursing her lips and stalling, Lucia quickly ran all the equations and possibilities in her head before coming to the certain conclusion that Quinn was the perfect co-conspirator. "I have a plan and could use your help."

He put a marker in the book and closed it. "Sure."

"But you can't tell Ethan."

Now his head snapped back. "Well..."

"Just not yet. I'm going to tell him. I have to, but before he has a chance to talk me out of it, I want to have all the pertinent information." She walked around the end of a long table to face Quinn. She needed him and his big brain on her side for this.

When she had lain beside Ethan watching his handsome face relax, Lucia hadn't been able to keep her attention off his wrist. Even in sleep he covered the bracelet with his other hand. He guarded it.

The band that was supposed to save him had become a shackle. He looked over his shoulder every time he knocked the piece of jewelry against the wall. If he almost let it slip off in the shower.

He was more nervous with the band than he'd ever been without it. He'd fulfilled his lifelong search, only to find himself chained to the beast.

But Ethan wasn't the only one dreading the demon. Now Lucia was, too. And she'd be damned before she let a snake-faced peeping-Tom Seraphim dictate their love life. Or any part of their lives.

A tingle coursed through her before settling inside her chest with a great squeeze. Half joy, half bittersweet pain. She and Ethan would have a life together, a long, happy, adventurous one.

But three was definitely a crowd.

She made her lip stop curling and schooled her expression

into one of wisdom. She hoped. "Ethan said something to me once, when we were in Peru. There might be a way to save him, but we need specifics." She tapped one finger on the book Quinn had put aside. "And I need the master researcher to help me find them."

She held her eyes on his as the request and its meaning sank in. Quinn knew better than anyone how long Ethan had suffered. How much he'd been denied.

"You *will* tell him once you find what you need?" Quinn tilted his head in question, but she could see the light in his eyes. Quinn loved exploring as much as Lucia did. He just worked better with books.

She nodded solemnly. "*Te lo juro*. I swear."

Quinn lifted one side of his mouth. "Then let's do it." He gazed around the vast library, and Lucia could practically hear him mentally naming the sections. "Where should we start?"

Lucia imagined Ethan's sleeping face, and how he might look if he could rest with no worries at all. "At the risk of beating the long-buried horse, we have to go back to demons."

With his brow beetled, Quinn turned back to her. "Why?"

Lucia firmed her shoulders and said, "I need a name."

36

"Are you sure you don't want us to come with you?" Quinn asked the next evening. He and Anna had been filled in on Lucia's plan, and concern shone from their two sets of sapphire-blue eyes.

"I need to handle this privately." Tugging on the hem of her black tank, Lucia prepared herself for what might end up being the most dangerous feat she'd ever attempted. Only Quinn and Anna knew what was about to happen, and neither of them was crazy about the idea of her going it alone.

The rest of the coven hadn't been told, because Lucia couldn't keep Ethan in the dark while everyone else sat on the sidelines watching his destiny unfold.

Or cartwheel into destruction, depending on the reliability of the data Lucia and Quinn had gathered.

"Don't come out unless it sounds like..." She gathered her brows, unwilling to face the possibility. But finally she clarified, "Unless it sounds like everything's gone wrong."

"How will we know?" Quinn asked, pacing now and glancing at her in exasperation.

"Oh. You'll know," Lucia told him before going to stand in front of him and halt his nervous march. "And Quinn. I couldn't have done this without you. So thanks."

She hugged him tight, Quinn St. Germaine. Honorary brother to all of Anna's witches.

When Lucia felt a silken brush against her leg, she bent down to pick up Iris. Poor thing, she hadn't had her human's attention for far too long, but the oversight would soon be remedied. If Lucia had her way, the black cat would be spoiled rotten for days on end.

And after tonight, she would have two humans to do the spoiling.

"Lucia, I want to tell you," Anna said, a gentle smile on her lips. "I was wrong about my vision, the one I had at the start of your trial."

"Wrong?" Lucia shook her head. "How can that be? Everything since then has come true. The dagger. The jungle."

"I know. But the bird in the cage. The one that changed to red and then flew away?" She put her hand on the side of Lucia's face. "It didn't represent you after all."

Crystal clarity thrummed through Lucia before Anna said, "The bird that needed to be set free." She smiled. "I think it was Ethan."

The power of providence welled up in Lucia as her heart trembled and her eyes watered. She set her cat down after a final hug and walked resolutely down the slate-floored corridor. "Then I know I'm in the right," she called, walking backwards and smiling through her fear. "I know it."

The moon was high in the sky when she entered the gardens, much as it had been the night Anna had her premonition.

Lucia took a long, winding route, enjoying the cool, silent night and the soothing gardens. She came around the last bend and felt love trickle through her.

Ethan was waiting for Lucia near the pond, just as requested.

He didn't know it, but he was being set up, conned, because Lucia knew there was no other way. She had to take him completely by surprise, because he would never take the required risk.

She would have to force his hand.

She carried a satin bag, its contents a mystery to the casual observer. Ethan didn't inquire when she went to him. He didn't question when she eased closer, touched his face, and fell straight into his arms.

They'd been in a type of honeymoon phase since making love. Lucia had spent the rest of the night in the library with Quinn, but once they'd gotten what they needed she'd slipped quietly back into bed beside Ethan.

And this morning, he'd found an inventive way to wake her up.

Lucia shivered as she recalled the delightful yet sinful tricks Ethan had shown her. She intended to have plenty of mornings with him. And days. Afternoons. Nights.

Plainly put. She wanted forever.

"What are you up to?" he asked after kissing her to distraction and lifting her to her toes. She found she quite enjoyed a tall man as her partner. He still made her feel feminine.

"I've brought you out here to the most romantic spot on the estate for good reason." She fluttered her eyelashes and laughed at her failed attempt to play coy.

"Out with it, witch," he teased. "I can tell you want something."

She nodded then slipped away to set the bag on the stone wall that surrounded the pond. As she stared into the shimmering surface, she prayed to her God and to any eavesdropping deities that they would guide her in this endeavor.

That they would protect her and the man she loved.

"Believe it or not, I'm grateful to your demon. To the Seraphim." She turned to face him, and as expected, his expression had changed to granite. "Oh, not much. After all, he is evil, and he hurt you."

"And you," he said in a tone that would sound menacing to

most, but Lucia knew he was just feeling protective.

"Still," she said, "if the Seraphim hadn't been an issue, I might not have realized how much you really love me."

Ethan looked like he would choke. "Don't. Don't talk about it, not yet. I need more time to get used…"

"To the bracelet?" she asked. "You think time will tell you anything more about how strong it is? Or isn't?"

"I don't know, dammit, but I won't have you risking your life by declaring my love for you." He rammed his hand through his hair. "It's like tempting the devil or something. Besides," he said with more heat, "it's my right to tell you how I feel when I'm ready."

"And when will that be?" She gestured to the silver band. "You have the bracelet. The artifact that was supposed to save you. To save me. But that thing hasn't given you your freedom. You've been a nervous wreck since you put it on at Kuelap."

He closed in on her. "Have you forgotten what happened between us last night? Didn't I show you how I feel?" His eyes grew tender. His fingers cupped her cheek. "Don't you know?"

"Yes," she answered gently. "But I need to hear it. And not only for my wounded pride."

Without explanation, she turned to the bag and retrieved her sword.

"What are you doing with that?" he asked.

Ignoring him, Lucia channeled her magic down her arm and infused the metal until it glowed a brilliant blue. Then she set it back down. "You might need it."

"Why?" he demanded. "What are you doing?" His eyes danced between her and the weapon, panic rearing as he sensed an oncoming threat.

"I have a name for you, Ethan." She moved back to him and put her arms around his neck. She stood on her toes and slanted her mouth against his. Kissing him as if it were her last day on earth.

She hoped it wasn't.

Nuzzling her neck, Ethan held her to him, so tightly, fearfully. She felt him tremble. His heart was thundering and so was hers. Together they beat as one, breathing each other in.

Lucia clung to Ethan and whispered in his ear. "I love you so much, Ethan. Please don't keep from me the one thing I need most."

"I can't." He shook harder. "I won't risk you. Why are you doing this?"

"Because I have faith after all. Love is the greatest power there is. Now, please," she placed a light kiss on his temple. "Give me yours."

Her hands shifted to his shoulders as he drew a ragged breath. They fell to his forearms when he said her name.

And her fingers tingled, holding onto his when he told her, "I do love you."

In a flash she ripped the silver band from his wrist, tossing it to the stone path to buy some time. If only a few seconds.

To allow the demon to come.

"No!" he yelled. "What have you done?" He tried for the bracelet but she intercepted him.

"Please! We have no time!" Lucia sank her fingers into his arm to hold him. "His name is Moros. Your Seraphim. We found his name."

"It doesn't matter. I have to get the band!" He threw her off, fearing for her life.

Lucia jolted and let out a keening moan when what felt like acid filled her intestines. She bit back the pain that wanted to tear from her throat. "Your things are in the bag! His name is already written." She doubled over as the searing liquid funneled into her chest cavity.

Dios! Would her organs melt inside her?

"The demon is attached to the bracelet, Ethan. Please! You

have to trust me. Trust Quinn. You have all you need to be rid of the Seraphim. Destroy the bracelet and destroy him."

Now she did scream, because the agony was unbearable. She was afraid Quinn would already be running for the door and soon into the gardens.

The world went yellow, and a strange, foreign laugh escaped her. It stung her throat as it climbed from something dark and rotten inside.

"Your eyes," Ethan said, stunned. Then he clenched his fist. "Leave her alone, you bastard! Get out of her!"

"I knew you wouldn't last," the invading spirit said, speaking through her. "A deal is a deal. Now watch your woman suffer. Again."

Ethan yelled from the base of his soul, roaring to shake the very stars from the sky. He dove for the bracelet and set it on the stone wall then he emptied the contents of the bag. Salt. Lighter. Paper with the Seraphim's name written.

He picked up the scrap and read the cursed name out loud. "Moros."

You won't have me! Lucia screamed inside her head. *Ethan, hurry!*

Lucia fell to the ground and writhed as the burn spread everywhere. Her brain felt like it was boiling. Her arms and legs. Eyes and throat.

Ethan was chanting when he lit the paper with the demon's name then he held it up to make sure it burned completely. Grabbing the salt, he poured it over the bracelet, cleansing the area around and underneath the talisman.

He paused when his gaze fell to the glowing sword. Lucia's magic and titanium. Weapon enough to kill a demon.

He turned, eyes crazy with terror. "If I destroy the bracelet, you'll die."

"No. The demon will." Quinn was with them now, and thank heavens, because Lucia couldn't speak through the ongoing torture. "Hurry, Ethan. You have to crush the bracelet. It's part of your demon and has been since the moment you used it to block him. Do it."

Lucia screamed as her mind ripped apart.

"Do it," Quinn said, on the verge of panic. "Do it now!"

A streak of blue lifted into the night sky, blurry and misshapen to Lucia's eyes. But somehow she knew it was her sword. A sonic blast rolled over her as the air thundered and filled the gardens with her magic.

The blue seemed to displace the air. The oxygen. Sweeping over everything like a mystical aftershock.

Then the world was clear again, and metal clattered onto stone.

Ethan kneeled beside her as the boiling pain receded. As the acid leached from her system. "Lucia, talk to me. Are you still with me? Please." He cradled her like a child and pulled her into his lap.

She could smell him. Ethan. Her love. He pulled her back from the brink of unconsciousness, talking and soothing. Whispering again and again, the words he'd been banned from saying for so long. "I love you. I love you."

He brushed her hair from her face. "Witch, wake up. I'm telling you I love you. And if you're going to resort to a near-death experience to have me say it, then you'd better wake your *trasero* back up and listen."

Her eyes fluttered open as humor tickled in her stomach. "*Trasero?*" she mimicked, as life and strength rushed back into her.

He shrugged and grinned. "I pay attention."

She tried to stand but he wouldn't let her. Instead he lifted her straight from the ground and into his arms.

"I can walk, demon hunter." But she laid her head on his shoulder. "Thank you for trusting me."

He made a disgusted sound. "As if you gave me a choice."

He passed a grinning Quinn and gave his friend a pointed look. "I'll be dealing with you later."

"Sure. Okay." Quinn blew out a breath. "Man, I'm just glad that worked."

Anna had met them halfway and heard the last. The usually serene woman hauled off and punched her brother in the arm. "What do you mean you're glad it worked? You said there was no doubt."

"I said less than one percent chance of failure." Quinn rubbed his arm as they walked back to the house. "Your memory's defunct."

Kylie was the first to pour out of the back doors, followed closely by Claudia and the others.

Lucia wiggled. "Okay. Now you need to put me down." She flashed a grin to Ethan. "I've got a rep to protect."

He kissed her hard and long then released her. Steadying her when she wavered.

When everyone started asking at once about the noise and what had happened, Anna calmly explained and answered questions.

"But you're all right?" Willyn asked, her golden waves shining in the moonlight.

"Yes."

"And Ethan's demon is gone. For good." Viv edged closer and looked over her glasses at Lucia and Ethan. "Because you could have let us help, you know."

"I know, but it was better this way." Lucia put an arm around Ethan's waist. "I needed his full attention."

When Ethan gave her a lusty look and leaned down to kiss her again, Hayden murmured. "Looks like you got it."

"Good," Kylie said. "Then we can get back to our movie. We're trying to educate Viv on middle-earth and other important things."

Paige had a strange look on her face as she stared at Lucia.

She blew her light bangs out of her eyes. "Wait a minute. Everything's not all right."

Lucia had wanted to revel in the joy of having Ethan free and clear. And without his ancient, silver shackle. But Paige was right, and now, Lucia was at a loss. She had run out of ideas, and didn't know what else to do.

She tapped a finger to her amulet, to the crimson stone that was still silent. "No. Not okay by a long shot."

"You still haven't heard anything?" Shauni asked, green eyes concerned. "After all you've done?"

"Nope." Lucia steeled herself for the reality they all now had to face. "Not a peep."

"But that means..." Anna stepped forward and put her hand to her mouth.

"I know," Lucia said, "and I'm sorry." She held tight to Ethan's hand, and he supported her when she needed it most.

Clearing her throat, Lucia notched up her chin, and she tried so hard to be brave. "My trial's not over."

Suza Kates writes both paranormal romance and romantic suspense. She lives in Savannah, Georgia with her family and three ridiculously spoiled cats.

For more on Suza and her books visit

www.suzakates.com